Other books by Bob Mayer

*Eternity Base*
*Cut-Out*
*SYNBAT*
*Dragon SIM-13*
*Eyes of the Hammer*

# Bob Mayer

Z

*A
Dave Riley
novel*

LYFORD
Books

Copyright © 1997 by Bob Mayer

LYFORD Books
Published by Presidio Press
505 B San Marin Dr., Suite 300
Novato, CA 94945-1340

**Library of Congress Cataloging-in-Publication Data**

Mayer, Bob, 1959-
    Z : a Dave Riley novel / Bob Mayer.
       p.   cm.
    ISBN 0-89141-510-6 (hardcover)
    I. Title.
    PS3563.A95227Z18   1997
    813'.54—dc20               96-43054
                                    CIP

Printed in the United States of America

*Corey Andrew Cavanaugh,*
*a special person*

# Prologue

**Cheyenne Mountain, Colorado, 21 May**

Eight hundred feet underground, the monotony of watching computer screens was broken by one of the six men on duty calling out to the shift commander: "Sir, we've got a break in orbit on a known."

The Warning Center watch officer, Major Sinclair, looked up from his computer chess game. "Whose is it?"

"Code is RG-fourteen," the screen watcher replied.

The code told Sinclair several things: The *R* meant it was Russian. The *G* represented the year the object went into space, and since it was the seventh letter in the alphabet that meant it had been launched this year. The *14* indicated it was the fourteenth object launched into space by the Russians since January 1. "That's very current," Sinclair commented. "What's the break? New orbit?"

"No, sir. It's a decay. She's coming down."

"Damn," Sinclair muttered. "How long before she reenters?" he asked as he figured out who to call and how soon he would have to call. He hoped they would have a couple of days before reentry so he could just log it and let the center's operations officer take care of the situation during normal duty hours.

The screen watcher hit the keys on his computer, then whistled. "Twelve minutes."

Sinclair almost spilled his coffee. "What?"

"Twelve minutes, give or take twenty percent. It's decaying rapidly," the man added in a bit of an understatement.

"Put it on the big screen," Sinclair ordered. The large screen in front of the room displayed a Mercator conformal map of the entire world's surface. With a few commands, the data that was being downloaded from Defense Support Program (DPS) could be selectively displayed on the screen. A glowing dot appeared on the screen moving from left to right across the South Atlantic.

The U.S. Space Command's Missile Warning Center is located deep inside Cheyenne Mountain on the outskirts of Colorado Springs. The Space Command, part of the air force, is responsible for the DSP satellite system.

DSP satellites blanket the entire surface of the earth from an altitude of over twenty thousand miles up in geosynchronous orbits. The system had originally been developed to detect ICBM launches during the Cold War. During the Gulf War, it had picked up every SCUD missile launch and proved so effective that the military had further streamlined the system to give real-time warnings to local commanders at the tactical level.

Every three seconds the DSP system downloads an infrared map of the earth's surface and surrounding airspace. Most of the data is stored on tape in the Warning Center, unless, of course, the computer detects a missile launch, or something different happens to one of the objects already in space that the Warning Center was tracking.

The staff at Space Command delineates four categories of objects in space. The first is a known object in stable orbit, such as a satellite or some of the debris from previous space missions. Each of those has a special code assigned to it, and its data is stored in the computer at Cheyenne Mountain. There are presently over eight thousand five hundred catalogued items orbiting the planet.

The second category is a known object whose orbit has changed, such as when a country or corporation decides to reposition one of its satellites. The third is a known object whose orbit is decaying. When that happens Space Command puts the tracking and impact prediction (TIP) team on the job to figure out where it will come down. TIP teams were instituted as a result of the publicity after Skylab came down years ago. The fourth category is an object that has just been launched and has yet to be assigned a code.

The man who had first picked up the discrepancy explained the movement. "She's running roughly east-west along about ten degrees south latitude."

"Do you have an impact point?"

"Computer's working on it, sir."

Hell, Sinclair thought, by the time the computer figured it out, the thing would be down. He got out of his chess game and entered the code for the object. The entry on his screen was very short.

RG14: Proton final stage booster.
Orbit: Free, plotted, and logged.
Launch: 18 May 1997
Launch Site: Kazakhstan
Comments: Final stage booster for Proton launch of communications satellite contracted out to SINCOM, European Communications. Payload is listed as EG36.

The dot was simply the last stage of a Russian Proton booster rocket, which was some relief to Sinclair. At least it wasn't a nuclear power source, of which he knew the Soviets had several in space giving juice to their space lab and some of their satellites. If one of those started coming down, there'd be hell to pay. The fact that a Russian rocket had put a European satellite into orbit was not strange at all. The Russians were so strapped for cash that they had begun putting their space program up for hire several years previously. The booster itself was garbage and of no concern, unless of course it landed on someone's roof.

"Why's it deteriorating so fast?" Sinclair asked out loud.

The man who had first spotted the decay was just as confused. "I don't know, sir. It shouldn't be deteriorating at all. Those Proton final stage boosters usually stay up there for quite a while before they go down the gravity well."

"Could the Russians be bringing it down?" Sinclair asked.

"No, sir. According to our data on the Proton booster, it's dead weight. No thrusters."

"Dead weight doesn't decay its own orbit and defy the law of gravity," Sinclair remarked. "Maybe they're trying to recover it to use it again."

"They wouldn't be bringing it down at that latitude," the man said. "And they've never brought one down before."

They continued to watch as the small dot moved across the ocean.

"She's coming down somewhere in Africa," the man said as his computer finally yielded its projection. "Maybe Zaire."

The dot touched the western shore of Africa. It started across Angola, then suddenly disappeared just short of the border between that state and its neighbor Zaire.

"She's down."

"Put a lock on the tape," Sinclair ordered. The center recorded everything that the GPS satellites picked up. The lock would ensure that the tape with this particular action would not be reused. Due to budget cuts, they were starting to reuse old tapes that had nothing of significance on them.

"At least it didn't strike a city," the screen watcher joked. "Maybe some farmer just saw what he thinks is a meteorite."

"It probably just hit jungle," Sinclair said, noting the location where the dot had disappeared: on the edge of the Congo basin. The heart of darkness in the title of Conrad's novel. Better Africa than North America, Sinclair thought.

As things settled back down, Sinclair stared at the screen at the front of the room and the traces of the political borders in Central Africa that were on it. Something wasn't right about this. Like he had said, the booster should not have come down that fast, if at all. A normal gravitational decay usually occurred over the course of several weeks to months to years, depending on the height of the orbit and the object's velocity, yet this thing had come down less than fifteen minutes from the first change in orbit being noticed. Maybe the booster had hit something, Sinclair reasoned. There certainly was enough debris floating around in orbit. But that didn't sit right either.

Sinclair shrugged and entered one line in his duty log concerning the event. He noted the date and time group for the computer tape of the incident. Then he turned his computer game back on.

# Chapter 1

**Angola, 9 June**

"What do you think?" the corporal driving the truck asked Sergeant Ku. The patrol was deep inside rebel territory and the men were very nervous. Ku knew Lieutenant Monoko, out front in the jeep, didn't want to admit that he didn't know *how* deep inside rebel territory they were.

They'd traveled for six hours over unpaved roads and trails since leaving the paved main road between the border post at Luau and Luena, the next major town on the road. Sergeant Ku had watched the sun the entire time, troubled about the direction it told him they were traveling.

"I think the lieutenant does not know where we are," Ku said. He was in the cab of the half-ton diesel truck with the corporal driving. The rest of the patrol—twelve men—was in the back. Ku was an old veteran of the civil war in Angola, having fought the Portuguese at the start, then beside the Cubans many years back. The allies and enemies had changed over the years but never the fighting. Ku's dark scalp was covered with gray hair and his slight frame was tense, ready for action.

They could see Lieutenant Monoko ahead in the jeep, looking at his map and scratching his head. The fact that the lieutenant's vehicle was out in front told the sergeant more than he wished to know about his new officer. Only a fool would want to be in the lead to trip whatever mines the UNITA rebels might have planted on the road. Of course, Ku's sense of self-preservation made him very grateful that in this specific area the lieutenant was ignorant. If Monoko had done as he should have and made the truck lead, the sergeant would not be sitting in this cab—he'd be in the backseat of the jeep with the lieutenant.

Ku climbed out of the truck and walked forward. This was their first chance in several hours to stop, and he indicated for the soldiers to take a break. Some were already urinating off the side of the truck. Ku snapped a salute, startling Monoko. "Sir, may I be of assistance?" The lieutenant was a very large and fat man, used to the easy life of the city. Ku wondered what circumstances had forced him into uniform and out to the bush.

Ku watched with detached amusement at the emotions that played across the broad black plain of his officer's face. Pride versus the reality of the situation. The amusement disappeared quickly, though, because the look on Monoko's face also confirmed what Ku had been fearing. They were indeed lost.

"I believe we are near Cangamba," Monoko said, vaguely stabbing his finger at the map.

Years of working with incompetence allowed Ku to keep his face expressionless. "Sir, we have been heading to the northwest all afternoon. We cannot be close to Cangamba."

"We have been traveling southwest," Monoko disagreed. He reached into his pocket and pulled out a compass, flipping open the plastic cover proudly.

There was no amusement left at all in Ku. "Sir, we never stopped to take compass bearings. How do—"

"I was checking all along," Monoko interrupted. "I can read a compass on the move. I do not need to stop."

Ku held out his hand. Monoko paused, then gave him the compass. "Sir, if you note, the compass now says north is that way"—he pointed to the right side of the road. Ku turned and walked several paces from the jeep. Monoko reluctantly got out of the jeep and followed. "If you would please note, sir, the compass *now* says north is that way." Ku pointed to the left.

Monoko blinked. "But how can that be? It is not supposed to do that!"

Ku bit the inside of his mouth to restrain himself. "Sir, the metal of the jeep affects the magnet in the needle. That is why we must stop to get compass readings away from the jeep or navigate off the direction the sun speaks." Ku pointed up.

Ku felt sick with himself for having allowed the officer to proceed in ignorance for so long. But it was Monoko's fault also, Ku reminded himself. Not only did the lieutenant not know how to use a compass properly, he had never told Ku what their orders were or where they were headed. Ku had assumed that they were going in the right direction, even if it was in the direction of the enemy. After all, they occasionally did have to go out and fight. Who knew what the idiots in charge in Luanda had thought up? Ku had been hearing rumors for weeks now that something big was getting ready to happen, and he had assumed this strange direction was tied to those rumors.

Monoko looked about at the undulating grasslands that surrounded them. He turned back to his platoon sergeant. "What do we do?"

"Let me see your map, sir." Ku took the sheet and stared at it. He found the last point where he had positively known where they were, then estimated. They'd been traveling for over five hours since then, mostly north and west. He placed an aged finger on the paper and traced a forty-kilometer circle just south of a town named Saurimo. "We are somewhere here. We must head due west as quickly as possible to get out of rebel territory before nightfall. I know for certain that there are many rebels in Saurimo."

The last thing Ku wanted was to spend the night in this province with a green officer and a platoon full of new recruits. They were on the edge of Lunda Sul, a diamond-rich area that made up northeast Angola and was completely in rebel hands. There was a government garrison at Cacólo, about one hundred kilometers away. With a little luck and good roads, they might make it before dark.

Monoko pulled himself together. "Yes. We must head west. Tell the men we must be moving."

Ku yelled out the appropriate orders, then made a difficult personal decision. "Sir, might I join you in your vehicle?"

A half hour later, they turned a corner in the road and the driver hit the brakes. Ku reacted instinctively to the tangle of fallen trees that blocked the road ahead. He rolled out of the backseat and took cover behind the jeep, pointing his weapon ahead, searching for the ambush he expected to explode out of the foliage all around as he screamed for the men in the truck to deploy.

The men reacted slowly, but eventually all were on the ground in the semblance of a perimeter and Lieutenant Monoko was at his side, peering ahead. "What do you think?" the officer whispered.

If there were any rebels about, there was no doubt in Ku's mind that the patrol's presence had been detected and whispering was not needed, but he played along. "I do not know, sir." He peered at the trees. They'd been hacked down and pulled across the road. Beyond he could see some smoke, maybe from cooking fires. There was a small patch of thatched roof visible above the fallen trees. "There is a village there." It was a logical location for a village: they were in low terrain and a river ran to their left.

"A rebel village?" Lieutenant Monoko asked.

This was rebel territory, but most of the villages Ku had encountered over the years were on neither side in this bloody civil war. The inhabitants probably wanted to just be left alone. But Ku needed to get through the village to continue on to the west. There was most likely a crossing site for the river on the far side of the village. "I will look, sir."

He stood and signaled for a couple of men to accompany him. He walked up to the roadblock and checked it for booby traps. Nothing. He went around the tangled limbs and looked. A small village of about ten or twelve huts was in a clearing on the gentle bank that led down to the river. There was no one moving about. A pile of smoldering logs on the right side of the village was the source of the smoke. There were also the remains of several huts that had been burned to the ground.

Ku frowned. The road was blocked on the far side also, and beyond it he could see a ford across the small river. What had the villagers wanted to stop? And where were they? Who had destroyed the huts?

He ordered his men to stay put and went forward. Then he caught a scent in the air and stopped in midstep. He recognized the horrible smell from past battles: burning flesh. Ku turned and looked more closely at the pile of logs and now saw that they weren't wood. They were bodies, tightly wrapped in soiled sheets, piled four deep.

"Remove the roadblocks!" he yelled at his men. "Quickly!"

Ku went to the first hut and used the muzzle of his AK-47 to push aside the cloth that hung in the doorway. The stench that greeted his nostrils was even worse than the burning flesh. The walls were spattered with blood. There was something that might have once been human lying on the floor, but the body had been destroyed by some terrible force.

Ku had seen many bodies in his service, but this one did not look like it had been killed by an explosion. However, that was the only thing he could think of that would cause the mangled flesh and the amount of blood splattered all around the interior.

Ku moved to the next hut, but paused as he heard Lieutenant Monoko's voice. "What is going on, Sergeant?"

"I do not know, sir. I have ordered the men to clear the roadblocks. We can proceed across the river when that is done."

Monoko wrinkled his nose. "What is that stink?"

Ku pointed. "Bodies. Burning."

The lieutenant's eyes widened. "What has happened here?"

Ku felt fear now, an icy trickle running down his spine and curling into his stomach. He pulled aside the curtain to the next hut with the steel of his rifle barrel.

Monoko cried out and turned away. Ku heard his officer vomiting as he stared at the sight that had greeted both of them. A woman was on a dilapidated mattress, her legs spread wide. Between her legs was an aborted fetus. At least that's what Ku hoped it was. All he could see was a pile of dark black blood and putrid flesh. The mother was dead also. Ku forced himself to stare and take note. Blood had poured out of the woman. Not just from between her legs but from her eyeballs, her nostrils, her ears, her mouth, every opening. The rags she had wrapped herself in were soaked with red as if she had even sweated blood. Skin that wasn't covered in blood had angry red welts crisscrossing it.

Ku finally turned away. Monoko was on his knees, still retching. Ku grabbed his arm. "We must go, sir! Now!"

Ku looked about. The men had figured out what the burned pile was. That was evident from the amount of effort they were putting into clearing away the trees. The first roadblock was clear and the second halfway done.

"We must look for survivors," Monoko whispered.

Ku shook his head. "There are none, sir."

"We must check all the huts."

Ku frowned. "All right. I will do it. Move the jeep and truck forward. We must leave as soon as the trees are clear."

Ku quickly ran to the next hut. It was empty. The next four held bodies, or what had once been bodies, but were now just masses of rotting flesh and blood. In the next-to-last hut, there was a person lying on the floor. A young woman. She turned her head as Ku opened the curtain. Her eyes were wide and red, a trickle of blood rolling like tears down her cheeks. Her skin was covered with red welts.

"Please!" she rasped. "Help me."

Ku stepped in, every nerve in his body screaming for him to run away. He knelt next to the woman. Her face was swollen and her breathing was coming in labored gasps. From the smell, there was no doubt she was lying in her own feces.

Suddenly the woman's hands darted forward and she grabbed the collar of Ku's fatigue jacket. With amazing strength she half-pulled herself off the fouled mat, toward Ku's face. Her mouth opened as if she were going to speak, but a tide of black-red matter exploded out of her mouth into Ku's face and chest. He screamed and slammed his arms up, but couldn't break her grip. Struggling to his feet, he moved backward to the door, but the woman was still attached to him.

He jammed the muzzle of his AK-47 into her stomach and pulled the trigger. The steel-jacketed rounds literally tore the woman in half, but even in death her hands held on. Ku threw his gun out the door, then pulled his bloodied shirt up and over his head and left it there, clutched in her dead fingers.

He staggered out into the clearing as soldiers ran over, weapons at the ready. "We go!" Ku screamed at them as he wiped at the blood and vomit on his face. "We go!"

# Chapter 2

**Aragon Island, 9 June**

The helicopter was barely twenty feet above the tops of the trees, moving at over a hundred miles an hour. Inside, soldiers with camouflage paint on their faces and the double-A patch of the 82d Airborne Division on their left shoulders pulled back the charging handles on their M-16s and put a round in the chamber, ready for action.

In one of the center seats facing to the rear, Dave Riley's hands twitched, missing the feel of a weapon in them. It was instinctual, and as he caught himself doing it, he smiled and forced his muscles to relax. He glanced to his left at Conner Young. She wore the same armband he did over the loose-fitting khaki, indicating she was with the press. On Riley's right, their military escort, a young captain from the Pentagon named Kanalo, was watching the actions of the paratroopers with wide eyes. From the shield insignia on the left collar of Kanalo's battle-dress uniform, Riley knew that the closest the officer had ever come to a situation like this was probably in his basic officer-training course. The shield with stars on it indicated Kanalo was in the adjutant general's corps, and the rest of the army had a saying about that branch of service: Twinkle, twinkle, little shield, keep me from the battlefield.

The battlefield was not a place that Riley had been kept from in his eighteen years of active duty. In his time in the Special Forces, he had been on covert combat missions into Colombia and mainland China; even live operations in the United States itself that had involved death and destruction. After leaving the army two years ago, after the death of the woman he loved—a Chicago police officer he'd met on his last mission under the streets of Chicago—Riley had worked for an international security firm and gone down to the wastelands of Antarctica, where he'd run into commandos from North Korea trying to appropriate atomic weapons.

His official job now was to watch over Conner Young and keep the reporter safe. Hard to do with no weapon, he reflected, as he noticed the crew chief indicate one minute out to the lieutenant in charge of the soldiers. The landing zone was supposed to be clear, but from the intelligence reports Riley had looked at, over the course of the past week—ever since this unit of the 82d had deployed here to bring peace—the rebel forces had had a strange habit of showing up, at just the worst time, in places that had been "secured."

Riley was shorter than most of the men in the helicopter at five and a half feet. He was dark skinned, an inheritance from his mother's Puerto Rican side. His muscles were like rubber stretched over his bones. His body emanated barely restrained tension as the helicopter began slowing, but his dark eyes reflected the patience he'd learned over the past thirty-seven years—from the streets of the South Bronx through all his years of service.

The lieutenant reached over and tapped Conner on the knee, ignoring Riley and Kanalo. "We're one minute out!" he yelled to be heard above the sound of the engines and rotor blades.

Riley understood the reason he was being ignored. He knew the effect Conner had—any man would. She was a beautiful woman, with dark eyes, a thin nose, and a wide mouth. Her skin was the most alluring aspect of her face: soft and white, it highlighted her features to maximum advantage. She had not applied the camouflage stick that Riley had given her earlier this morning and he understood her reasoning behind that, but it was something he noted for future reference. Tucked under the bush hat that Riley had given her was Conner's trademark—thick black hair, cut short and framing her face.

Riley knew that Conner knew the effect she had, and he also understood that was partly the reason she wasn't wearing camouflage paint on her face. And he respected her for that self-knowledge, and for the fact that, while she did use it to her advantage in her job, she didn't complain about the times when it worked against her and people treated her like she was just a pretty mouthpiece for the network. Even in the midst of all this, Conner's charm was working on the lieutenant, who should have been thinking about other things.

They cleared a tree line and the Black Hawk swooped down into an open field on the edge of a small hamlet. As soon as the wheels touched, the soldiers scrambled off, weapons at the ready, forming a loose perimeter as a second bird came in. Within a minute an entire platoon, over thirty infantrymen, was on the ground. Riley crouched with Conner on the inside of the hasty perimeter. The hamlet consisted of eight cinder-block buildings with tin roofs. A dirt road ran through the center.

"Let's move in," the lieutenant called out, and the men stood.

Two black men dressed in cutoff shorts and T-shirts appeared on the edge of the village. They had AK-47s in their hands.

"Put down the weapons!" the lieutenant yelled to the men.

"This is *our* village," one of the men yelled back. "You put down *your* weapons." Despite the rhetoric, the two men were not holding their rifles in a threatening manner. The paratroopers came to a halt, forming a line less than forty feet from the edge of the village.

An old black woman came out of one of the buildings. "Let me talk to your leader," she said, her accent similar to that heard in the hills of Jamaica. According to intelligence, this area was settled by descendants of runaway slaves from that island, and they valued their independence fiercely. Unfortunately, this village was in the buffer zone being established by the United Nations peacemakers between the government and a dissident rebel group.

Riley could see that the lieutenant had not expected this type of challenge. "I'm in command," he said.

"I lead this village," the woman replied. "What do you want?"

"We're here to protect you," he said.

The woman held up her own rifle. "Ourselves, we protect. You, we don't need. You will only bring the infiltrators here."

The lieutenant was sticking to what he'd been taught and ordered. "We can help you defend yourselves."

"Ourselves, we have done that quite well. Your help, we don't need."

"We can add our strength to yours," the lieutenant said.

"For now," the woman agreed. "Maybe. But what about when you leave?"

"We—" the officer began, but he was cut off.

The woman spit. "Somalia, you left. Vietnam, you left. A long history you Americans have of offering to protect people, getting them to join you, then abandoning them and leaving them worse than they were before you came with your fine help."

If the lieutenant's face had not been painted green, Riley would not have been surprised to see it get red. "We are here to enforce the United Nations resolution regarding the peace between—" he tried, but again the woman interceded.

"What do we care for the United Nations, eh? Over a hundred years we have lived here. Our land this is and we want no outsiders here. Leave us alone."

"I can't do that," the lieutenant said. "My orders are to secure this village. A demilitarized zone is being—"

"This village is secure!" the woman yelled. Several other villagers had joined her so that there was now a small crowd of ten, eight adults and two children. All the adults were armed. The lieutenant shifted his feet nervously. This was not at all going the way he had hoped, and they hadn't covered this type of scenario in his Infantry Officers' Basic Course at Fort Benning and most certainly not in Ranger School.

The woman looked at the soldiers for several moments. "How do I know we can trust you?"

The lieutenant was taken aback. "We're Americans. We're here at the bequest of your government and under United Nations charter to—"

"Our *government!*" the woman's voice was full of scorn. "What does our government care about us? They'd rather see us dead out here in the swamp. Tell me, American man, why should we trust *you?*"

The lieutenant glanced at his platoon sergeant, searching for advice, but the woman beat him to it. "Lay down your weapons and I will believe you. I will let you into our village and we can talk."

"I can't do that," the lieutenant said.

"Then leave. We will never allow you in our village with your weapons." The woman turned away.

"Wait!" the officer cried out. The woman paused.

Riley knew the lieutenant was seeing his career go down the tubes with the failure of this mission.

"I will put down my rifle and join you. We can talk."

"And leave thirty armed men waiting to attack my people?" the woman replied.

Conner leaned close to Riley. "What do you think?" she whispered.

"I think we're going to see a fuckup," Riley quietly replied. He was looking about, checking out the buildings, the wood line. He had a very bad feeling in the pit of his stomach. The paratroopers were strung out in the open, waiting for their leader to make a decision. The lieutenant had become so preoccupied with the confrontation with the woman, he had lapsed in control of his platoon and the over-all tactical situation.

The woman smiled and took the magazine out of her AK-47. She tucked it into her waistband and ejected the round still in the chamber. "There. See?" She gestured and the other men did the same. "We are willing to compromise. Unload your weapons and join us in the village."

The lieutenant stood a bit taller. He turned to his platoon sergeant. "Have the men unload."

The veteran NCO stared at his officer. "But, sir—"

"Now!" the lieutenant ordered.

"Yes, sir," the sergeant said reluctantly. "Magazines out of weapons, chamber empty."

In the tradition of the 82d, the men did as they were ordered. Satisfied, the woman turned toward the first building. "Come, join us." She disappeared into a doorway. The platoon had started moving forward, when the rooftops suddenly erupted in a cacophony of small arms fire. Riley dragged Conner down to the ground as firing also roared out of the tree line to their left.

The paratroopers dived for what scant cover there was in the open field, tearing magazines out of their ammo pouches and desperately jamming them back into their weapons.

"Fuck, I'm hit!" one young soldier called out.

A loud beeping noise chirped off of Conner's web gear. "What is that?" she asked above the sound of weapons firing.

"You've been shot," Riley said. He reached into her combat vest and pulled out a small envelope, tearing it open. It had been placed there at the beginning of this exercise and now he read it. "At least you're not dead. According to this you've suffered a wound to your stomach. You need to call for a medic."

"Great game you men play," Conner muttered.

"I don't hear you crying out in pain," Riley noted. "Wounds to the stomach tend to hurt."

"Screw you, Dave," Conner said. "Keep it up and I'll show you hurt."

Most of the MILES harnesses on the men in the platoon were already activated, indicating that they had been hit by laser beams from the ambushing force. It was over quickly. A surviving squad leader rallied the remnants of the platoon and retreated to the far tree line, calling on the radio for reinforcements. Riley's MILES vest was silent, but he simply rolled on his back and stared up into the blue Louisiana sky.

"How do you shut this damn thing off?" Conner asked.

"The controllers will sort this out in a few minutes," Riley said. "Give the squad leader a chance to finish his radio calls for help." He looked around. The lieutenant took a key out of his rifle laser—making the emitter inactive—and placed it in his MILES harness, turning off the beeper. Not a happy camper, Riley thought, but unloading weapons—that was stupid, and the whole purpose of this exercise was to have people like the lieutenant do stupid things here where the price paid was a little humiliation rather than blood and guts.

A man wearing an OC—observer-controller—armband walked over. "What have we here?" he asked, stooping over Conner. "A dead reporter?" He looked at the card. "Ah, just wounded. Still, very bad for publicity," he said loudly enough for the lieutenant to hear. He took his controller key and turned her MILES gear off. He looked at Riley. "How come you didn't run with the others? You're still alive."

"I'm signed for her," Riley said.

The OC laughed. "Well, welcome to peacekeeping 101. As you can see, the natives aren't too friendly."

# Chapter 3

**Cacólo, Angola, 11 June**
Sergeant Ku buttoned his fatigue pants and threw several bills on the ground. The whore scooped them up and they disappeared into the robe she wore. She hadn't even bothered to take it off for their brief coupling, simply hitching it up at her waist. Prostitution was not exactly an art form in the Third World but rather a matter of everyday life.

Ku walked out of the "house" made of cast-off cardboard from relief packages and squinted up at the sun. There was the sound of a helicopter, and he watched as the aircraft banked across the sky and headed to the west. It was a pretty thing to watch. The Americans certainly had better equipment than the Cubans had had.

"There you are!" A soldier who had been in the patrol the previous day sauntered up. "The major wants to see you."

Ku frowned. "What for?"

"How should I know?" The soldier pointed at the hut with a knowing smile. "How is she?" He didn't wait for an answer, disappearing into the black hole of the doorway, already tugging at his pants.

Ku walked toward the garrison headquarters, wondering why the major in charge of the garrison here would want him. There was more going on in Cacólo than had happened in years. The Americans were coming and everyone was excited. After the patrol's arrival late yesterday evening, the officer in charge of the Cacólo garrison had absorbed Lieutenant Monoko's men into his own force regardless of Monoko's original orders. Not an uncommon occurrence in

Angola, where communication over distances was slow and erratic at best.

A guard lounging in the shade didn't even acknowledge Ku's approach. He knocked once, then entered. "Sergeant Ku reporting, sir."

Major Gungue, the garrison commander, looked up from some papers on his desk. There was another man in the room, a white man dressed in camouflage fatigues.

"Sergeant Ku. Welcome, welcome!" Major Gungue smiled. "This is Major Lindsay, the commander of the Americans who will be helping us."

Ku stood a little straighter. "Sir!"

The American returned his salute.

"I am assigning my most experienced men," Gungue said in Portuguese, the official language of the country and military, "to work with the American soldiers who will be coming here. You," he said, looking at Ku, "will work with one of the units that will be stationed here at Cacólo."

The American spoke for the first time, also in Portuguese, which surprised Ku but explained the fulsome way Gungue had just spoken about him. "Sergeant Ku, you will be working with Operational Detachment three one four."

"Yes, sir," Ku said, for lack of anything else to say. He had no idea what an operational detachment was, or what the numbers represented. He also wondered why he was being sent to the Americans. Gungue didn't have a clue whether Ku was experienced or not. Obviously the major didn't want to spare any of his own men.

"You will be the unit's interpreter and guide," Major Gungue said.

"Guide?" Ku asked.

Gungue smiled and now that smile made Ku nervous. He'd seen that look before on officers' faces, and it usually spelled trouble. The major walked over to the map pinned to the wall. "The Americans are going to clear this area of rebels. You must show them around." Gungue's hand swept across the northeast part of the country on the map. Ku knew next to nothing about the area. How could he? It was rebel territory. He felt trapped, knowing there was no way out of this assignment.

Then Ku thought about the heavily armed helicopter he had just seen flying away, the American helicopter. They had hundreds of those, from what he heard. Maybe this was not going to be as bad as it looked.

"The team will be here on Saturday," the American major said. "Do you have any questions?"

Ku had hundreds of questions, but he could tell by the look that Major Gungue gave him that it was best to keep his mouth shut. He found it strange that the American would ask such a question. Officers usually did not answer questions of sergeants in the Angolan army. Maybe the Americans were different, Ku thought. He eyed the combat vest the white man was wearing: top-notch equipment. If all the soldiers coming had such gear . . . Ku's head swam with the possibilities, not in terms of combat potential but in terms of the black market.

"No, sir. I have no questions."

### Fort Bragg, North Carolina, 11 June

"We are very pleased to have you here, Ms. Young, and to have you work with us." The 3d Special Forces Group commander, Colonel Burrows, walked around his desk and extended a hand.

"I'm pleased to be here," Conner Young replied, taking the hand.

To her left, the large young man in uniform snapped to attention. "I'm Captain Kanalo, sir. I'm Ms. Young's escort from the Department of the Army public affairs."

Burrows acknowledged the captain's presence with a hearty handshake, but his attention was focused on the lone woman in the room. To Conner's right, Dave Riley went unnoticed as Colonel Burrows introduced the other members of his primary staff to her. The Conner effect was in full force, Riley thought.

"This is Mr. Riley, my assistant," Conner said, breaking up the group in front of Colonel Burrows's large desk.

Burrows nodded. "Mr. Riley."

Riley forced himself not to snap to attention and salute. He simply nodded back. "Colonel." He felt uncomfortable. His years in the service had instilled in him many habits that the past couple as a civilian had not quite erased. It felt strange to be around men in starched camouflage fatigues while wearing khaki pants and an open-collar, short-sleeve shirt.

Riley could read the cloth markings sewn on the men's fatigues: Combat Infantry Badges (CIBs), jump wings, Ranger and Special Forces tabs, scuba badges, and others. From his own personal history, he knew what was needed to earn each of those, and thus he knew a little about each of the men in the room.

He wondered what they knew about him. He had never served with any of the officers present and for that, in a way, he was grateful. He preferred not to have anyone take interest in him. Of course on this job, that wasn't so hard. One thing he had learned in the past six months while working with Conner was that he could be wearing a clown's costume and doing backflips and most men would not notice him if he was in the same room with her.

"You had no trouble finding us?" Burrows asked.

The 3d Group headquarters was away from the hustle and bustle of the main post at Fort Bragg. It was set in the midst of a grove of pine trees off Yadkin Road on the edge of the reservation. Special Forces had been started on Smoke Bomb Hill on the main reservation, but as the years had gone by and the forces modernized, both the 3d and 7th Special Forces Groups along with the brand new Army Special Operations Command had moved over to this area of the post. In his last assignment, Riley had worked with the Special Forces Training Group just down the road and had seen the construction begun on these buildings, so it had not been a problem to find them.

The facility consisted of a group headquarters, three battalion headquarters, barracks for the unmarried soldiers, an isolation facility for mission preparation, and space for team rooms. It was a long cry from the old World War II "temporary" barracks that had housed Special Forces at Fort Bragg for forty years.

Riley didn't like the new buildings. They seemed too impersonal. The old white-sided buildings on Smoke Bomb Hill had history hanging over them like a fog. One could almost imagine one of the first members of Special Forces walking about and working there. These glass-and-brick pieces of architecture seemed more fit for the MTV generation. Riley smiled at that thought. He still thought of himself as a twenty-something soldier, and he had to remember that he was much closer to the forty-something, nearing-retirement age he had thought was so old when he'd first come on active duty.

Conner shook her head. "No, none at all. My cameraman is taking some background shots outside. Your compound here is most impressive. Captain Kanalo told me that would be no problem."

"No, that's not a problem." Burrows gestured toward the door. "Well, let's go down to the conference room and we'll get you up to speed on what's going on."

They moved down the carpeted hallway to a large room with a wood table as a centerpiece. The Special Forces crest was carved into the middle of the table, and the walls of the room were crowded with various plaques and photographs from the military elite of other countries around the world—places 3d Group teams had visited or hosted visits from.

Riley noticed that they had reserved one seat for Conner next to the group commander, one farther down the table for Captain Kanalo, and none for him at the main table as the staff filled in the rest of the leather chairs. He took a hard plastic chair along the back wall along with a few captains and a couple of NCOs.

Colonel Burrows didn't sit down right away. "As you know, Third Group has been tasked to support Operation Restore Life. An essential part, if I might say so. I will let my operations officer, Lieutenant Colonel Waller, brief you on the details of our tasking." With that, Burrows settled down in his seat and a gray-haired officer took his place.

The lights dimmed and Waller began speaking, remote in his hand. A slide came on the screen built into the wall. "On the twenty-third of May, 1997, this headquarters received a Special Operations Command mission letter. The Third Special Forces Group was ordered in this letter to support Operation Restore Life in Angola. Our specific mission guidance has two phases." Waller used a laser pointer on the wire diagram as he spoke.

MISSION GUIDANCE: OPERATION RESTORE LIFE
*PHASE I:* ESTABLISH ONE SFOB AT LUANDA
*PHASE II:* ESTABLISH AS MANY AOBs TO SUPPORT MISSION IN COUNTRY AS MISSION PLANNING DETERMINES.

"What these two phases mean is that we must deploy our group headquarters to establish a Special Forces forward operating base, SFOB, at the capital city of Luanda. That FOB must be prepared to send out our company headquarters, augmented, to establish advance operating bases, AOBs, at sites to be determined by the SFOB commander, Colonel Burrows, to support assigned missions."

"Excuse me a second," Burrows interrupted. He turned to Conner. "I hope all these terms aren't a bit overwhelming. Are they?"

"Not at all," Conner said. Riley could see the flash of white teeth as she graced the commander with a smile. If only Burrows knew what she knew, Riley thought. He wondered how long she was going to wait before bursting Burrows's bubble.

"Go ahead," Burrows indicated.

A new slide came up. Waller was indeed keeping it at a base level as he continued. "The Third Special Forces Group consists of a group headquarters, a headquarters and headquarters company, a support company and three Special Forces battalions.

"For this mission," Waller said, "we have formed a task force out of the group assets to conduct the mission: Task Force Angel."

Riley winced. He wondered who made up these names. He could well imagine the reaction of the actual men on the teams to being part of a task force with such a name.

Angel consists of the Group headquarters augmented by the First Battalion staff at the SFOB. The three AOBs, the three line company headquarters from First Battalion, are augmented by personnel from C Company, Second Battalion. And fifteen operational detachment alphas, or ODAs, commonly called A-teams, will be doing the on-the-ground work.

"The SFOB will be established in the capital city of Angola, adjacent to the Joint Task Force headquarters. Each of the AOB titles tells you the town where they will be established."

Waller paused. "Would you like me to give the background information on the situation in Angola and the strategic-level concept of operations?"

"I understand most of what is happening," Conner replied in a quiet voice. "Perhaps a brief summary from your perspective would be helpful, though."

Waller nodded. "I'm sure you know that this is to be a humanitarian mission into Angola with the dual goals of ending the decades-long civil war there and relieving the chronic famine that the country experiences. Basically you might call it an attempt at nation building.

"This attempt, though, is to be different from previous similar attempts, such as the failed one into Somalia several years back. Although the United Nations is sponsoring the mission, command of forces on the ground is to remain with participating countries. Because of that, Angola has been cut in half in operational terms."

A map of Angola came up on the screen. A red line ran across the middle of the country, splitting it into two almost equal portions, north and south.

"The United States Joint Task Force—JTF—area of operations is the northern half of the country. The southern half—and another difference in this operation—belongs to a Pan-African force spearheaded by the South African Defense Forces. The UN has issued the mandate. It is up to us and the Pan-African forces to enforce the mandate in the manner we see as best accomplishing that."

A new slide came up. "In support of United States missions in the northern half of the country, Third Group has three initial operational tasks: (a) conduct reconnaissance and targeting in advance of regular forces; (b) provide liaison with Angolan army forces; (c) conduct special operations as dictated by Joint Task Force commander.

"We have already deployed advance elements of our SFOB to Luanda, and they are in place and operational. The rest of the Group Staff, and you with us, will deploy on Friday. Two of the three AOBs are also in place, and the third is currently en route. Our first operational detachments deploy later this week to conduct reconnaissance missions and initial coordination with the Angolan armed forces."

Riley rubbed his chin in the back of the room. There was a lot that wasn't being said. Tasking C left a lot of possibilities open. One mission that Riley knew the group had to have under the broad title of "Special Operations" was E & E—escape and evasion for downed pilots. The aircraft carrier *Abraham Lincoln* was off the coast of Angola and air force units were at a Namibian airfield to the south of the country, all prepared to carry out a "no-fly" order in support of Operation Restore Life. Some of the teams of 3d Group were going to be out there in the hinterland prepared to pick up any downed pilots. The rebel forces did have access to ground-to-air missile systems and a fledgling air force, so there were bound to be some shootdowns.

There was also the possibility that 3d Group had some classified "special operations" tasked to it that they couldn't show Conner. The one that came immediately to Riley's mind, based on his study of the situation, was the capture or possible assassination of rebel leader Jonas Savimbi. That action would go a long way toward ending the civil war with one fell swoop. After the way the warlord Aidid had embarrassed U.S. forces in Somalia, Riley had no doubt that the people in the Pentagon wanted to be better prepared this time around. While assassination as a tool of foreign policy was technically illegal, Riley was certain no tears would be shed if "someone" took out Savimbi at long range with a sniper rifle, so long as that "someone" was never identified.

The history of the civil war in Angola was long and convoluted, and Riley had spent many hours studying it to grasp the changes that had led to the present situation. For most of the civil war, the United States had actually supported Savimbi and his rebel forces, both in the international political arena and with hundreds of millions of dollars of military equipment. The CIA was reported to have even supplied training for some of Savimbi's troops. As was not unusual in the modern world, the United States was going up against a force it had once helped train and arm.

It had taken Riley a little while to get the various groups straight in his mind. Savimbi led UNITA, the National Union for the Total Independence of Angola. The government party of President José Eduardo dos Santos was the MPLA, the Popular Movement for the Liberation of Angola. As the names of both factions indicate, they had originally been formed in the sixties and fought against the Portuguese colonial government. In early 1975, after a military overthrow of the government in Lisbon, Angola was granted independence from Portugal.

As usual, after independence is granted in a country, there was a battle between competing guerrilla forces to fill the power vacuum left by the withdrawal of the occupying power. In the struggle between the MPLA and UNITA for control of the country, the Cold War came to Angola. The Soviet Union supported the communist MPLA and the United States began sending money to UNITA. Not because it was a democratic movement (in fact, it was modeled along Red Chinese lines), but more because it opposed the communist MPLA. Riley knew that flawed logic well: the enemy of my enemy is my friend.

Because the Soviets acted more quickly and with more money, advisers, and weapons, the MPLA took over the capital city of Luanda and announced the establishment of the People's Republic of Angola on 11 November 1975.

By January of the following year, with the aid of ten thousand Cuban troops and over $250 million in Soviet military aid, the MPLA emerged as the dominant military power.

The U.S. supported UNITA with overt aid for a while, but the recent memory of the debacle in Vietnam caused a large outcry against any possibility of being drawn into another such conflict, which was what the war in Angola seemed about to turn into. As a result, the Clark Amendment was passed by the United States Congress, which ended all overt aid to UNITA. The MPLA was finally recognized by the OAU, the UN, Portugal, and over seventy other nations.

UNITA and Jonas Savimbi did not disappear, however. They simply found another supporter closer to home who did not like the idea of a communist government in power in Luanda. With South African backing, Savimbi slowly began a guerrilla campaign against the government. The MPLA was experiencing much factional infighting throughout this process, which further contributed to the confusion. In 1979 President dos Santos of the MPLA came to power in Luanda and another factor came to play in the Angolan story—Namibia, a province of South Africa to the south.

The South Africans in Namibia supported UNITA. The Cubans in Angola supported the MPLA. Both sides wanted the other to back off. Naturally, the South Africa government wasn't too keen on this idea and in 1981 launched assaults over a hundred kilometers deep into Angola against MPLA bases that were said to be supporting Namibian guerrillas. A decade of war followed between UNITA and the MPLA, with hundreds of thousands of casualties on both sides.

Eventually, as the Cold War wound down and changes occurred in South Africa, the external powers backed off, with the Cubans going home and the South Africans pulling back. But the Angolans themselves continued at each other's throats, as they were already home and had no place to go. And there was still considerable covert foreign interest in Angola due to the natural resources the country possessed—primarily oil and diamonds.

The story got even stranger, Riley knew. The international community, along with the UN, finally managed to get both sides to agree to a country-wide election in 1992. UNITA received 34 percent of the vote, while the MPLA took over 53 percent. Instead of standing by the results as he had promised, Savimbi took to the bush and continued his fight to militarily seize what had just been denied him by popular vote.

The last U.S. administration had finally seen the light and reversed decades-long support for Savimbi and recognized the rightfully elected government in Luanda: the MPLA. Times had changed and the red threat was no longer an issue.

Still, the fight had continued until late 1995, when Nelson Mandela had helped negotiate another cease-fire and apparent compromise between Savimbi and the ruling MPLA. Savimbi was given the second slot in the government in exchange for peace. The solution had worked for a while, but then last year, Savimbi had attempted a coup that had just barely failed. He had succeeded, however, in seizing half the country, including the critical diamond-mining region.

Riley's analysis of the military situation in the country was the same as most other military men's: without outside influence, neither side was likely to win and the war was going to drag on, with the majority of casualties coming from disease and starvation among the civilian population. It was a disastrous recipe that the United Nations wanted to abort but had always lacked the willpower and firepower to do so, especially after what had happened in Somalia. It was only after South Africa and the Organization of African States, the OAS, had proposed this joint plan, with U.S. support pledged, that action had been agreed upon.

Thus it had been decided that the U.S. and South Africa, along with other African nations, were going to go into Angola and defeat the man whose forces the U.S. and South African governments had supported for so many years. Typical, Riley had thought, reading the Angolan country study in preparation for this assignment.

Riley kicked back in his chair as Waller continued, giving Conner information Riley knew she already had in her laptop computer. He had to admit it felt good to be back around other Special Forces types after the past several years in the civilian world.

Riley perked up as Waller started outlining the schedule they'd prepared for Conner. There were numerous briefings for her with various elements of the SFOB staff and visits to the various AOBs planned. Riley watched as she raised a hand, interrupting the S-3.

"Yes?" Waller paused.

"I'd like to work with an ODA."

"Excuse me?" Waller's gaze shifted to his commander.

Colonel Burrows turned in his seat. "We have a complete schedule worked out for you, Ms. Young. You'll get a much better idea of what's going on at the SFOB and—"

"I'd like to accompany an ODA on their mission," Conner repeated.

Riley leaned forward in his seat. He'd coached Conner on this part and he was interested to see how it played out. They'd already set the ground work at the Pentagon the previous week. One thing Riley had learned the past year—Conner represented SNN, the Satellite News Network, and as such she was a very powerful person. The media was going to be an essential part of this mission as the administration tried to keep the voting populace behind the plan. Persons of power in Washington and around the Beltway understood that. He hoped Burrows would also.

"Going out with a team would be too dangerous," Burrows said. "This is a live combat zone and our rules of conduct—"

"That's the story I was sent to do," Conner interrupted. "There will be other people from my organization in Luanda to cover whatever happens at the SFOB. I'm here now," Conner continued, "for the purpose of getting down on the ground and showing the American people what is really going on."

"I'm afraid I can't take the risk of allowing you—"

Conner cut in again, probably the only time the group commander had been interrupted in his own conference room. "I'm afraid, Colonel, that this really isn't a matter that is open for debate. I appreciate your concerns, but I've already discussed this matter at length with quite a few people in—what do you call it—your chain of command?" She graced Burrows with a bright smile as he nodded. "Anyway, your chain of command thinks it's an excellent idea. General Long was most enthusiastic."

That was a bit of an overstatement, Riley knew. He'd been there in Long's office with Conner when the phone call from the secretary of defense had come in, ordering Long—commander of U.S. Special Operations—to allow Conner Young of SNN free rein on this assignment. The Department of Defense had a long history of being burned by the media, and many of the wounds were self-inflicted. Obviously, the new administration wanted to change history. Long had grimaced and accepted the inevitable, as Burrows was going to have to do. If you can't beat them, join them, seemed to be the unhappy new assessment of the Pentagon regarding the media.

Burrows turned to Captain Kanalo. "Is this correct?"

Kanalo was not a happy man, to be looking down the double barrel of a full colonel's glare. "Uh, yes, sir. She has complete authorization from the Pentagon, sir."

"But, Ms. Young, you don't seem to understand," Burrows said, trying to change his tactics. "These teams will be going out into the bush. They'll be going in fast and hard and—"

"Mr. Riley," Conner cut in again, turning her head toward the rear of the room, "has fully briefed me on the type of operations that will be conducted. He has had fifteen years of active duty service in the Special Forces."

Riley sat up a bit straighter in his chair as every eye in the room fixed on him, as if he were to blame for this unexpected change of events. Now he was glad he wasn't wearing a uniform.

"Mr. Riley and I spent the last three days down at the Joint Readiness Training Center at Fort Polk getting familiarized with peace-

keeping operations and media-military interface," Conner continued. "Everything has been arranged, Colonel."

"But—" Burrows sputtered.

Conner kept the initiative. "I understand the teams are in isolation and will be briefing back this week. I would like to get linked up
with one of your teams and sit in on their briefback."

"The briefback?" Burrows said, surprised at her use of Special
Forces terminology.

Conner smiled. "Yes. The briefback."

"I have to reiterate," Burrows said, "that the teams will be going
into very dangerous areas. We can't be held responsible for your
safety."

"You will not be responsible," Conner sweetly replied. "This has
already been cleared by SNN's legal people with the judge advocate
general's office. Also, to help ensure my safety, Mr. Riley is with me."

Burrows looked at Riley. "What was your MOS?"

"I was a one-eight-C before I went warrant," Riley replied, indicating that he'd been a Special Forces engineer while an enlisted
man, then had received a warrant officer commission.

"What units have you served with?"

"First, Fifth, and Seventh groups. Ranging in duties from junior
demo sergeant through team leader. My last tour was with the Special
Warfare Center assigned to the officer committee of the Q-course."

Burrows frowned. "Your name sounds familiar. Have we served
together?"

"Not to my knowledge, sir."

Burrows took a deep breath. "Well, as long as you understand that
we can't be held responsible for your safety and it's been cleared."
He turned to Waller. "Which team's briefing back soon?"

Waller grabbed a file folder and flipped it open. "We've got—" He
paused as he scanned the page. "Uh, I would suggest ODA three one
four, sir. You're taking their briefback at eighteen hundred hours
today."

Conner stood. "I won't take up any more of your time, then,
Colonel. I'll see you at the isolation facility at eighteen hundred
hours. Please make sure to put myself and Mr. Riley on the team's
access roster."

She shook hands with Colonel Burrows and walked out the door, Riley on her heels. They left the group headquarters. Mike Seeger, Conner's cameraman, was waiting outside, his rig lightly tucked under one arm. He was a huge man, well over six and a half feet tall with a bushy gray beard. He appeared to be the classic Harley biker, which was misleading because outside of his job he was a minister in his local church outside Atlanta and one of the gentlest men Riley had ever met.

"Are we in?" Seeger asked.

"We're in," Conner said as she led the way to their van.

"Burrows will call General Long," Riley warned.

"And Long will tell him that we're to go with the team," Conner said. "I called Long's bluff and we played his little war game in Louisiana for three days," she added. "Now he has to back up his end of the deal."

"I know that," Riley said. He paused and lightly touched Conner's arm. "I know you had to do that to get in with the team, but remember something. Burrows runs the SFOB and when we go in on the ground with the team, the SFOB is heaven and Burrows is god. He controls the most important thing to every team." Riley could tell that Seeger was annoyed with his religious analogy.

"What's that?" Conner asked.

"Exfiltration," Riley said. "We go in with a one-way ticket and Burrows and the SFOB control the ticket out, so don't get too far on his bad side."

"I'll remember that," Conner said.

"This colonel is just a man," Seeger said, putting his camera into the rear of the van. "I put my trust in no man. My trust is in God." He walked around to the other side to get in the driver's door.

"I don't know if God spends too much time on the ground in Angola," Riley muttered.

"What was that?" Conner asked.

"Nothing."

**Vicinity Luia, Angola, 11 June**
"I can't see a fucking thing in this jungle," a man with an Australian accent whispered in the dark.

Quinn tapped his top kick, Trent, who scooted back and edged down the line of prone men, searching for the whisperer. Through night vision goggles, Quinn continued to scan the forty-foot section of trail that was directly in front of his position.

A grunt and a few hisses told Quinn that his senior noncommissioned officer had found the source of the errant whisper and there would be no more violations of noise-and-light discipline. His men didn't need to see a damn thing; he had the goggles and he could do all the seeing necessary. He knew the exact placement of every one of his eighteen men and their weapons. All they had to do was fire between the left and right limits of the aiming stakes they'd carefully pounded into the ground during daylight and the kill zone would become just that to anyone unfortunate to wander into it.

Quinn had chosen this spot because it was where the trail ran straight for a while, with a steep slope on the far side. Anyone on the trail would be caught between the weapons of Quinn's men and the slope, which was carefully laced with some of Trent's "specials," as Quinn liked to call them.

Trent and Quinn had served together for four years now. A very long time in the life of a mercenary, in fact well past the effective life expectancy of those who stayed in the job. There were four or five men in the group that Quinn felt comfortable working with. The rest, well, they were what one got on the international market. Men searching for quick money and life on the edge. The problem was that most of the men wanted the first and weren't too keen on the second. Nine of the sixteen men were brand new to Quinn, picked up just before they'd crossed the border from Zaire into Angola two weeks ago.

They were here because the money was here, Quinn knew. He himself had earned enough here in Angola over the past three years to easily retire in comfortable style. It was such a perfect scam that even Quinn, hardened as he was by combat in half a dozen spots around the world, had to wonder sometimes.

He got paid by the Angolan government to kill rebels, and then he got paid again by a private party to collect what those he killed carried. It all added up to quite a bit of change.

But the money didn't matter much to Quinn. Even if he wanted to retire, he wasn't sure where he could go. Not many countries hung out welcome mats for mercenaries. He'd always planned on South Africa, but that was out now with the recent changes. Maybe somewhere in South America, if one could stay away from the cocaine cowboys. Namibia was a possibility if rumors he had heard about the future of that country came to fruition.

There was no way he could ever go back to Canada. Dear sweet Canada, where the fucks in their fancy uniforms had been so readily done with him after what had happened in Somalia. He'd served, and served well, in the best that mother Canada had to offer: the Canadian Airborne Regiment. The reward for being the best was a paltry check and a kick out the door. He'd heard that they'd finally done away with the Regiment itself because of the Somalia scandal, and that was the last straw. He'd never go back there. Not that he would be allowed back in.

Quinn interrupted his train of thought when he heard someone moving behind him. He assumed it was Trent, and that was confirmed when the NCO tapped him on the shoulder. "Andrews has a message on the SATCOM. He's copying it down."

Quinn twisted his head and looked over his shoulder into the thick jungle. Andrews was back there with satellite radio, their lifeline out of this hellhole. What did those niwits want now?

No time for it, Quinn realized as he heard noise coming from down the trail. He returned his attention to the matter at hand. There was the sound of loose equipment jangling on men as they walked; even some conversations were carried through the night air.

Bastards must think they're damn safe, Quinn thought. And they should be. This location was over two hundred kilometers inside rebel territory. And you could be sure the Angolan government forces, the MPLA, wouldn't be out here in the daytime, never mind the dark.

The point man came into view. Jesus, Quinn swore to himself, the fool was using a *flashlight* to see the trail. And not even one with a red lens! It looked like a spotlight in the goggles. They must be in a real hurry, he thought. Quinn adjusted the control and looked for the rear of the column.

There were thirteen men and two women in this group. There were more shovels than weapons scattered among them. They were also carrying two of their number on makeshift litters—ponchos tied between two poles. They were excited about the closeness of the border with Zaire and getting out with their load of contraband, and they must be in a rush because of the two wounded, Quinn thought.

Quinn pulled off the goggles, letting them dangle around his neck on a cord. He fitted the stock of the Sterling submachine gun into his shoulder. His finger slid over the trigger. With his other hand he picked up a plastic clacker.

The man with the flashlight was just opposite when Quinn pushed down on the handle of the clacker. A claymore mine seared the night sky, sending thousands of steel ball bearings into the marching party at waist level.

As the screams of those not killed by the initial blast rang out, Quinn fired, his 9mm bullets joining those of his men. The rest of the marchers melted under the barrage. A few survivors followed their instincts instead of their training and ran away from the roar of the bullets, scrambling up the far slope, tearing their fingernails in the dirt in desperation.

"Now," Quinn said.

It wasn't necessary. Trent knew his job. In the strobelike flashes from the muzzles of the weapons, the people fleeing were visible. Trent pressed the button on a small radio control he held in his hand and the hillside spouted flames. A series of claymore mines Trent had woven into the far slope at just the right angle to kill those fleeing and not hit the ambushers on the far side of the kill zone wiped out the few survivors.

"Let's police this up!" Quinn called as he stood. He stepped among the bodies and pulled off his bush hat, placing it, top down, on one of the few parts of the trail that wasn't covered with blood and viscera. "All the rocks in the hat."

He pulled up his night vision goggles and watched. Trent took up position at the other end of the kill zone. Quinn's mercenaries descended like ghouls upon the bodies, hands searching. A shot rang out as one of the bodies turned out to be not quite dead.

Quinn pulled a Polaroid camera out of his butt-pack and popped up the flash. He took several long-range pictures of the bodies. Then he took close-ups of faces and made sure he had each body accounted for, stowing the pictures in his breast pocket as the men continued their search. In the brief light of the flash, various black faces appeared, frozen in the moment of their death. Some of the faces were no longer recognizable as human, the mines and bullets having done their job. Quinn was satisfied with getting an upper torso and head shot of those.

As he got to the one of the bodies that had been carried, he saw a female's face caught in the viewfinder, the eyes staring straight up, the lips half parted. He could tell she had been beautiful, but she was covered in blood now and there was a rash across her face—broad red welts. Quinn walked over to the other makeshift stretcher. The body in there was in even worse shape. There was much more blood than the round through the forehead would have brought forth. The same red welts across the face. Quinn reached down and ripped open the man's shirt. His body was covered with them. Quinn snapped a picture, then slowly put the final picture in his pocket.

"Let's get a move on!" Quinn yelled out, moving back to his hat. After five minutes, the men began to file by, dropping their find into Quinn's hat until it bulged with raw, uncut diamonds.

# Chapter 4

**Fort Bragg, North Carolina, 11 June**

"ODA three one four's mission is to deploy to AOB Cacólo in the country of Angola and perform reconnaissance missions throughout Operational Area Parson at the discretion of the SFOB Commander."

Riley stood in the back of the briefing room, watching and listening. The officer who had just spoken, Captain Dorrick, was the detachment commander of 314. The rest of the team was seated in a line along the left side of the room. Colonel Burrows and his staff, along with Conner Young, were seated in a cluster of chairs in the center faced forward. Behind the captain were maps showing Angola.

Riley checked the right side of the room and smiled. The team's code names and other essential pieces of information were listed on easel paper taped to the wall—all within view of the team so that, when they were questioned, a memory lapse could be covered up with a quick read of the opposite wall. Riley had always had his team do that trick, and he was glad to see that it was still alive and well.

"The politico-military implications of this mission," Captain Dorrick continued, "are immense."

Riley glanced down at the mission briefback format he had xeroxed out of the new FM31-20, Doctrine for Special Forces Operations. This part of the briefback was new, and it was one that Riley had never heard briefed before.

Dorrick began explaining why the implications were immense. "The United Nations has issued a mandate in conjunction with the

Organization of African States, OAS, regarding Angola. Our mission is in support of enforcing that mandate. The political and military goals are fivefold.

"First, to end the civil war that has raged off and on in that country since 1975. Second, to prevent intertribal and ethnic warfare from breaking out upon the cessation of the civil war. Third, to end famine and introduce new agricultural techniques to the country to make it, at an absolute minimum, self-supporting in food. Fourth, to consolidate the natural resources of the country for the benefit of the majority of the people. Fifth, to improve the health and educational infrastructure of the country.

"Our higher commander's intent," Dorrick said, looking directly at Colonel Burrows, "is to focus our primary efforts on reconnaissance and intelligence gathering in the Lunda Norte province of Angola in preparation for the deployment of elements of the Eighty-second Airborne Division into the region.

"My intent, as commander of this team, is to divide the team into two reconnaissance elements to accomplish all assigned missions."

Riley looked down the team and focused on the team sergeant. The man was huge: a six-foot-three-inch rock of ebony. His name tag said "Lorne" and his patches showed a combat infantry badge, master parachutist, and Ranger tab. Lorne appeared competent, but the look on the man's face told Riley he didn't think the same of his own team leader. Riley had to agree with that assessment after hearing the captain's intent for his team: not original, to say the least, or well thoughtout.

As if sensing Riley's thought, Dorrick turned toward the team sergeant. "Each member of the detachment will introduce himself, and then the detachment's acting intelligence sergeant will brief the intelligence preparation of the battlefield."

Lorne snapped to his feet and his deep voice boomed out. "Master Sergeant Lorne. Detachment operations sergeant and senior noncommissioned officer." He remained standing as the introductions went down the line.

"Sergeant First Class Comsky, senior medic and acting intelligence sergeant."

Riley surpressed a smile as he looked at the squat, barrel-chested medic. Comsky and he had served together back in 1989 on the same team in Korea. They'd participated in a mission into mainland China that was still highly classified. It was a mission during which Riley had been shot and Comsky's medical skills had saved his life. Riley had felt great relief upon entering the briefback area when he'd spotted Comsky seated among the team members. There was at least one man present he knew he could trust.

"Sergeant Hoight, junior medic."

"Staff Sergeant Oswald, senior weapons."

"Sergeant Byers, junior weapons."

"Sergeant First Class Pace, senior communications sergeant."

"Sergeant Hampton, junior communications sergeant."

"Staff Sergeant Brewster, detachment senior engineer."

"Sergeant Tiller, junior engineer."

Lorne executed a right face. "Detachment. Take seats."

All except Comsky sat down. Captain Dorrick joined them, sitting next to Lorne. Comsky walked up to the maps at the front of the room and picked up a pointer.

"I will be doing the intelligence portion of this briefback. Operational Area Parson is in the northeast corner of Angola. It is bordered on the north and east by the international border with Zaire. On the south by Route 2, the major east-west highway in Angola, which is also the line of demarcation between American and Pan-African forces. Our western boundary is the Cuango River. Total area is approximately four thousand square kilometers.

"The land is primarily plateau grassland with rolling hills. In the river valleys and other low areas, particularly the northeast part of the AO, the terrain is heavily vegetated jungle.

"The immediate threat in the area is the UNITA rebels, under the overall command of Jonas Savimbi." Comsky slapped the pointer onto the map. "Savimbi is headquartered in Huambo, which is not in our AO. The chief rebel stronghold in our area is in Saurimo.

"This area, while not on the front lines between UNITA and the MPLA, is critical. Lunda Norte and adjacent Lunda Sul are the center of the diamond-mining area in Angola. Illegal exportation of these diamonds is UNITA's primary source of monetary support. There have been reports that UNITA representatives have directly traded raw diamonds for arms on the international black market.

"Intelligence analysis at Special Operations Command places control of the diamond mines as the third priority for our forces, after the destruction of the UNITA armed forces and neutralization of—"

"Excuse me, Sergeant," Colonel Waller, the group S-3, quickly cut in. "But, please, confine yourself to your team's area of operations and missions."

Comsky stared at the colonel. His bushy eyebrows turned in the direction of Conner, then back to Waller. "Yes, sir. To continue." He walked over to the map and dropped an acetate overlay down over it. "The rebel order of battle in the area is very incomplete." Comsky scratched his head. "I suppose that it's our job to figure it out when we get there. The AOB is working on several initial targets that we will designate for air interdiction upon arrival in country. After that, we will be searching for the enemy."

Riley smiled. Sergeants often had a way of saying things bluntly, and it cut against the formal grain of language in mission letters and operations orders. From his time serving with Comsky, he knew that the man would probably summarize their mission in one sentence and that would be that: We go in, eyeball the place, and report what we see.

"Although we don't know the disposition or strength of the rebel forces in our area, we do know their capabilities. They have individual and crew-served weapons, to include heavy machine guns and mortars. Hand-held air-to-ground missiles of the SAM-7 type are common throughout the country. There have been no sightings of armored vehicles in our area, but the rebels do possess various types of armor and contact cannot be ruled out.

"The local population . . ." Comsky paused and shrugged. "We don't really know what the local population thinks or feels. The indigenous population is most likely concerned with survival. There are numerous smugglers and black marketers in the area working the mines. There is no doubt they aren't going to be happy to see us show up. In some cases these criminal elements are armed as well as, if not better than, the rebel or government forces."

Captain Dorrick stirred and made a small hand gesture, indicating for Comsky to stay with the planned briefing and cut his editorial comments.

Comsky coughed and looked at the map, rerailing his train of thought. "Uh, the effect of terrain and weather on our operations.

Movement by air should be unrestricted, and we expect to have complete air superiority. However, if our air assets are not available, movement on the ground will be difficult at best. Maps show few roads, and the reliability of the roads marked is questionable." Comsky smiled. "We always have our feet, of course."

"You'll have air assets," Colonel Burrows growled. "You won't have to worry about that."

"Yes, sir," Comsky said, throwing a glance toward Riley at the back of the room. They'd both been on board the Black Hawk that had gone down on their way out of China in '89. They'd done a lot of walking there after having been assured they would have air support.

"This time of year is winter in Angola, but since the country is so close to the equator, the temperature is mild at best and hot at worst. It isn't the monsoon season, so rainfall won't be a major problem."

Riley listened with only half his brain as Comsky droned on about Angola and the intelligence the team was supposed to gather on their reconnaissance. Riley was troubled. Comsky had yet to say anything that Riley and Conner didn't already know from their research on a computer database available to any citizen. That meant, as usual, that the intelligence people in the Pentagon didn't know squat about the situation on the ground in Angola. Of course, Riley reminded himself, that was the whole purpose of these advance teams going in. To gather intel before the 82d Airborne, the big force, came in and cleaned things up.

It was better than the way the military had gone into Somalia and Haiti. In one case they'd been unlucky. In the other, lady luck had smiled on them. Obviously, the army didn't want to trust to luck in Angola. Riley had accompanied Conner to Washington, and he'd listened and watched. This Angola mission was a gigantic political gamble. If it worked, it would reverse the trend in the United States to back away from working in the international arena. If it failed, the administration would go down the tubes, not to mention the soldiers who would die as the down payment on the gamble. Operation Restore Life was being mounted against a massive groundswell of isolationism in the country.

The point that had allowed the president to sell the mission to Congress was the modified chain of command. At no time in the operation would U.S. troops work under UN command. There was a

UN mandate authorizing the mission, but both the UN and Pan-African forces would be answerable to their own governments.

While that made for good home-front politics, Riley wondered what would happen if something occurred to make the coalition unravel or if different countries developed different objectives during the course of the operation. There would be no overall commander to coordinate things.

Riley knew from talking with men he'd served with who had done some UN duty that by far the biggest complaint military personnel had with working under UN command was not what civilians and politicians would expect or understand. The media made a great issue out of the lack of resolve by the UN Security Council to employ force in such places as the former Yugoslavia, but the soldiers were much more concerned about the lack of logistics support and expertise shown by the UN Security Command. Modern warfare demanded a high volume of logistical support, and the UN had neither the resources nor the expert personnel to do it anywhere near adequately. United States forces working under U.S. command could at least count on their own logistical support. Without beans and bullets, the best-trained army in the world was worthless.

Comsky wrapped up the intelligence portion and Master Sergeant Lorne replaced him at the podium. Lorne went through the team's deployment from Fort Bragg through arriving at the AOB in Cacólo. Riley tuned back in when Lorne outlined the rules of engagement. Lorne's deep voice calmly enunciated orders that made it clear that the team was going to shoot first and ask questions later. They'd come a long way from marine guards standing outside a compound without a magazine in the chamber while a suicide truck bomb drove by.

The rest of the briefing told Riley little more other than to show that the team had done its homework and was prepared to deploy. Unlike a normal mission briefing, this one was short because no one really knew what was going to happen until they arrived at the AOB and the commander on the ground there gave them their specific mission taskings.

At the end, Captain Dorrick stood back up. "Sir, as you can see, ODA three one four is prepared to conduct any and all missions it might be assigned. What are your questions?"

Colonel Burrows nodded. "It sounds like you have prepared well, Captain. I notice you're short a team executive officer and an intelligence sergeant. Will that affect your ability to perform your mission?"

"No, sir. Sergeant Comsky is qualified to act as the team's intelligence sergeant."

"What about the possibility of contact with rebel armor that Sergeant Comsky mentioned?" Burrows asked. "Are you prepared for that?"

Staff Sergeant Oswald, the senior weapons man, popped to his feet before Dorrick could answer. "Sir, we will be carrying AT-4 antitank rockets. I have trained every member in the use of the rockets, and it will stop the types of armor we have been told the rebels might possess. Every member is also trained on laser designation of targets for air interdiction and how to call for fire support from air assets."

Burrows opened the floor up to the rest of the staff, and they asked several questions. Riley could tell it was mainly a show for Conner's sake. He wouldn't be surprised if the team hadn't done a briefback earlier in the day for Colonel Waller to make sure that they didn't screw up in front of the reporter.

By the time it was over, it was past eight at night, and Colonel Burrows escorted Conner out of the isolation area, back to Group headquarters. Riley waited as the rest of the hangers-on filtered out, until only the team was left. Comsky walked over and gave him a bear hug, lifting him off his feet.

"How the hell are you, Dave?" Comsky asked.

"I'm doing good, Ape Man. Nice show," Riley commented. The nickname was one that Riley's team in Korea had given Comsky. Both for his looks and his attitude. "I can't believe they've got you as intelligence sergeant. Talk about a contradiction in terms there."

"Keep it up, smart-ass. I can call you that, now that you're a civilian puke."

Riley pointed at the maps. "Sounds like you all are squared away."

Comsky grimaced. "Shit, you don't know the half of it. This is the biggest jug-fuck I've ever been associated with." Comsky scratched his underarm idly. "Well, maybe not the biggest," he amended, "but close to it. It sounds good but this place—"

"Comsky!" Lorne was suddenly there, towering over the two men. The team sergeant looked at Riley. "We've got some things to go over," he said, pointedly shifting his gaze to the door.

Comsky slapped the senior NCO on the arm. "Hey, Top, Dave here was my team sergeant in Korea. He's all right."

"He's not wearing a uniform now, as far as I can tell," Lorne said. He stared at Riley and the other returned the look. They remained like that, visually locked together, until Captain Dorrick walked up and stepped between them. "You'll have to leave now," he told Riley. "We may have had to let you civilians into our briefback, but we don't have to let you hang around."

Riley broke his gaze away from Lorne and looked at the captain. "All right." He tapped Comsky on the shoulder. "I'll talk to you later."

"Sure thing, Dave."

Riley walked out of the isolation area deep in thought. The SNN van was waiting for him, Seeger at the wheel and Conner in the back. She was looking at the screen of her laptop. Sometimes Riley wondered if she wasn't surgically attached to the computer.

"Well?" she asked.

"Well, what?"

"Come on, Dave." Conner turned off her computer. "You've attended a lot of those briefbacks. What was your feel?"

"I think the team is screwed up," Riley said.

That wasn't exactly what Conner had expected. "The team?"

"That Captain Dorrick has his head so far up Colonel Burrows's butt that he can't see the mission ahead. I don't know about the team sergeant. The team seemed organized well. I just didn't like what they were saying, but I think they were censored. Maybe by Dorrick, more likely during an earlier run-through by the Group S-3."

"Censored?" Conner repeated. "About what?"

"Let's put it this way," Riley said. "I hope they were censored."

"Why?"

"Because if they weren't, they don't know diddly-shit about where they're going or exactly what they're going to be doing when they get there."

"Hell, Dave, we've been researching Angola for the past two weeks with all the resources SNN has available and we don't know too much, either, about what's going on in that country right now."

"Yeah, but no one was shooting at you."

"Besides the team," Conner said, "what do you think of the mission?"

"I don't know yet. I'll tell you when we get on the ground. I'm going to pump Comsky for more information on the flight going over. At least we'll hit the ground running with those laser targets from the AOB as soon as we arrive."

Riley remembered the other parts of the censored operations plan he'd been allowed to read. Apparently the idea was to get the SF troops on the ground on day one of the air war. Take out all known targets before the rebels were ready or could hide in the countryside. After those initial targets, the teams would scour the countryside in conjunction with air surveillance, searching out new targets while the regular ground forces came in country.

It was this sequence of events that the military wanted to keep under wraps. They hoped to eliminate most of the MPLA armor and aviation on that first day, along with all fixed bases and lines of communication. That, hopefully, would prevent major, pitched battles as the 82d hit the ground. It actually wasn't a bad concept, in Riley's opinion. After Haiti and Somalia, everyone who watched SNN expected the military to move slowly and with great preparation. This fast knockout punch might just do the job. Then again, Riley knew, it might not.

Conner closed her eyes and leaned back. "Talk to Sammy lately?"

"Yeah, last night," Riley said.

"How is she?"

"The same."

Conner's sister, Sammy Pintella, had been the one who had brought Riley in contact with Conner the previous year, when she'd discovered information about a secret military base in Antarctica and they'd gone south to investigate. The three of them had been the only survivors after a run-in with North Korean commandos on the ice pack.

Conner's stock with SNN had risen greatly, based on the story that came out of the whole episode with Eternity Base, to the point where she now was able to pick and choose her own stories and investigate them with her own team. Sammy had stayed at her job at the National Records Center in St. Louis, where she had discovered the information. Riley saw her every once in a while and talked to her on the phone when the schedule permitted.

While Sammy was slow and steady, Conner was fast and brilliant. Technically, Riley knew he was being paid as a security consultant, but Conner had come to rely on his common sense more and more to balance out her driving instinct for the story that sometimes blinded her to other realities. This mission especially, because it was in Riley's area of expertise, she was counting on him. He didn't plan on letting her down.

# Chapter 5

**Luia River, Angola, 12 June**

The patrol looked like a party of ghouls as the sun revealed details. Most of the men were splattered with dried blood, and all were covered in mud. They'd made good time in the darkness, following the riverbed away from the site of the ambush. Steam was rising off the surface of the river, mingling with the trees that hung over it. The foliage almost touched in the middle overhead, making the band of water a dark tunnel with splotches of light playing along the surface.

"All right. We'll break here," Quinn called out. Daylight revealed him to be more than just a voice in the dark. He was a tall, thin man, his hair completely white, unusual for a man of thirty-six, but not for someone in his line of work.

Trent placed outflank security on either side and the rest of the men slumped to the ground, exhausted. Trent was the opposite of Quinn in body type: short and stocky with heavily muscled arms and legs. He'd been the heavyweight boxing champion of the regiment before Quinn and he had been cashiered after the episode in Somalia. His nose and ears showed the results of those fights, squashed and battered up against his skull.

"I suggest everyone take a bath and get cleaned up," Quinn said in a voice that carried across the patrol.

"Fuck, we're just going to get dirty again," one of the new Australians replied, pulling his bush hat down over his eyes. Those who had served with Quinn before were already beginning to strip down.

Quinn had Australians, English, French, Germans, and quite a few East Europeans in his group, along with several black Africans—the latter a fact that didn't bother him in the least, but had caused four South African merks to quit just before this latest foray into the bush. Good riddance was Quinn's view. Bullets were not a discriminator and the blacks were good men. They kept their mouths shut, followed orders, and did their job well. That was all that Quinn was interested in. The white South Africans had bitched too much anyway about things that they no longer had any control over. Change with the times or become a statistic was one of Quinn's mottos.

"Yes, but cleanliness is very important," Quinn replied, keeping his voice neutral.

"I'll clean when I get out of this pigsty of a country," the Australian joked.

Quinn pulled the bolt back on his Sterling, the sound very loud in the morning air. "You'll clean now."

The Australian stared at him. "What the hell, mate? You fucking queer or something?"

"I'm not your fucking mate. I'm your commander. Take your clothes off, put them on the riverbank, then get in line."

"You ripping us off?" the man stood, his weapon not quite at the ready.

"No," Quinn said with a smile. "I'm making sure you aren't ripping your buddies off." He centered the muzzle of the submachine gun on the man. "Now strip."

Soon there was a line of naked men standing waist deep in the water. The white ones had farmer's tans, their torsos pale, their faces and forearms bronzed from the sun. Quinn and Trent went through the men's clothes and gear, very slowly and methodically. A diamond was a very small thing to conceal, but they had experience. Trent had briefly worked security in South Africa at the diamond mines and knew the drill, and Quinn had followed his lead enough times to pick up the science of the search. It was just like customs officials. They knew the way people tended to think when they wanted to hide something, which usually led to the same common hiding places being used.

Quinn held up a plastic canteen and shook it. He turned it upside down, draining the water out, then took his flashlight and peered in. "Ah, what do we have here?" Quinn asked. He drew a knife and jabbed it into the canteen, splitting the side open. A small, soaked piece of cloth fell into his hand. He unfolded it. Four rough diamonds fell into his palm.

"Whose gear?"

The men all turned and looked at one of the Australians who had just joined them for this mission. The one who had bitched about taking a bath. "Come here, mate," Quinn called out with a smile.

The man walked out of the water, his hands instinctively covering his groin. "Going into business for yourself, are you?" Quinn asked.

"I didn't—"

The first round caught the man in the stomach and Quinn casually raised his aim, stitching a pattern up the chest. The man flew backward into the river, arms splayed, blood swirling in the brown water. Quinn turned to Trent, who had finished with his share of the gear. "Get to work, Doctor."

Trent reached into his backpack and pulled out a small cardboard box of surgical gloves. He pulled a pair on and gestured for the first man. "Come on, let's get this over with." The man walked up and Trent checked his mouth, nostrils and ears, then down the body to his groin. "Turn. Bend." The man grunted as Trent checked his anus, fingers probing.

"Next."

When Trent was done, the men redonned their clothes and gear. "Make sure you drink upstream from that shitpile," Trent advised the men, pointing at the body of the Australian, which was slowly floating away downstream. "We'll rest here for a few hours."

Quinn retired to the shade of a tree. He took the four diamonds and added them to the group in a leather pouch tied around his neck along with his old ID tags. Trent joined him there and handed him a sheet of paper. "The message Andrews received last night."

Quinn looked at a long list of letters that made no sense. "They encoded it. Must be getting worried about the Americans listening in."

Trent didn't reply. He took his knife out and began sharpening the already gleaming edge.

Quinn retrieved a Ziploc bag from his breast pocket. Inside it was a small notepad. He turned to the eleventh page—equaling the day of the month they received the message—and began matching the letters of the message with the letters on the page. Then, using a trigraph, a standard page that had three letter groups on it, he began deciphering the message. It was slow work, made more difficult by the need to figure where one word ended and the next one began. After twenty minutes, he had it done:

TO QUINN
FROM SKELETON
LINK UP WITH PARTY—VICINITY CHILUAGE ACROSS BORDER IN ZAIRE—AT COORDINATES SEVEN TWO THREE SIX FOUR EIGHT—DATE TIME SIXTEEN JUNE ZERO NINE ZERO ZERO GREENWICH MEAN—FOLLOW ALL ORDERS OF PARTY TO BE MET—BONUS ASSURED—CONFIRM ORDERS RECEIVED
END

Quinn pulled out his map and looked at the coordinates. About eighty kilometers upstream and then slightly to the east across the border into Zaire. He handed the message to Trent.

"Why the fuck don't they just drop this party off at one of these dirt runways in country?" Trent asked.

Quinn pulled a small Walkman radio out of his backpack. "You haven't been listening to the news. I pick up SNN radio broadcasts out of Kinshasa on this. The Americans have moved an aircraft carrier to just off the coast. They're going to start enforcing the UN's no-fly rule."

"But Skeleton could still—"

"He's got to cover his ass," Quinn cut in, looking around to make sure none of the others were in earshot.

"Why through Zaire?" Trent asked. "Skeleton's in Namibia."

Quinn had already considered that. "Northern Namibia is hot right now with the SADF and the other Pan-African forces. Easier to send someone around through Zaire. Besides, it's closer to us."

Trent looked at the map. "It's still a long fucking walk."

"We've got three full days to make it." He rubbed the stubble of his beard. "I wonder what the hell Skeleton wants us to do after we link up with this guy?"

Trent was anything but stupid, and he had been thinking about the upcoming changes. "Probably Skeleton wants us to eyeball the mines. Get ready for when Van Wyks gets them under his control. After all, Skeleton is his chief of security."

"That will put us out of business," Quinn said. "But I think we've played this one as long as we can. And he does promise a bonus. Exactly how much, though, I think we can negotiate over the radio the next few days, seeing as they apparently need us."

"We need Skeleton, too, though," Trent noted. "For the diamonds."

"No," Quinn disagreed. "We don't need him. Push comes to shove, we can take the rocks on the black market."

Trent nodded toward the merks. "Speaking of that, some of these boys just want to take their share of the diamonds and split."

Quinn laid a hand on the stubby barrel of his Sterling. "We move out in two hours."

## Atlantic Ocean, Vicinity 12 Degrees East Longitude, 12 Degrees South Latitude, 12 June

"Hawkeye Three, you are clear to launch. Over."

"This is Hawkeye Three. Roger. Out."

The catapult roared and the Grumman E-2 Hawkeye accelerated down the flight deck of the *Abraham Lincoln* and was airborne in less than three seconds. It turned due east and within twenty minutes a dark line appeared on the horizon through the cockpit window.

The twenty-four-foot-diameter radome piggybacked on top of the fuselage began rotating, and inside the craft the radar officer checked out his equipment. He picked up the CAC—combat air cover—over the *Abraham Lincoln,* then he began coding out all known civilian flights in the area, of which there were currently only four recorded.

As the Hawkeye went farther east over Angola, the four-hundred-mile reach of the radar covered more and more of the sky above that embattled country. A pair of F-14 Tomcats roared by, waggling their wings: the power to enforce the no-fly rule in case the electronic eyes picked up a target. The pilot of the surveillance craft kept them in a figure-eight pattern over the center of Angola as they settled in to their duty.

They had their first unknown contact exactly two hours and twenty-two minutes into their tour of duty. The combat information officer was very careful to note the time in his log. After the debacle in 1994 over Turkey where air force jets downed two army Black Hawk helicopters, killing all on board, already tight procedures had been given a few extra turns of the caution screw. The CI officer knew that there *were* Black Hawks from the Special Operations Command operating below. And this target was moving in a manner that told the radar operator it was a helicopter. The contact was over what was tentatively identified as rebel territory in the north central part of the country. It was moving to the north.

The CI keyed his radio as his fingers flew over his keyboard. "Stallion One, this is Hawkeye Three. I'm feeding you an unidentified bogey. Looks like rotary wing. Over."

The pilot of the lead F-14 confirmed he had the target information in his computer. "I've got it. Over."

"Vector in. Over."

"Roger. Over."

The CI checked to make sure he had all listed army flights accounted for. Then he double-checked. Then he triple-checked. He interrogated it, looking for a transponder code. Nothing. He tried calling the rogue flight on the radio. Nothing. Regardless, he started broadcasting a warning, ordering the flight to immediately set down, giving flight instructions to the nearest government airfield.

"Any change?" the CI asked the radar man.

"Yeah, he's going lower, trying to get into terrain masking. Must think he got picked up by ground radar." That was the advantage of the E-2's radome—it wasn't blocked by intervening hills, since it was looking down.

"Stallion One, this is Hawkeye Three. I have you intercepting in thirty seconds. Over."

"Roger. We're slowing. Wait one. Over."

The CI watched the dot representing the two F-14s merge with the target.

The pilot came back on. "We've got one MI-8. No markings. Over."

The CI knew that both the rebels and the Angolan government had MI-8s. He made communication through the *Abraham Lincoln* with the coordination cell of the Joint Task Force headquarters in Luanda to check whether it might be a government aircraft that had both failed to file a flight plan and was in the wrong place. The JTF headquarters confirmed that it was not a government flight.

Satisfied that this was not a friendly and, just as importantly to the CI officer, satisfied that he had all these confirmations on tape, he contacted his commander aboard the *Abraham Lincoln*. Eight minutes had now passed since the first contact.

"Six, this is Hawkeye Three. Over."

The reply was immediate. "This is Six. I've been monitoring. Break. Stallion One, this is Six. Over."

"This is Stallion One. Over."

"This is Six. You are clear to fire. Over."

"Roger. Out."

Eighty miles to the north of the Hawkeye, the lead Tomcat dived. The pilot of the MI-8 must have finally realized that something dangerous was happening, because the helicopter tried to evade. It was a futile effort.

A Sidewinder air-to-air missile leapt off the wing of the F-14 and was in the engine outtake of the helicopter in four seconds. A blossom of flame appeared above the jungle canopy, then disappeared into the sea of green.

The CI officer turned to the radar operator. "They seem to be taking this seriously," he understated. He knew it was important that they keep the sky clear for the next forty-eight hours to allow the coming infiltration of surveillance and targeting teams to occur unobstructed.

"About time," the radar operator said. "Show these people we mean business right from the start."

### Pope Air Force Base, North Carolina, 12 June

The C-141 Starlifter transport roared down the runway and took off. The interior was packed with pallets of equipment and people. Riley, Conner Young, and Mike Seeger were near the front of the aircraft, next to the pallet on which their camera and communication gear were packed.

Conner had a modem from her cellular phone hooked into her computer. She leaned over and tapped Riley as something new came in on it from SNN headquarters. "Navy F-14s off the *Abraham Lincoln* just downed a UNITA helicopter that was violating the no-fly rule."

This wasn't going to be like Haiti, Riley knew. Savimbi and the UNITA rebels weren't going to just give up their guns. The die was cast and they were now airborne for a war zone.

### Oshakati, Namibia, 13 June

The area around Oshakati was lined with washes, running from north to south where they fed into the Etosha Pan. That is, they ran when the rainy season was upon the land. Right now, the washes held not water, but men and their machines of war. Wheeled armored personnel carriers and gun carriers were spaced out, hull down, in the low ground, their crews resting in the shade created by ponchos stretched out.

The overall commander of these troops—the Pan-African Force (PAF)—was South African, both because the South African Defense Force (SADF) formed the majority of the military might and also because the SADF had the most experienced officers in conventional warfare. General Nystroom had served for thirty years in the SADF and he had weathered the many political and military winds that had swept his homeland. He had steered clear of the right-wingers and thus had survived the change in government. He did this not because he was particularly politically astute but because he had always viewed himself as simply a soldier, not a politician. He was one of the very few white officers of high rank left in the SADF. He wasn't sure why he had received this assignment and he didn't really care. Orders were orders.

Right now, Nystroom was standing in one of the top hatches in his South African–made Ratel armored command vehicle. He scanned the surrounding terrain through binoculars, noting the various types of vehicles that were scattered about the perimeter.

Unlike the campaign in Desert Storm, these troops had very few tracked vehicles. The SADF had long ago made the decision to mostly go with wheeled armor, sacrificing protection and weaponry for speed and efficiency. The distances involved in the war that South Africa had waged—prior, of course, to Mandela coming to power—in the forbidding terrain of Namibia, had been the first factor in canceling out the effectiveness of tanks. Most nonmilitary types, Nystroom knew—and many military who have never served in armor—did not realize that tanks were rated in gallons per mile, rather than miles per gallon, necessitating a tremendous logistical tail to any armored beast. A tail that the long distances involved in the desert made almost impossible to maintain.

The wind blew a veil of sand across the top of the vehicle and Nystroom felt it rub against his skin, reminding him of the most important prohibitor of tracked armor in this terrain. The sands of Namibia were soft and shifting. A sixty-ton main battle tank would bog down where an eight-ton wheeled personnel carrier would be supported.

All this knowledge and expertise Nystroom had learned and honed in the fierce guerrilla battles in the buffer states around South Africa while the whites tried to remain in power. It was an irony not lost on Nystroom or many of the soldiers now waiting in the northern Namibian desert that they now were to turn that expertise to the aid of their traditional black foe.

While the Americans were beginning to move by air and sea, the Pan-African Forces, of which the South Africans represented the most potent and skilled part, were spreading out across the desert, just south of the border with Angola, prepared for their historic mission. A map in the cargo bay below Nystroom showed the deployment of the forces in a loose line from Quedas do Ruacan in the west to the Capriva Strip to the east—a thin stretch of Namibia that ran between Botswana in the south and Angola and Zambia in the north.

Nystroom had been here before, and sometimes even he had to stop a moment and sort out in his mind the strange history of this area and the shifting alliances, of which this was just the latest.

The Ovimbundu people who populate northern Namibia are also the predominant tribe in Angola. After the United Nations had declared South African rule of Namibia to be revoked in 1966—which the leaders in Pretoria simply ignored—and the International Court of Justice declared the continued occupation to be illegal, the South Africans responded by beefing up their forces in the country. Nystroom had been a young lieutenant then and had traveled north for the first time in Namibia. The Ovimbundu had responded by forming SWAPO—the South-West African People's Organization.

The guerrilla war waged by SWAPO was weak at best. Open desert is not friendly to either side, but it is very difficult terrain for guerrillas to hide in. No taking to the hills or jungle here, Nystroom knew.

To further confuse the historical picture, when the Portuguese pulled out of Angola in 1975, the UNITA nationalist movement—also composed mostly of Ovimbundu—rose up. For a few years UNITA and SWAPO worked together and, with safe bases in Angola from which to strike and return, SWAPO started achieving some success. South Africa responded in Israeli fashion, taking the war into southern Angola and attacking the base camps. Thus Nystroom was not only not new to his upcoming mission, he was also familiar with the locale. He had been in the terrain in southern Angola that they were now preparing to invade.

Back then, though, in an even more shrewd move, South Africa had lined up with Jonas Savimbi's UNITA against the communists in the MPLA government, who were supported by Cuban troops. This alignment left SWAPO out in the cold.

Then, just a few years back, everything had changed once again. With Mandela in power in South Africa, the policy shifted and now the MPLA government was in favor with both Pretoria and the international community. Even the Americans, who in their blinded antired vision had supported Savimbi against the MPLA and the Cubans, had shifted and now endorsed the elected MPLA government.

The cease-fire of '95 had brought hope that the long civil war would be over. Mandela had staked much of his international reputation on bringing Savimbi into the fold, and when Savimbi had broken his word and taken to the bush again the previous year, Nystroom had felt it would only be a matter of time before Mandela did something about the betrayal. Black or white, the leaders in Pretoria seemed to respond the same.

In Namibia, SWAPO, after decades in the desert, was brought into the fold and now SWAPO guerrillas sat in the desert next to their former enemies in the South African Defense Force. There were also troops representing other former enemies of South Africa present in the Pan-African Force (PAF): soldiers from Zimbabwe (formerly Rhodesia), Mozambique, Tanzania, Egypt, Cameroon, Senegal, and smaller contingents from several other countries.

Namibia, now technically independent, was still heavily dependent on South Africa for everything. SWAPO had some representatives in the government in Windhoek, but there wasn't much in Namibia to govern. The largest industry was diamond mining, and that was in private hands. There was talk among some of the right-wingers in South Africa of creating a white homeland by carving a chunk of land out of Namibia, and Nystroom wasn't too sure whether Mandela would or would not let that happen if the right-wingers tried. So even though he was oriented northward, Nystroom still had to keep an eye looking over his shoulder to the south.

Nystroom knew the entire operation was a gamble politically. He felt confident that the PAF and Americans would defeat Savimbi's UNITA rebels. The question was what would happen then? Would the country unite? Would it disintegrate into tribal warfare like Rwanda had? Could they hold on to the victory or would the pictures of dead and wounded cause the public to cry out for the troops to come home and give up what they had won? There was a good chance the Americans would leave, Nystroom felt. This was not their continent or their fight. But it was his.

Angola was to be the first test of a new African consciousness, a consciousness Mandela had forced upon the other heads of state on the continent because of the apathy of the outside world. The help of the Americans was necessary both militarily and politically, but the bottom line was that it was the PAF that was going to be left on the ground after the Americans withdrew.

Nystroom ran a hand through his thick beard. He looked more like a friendly grandfather—which he was—than a thirty-year soldier. He had a large belly and sharp blue eyes peering above the white of his beard. His portly presence tended to make others think less of his mental abilities, as if there were some correlation between weight and brainpower. But Nystroom was still in uniform and in command where the vast majority of his contemporaries had been sucked under by the sands of time and political change.

Nystroom considered himself a professional soldier first and foremost, and he had read the great writers of military strategy such as Sun Tzu and Clausewitz. He knew there were factors other than pure military operations and political maneuvering involved here, of course. Mandela was not just concerned about the politics of nation building in Africa. There was the threat that the entire region could destabilize if all these civil wars were allowed to rage unchecked. Borders were lines drawn on maps. In Africa many of those lines had been drawn by the colonizing powers with little regard for tribal, geographic, or economic factors. The result was that civil wars in Africa often spilled over such borders. There was most definitely a self-preservation drive in Pretoria to keep such a war from coming south by going north first with peacemaking efforts.

Economics added into it also, Nystroom knew. That was an area that was very sensitive and one he tried to steer clear of. There were shadowy forces at work both in Pretoria and out here in the PAF, all involved in complex maneuvering. There were oil and diamonds in Angola, as there were diamonds here in Namibia. The right-wingers were just one of several factions with interests in this part of the world.

The South African government had publicly maintained for decades that its involvement in Namibia was for protection against incursions by terrorists and guerrillas, but what had not been so public was the vast amount of capital that was flowing out of the diamond mines in the southwest portion of the country. There were over a thousand square miles of coastal area near Lüderitz that were a restricted area and highly policed with private armies—the backbone of the Van Wyks diamond empire. No one outside of the Van Wyks inner circle knew how many diamonds came out of that land, since the Van Wyks Corporation controlled over 80 percent of all diamond sales on the planet.

There was little doubt in General Nystroom's mind that Pieter Van Wyks, the elder statesman of the family, had given more than a little nudge in support of this operation to stop the black market trade in diamonds by UNITA rebels and to try to bring the mines in Angola under his cartel's control. How strong that push was, Nystroom preferred not to know.

He knew that the officer corps of the SADF under his command was riddled with men drawing more money from Van Wyks under the table than in their paychecks from Pretoria. Nystroom would prefer not to have to find out where their loyalties really lay. When Mandela had come to power, the country had held its breath, waiting to see which way the military would turn, which in reality meant which way Pieter Van Wyks ordered those he controlled to act. It was something of a surprise that Van Wyks had discreetly let it be known that the peaceful transition was to be supported.

Nystroom and many others did not know what to make of that. Perhaps there was some secret deal between Van Wyks and Mandela. Or perhaps Van Wyks had other plans. Whichever it was, Nystroom was not going to worry about what he did not control and did not know.

Nystroom grabbed the rim of the hatch and lowered himself down. He had enough to concern himself with simply keeping the military coalition together. It was the politicians' job to worry about the other aspects. While the SADF had fought in the area for many years, this was by far the largest deployment of force ever made in this direction. The desolate terrain of Namibia and the Kalahari Desert to the east in Botswana were very effective natural defenses for the homeland, and the SADF had always oriented the bulk of its forces to the east and south.

Nystroom looked at the bank of radios that took up most of the room inside the carrier. They were his link not only with his forces here, but with his higher headquarters over a thousand miles to the south, in the underground communications complex at Silvermine near Cape Town, and the American commanders to the north, already on the ground in Angola. Nystroom had several American liaison officers assigned to his staff, and he had sent several of his men north to work there in coordinating actions.

The report of the downing of the MI-8 helicopter had cheered Nystroom. It meant the Americans were here to do business. At least their military was, he amended. He just hoped that the politicians kept their hands out of the action that was coming, or else they could end up with another fiasco like Desert Storm had turned out to be: a military victory cut short of achieving the strategic goal. While Nystroom tried to keep his own hands out of political affairs, he wished politicians would reciprocate and keep their nose out of the military's once the die was cast.

Nystroom settled onto a stool and looked at the map of Angola. So much was going to happen in the next several weeks. The operations plan for the PAF movement into southern Angola was over three hundred pages long. And from his long military experience, Nystroom knew there was one truism he could count on: Something they had not planned for would develop and have to be dealt with.

### Airspace, Southeast Atlantic, 13 June

They had refueled in Cape Verde and were on the final leg of their long journey. Not only did they have to travel across the Atlantic, but they also had to go from northern hemisphere to southern.

Riley walked along the thin pathway between soldiers and pallets. Men were spread out everywhere, huddled under poncho liners, trying to get a few hours of sleep before they arrived in Angola. He found Comsky snug as a bear in his cave in the slight space afforded between two pallets of duffel bags. Even above the roar of the jet engines, Comsky's snores could be clearly heard.

"Hey. Hey," Riley said, nudging the sergeant on the shoulder.

"What?" Comsky muttered, not bothering to remove the poncho liner over his face.

"It's me, Dave."

"Yeah, and?"

"Stop dicking around," Riley said.

Comsky slid the liner down and sat up. "So you decided to come along anyway. Didn't you get enough of this shit when you were active duty?"

"The pay's better on this side," Riley said.

"Really? They need a medic at SNN?"

"You know a good one?" Riley asked as he squeezed into the hole and sat next to Comsky.

"Very funny," Comsky said.

"You still work under the proven medical theory that you're only sick if you're bleeding?" Riley asked. It had been a standing joke on the team they had both been on.

The smile left Comsky's face. "Not on this trip. You got all your shots?"

Riley pulled out a yellow card from his pocket and handed it to his former teammate.

Comsky read down. "Yellow fever, anthrax, botulism, Q fever, tularemia. Yeah, they gave you the works. Have you had your hepatitis series?"

"Yes."

"Then they've given you everything they could give you."

"You worried about something?" Riley asked.

"Every time I go to Africa, I get worried. Man, we're just south of the Kinshasa highway. Know what they call that? The AIDS highway. And there's no innoculation for that particular bug."

"I'll keep my dick in my pants," Riley said.

"Yeah, well you'd also better watch whose sucking chest wound you try to bandage up, too, if there's blood all over the place. And AIDS is a level three bioagent. They've got shit over there that would make you wish you had AIDS."

The first sentence brought to Riley's mind the flight out of China years ago with Comsky desperately trying to stop both the air and the blood from flowing out of a wound in Riley's torso. He rubbed a hand across the scars knotted on his chest. "I owe you."

"It was my job. Still is. Besides, you were bleeding, so I knew you were really hurt, not like some of these wimps that are always complaining about something or other bothering them."

"What else are you worried about, besides little bugs?" Riley asked.

Comsky wasn't done with his warnings. He wouldn't be a good medic if he stopped here. "Don't drink the water if I or another medic haven't specifically cleared it for consumption. And don't eat any local meat. Anything that might have blood in it, human or animal, stay away from. Stay with MREs the entire time."

Comsky shook his head. "First time I deployed to Africa I thought I knew my stuff. Hell, I'd been to the Far East and South America and seen some bad things. Boy, was I in for a rude awakening. I got told, but I didn't quite believe it. It was a year and a half ago. I went to Liberia on a MEDCAP."

Riley knew a MEDCAP was a peaceful mission where Special Forces medics worked with aid agencies on health problems in the country they were deployed to. It was SF's way of waging peace.

"We went in there with big hearts," Comsky said. "You know, save the children and all that. And we did save a whole bunch of people. But after a while, man, you just can't take it anymore. Don't shake hands." Comsky didn't smile at the sudden change in his speech. "I'm serious, Dave. You get to the point after watching all your buddies get the cruds that you don't even want to shake hands anymore and catch something from that. I *triple*-gloved every time I had to give a shot or work around blood.

"It's a fucking mess. And the people, I hate to say it, but they're used to it. A lot of them don't give a fuck. You teach them proper sanitation one day and walk down by the river the next and there they are letting their animals take dumps and urinate in the river while they're drawing water to drink not ten feet away."

Riley was quiet. He'd never seen Comsky so animated and emotional. That MEDCAP must have been a traumatic experience. It was one aspect of all these missions that the media hadn't caught on to yet—the emotional toll on the peacekeepers who had to live among the death and dying that the rest of the folks back in the states got in thirty-second clips every night on the news. It was something he wanted to impress upon Conner. When they got on the ground, he needed to have her interview Comsky. Of course, they'd have to clean up his language and some of his slant. Riley had been around Washington and Atlanta enough to know what was politically acceptable and what wasn't.

"I tell you," Comsky continued, "it's a damn mess. I can blame some of the adults, they should know better—at least after we teach them, they should—and choose not to, but it's the kids that get to me. They didn't ask to be there. And they're the ones that get it worst. You know how many amputations from mines I had to do? Kids out playing and they blow themselves up? You know how many millions of mines are out there all over the world, just waiting to get tripped? Hell, I could go to work in any emergency room in the United States with my experience." He lapsed into silence and Riley let it ride for a little while before pushing on.

"How do you feel about this mission? You shouldn't have much contact with the natives."

Comsky sighed. "Ah, I don't know, Dave. Captain Dorrick's been kissing everyone's ass who outranks him. Lorne just joined the team about three weeks before this mission. He was in training group with the Camp Mackall survival committee before this. He's got a good rep but we don't know him. We don't have a warrant officer and our top two guys are question marks. Doesn't it give you a warm and fuzzy feeling on the inside, especially when you're getting ready to go on a live mission?

"The recon mission looks pretty simple on the surface, but you and I know that simple on the surface gets pretty deep if you break through the ice," Comsky continued.

"You'll have air superiority," Riley noted.

"Yeah," Comsky said without much enthusiasm.

Riley waited, but there wasn't any more forthcoming. "Listen, Ski, I haven't had a lobotomy. That briefback was a bunch of bullshit. There was no mission there. You're just going in to look at what specifically? And what are you going to do about what you're looking at?"

Comsky looked at him. "Between you and me? No forwarding this info to the news lady?"

"You got my word."

"Okay, the big thing is the first two days of this operation. These UNITA guys got armor and artillery. They have some air assets. Hell, they control a good portion of the country. We're going in to put them on their knees before the infantry guys come in to do the cleanup."

That confirmed what Riley had read in the classified operations plan that a friend of his had allowed him a brief look at. He had not told Conner what he knew because that would be violating the trust his friend had put in him. He had read it in order to be prepared for whatever might be coming. "The air force sold a bill of goods on this one, didn't they? They're still thinking Desert Storm and smart bombing."

"I hope it's a real bill of goods," Comsky said, "because our butts are going to be hanging in the wind."

"They can't be totally counting on knocking out all that equipment from the air," Riley said.

"Well, actually, Dave, I think they do believe they can do it. You and I know better, but the people up in the big house—well, it's a lot nicer to bomb from ten thousand feet than to have to send in the poor bloody infantry to dig the bastards out at the tip of a bayonet. But that's the way it's going to end up. We just hope the flyboys take out all the major stuff and break down the rebels' infrastructure so the Eighty-second can take them down piecemeal."

"And if some of the rebels' armor survives?" Riley asked.

"You know that the Eighty-second with air assets from the Eigteenth Airborne Corps is doing the majority of the groundwork, right?"

"Yeah."

"What you don't know is that they got elements of the Twenty-fourth Infantry on a ro-ro off the coast with the carrier task force."

Riley knew what a ro-ro was—a roll on, roll off cargo ship, capable of rapidly landing armor. And the 24th Infantry out of Fort Stewart, Georgia, was mechanized. "Bradleys?" he asked, referring to the army's top-of-the-line armored personnel carrier.

"A mechanized battalion—two companies of Bradleys and one company of Abrams tanks." Comsky shrugged. "It's a nice thought— I guess the secdef doesn't want to catch any shit after the stink about ignoring the armor request from Mogadishu. But the terrain isn't favorable for cross-country movement to our AO. Maybe if they get into a firefight in Luanda, which ain't likely." He chuckled. "Maybe they could airdrop one of those Bradleys in our AO.

"What *does* make me feel good, though, is that they got a Ranger task force on the *Abraham Lincoln*. That's real hush-hush, but they told us on the teams that in response to the overall feeling that our dicks were going to be hanging out in the wind until the Eighty-second landed. If the rebels get together in more than squad size, we could be in deep shit, but knowing those Rangers can fast-rope in makes it a bit better."

"Why is it hush-hush?" Riley asked. "I understand keeping the air strikes secret so the rebels don't hide their equipment, but it seems like they would publicize the Rangers and the armor to the max.

Make the rebels worry and maybe even fool them into forgetting about the air stuff."

Comsky didn't say anything.

"You were going to say something about another mission during the briefback and the Group S-3 cut you off," Riley said. "What were you going to say?"

Comsky shook his head. "Just rumors that I heard around Bragg before we went into isolation. You know how people talk." He shook his head. "Nothing, really."

Riley looked him in the eyes and Comsky returned the look. Riley nodded and tapped him on the shoulder. "Thanks."

Comsky pulled his poncho liner back over his head. He was snoring before Riley got out from between the pallets.

### Luia River, Angola, 13 June

"We got a reply," Trent said, handing Quinn a piece of paper with a string of letters on it.

"Put out a perimeter," Quinn ordered. "We'll spend the night here."

He sat down and pulled out his code book to break the message. When he was done, he handed it to Trent.

```
TO QUINN
FROM SKELETON
   VICINITY CHILUAGE ACROSS BORDER IN ZAIRE AT CO-
ORDINATES SEVEN TWO THREE SIX FOUR EIGHT—DATE
TIME SIXTEEN JUNE ZERO NINE ZERO ZERO GREEN-
WICH MEAN—LINK UP WITH PARTY—FOLLOW ALL OR-
DERS OF PARTY TO BE MET—PARTY TO BE ONE MAN TO
BE TAKEN TO LOCATION NORTHEAST ANGOLA THEN
BROUGHT BACK TO PICKUP POINT—YOUR CONFIRMA-
TION RECEIVED—BONUS ONE MILLION TOTAL HALF
ALREADY IN YOUR ACCOUNT OTHER HALF WHEN YOU
RETURN PARTY
   END
```

"A million? They already put half in?" Trent whistled. "They must want us to do this job real bad."

Quinn pulled out a match and burned the paper with the message on it. "Skeleton's never been stingy. A million isn't that much to him or the man he works for."

"It's a lot to *me*," Trent said. He looked over at the men spread about the area. "How about them? What do you want to tell them?"

"We'll cross that bridge when we get to it," Quinn said.

"You mean we'll destroy that bridge when we get to it," Trent said with a smile.

"Maybe."

"Some of 'em are good men," Trent said. "We could let the rest go when we get to the border. Just take a couple with us and that will increase the shares on the million."

"Yeah, maybe," Quinn replied. "Like I said, we'll deal with that when we have to. We'll need a few of them to do this. We might run into some of Savimbi's boys."

"So what do you think this fellow is going to do in northeast Angola?"

"I don't have a clue."

"Can't be diamonds," Trent said. "We've got that base covered already. And that's the only thing in this whole stinking place that's worth that much money."

"Well, obviously there's something else to be done or found around here that's worth a million now."

"I wonder if Skeleton's boss is behind this whole Angola thing," Trent said. "I've got my theories about—"

"You ought to be keeping such talk to yourself," Quinn cut in, looking around. "Skeleton and his people would as soon kill you as look at you. You and I both know he works for Pieter Van Wyks, and you should know even better than me that *he* don't like people talking about him." Quinn leaned closer to Trent. "I wouldn't doubt but that one or two of these fellows we've got with us answer directly back to Skeleton. Making sure we don't keep any of the diamonds and go into business for ourselves."

The look on Trent's face told him that his top NCO had not even considered the possibility of a double agent in the patrol. "You have any idea who the bastards are?" Trent asked, his hand slipping to the butt of his knife.

"I don't even know for sure there is a spy or spies, but I wouldn't put it past Skeleton. He's a mean dude." Quinn tapped him on the shoulder. "Let's just watch each other's backs, right?"

## National Security Agency, Fort Meade, Maryland, 13 June

Tim Waker carefully dipped the tea bag in a mug of hot water. He placed it on a spoon, then wrapped the string around, squeezing the last drops out, and discarded the bag into the waste can next to his desk. He cradled both hands around the mug and leaned back in his large swivel chair, staring at the oversized computer screen in front of him. He had six programs accessed and his eyes flickered from one to another.

The NSA was established in 1952 by President Truman as a replacement for the Armed Forces Security Agency. It is charged with two major responsibilities: safeguarding the communications of the armed forces and monitoring the communications of other countries to gather intelligence. The term *communications* had changed from the original mandate in 1952. Back then the primary concern was radio. Now, with the age of satellites and computers, it involved all electronic media.

Waker had been "given" Angola yesterday. Normally, the NSA didn't invest much time in the entire continent of Africa, never mind a single country. There just wasn't that much being generated there to zoom in on, besides the relative lack of strategic interest in the area. But with the recent deployment of U.S. forces, the NSA director had passed the order down and it had stopped at Waker's desk. Waker, and the two men picking up the other shifts, were to keep the NSA's electronic eye on Angola.

So far it had been interesting, but mainly because he had spent the last several hours sifting through the communications and signals generated by both the U.S. forces and the Pan-African forces. His ears and eyes were a battery of sophisticated and tremendously expensive equipment.

A KH-12 satellite had been moved to a fixed orbit over Angola for the duration of the mission. Hawkeye and AWACS surveillance aircraft provided radar coverage of the airspace. A JSTARS plane was on call to paint a more complete picture of what was happening on the ground across the light spectrum.

Right now, the KH-12 had divulged some interesting information. Someone in the Lunda Norte province had transmitted several hours ago on a narrow band to a satellite and a reply had been sent back down just fifteen minutes ago. Waker put the tea down and leaned forward. He accessed information from the database on the satellite that had been the middleman on both transmissions and found out it was a commercial one that had hundreds of corporate clients. Because of that, the other end of the message was more difficult to trace. He was only able to tell that one end of the relay was in Lunda Norte because the U.S. military had its own satellites overhead and they had picked up the uplink coming out of Angola. If it was essential, Waker knew he could use other means to get information out of that civilian satellite, which, according to the computer, was owned by a French communications consortium.

But the only way to know if it was essential would be to know what the message was. Not being in the direct uplink of the broadcast, the KH-12 had only picked up part of the transmission. As he had expected, what the satellite had intercepted was not decipherable. The computer's best guess was that it was encoded in a one-time pad format.

Waker summarized the information and put it in his duty log. Then he ordered the computer to alert him the next time a message was picked up. Until then, it wasn't that important.

### Airspace, Angola, 13 June

"I've got a faint image," one of the radar operators in the back of the Hawkeye announced. "Helicopter. She keeps popping up and down. Staying real low."

"Location?" the combat information officer asked.

"Departing Huambo. Heading northeast."

The CI checked the overlay. He was supposed to have four F-18s on station, but one had mechanical problems and its partner was staying close to the carrier offshore. That meant he only had two warplanes in the sky. This was very bad timing. He had to keep the pair in close to his own position for defensive purposes on the off chance the rebel air force launched some sort of preemptive strike against either the Hawkeye or a quick cross-border attack against the PAF forces massing in Namibia.

After the downing of the MI-8 earlier today, everyone was operating on a higher level of anxiety. He could ask the op center on the *Abraham Lincoln* to give him two more planes, but the CI knew that the officer in charge of the planes on board the carrier had a lot on his mind right now and they were in the middle of important preparations.

"Still up?" the CI asked.

"He's staying low, now following the main road to the east."

That meant the chopper was on the dividing line between the U.S. and PAF forces. It could go either way before he could get planes on it.

"Let it go," he decided. "It will probably land before I can get something in the air to take care of it. Log the sighting and transmit the information to headquarters."

"Yes, sir."

# Chapter 6

**Cacólo, Angola, 14 June**

"How come you military people always do things in the middle of the night?" Conner Young asked.

"Because it's more uncomfortable," Riley replied facetiously. "And also more difficult for reporters to see what they're doing in the dark. Never mind that it might catch the bad guys off guard." They were on a UH-60 Black Hawk flying east over the Serra da Chela mountain range, heading up to the high plateau that made up the western part of the country.

From the inbriefing that Riley had given her, Conner knew that Angola was split into three distinct geographical regions: a coastal lowland, an escarpment of hills and mountains of which the range beneath their aircraft was a part, and the high plateau flowing out of the escarpment to the east.

The capital city of Luanda was located in the western part of the country. Conner and company had landed there four hours ago. With quite a few aircraft flying in and out, the activity at the airfield had appeared confused to Conner, but in surprisingly short order they had been cross-loaded onto the Black Hawk. Their gear was put onto another helicopter, and they were flying east to Cacólo with ODA 314 along with a second team that was going to be working out of the AOB there.

They were leaving the western part of the country, where the majority of the population of Angola lived. Conner wondered, not for the first time, if she had taken the wrong bus and everyone else was

68

headed for center stage and she was going far off Broadway. Luanda was where the U.S. contingent in this operation was going to be head-quartered. It was where the other networks, along with a bigger SNN crew, were going to be descending like flies in the next few days to record the latest international peacekeeping effort. And Conner was half afraid she was going to be out in the boonies counting trees. Too late for that, she thought, looking out of the helicopter and mentally focusing on where they were going.

The northeast section of the country was on a high plateau. The rivers in the area drained into the Congo, north in Zaire. Signs of civilization were few and far between. The dominant industry was di-amond mining, and Conner had more than a passing interest in that fact. She knew the Van Wyks cartel had a shady past and she won-dered where the long hand of that organization would touch down during this operation. The major reason, though, that she was go-ing out here was simple reverse logic. At least that was the way Riley had explained it. All the other news agencies were going to be at JTF headquarters on the west coast in Luanda. "So be where they aren't" had been Riley's suggestion.

Conner looked across the dimly lit cargo bay at Riley. He was still, but she could see the glint of his eyes as he looked out the open door at the moonlit terrain. He was a strange man. She knew Sammy, her sister, and he talked quite a bit. At first she had been hopeful that maybe Sammy had finally found herself a good man, but after watch-ing and listening to them one time when they passed through St. Louis on a story, Conner had finally resigned herself to the fact that Sammy had found herself a good friend who happened to be a man.

Conner wasn't quite sure what was going on with both of them, and she really didn't have the time to concern herself with it. She'd been busy this past year, racing around the globe, always against a deadline, trying to keep the status she'd earned with the Eternity Base story.

Not only the location but the angle on the Angolan mission—go-ing on the ground with a team—had been Riley's suggestion. Con-ner had thought long and hard about it. There was no doubt it was a gamble, but you didn't stay on top by taking the safe route. On the positive side, Conner knew she'd have a camera on the ground with a live satellite feed long before any of her competitors, who were going to be content to sit in the hotel in Luanda and get the daily military briefing. On the negative, she could end up with a live feed of not much.

The fallback position, a term she had picked up from Riley, was that she would most certainly have a unique perspective. One of the greatest criticisms of the media during the Gulf War had been the contentment of correspondents to sit in Riyadh and accept the military daily briefings with very little effort made to get out on the ground to see what was really happening.

However, a unique perspective wouldn't be enough if there wasn't a story to get a perspective on. And Conner also had to remind herself of the one news crew that had gone out on its own during Desert Storm to try and get a story and ended up getting captured by the Iraqis for their trouble. She looked at Riley's silhouette one more time and felt that at least she held an advantage over that team with his expert presence.

Conner was distracted from her thoughts as the crew chief made some sort of gesture with his hands. Next to her, one of the Green Berets from the briefback pulled a magazine out of his vest and slammed it home into his weapon. He placed the gun between his knees, muzzle pointing down. This time, though, there were no blank adapters on the end of the weapon's muzzle, nor a MILES harness strapped on top of their load-bearing equipment. There were live bullets being loaded.

The combination of the thud of the blades above her head, the wind, the soldiers, and the loading of weapons, and suddenly Conner felt a strange sensation in her stomach. While she was puzzling over what it was, the young soldier suddenly turned and looked at her. He smiled and leaned close. "Just a precaution, ma'am. The AOB is secure, but it never hurts to be ready."

Conner nodded and looked out the open door. She could see a scattering of lights on the ground up ahead—Cacólo. The helicopter suddenly plunged earthward toward the landing zone, rapidly descending into and through SAM-7 range.

On the ground in Cacólo, Sergeant Ku rubbed the sleep out of his eyes. He was tired and his head hurt. Damn these Americans. Why did they have to do this in the middle of the night? What was the rush? As long as Ku could remember he'd been at war. What would another night matter?

Three helicopters landed, one after another, and men and matériel poured off. The aircraft shut down their engines and silence descended on the AOB. ODA 314 and another team, ODA 315, stood there in the darkness. Major Gungue and the American major, Lindsay, walked out and greeted the team; Ku reluctantly followed as he was instructed.

Cacólo's population could never really be tabulated because it was determined by the flow of refugees from the surrounding countryside, which depended on two factors: the way the war was going, and the way the crops were growing. Currently, the town had over thirty thousand souls crammed into it. A few relief agencies had set up camp and were supplied from the small dirt landing strip on the east side of the city.

The AOB advance had appropriated several buildings near the landing strip and turned them into an SF camp with barbed wire all around the perimeter and sandbagged gun positions guarding all avenues of approach. There was more open land to the north of the AOB for the 82d Airborne to take over when it arrived.

Lindsay greeted the two team leaders and team sergeants and linked them up with their indigenous guides. He took the entire party back, along with the pilots of the helicopters and the news team, to the AOB operations center, a former garage when there had actually been cars that ran in Cacólo. Ku reluctantly followed, wishing the headache that throbbed in his temples would go away.

Riley looked at the setup as he entered the garage with Conner and Seeger. It was typical of a Special Forces operation. Everything jury rigged, but jury rigged well. Maps lined the wall and radios were manned by men pulled from other teams to supplement the AOB.

He'd spotted a team on the roof of the garage with .50 caliber machine guns well sandbagged in at opposing corners. They were taking security seriously here, which made him feel better.

Lindsay didn't spare any punches. "We're putting you in before dawn." He turned to Dorrick. "You first." Lindsay used a pointer on the map. "ODA three one four will go in to two locations."

Riley listened carefully, making notes as Lindsay rattled off grid coordinates, time of departure, flight paths, false insertion points—the entire operations order.

Conner tugged on his elbow. "This morning? Already?"

Riley nodded. "No wasted time."

"Who do we go with?" she asked.

"I'll talk to Captain Dorrick after the OPORDER is over," Riley said.

He could tell from what Lindsay was saying that 314 had two targets to be reconned and targeted. One was the airfield on the southeast side of Saurimo, the local rebel stronghold. The other was the road leading north out of Saurimo where a bridge crossed a deep streambed. The airfield team was to help in the destruction of both the field and the planes currently stationed there. The bridge team was to laser-designate the bridge so that it could be destroyed with smart bombs. The intent was to sever Saurimo's major ground link to the north.

Riley was impressed with the intelligence and the professionalism of Lindsay's briefing. It more than made up for the lack in the briefback at Bragg. The AOB had certainly done its homework.

Lindsay wrapped up the order. "You load in sixty minutes. Depart at zero five twenty local time. It's under eighty miles to the furthest insertion point. Both your teams will be on the ground before daylight. Your commo men need to link up with my AOB commo chief and get all frequencies and call signs. Questions?"

There were none, and the teams split out to prepare. Riley followed Captain Dorrick out and grabbed him. "Sir, which split team do you want us to go with?"

"I don't want you to go with either," Dorrick said irritably. "But if I have to, which I've been ordered to, then you go with the bridge team. I'm sending it in light. The airfield team has more likelihood of contact, so there won't be room on that bird. Get with Sergeant Lorne. He's taking the bridge element."

## Namibia-Angola Border, 14 June

General Nystroom watched through a night vision telescope as the first scouts moved out, slipping across the border. They were part of two units: No. 32 Battalion, which was manned by native Angolans recruited by the South Africans during their long-running war in the area; and the Reconnaissance Commandos, the elite of the South African army. Many of the men walking out into the darkness had been here before, but fighting each other.

The scouts carried four days of food and water along with heavy loads of ammunition. Also, they carried the laser designators that they'd spent the last month training on. This was the most critical part of the entire plan, in Nystroom's opinion. He wasn't as confident as the American air force general who'd briefed the PAF staff three weeks ago in Silvermine. Nystroom looked back over his shoulder. An armored antitank gun was parked near his command vehicle. If the next forty-eight hours didn't go as the American general had promised, there was going to be quite a lot of work for that gun.

### Fort Bragg/Fayetteville, North Carolina, 14 June

In quarters and houses across Fort Bragg and Fayetteville phones began ringing. There was no surprise with this alert—they had all known they would be going sometime soon—and very little irritation at the timing of it. For some strange reason, practically every alert, real or practice, called by the army comes in the middle of the night and the soldiers of the 82d Airborne Division and the 18th Airborne Corps were used to alerts. At least this one was early enough that most weren't even in bed yet.

The major difference about this one, though, was that they all knew it was the real thing. They had been training up for Angola for two months now, ever since the president had announced support of the proposed peacekeeping mission. So this time, the good-byes were longer and harder, and spouses woke children up and put them in the car to drive onto the post and watch their other parent walk away into the darkness. And in the back of everyone's mind was the question if everyone who left was going to come back alive.

### Cacólo, Angola, 14 June

Conner ran a hand across the green markings on her face that Riley had just rubbed on using a small tube. "This isn't going to come off easy, is it?"

"No, it isn't," Riley said, now checking the combat harness she had put on earlier. "Most soldiers use bug juice to get the camo to go on easy but that defeats the purpose, which is not, as you would think, to turn your face green. It's to remove the shininess of your skin so you won't be spotted as easily. Jump."

"What?"

"Jump up and down."

Conner followed his instructions and Riley tightened down a flap on the vest. "All right. Again."

She jumped and this time made no noise. Riley stepped back and carefully inspected both Conner and Seeger. He glanced at Master Sergeant Lorne, who'd looked as if he were being asked to jump into shark-infested waters covered in blood when Riley had informed him that they were going with him. "Okay," the senior NCO said reluctantly. "Let's load."

Riley trailed as they ran out to the Black Hawk. Besides Lorne, this recon element consisted of Comsky as medic, Pace on the radio, and the junior engineer, Sergeant Tiller, carrying a laser designator. Sergeant Ku was their indigenous representative and appeared quite confused.

Riley pushed in next to Conner, while Seeger began doing his job. The camera he was using was specially fitted with a night vision adapter over the normal aperture. The recording would be very similar to what everyone else on the bird was seeing as they pulled up their night vision goggles and turned them on—everything brightly lit in a green haze.

Riley leaned over and helped Conner adjust her goggles. "Can you see?" he asked, yelling to be heard over the whine of the turbine engines starting.

"Yes." Conner's head was turning about as she got used to the new view of the world.

"You might have problems with depth perception," Riley advised. "Be careful when you get off the helicopter."

The wheels of the helicopter parted company with the ground and they gained altitude quickly. The aircraft was blacked out and the pilots were wearing their own goggles and using the cutting-edge technology of the aircraft cockpit to guide them to their destination.

"Remember," Riley yelled, "first time we touch down, don't get off. That's the false insertion. We get off on the second one."

"Second one. Got it."

Riley grabbed Seeger and reminded him one more time. He'd seen anxious soldiers jump off at false insertion points, which made for a bad scene as the chopper had to come back and get them. The point of the false insertions was to keep any enemy who might hear the helicopters from getting a fix on the landing zone that the team would use by repeating landing signatures throughout the area.

Conner's head was still darting about, the snout of her goggles looking this way and that. It was more than just getting oriented. Riley placed a hand on her forearm. "Yeah, it's real. We'll be all right."

He'd been with Conner in Antarctica where they'd been shot at, but that had been thrust upon them. Here they were deliberately going out and seeking danger. Riley always found the time before actually being in action the worst. If not dealt with, the anticipation of the unknown could incapacitate a person. In his experience, people tended to fall into two categories when faced with crisis. There were those who did what they had to do, shutting down their emotions for the duration; and there were those who panicked, overwhelmed by emotion, who shut down their ability to think and function. From what he had seen of Conner in Antarctica, Riley had no doubt that she was one of the former. The other people on the helicopter—well, he trusted Comsky, but beyond that, any person who had not been in combat was a question mark. Riley had seen men with all the proper training and little badges on their uniforms freeze when the time came to get the job done. He didn't blame them, but he didn't want to be around them either.

They were flying low, against the possibility of going over a rebel force armed with surface-to-air missiles. Coming in from Luanda they'd flown high, out of range, but now, since they had to land somewhat surreptitiously, they were staying down on the deck and hopefully would be past anyone armed with a SAM before they had a chance to get a lock and fire. Whizzing along at twenty feet above the terrain in the pitch black at a hundred and ten miles an hour was a sensation that Riley knew Conner had never experienced.

"Five minutes to the first false insertion," Riley yelled in her ear.

The helicopter swooped down into a creekbed, trees on either side appearing dangerously close to the blades overhead, in Conner's opinion. She looked around the inside of the bird. Riley and Lorne were doing the same thing—looking at a map and staying oriented to the terrain below. A crewman sat in each forward window manning an M-60 machine gun, the muzzle traversing the terrain on either side. The pilots were two large helmeted heads in the front, silhouetted by the dim glow of their instrument panels. Sergeant Ku was directly across from Conner. He was the only one who didn't have goggles on and his eyes were wide open.

"All right," Riley yelled as the helicopter slowed. "Stay on."

They lifted up over the trees lining the creek to the open land on the south side and settled down, wheels briefly touching. Conner counted to three, then the bird lifted again, back over the trees into the creekbed. From what she remembered, the bridge they were to target was across this very same creek.

"Thirty seconds," Riley said. He unbuckled her seat belt.

They rose out of the creekbed, this time to the north. Open land appeared and then they were down. Riley had a hand on her shoulder and he was pulling her. She stumbled as she felt her feet touch ground but Riley's hand kept her moving. She followed his lead as he ran out away from the bird and then pulled her to the ground.

She heard the engines increase power and felt the downwash as the helicopter lifted and flew away. The sound diminished to the south and west until there was only silence. It was extremely unnerving. Conner felt totally exposed and naked.

Riley tapped her and tugged up. She got to her feet and fell in behind him. The five soldiers formed a triangle and moved downslope toward the creek, Riley, Conner, and Seeger in the middle of the triangle.

### *Abraham Lincoln* Task Force, 14 June

"Questions?"

The pilots gathered in the ready room were just that—ready to go—and there were no questions. They were, in pilot jargon, "in the zone"—minds already in the cockpit and flying. They filed out, maps tucked under their arms. Their boots rang out on the metal ladders as they went up to the flight deck where their jets waited: sleek F-14 Tomcats and F-18 Hornets with missiles loaded under the wings, along with stubby A-6E Intruders with bomb racks bulging with more firepower than the largest bomber ever carried in World War II. They all waited for their riders.

The massive ship was already turning into the wind as the pilots and crew boarded their jets and strapped themselves in. With a roar of steam, the catapult vaulted the first aircraft into the air. The next was immediately wheeled into place.

### Oshakati, Namibia, 14 June

The lead A-10 "Warthog" taxied to the end of the runway and paused as a string of similar aircraft waited in line behind it. The official air force designation for the A-10 was the Thunderbolt II, after the famous P-47 Thunderbolt of World War II. Pilots, of course, were not known for following the official line and shortly after entering service, the A-10 was affectionately being called the Warthog by those who flew and those who didn't.

The majority of air force pilots detested the plane and stayed as far away from it as possible. It was ugly and it was slow and its mission was dirty: close air support of ground forces. No racing through the sky at Mach 2 and engaging in aerial gunfights. The A-10 was not what jet jocks dreamed of.

Those who flew the Hog loved it because it was built to fly low to the ground, carry a tremendous amount of bullets and bombs, and designed to survive an incredible amount of damage. A-10 pilots were the air force's version of paratroopers.

The plane was practically designed around its gun system—a 30mm Gatling gun whose multibarreled snout stuck out underneath the nose of the plane. Firing at either 2,100 or 4,200 rounds per minute, the A-10 could put out a tremendous number of milk-bottle-sized bullets in a hurry. The wings could handle an amazing variety of ordnance, from bombs to air-to-air missiles.

These A-10s had a mixture of laser-guided "smart" bombs on the wings and cluster bombs, designed for ground targets. A few, with special missions against the MPLA airfields, had "runway busters" loaded.

On an adjacent runway, a different line of planes queued up. South African Impala IIs, Liberian F-4 Phantoms, Egyptian-owned Soviet-made MIGs—the aircraft of the PAF prepared to do their missions in the southern half of the country.

Forty-five thousand feet, more than eight miles, above Oshakati, a Boeing E-3C Sentry AWACS—airborne warning and control system platform—picked up the lead A-10 and South African Impala as they launched. From the west, the crewmen in the back had the strike squadrons from the *Abraham Lincoln* as a series of small triangles over a blank sea.

The officer in charge (OIC) of the management station, Col. Tom Harris, knew the AWACS had the capability to provide flight and strike control for five times as many planes as were in the sky. Most of his crew were veterans of the Gulf War and nothing could compare to the first night of the air war there, when over a thousand airplanes and helicopters had been in the sky at the same time. Compared to that, the present action was a cakewalk, though he wasn't going to allow his crew to be slack.

The colonel spoke into the boom mike that hung in front of his lips. "Any signatures?" He could talk to all crew members on intercom and, with the right call sign, with any of the one hundred and twelve war jets and helicopters in the air below. They had native-language speakers on board for those craft that didn't have English speakers as pilots.

"Skies clean. Luanda International is shut down also." There were no radars on in the entire country of Angola, as usual at this time of the morning. There was no way the rebels could know the sky was going to spit thunder and lightning in less than an hour.

## Vicinity Saurimo, Angola, 14 June

Lorne held up his hand palm out. The team halted while the sergeant crawled forward with Ku. They were back in less than five minutes. "Bridge is just ahead," Lorne whispered. "One guard. There's a hut on the south side."

"Can we get a shot?" Conner quietly asked.

Lorne bit his lip and looked at Riley as he thought. "All right. But you make sure they keep it quiet and stay down from Tiller and the laser," Lorne said.

Riley nodded. He felt for Lorne. Riley had been both a team sergeant and a team leader in his time in Special Forces, and he could well imagine Lorne's concerns: Number one would be the safety of his men. Second would come mission accomplishment. Lorne had been ordered to allow Conner and her man to do their job, but if that came close to violating concern one or two—well, Riley had also been in that situation and he knew what would happen.

"Let's go," he said to Conner. He pressed Seeger and her down to the ground and they low-crawled up along the north side of the streambed, behind Lorne and Tiller, who had the laser designator. Comsky and Pace were following, manning the radio and providing rear security.

Lorne halted and Tiller climbed farther up the bank and looked over where the stream turned to the south. Riley indicated for Conner to stay still and nudged Seeger farther along in the water, which was up to their chests. Just below Tiller, the large roots of a tree extended out of the bank and dipped into the water. Seeger rested his camera on top of a root and zoomed in on the bridge.

It was sixty feet long, double wide, concrete with multiple supports. A tough target for a man with a backpack of demo, Riley knew—contrary to what is shown in movies. But for a man with a laser designator, a satellite radio, and the resources of the U.S. air force and navy at his beck and call, not a tough target at all.

A lone guard stood smoking a cigarette at the south end. A shack, probably holding other guards, was next to the road there.

Comsky keyed the SATCOM radio. "Sierra Romeo Three Four, this is Sierra Romeo One One. Over."

Eight miles up and five hundred miles to the south, Comsky's call was picked up and redirected by the crew on board the AWACS. At a bank of radios and computers, officers and NCOs linked up ground teams with their planes in an intricately coordinated dance of man and machine.

"Uh, One One, this is your Three Four. Go ahead. Over." The attention of the bombardier-navigator in the lead of two A-6 Intruders was totally inside his small world, watching information scroll up on his computer screen.

"This is One One. We're on target and waiting for the train. Over."

The officer smiled. He didn't understand ground pounders. Why would they want to be down there in the dirt and mud when they could fly high and safe and go back to a hot meal and warm bed at the end of every mission? His squadron of A-6s was the last one still on active duty. The plane was being phased out, and this action over Angola was most likely going to be its last mission. They all wanted to go out with the same proud record the plane had earned over the past several decades in numerous other conflicts.

"Roger, One One. We'll be pulling into station in"—he checked his display—"at my mark, one minute and twenty seconds. Over."

On the ground, Comsky keyed his FM radio and spoke into his teammates' ears. "Fast movers are one minute out. Light it up."

Tiller turned on the laser designator and the invisible beam of light touched the center span of the bridge.

"Three Four, your station is lit. Over."

The bombardier-navigator was doing several things at once. "Roger. I'm searching." He armed the outermost pair of air-to-ground smart bombs on the plane's wings, gave the pilot an update on course, and, with the forward-looking radar, continued to scan the ground ahead for the laser. A bright light appeared in the center of his screen. Right on. "I've got you, One One. Twenty seconds. Over." He ensured the bombs had the same acquisition on the laser, then flipped up his firing switch.

The wings of the Intruder lit up and the two bombs were gone. "Away and tracking good. On to secondary target. Thanks, One One. Out." The pair of Intruders turned away, leaving the missiles to finish the job.

Riley twisted his head and watched the two streaks of lightning come out of the sky. Both bombs hit and the bridge disappeared in a globe of flame. Chunks of concrete and twisted steel flew through the sky, somewhere among that a little bit of flesh and blood from the unfortunate guard.

"Dear Lord!" Seeger exclaimed, keeping the camera steady.

Riley noticed that Conner had come up next to him and was looking at the remains of the bridge. "Did you get it, Mike? Did you get it?" she asked.

"I got it!"

"This is going to be great," Conner said.

"Let's go," Lorne said, sliding down the bank with Tiller. He grabbed Sergeant Ku, who was still staring at where the bridge had been, his mouth agape. They retraced their way back along the streambed.

On the outskirts of Saurimo, Captain Dorrick's element watched as A-10s swooped out of the sky and destroyed eight rebel aircraft on the ground. With brisk efficiency, the runway was cratered and the control tower disappeared in a series of explosions. Job done, Dorrick and his men moved out toward their pickup zone.

In the AWACS, Colonel Harris listened to the jubilant calls of the pilots as they hit their targets. Not a single rebel aircraft made it off the ground, and as the tally came in of aircraft confirmed destroyed, Harris felt reasonably secure that they had made an almost complete sweep of the UNITA air force. They might have missed a few helicopters hidden around the countryside, but as far as fixed-wing craft went, the rebels were done. All rebel armor that had been targeted had been plastered under a rain of five-hundred-pound bombs and precision-guided munitions.

Colonel Harris sat back in his command chair and got a direct line to the command center on the *Abraham Lincoln,* which was hooked in to the Pentagon and the PAF headquarters in Silvermine outside Cape Town. Phase I had gone as planned and the road was paved. Now it was time for the main force to come in.

### Vicinity Huambo, Angola, 14 June

The sound of secondary explosions died out as the sun rose. Smoke drifted up from the wreckage left behind at the main UNITA military post. At the edge of the jungle, two thousand meters from the building that CIA intelligence had pinpointed as Jonas Savimbi's headquarters, three men waited in the shadows. They were almost invisible to the naked eye in their Ghillie camouflage suits. They'd been watching the building for the past three days, keeping track of every person who entered and exited.

They knew Savimbi wasn't in the building—or rather the wreckage of the building, since it was now nothing but a stack of crushed concrete and twisted steel. They'd seen him exit the previous afternoon, climb into an armored BMW, and drive off. To where, they didn't know. He had not returned.

"Break it down," the leader ordered.

The sniper took his rifle off its tripod and broke it into two parts, sliding them into his rucksack, then folding up the tripod itself.

"We should have taken him last night," the third man said.

"That would have tipped off the bombing," the leader said absently, still looking over the destruction through his binoculars. "We'll get another shot."

The three turned and slipped away into the jungle.

# Chapter 7

**Vicinity Luia River, Angola, 14 June**

Quinn and Trent had listened to the distant roar and rumble and scanned the early-morning sky in an attempt to see the source. A flight of warplanes had gone by less than forty-five minutes ago, but it was too dark to tell what kind they were. All they could see was the flames from the planes' jets race across the sky and the following thunderclap.

The mercenary patrol continued on its way toward their scheduled rendezvous. Quinn pushed them until it was daylight, then considered it prudent to get under cover.

"We stay here until dark," he announced when they had reached a point where a side stream entered the Luia River and the overhead cover was thick.

The merks faded under the cover of the foliage that surrounded the stream and Trent set out the perimeter, then rejoined his commander.

"Two of the boys aren't feeling too well. Running a fever."

"Give 'em some aspirin," Quinn said. "We don't have time for any slackers."

"Already did," Trent said. He settled down in a rucksack flop. "What do you think?"

"About what?" Quinn replied.

"Sounds like somebody bombed the fuck out of Savimbi's boys."

Quinn wiped the sweat off his forehead with an old rag tied around his throat. "Yeah, that it did."

Quinn squinted as they heard a roar come out of the south. A flight of F-14s flew by at a thousand feet up. In the sunlight there was no mistaking the plane's double vertical tails, and also no doubt about the star and stripe on the wings.

"Americans," was Trent's succinct comment.

"Means we're out of business here," Quinn said. "They'll get the diamond mines under control so we won't get paid there, and the government won't pay us bounty on rebels killed either. Not when they can get the bloody Yanks to do it for free."

"Well, it was fun while it lasted," Trent said. "Do this last bit, then be on our way."

Quinn felt the diamonds resting against his chest in their leather pouch. "Maybe we should screw this mission, Trent."

Trent blinked. "Say again?"

"Maybe we should just go, cross the border into Zaire, dump the stones on the black market, and move on."

"We won't get as much on the black market," Trent pointed out. "And we won't get the MPLA bounty on the rebels we killed to get the stones if we dump them on the market. Five thousand American dollars for each of your photos is nothing to sneeze at."

"Money doesn't do you any good if you aren't around to spend it," Quinn said.

"It's a million for just a little escort job," Trent said. "And this thing should be easier with Savimbi's boys running from the Americans. No one will bother us."

"I know," Quinn said. He twisted his head and listened to the sounds of the jungle. "I don't feel right. Something isn't jibing about this mission."

"I've never heard you worry like this," Trent said. "Besides, what if Skeleton does have a spy among the patrol? Skeleton's got contacts in Zaire. Hell, all over the world. We don't need him after us." He reached over and slapped Quinn on the shoulder. "Hey, it's an easy one. A cool million."

Quinn leaned back against his ruck. "Aye. A cool million." But the thought of the money didn't comfort him. He reached into his pocket and pulled out the Polaroid of the female rebel and looked at it for a while, then slowly put it back.

**Cacólo, Angola, 14 June**

Conner was looking at a different picture through the viewfinder on Seeger's camera, replaying the bombing of the bridge. "Christ!" she said. "No one's got footage like this. No one. This is great."

She turned to Seeger, who was setting out a small satellite dish. "Are you ready to transmit?"

"I will be in a couple of minutes," Seeger replied.

"They'll eat this up in Atlanta," Conner said.

Riley was watching her. He knew that the transmission would actually go through military satellites to a downlink at the Pentagon, where government censors would take a look and then forward to SNN at Atlanta whatever met the guidelines they had worked out with the news agency to get permission to be on the ground. There should be no problem with the recording from the bridge. After all, it showed the military was doing its job. It was all part of the agreement. The government's justification had been that they couldn't allow uncensored film to go directly on the air. What if it showed Mrs. Jones's son getting blown up before the Pentagon had a chance to officially tell Mrs. Jones her son had been blown up?

He could tell Conner was excited. Exhaustion from the long trip and the night-long mission would settle in soon, though. Riley stepped forward and tapped her on the shoulder.

"Yes?"

"Can I talk to you for a second?"

Conner glanced at Seeger, who was still connecting cables. "Make it quick. I have to do a voice-over to go with the footage."

Riley led her out of earshot, then pointed back at the camera. "Do you know what you have on film there?"

"Best damn footage America's going to see when they wake up today," Conner said. "The other networks are probably scrambling to get footage from the military. You know, gun camera shots of the smart bombs going in, but we got the—"

"Conner," Riley said quietly.

"—real thing. We have it in color too! Mike had the perfect angle on the bridge when it blew. I think that if we continue—"

"Conner," Riley said sharply.

She stopped and looked at him quizzically. "What?"

Riley spoked slowly. "There was more than a bridge that got blown up, Conner. There was a man, a boy, on the bridge."

"I know there was someone on the bridge. I saw—" Conner began, but Riley stepped in close and cut her off again.

"This isn't a game, Conner. This isn't a movie set where your chief worry is to get the best angle for your shots. There was some kid on that bridge. Maybe fifteen, sixteen years old with a gun about as big as him, probably thinking about what was for breakfast when those bombs hit and killed him. The OC doesn't come over with a key and turn people back on alive again here. When you're dead, you're dead."

Riley pointed at the town around them. "These people are real. This is their home. They don't get to climb on a plane and fly away from all this when it's over and the story's filed." He nodded toward the tent where the members of ODA 314 were getting debriefed. "Those guys' lives are on the line. This is real, Conner."

Conner was speechless. In all the time she'd known Riley, she'd never seen him so worked up.

"You know what we just saw?" he continued. "We just saw a four-hundred-thousand-dollar bomb used to blow up a little old bridge and kill one enemy soldier. Did you know that if we had simply divided the amount of money we spent on bombs in Vietnam by the number of people in the country and given it out at the beginning, we probably could have *bought* their damn hearts and minds?"

"What's wrong, Dave?" Conner asked.

Riley's hands gestured at his clothes. "I wore a uniform for almost twenty years and did what I was told to do. I'm not one of them anymore. I'm a civilian now. You are too. Our job here is different. I know you have to get the explosions and all that for your bosses in Atlanta, but there's more to this mission than that. There'd better be. There has to be a purpose to it all."

Conner stared at Riley for a few moments, then nodded. "All right. It's real. And there's a purpose."

Riley's form relaxed slightly. "Then maybe, just maybe, we can resurrect some good out of all the death and destruction that's happened and is going to happen here," he said.

"Do you have any suggestions?"

Riley nodded. "I thought you'd never ask. But first, you'd better do your voice-over."

Two hundred meters away, Sergeant Ku rubbed his crotch. His testicles ached. It was not the first time he'd had trouble in that part of his body. He knew the source. That damn whore from yesterday.

As he reached into his pants and scratched, Ku reflected on the night's events. The Americans knew what they were doing. From what he understood, there would be more Americans coming to his country to go into the field after the UNITA rebels.

Ku had mixed feelings about that. On one hand it would be good for the war to end. But on the other, he was concerned about his future. Without the war, would he have a job? The military was all he knew, and in Angola soldiering and grave digging were two occupations that had always been secure for the past thirty-five years. Ku knew that across the border in Zaire, the only government agency that President Mobutu ensured was paid on time was the military. He'd failed once in 1991 to do that and the country had been torn apart by the military. In Africa, the man with the gun ruled supreme and Ku enjoyed being one of those with the gun.

Ku cursed. The ache was under his skin and no amount of scratching was going to make it go away. He checked his watch. He was going to have to get the cure.

Sergeant Ku walked away from the American compound to the Cacólo Mission Hospital. A rather ostentatious name for a few shacks sitting off to the side of the Catholic Church. It didn't even have a doctor in attendance. The hospital was administrated by Danish nuns. The primary problems they saw were malnutrition and malaria, but they also dealt with every possible type of injury and illness in a country where there was an average of only one doctor per ten thousand people.

Each day at eight in the morning the hurt and sick lined up outside the hospital. Some had walked many days out of the surrounding countryside to get there. Ku pushed his way to the front of the line. He was a soldier, after all, and, most importantly, he had a gun.

The young nun working the reception table asked him a few questions. Her face didn't register anything as Ku explained that he had a venereal disease. It was most common here, and Africa was one place where the sheer number of people dying outweighed anyone's sense of moral or religious decorum.

The nun gave him a piece of paper, and he walked over to another table where an older sister held court with a shiny hypodermic needle. She looked at the paper, dipped the syringe in a dish of warm water, then drew out the appropriate medicine from a vial on the shelf behind her. She jabbed the needle into Ku's buttock and pulled it out. He was done.

As he walked away, the nun dipped the syringe into the warm water, pulled up and down on the plunger to clear out the inside, then checked the piece of paper from the next client, a young boy shivering from malaria. She picked up the appropriate vial and gave him a shot, looking up with tired eyes at the line of people behind the young boy. It was going to be a long morning.

Ku walked back to the American compound and decided to get some sleep. He did not feel well at all and surely the Americans had nothing planned for today. He curled up in the shadow of the headquarters building and pulled a poncho up over his head, slipping into a very uneasy slumber.

**Luanda, Angola, 14 June**
In the harbor district, hard-eyed men with automatic weapons guarded an old warehouse. Inside the building, other men looked at maps and studied satellite imagery being fed live to them from a Keyhole satellite currently in orbit overhead. With the return of the team from outside of Huambo, the intensity of the search had increased.

"I've got Savimbi's chopper!" one man called out, holding up a photo he'd just ripped out of a laser printer.

"Give me a grid," the commander ordered.

The man read off the numbers and a pin was placed in a map. Northeast Angola, south and slightly to the east of Saurimo.

"He must have flown there last night. I've got the Sentry's records and they picked up a chopper out of the Huambo vicinity going in that direction."

"How come they didn't intercept?" the commander wanted to know.

"The CI officer on the Sentry only had two planes on call. Everyone else was getting ready for their missions this morning. It was bad timing."

Worrying about what was done was futile, the commander knew. At least they had the chopper and they knew Savimbi wasn't in Huambo. That meant the odds were very good that he was with his helicopter.

"What would he be doing up there? Checking on the diamond mines?" the commander asked.

"There's no mine right in that area. In fact, there's nothing up there that we know about."

The commander wasn't happy with that answer. "Yeah, well, what we know about this place is only exceeded by what we don't know. It's close to the border with Zaire. Maybe the bastard is going to make a run for it."

He looked at the photo of the MI-8 helicopter sitting in a small field. There was a village on the edge of the photo. There was no telling how long Savimbi, if he was there, would be staying. "Launch a strike force. Squadron-sized. Take that place out."

### AOB, Cacólo, 14 June

"Rise and shine," Riley said, tapping Conner on the shoulder.

"What?" she muttered. They were housed in an old service station, sleeping on cots surrounded by mosquito netting.

"We have a mission."

Conner sat up and looked at her watch. "I've only been asleep twenty minutes, Dave."

"No rest for the wicked," Riley said. "These guys have less than forty-eight hours to take out everything they can before the eighty-deuce is in the field. I told you we were going to be on the go pretty much nonstop. Seeger's waiting at the chopper. The air force has picked up some truck movement on the main road west of Saurimo. The team is going in to eyeball whether they should bomb the trucks. We got two minutes."

"All right, all right," Conner said, swinging her feet down to the ground.

## Northeast Angola, 14 June
"Savimbi's helicopter is taking off!"

The commander of the assault force checked the data relayed from the AWACS to him in the back of his UH-60 Black Hawk. A small blip had appeared in the target area. The MI-8 was airborne. He looked left on the display. The three red dots indicating his helicopter and the other two, one on either side carrying his men, were still forty miles out from the helicopter that they suspected was carrying the rebel leader, Savimbi.

The MI-8 had slipped out of Huambo the previous evening and escaped interdiction for several reasons, but none of those were working this morning. The commander keyed his radio. "Dragon Leader, this is Key One. Put down the MI-8. Over."

"Key One, this is Dragon Leader. Roger. Out."

Forty miles away the MI-8 was flying just above the grass of the plateau, following the contour of the land. From above two A-10 Warthogs swooped down out of the sky. The pilot of the MI-8 saw them, but it was already over as the helicopter started to bob evasively. The 30mm Gatling guns in the nose of both planes spit out a solid line of bullets that intersected with the thin skin of the helicopter.

The chopper disintegrated under the barrage. The main part of the airframe slammed into open ground and exploded. The two A-10 pilots banked and did a flyby.

"Key One, this is Dragon Leader. Target is down. Over."

"Any survivors? Over."

"You're going to have to pick the bodies up with an ice cream scoop. No survivors. Over."

The commander nodded. "Let's go in and confirm," he ordered the pilots of the Black Hawks.

The three helicopters continued on course and soon the circling A-10s came into sight, like two circling buzzards. The helicopters set

down near the wreckage. The fire was out and the smoldering remains of the MI-8 littered the ground amid the charred grass.

While his men secured the perimeter, the assault leader walked
over to the main compartment. Or what he assumed was the main
compartment—it was hard to tell what was what amid the twisted and
blackened metal.

There were bodies in among the wreckage; more accurately,
pieces of bodies. The commander tried to determine exactly how
many there were, but the number of legs, arms, torsos, and heads
scattered about didn't quite make the math easy. At least ten dead,
he estimated. A positive ID here was going to be impossible.

"Let's bag these!" he called out. They were going to have to haul
all this back and let the forensics people check dental charts.

Men grabbed body bags and began the grisly task of collecting
pieces and parts.

**West of Saurimo, Angola, 14 June**
This mission had gone as smoothly as the first. Conner was satisfied
with the results. Seeger had six minutes of air force fighters strafing
MPLA trucks desperately trying to escape to the east. They'd chop-
pered in ahead of the trucks, set down on a hill overlooking the road,
then checked out the vehicles as they drove into view a few minutes
later.

Captain Dorrick had confirmed the target and the next thing they
knew death had descended from the sky, blasting the vehicles. The
choppers showed up, and they were back on board. Conner's head
was spinning from the speed of it all.

Seated next to her, Riley was tired. He knew they all were. The air
force could have just taken out those trucks, but everyone seemed
to be playing this whole operation very carefully, making sure that
all targets were double-checked and confirmed. He knew that Conner was part of the reason for that. In the modern world a minor
event could have consequences far exceeding its actual impact if the
media seized upon it. Public relations had become as important as
—if not more important than—the actual conduct of the mission.

Riley noticed that the pilots were engaged in an extensive con-

versation and gestured for one of the crewmen to give him a headset. He settled the cups over his head. The pilots were talking to an
AWACS, getting flight path instructions. The skies were crowded and
a midair collision would make you just as dead as getting shot.

One of the door gunners called out an aircraft sighting to the pi-
lots and Riley looked in the indicated direction. Three Black Hawks
were off to their left, about four hundred yards away, also flying low.
Riley squinted. The aircraft had refueling probes under their noses.
That identified them to Riley as specially modified MH-60s from Task
Force 160, the army's elite helicopter unit. The doors were open and
Riley could make out some men dressed in black in the rear.

He noticed that Seeger was filming the aircraft. Riley leaned forward and tapped him. "Might as well stop. They're going to cut that."

Even as Riley spoke, the three aircraft turned away to the south
and disappeared.

On the other side of helicopter, Sergeant Ku struggled to keep
down his breakfast. Sweat was running down his back and he could
feel the blood pounding in his forehead, behind his eyes.

A crew member noticed his distress and handed him a couple of
barf bags. Ku bent over and vomited, filling the bag. He looked up,
full bag in hand, embarrassed in spite of the way he felt. The American crewman pointed out the door and Ku chucked it out. By the
time they got back to Cacólo, he had gone through three bags.

**Pentagon, 14 June**
In the War Room, deep underneath the Pentagon, the chairman of
the joint chiefs of staff, General Lowell Cummings, watched the tape
of the satellite feed that had come out of one of SNN's crews—SNN-
E1. He nodded approvingly at the sight of the trucks getting oblit-
erated by bombs and cannon fire.

There was a brief pause, then another scene came on. The three
Special Operations Black Hawks came into view. "We've deleted that
from what we allowed to go forward to Atlanta," the public affairs
colonel informed Cummings.

Cummings watched several other shots, mostly from Luanda,
showing the arrival of the troops and equipment, and footage from

the military's own cameras showing smart bombs destroying targets in Angola.

All in all, the morning had worked out almost exactly according to plan, and Cummings was a good enough general to understand how unique that was. The operation was going well, but that didn't mean Cummings was happy. He looked at the entire Angolan mission on two levels. The first was operational—the nuts and bolts of accomplishing the task the military was assigned by the president and Congress. Cummings's dissatisfaction came from a different level—the task itself. He saw little purpose to it when viewed through the prism of national security, which was the basic principle he'd been trained on since he'd stood on the Plain at West Point as a seventeen-year-old plebe, thirty-two years ago.

What security interest did the United States have in Angola? It was a question Cummings had raised with the president and never received an answer to. In fact, he'd been told the question was the wrong one. This application of military force had little to do with security interests. It had to do with humanitarian and political interests.

The army had even coined a term for this kind of mission in the early nineties: OOTW. Operations other than war. For the past several years, the military had slid along the scale from preparing to fight World War III to performing more and more OOTW. And Cummings was caught in a bind. He didn't like OOTW, but he also had to milk the OOTW cow in front of Congress to get funds to keep the force at a strength to be able to fight the real thing—war—if need be. And, ultimately, Cummings was a soldier. He would do what his commander in chief ordered.

But it wasn't only for national policy reasons that Cummings disliked OOTW. He was very concerned about the effect these types of missions had on the morale and training of the armed forces. Troops deployed on peacekeeping operations weren't training for war during the duration of the deployment. Those same troops had also joined the military for reasons other than acting as world policeman, feeder of the poor, and health-care provider. Especially most of the troops that were constantly being deployed on these missions: men who had volunteered for airborne or Special Forces duty did not exactly enjoy playing the role of peacekeeper.

Neither did these soldiers enjoy being gone from home months at a time on the numerous deployments these missions entailed. The toll on families and morale was very high. Cummings had sworn the same oath all the men and women in the service had—to defend the Country and the Constitution—and many OOTW missions didn't seem to have much to do with that oath.

Cummings looked at the current status report of the Angolan deployment. The 82d was doing well. On schedule, maybe even ahead of schedule. But that didn't thrill Cummings. His first line of defense to any world crisis—the army's only airborne division—was being sucked into this mission, and he didn't have another one to fill the gap if there was trouble somewhere else in the world. His only hope was that this would be over quickly with as little bloodshed as possible.

### Luanda, Angola, 14 June

The 82d Airborne was the army's most mobile division, priding itself on its ability to deploy rapidly anywhere in the world. It was outdoing itself in its effort to get to Angola. The first wave of troops had boarded C-141 Starlifters at Pope Air Force Base, adjacent to the Fort Bragg reservation, within two hours of the alert notification.

In-flight refueling had cut transport time down to pure flight time between North Carolina and Angola. The lead C-141 touched down at the capital city's airfield ahead of schedule, a fact that the division commander—General Scott—made sure to mention to the press representatives who dutifully filmed the first red-bereted paratroopers as they walked off the ramp of the aircraft.

Behind that first load of one hundred and fifty troops was an aerial line stretching across the Atlantic back to the States carrying two full brigades of the division—over ten thousand men. Their heavy equipment had been loaded onto ships three weeks ago and was already in port. Within seventy-two hours, General Scott promised the press and the world, the 82d would be here in full force, ready to fight.

### Angola-Namibia Border, 14 June

General Nystroom was satisfied as he reviewed after-action reports transmitted to his headquarters. The morning's air attacks had gone very well indeed. The American plan had worked as promised. In fact, even better than promised.

The UNITA Air Force didn't exist anymore. Over 80 percent of what they had estimated UNITA's armor strength to have been was confirmed destroyed. The Americans' 82d Airborne Division's first elements were on the ground to the north in Luanda.

Nystroom knew it would take the Americans a few days to get their infantry forces organized and begin combat operations. His own main elements were ready. He was just waiting for further intelligence from the scouts he had sent across the border.

He had two main questions right now. Would UNITA give up the fight or would it slip away into the bush and continue the war? And where was Savimbi? The answer to the first, no one knew and only time would tell. For the second, the American intelligence officers were being very coy. He knew they had plastered Huambo.

So with all the good news, Nystroom thought, he would have to look very hard to find something to worry about, but that was his job. He grabbed another batch of intelligence reports and began poring through them.

### National Security Agency, Fort Meade, Maryland, 14 June

A busy morning, Waker noted as he watched all the activity in the air and on the ground in Angola. The devices he was tied into were so sophisticated that they picked up much more information than any single person—or even a staff of people—could possibly ingest, never mind digest. So far, Waker's job had been simply to make sure that the devices were working and the information was recorded. No one had yet made any requests for information from the NSA. The commanders on the ground over in Africa seemed to be satisfied with the information fed to them directly from their own intelligence sources within the Pentagon and on the ground and sky over Angola.

Waker and the NSA computer were also supposed to look for patterns in the information, but the only pattern that was discernible so far was that things were going according to plan for the U.S. and Pan-African forces.

As part of his responsibilities, Waker was also checking out the countries bordering Angola. He had several different displays of the

Pan-African forces massing along the Angola-Namibia border, but that was in the operations plan. The waters off the coast were empty except for the *Abraham Lincoln* task force. Zaire to the north and Zambia to the east were quiet. No unexpected troop movements in either country, not that there had been any fear that there might be.

Waker hadn't forgotten the transmission out of the Lunda Norte region, but according to the computer, there had been nothing further happening there. With time on his hands, Waker decided to play around a little. He keyed in on the transmissions going to and from the headquarters of the PAF forces to their ground commander in Namibia and began giving the computer various attack angles to work on them. It couldn't hurt to break the South Africans' code system. It would give Waker something to put on his next evaluation support form.

One thing Waker found interesting after a cursory evaluation of the South African code and a comparison of it to the one that had come out of Lunda Norte the previous day was the difference between the two—the latter had been much more sophisticated. The question then was: who in Angola was using a more secure code than the South African Army?

### Vicinity Luia River, Angola, 14 June

Quinn pulled the earplug out and carefully coiled the headset, placing it in its special compartment on the radio backpack.

"What's the word?" Trent asked.

"The American Eighty-second Airborne is landing in Luanda. The American headquarters says they destroyed most of UNITA's planes and armor this morning."

Quinn thought one of the greatest intelligence breakthroughs in the last decade out in the bush was the AM broadcast out of Kinshasa of SNN's audio feed. Here in the middle of the African veldt, he could get the same words that the president of the United States and other heads of state watched on their TVs.

"Those two fellows aren't feeling any better," Trent said. "And now a couple more aren't feeling too good."

"What's wrong with them?" Quinn asked.

"Fever, sick to their stomach. Headaches."

"Malaria flare-up?" Quinn suggested.

"I don't know."

"Can they move?"

Trent smiled. "You bloody well know they'll move. No one wants to get left."

"They'd better stay close." Quinn looked at his worn map in its case. "We'll make the linkup in plenty of time."

"I hope this fellow we meet can do his job quick," Trent said. "Or we're going to be up to our necks in American paratroopers."

# Chapter 8

*Abraham Lincoln* **Task Force, 15 June**

The catapult fired and the F-18 Hornet accelerated down the deck. It was up and into the air, streaking to the east. Inside the cockpit, Lieutenant Theresa Vickers studied her CRT cockpit display. This was her second mission in support of Operation Restore Life. The first had gone like clockwork—a strike against the main rebel airfield outside Huambo.

This time she was simply going to be drilling a hole in the sky, flying overhead on-call cover in the northeast quadrant until she was needed. Her wingman, Lieutenant Chandler, had launched right after her and his F-18 slipped in off her right wing. At forty thousand feet they flew east.

After twenty minutes they were on station. Just in time to receive a call from the guardian AWACS to the southwest.

"Cruiser One, this is Eagle. Over."

Vickers acknowledged the call. "This is Cruiser One. Over."

"We're picking up FM radio activity on the ground in your sector. We've confirmed that it is not friendly forces. We need you to check it out. We're locking in to your computer and we'll put you on target. Over."

Lieutenant Vickers flipped up a switch on her control panel. "Roger that, Eagle. Ready for your control. Over." Her F-18 was now on a sophisticated form of autopilot—basically being flown by a controller on board the AWACS. She could override at any time and regain control, but it was a good way of efficiently getting the aircraft to the desired position, given that the AWACS controllers had a better view of the sky than she did in her cockpit. After glancing out to make sure her wingman was still with her, Vickers sat back and relaxed, letting the plane fly her.

### Cacólo, Angola, 15 June

Conner walked next to Sergeants Comsky and Brewster as they strolled through the town. Seeger followed, camera on them. Both had mikes clipped to their combat vests. They'd managed to get a couple of hours of sleep over the day and night, despite going out on one more mission to the edge of Saurimo to target several barracks buildings that had escaped the first wave.

She'd filmed footage a half hour earlier as the first CH-47 Chinook had come in, carrying paratroopers from the 82d Airborne. This was the beginning of the buildup of forces in the Lunda Norte area. The first few platoons had secured a designated area on the edge of town and, using supplies sling-loaded in, were beginning to build their base camp. There would be plenty of time to make it over there and get some stories. For now, Conner was doing what she had promised Riley.

After talking to him, Conner had decided on a rather unusual approach to this story. She was going to let the medic and the engineer talk freely. It was something she could edit when she got back to the States and make a story out of. Right now, she just wanted it straight.

And straight she got it. Brewster pointed down a street. "I checked with some of the local officials earlier this morning. That's the powerhouse down there. It uses oil, which they got plenty of here in Angola. The power grids are not interlocked in this country. What that means is that if a station goes down, the power stays down until that station goes back up. There's no way to switch power from somewhere else." They went down the street.

"As you can see," Brewster said, "this station has been out of commission for a while." Through large holes in the brick wall, they could see plants growing inside the building. Brewster kicked down a board that had been placed across the door, and they stepped into the dim twilight inside.

Brewster gestured. "Those are the generators." He shook his head. "From what I understand, the rebels were first to start taking down the power grid by blowing substations and the transmission lines. Then, when they captured this town four years ago, they tried to get the power back on line. So then the government, when it counterattacked, took out the powerhouse here." Two of the four generators were totally wrecked.

Brewster turned and looked at the camera. "Most people don't understand what happens when you lose your electric power source. Just think of all the things we take for granted. And not just luxuries but essentials. Without power you can't freeze anything, so food will rot. Medicines will go bad. You won't have electric light. Which means you can't even work inside during the day if you don't have windows. Sounds like no big deal until you have to live it.

"You also lose most of your manufacturing capability. No heavy machinery can be run in factories if you don't have power. Your water system is also down because you don't have power for pumping. Same for your sewage system."

They carefully edged their way out of the destroyed power plant. "This country has been on an economic slide since the Portuguese pulled out in 1975," Brewster said. "Angola lost a high percentage of their professional work force and foreign capital when independence was granted. Then add in twenty years of civil war. Railways and roads destroyed; crops burned in the fields; the men to work those fields carrying guns instead of hoes; the executions of those few professionals left by both sides because the intelligentsia is always viewed as a threat.

"The oil, diamond, and iron industries, the backbone of the Angolan economy, have been devastated by the war. It's hard to attract foreign companies when there is always the threat that their investment is going to get destroyed in the next government or guerrilla offensive. Stability is key for growth, and it's the most important factor missing in the Angolan economy."

Conner glanced at Seeger, who was panning over this section of town, capturing the shacks and war-ravaged buildings. She was impressed and realized Riley was right: this would make a good, indepth story. She was particularly caught by Brewster. The way he knew his subject matter and also the sense that he really did care about what he saw here.

At the Angolan army headquarters, Major Gungue was not impressed with Sergeant's Ku's muttered pleas to be released from duty. Granted, the sergeant did not look very well. In fact, he looked downright bad. Ku's face was puffy and his eyes were red. His words were barely audible and he did not make much sense. He was sweating profusely and he said something about vomiting a lot.

But Gungue had seen troops drink hydraulic fluid in attempts to get themselves sick enough to avoid going into combat. Ku getting excused from duty would start an epidemic of "illness" among Gungue's soldiers. He could not allow that.

Besides, if he allowed Ku to get out of working with the Americans, it would look bad. He gruffly ordered the sergeant to return to duty. He wasn't quite sure if Ku understood him or not as the man shuffled out the door, but the important thing was the other soldiers around the headquarters had seen that such malingering was not to be tolerated.

### Airspace, Northeast Angola, 15 June

"Cruiser One, this is Eagle. Returning control to you. Over."

Vickers's gloved hands took the controls. "I've got control. Over."

"We're still picking up FM radios in the area you're now on top of. Over."

"Checking it out. Wait one. Break. Chandler, you stay up here. Over."

Her wingman replied. "Roger that. Out."

Vickers banked and descended. The terrain below was rolling grassland, with heavy vegetation in some of the low area between the rounded ridges. It was also dotted with clumps of trees, any of which could be hiding UNITA forces.

Vickers spotted a flash of light and turned toward it. She saw the cause immediately: the sun had reflected off a windshield. A pickup truck was racing across the open grass heading from one clump of trees to another, a machine gun clearly visible in the bed.

"I've got a target. Am engaging. Over." Vickers slowed down

nearly to stall speed and armed her 20mm cannon. It almost didn't seem sporting to run it down like this, she thought as the distance rapidly closed.

"You've got multiple launches!" Chandler screamed in her ear.

At the same moment her missile alert light went on and a tone sounded in her headphones. Missiles were locked on to her. She jerked hard right, and kicked in thrust. A missile flashed by to her right. She jigged back left and rolled the plane onto its left side. Another SAM went by, just narrowly missing the belly of the plane. She leveled out and felt the plane shudder; the instrument panel went berserk as a third missile hit.

"I've got a fire warning light!" Vickers called out. She was reacting even as she radioed the situation to Chandler. Hours upon hours of training had imprinted the proper sequence. Her hands flew over the controls. "What do you see, Chandler?" she asked.

Her wingman was still watching out for her "You've got fire!" he yelled into the radio. "Punch out! Punch out!"

Vickers hit her ejection lever and was out into the air, her body slammed down into the seat by the powerful rockets that separated her from her plane. The chair fell away and her chute blossomed open. She twisted her head and watched her F-18 blossom into flame and explode.

It was only then, on her way down to the earth below, that emotion kicked in. Shit, she cursed to herself. She'd lost her plane.

### Cacólo, Angola, 15 June

"To top it all," Brewster said, "we're not helping much right now. The bridge we blew yesterday cut the main road out of Saurimo to the north. It was necessary militarily, but . . ." He paused. "Well, let me put it this way. In Special Forces, every time we look at a target, we engineers do what we call a CARVE formula on it. That stands for criticality, accessibility, recuperability, vulnerability, and effect of target destruction on the local area. The last one, E, is an important factor. When you go around blowing things up, you do more than simply destroy a military target. You affect the people living in the area for years.

"The only good side to all this is that once we get the rebels' forces destroyed, we can go in and rebuild. If the government doesn't pull us out before we get enough time to make the changes stick, we can help get this country back on its feet. We can rebuild that bridge. The power plant. Pave roads."

Comsky cut in. "That's if the people here want the change, and a better question is, if there are any people left."

"What do you mean?" Conner asked.

Comsky took a deep breath, then launched into his favorite topic. "The health standards here are—" He paused as Sergeant Lorne sprinted around the corner.

"Let's go, Comsky. We've got a pilot down!"

Riley had Seeger and his camera waiting at the Black Hawk. The blades were already turning as Conner and Comsky jumped on board, joining Ku, Lorne, Tiller, and Oswald. Riley didn't like the way the Angolan sergeant looked. The man had his head leaned back against the webbing behind his seat and he appeared out of it. His eyelids were droopy and what Riley could see of the man's eyes was red and puffy.

But Riley didn't have time for Ku. He pulled on a set of headphones and listened in as Lorne and the helicopter pilots coordinated with the AWACS flying.

Eight thousand feet and to the southwest, Colonel Harris was juggling several glass balls.

"Okay, Vickers, give me an update," he said calmly.

The pilot's voice was weak. The survival radio she was talking on didn't have the greatest power, but Harris was afraid there was more to the lack of radio strength.

"I'm down. I think I broke my right ankle. I can't move it. Just before I landed I spotted several vehicles moving around. Coming out of the trees. The whole thing was an ambush to draw me down into missile range. Over."

"All right. I've got help on the way," Harris said. "Stay on the air. We'll get you out of there."

"Roger."

Harris grabbed another mike. "Cruiser Two, this is Eagle. What do you see? Over."

Lieutenant Chandler's voice came in much stronger. "There's some vehicles moving toward my One's position. Over."

"How long until they're at her position? Over."

"Uh, I'd say about five minutes. Over."

"Take them out," Harris ordered.

"Roger that. Out."

"Be careful. Remember, they still have missiles. Over."

Harris took a deep breath. An F-18 was not exactly the greatest ground support jet. It moved too fast. Some of those vehicles would get through. Plus, he might end up losing the second F-18. The whole thing probably had been a setup. Sucking them in with the FM radios, the one truck in the open, and then ambush from other vehicles hidden in the trees. In Mogadishu the natives had quickly learned how to draw in helicopters and destroy them, and now it appeared in Angola they were learning to do the same with fast-moving jets.

Harris checked his board, searching for any A-10s that might be in the air. Nothing. They were all down, refueling and rearming from the early-morning missions. By the time he got one up and in the air, and then counting flight time from Namibia . . . Scratch that option, Harris decided.

A radar operator turned from his screen to Harris. "Rescue One is up, sir." Harris had implemented an alert plan as soon as Cruiser Two had called in the F-18 going down. They'd located the closest Special Forces unit to the crash site and ordered them into action.

"Rescue One, this is Eagle. You've got one pilot down. Injured. We have bad guys in the area. Her wingman is going hunting, but some of them are probably going to get through. They're about five minutes out from the pilot." Harris looked down at his display. "I have you with an ETA of . . . twelve minutes. We're going to try and slow them down. Over."

A deep, steady voice with blades thumping in the background replied. "Roger that, Eagle. This is Rescue One. We'll take care of this. Give me the pilot's freq and call sign. Over."

As Harris relayed the information he felt a surge of affection for whoever that voice belonged to. He'd heard about what had happened in Mogadishu years previously when those helicopters had gone down in the streets and Army Special Operators—Rangers, Special Forces, and Delta Force people—had gone in against all odds to pull the pilots out. There had been only two Medals of Honor awarded since the end of the Vietnam War and both had gone to Delta Force operatives who had gone in—knowing the odds were two against hundreds—to secure one of the downed choppers.

But those awards had been posthumous, and that was one thing Harris didn't want to see happen here. He looked at the situation board and noticed an aircraft listed on station over Luanda. Exactly what he needed. "Get me Spectre Four."

Riley heard Lorne order the radios switched over to the pilot's survival radio frequency, then the team sergeant handed a headset to the medic on board. "Pilot's down and hurt, Comsky. You'd better talk to him. Call sign is Cruiser One."

Comsky settled the cups over his ears. He keyed the radio. "Cruiser One, this is your help. We're en route to your location. Talk to me, buddy. Over."

They were all startled when a woman's voice replied. "This is Cruiser One. Good to hear your voice. Over."

"I'm a medic," Comsky said. "Describe your injuries and I'll have the aspirin ready when we land. Over."

Lieutenant Chandler was doing his best, but he only had so much ordnance. He had taken out three pickup trucks. The others had caught on and were laying low, scooting from one clump of trees to another. He solved that problem twice by simply taking out the entire clump of trees. He was gaining Vickers time, but that ate up the ordnance under his wings.

As he swooped out of another gun-run, his missile warning light went on, but he was prepared. He kicked in his afterburners and corkscrewed away, evading the missile.

Conner screamed as Sergeant Ku leaned forward and a stream of black-and-red liquid spilled out his mouth all over her and onto the seats of the helicopter. Ku's chest was rising and falling, his breath rattling loud enough to be heard.

Riley unbuckled her seat belt and pulled her out of the way. He slid in next to Ku and checked the man's pulse, ignoring the viscous material covering everything. His first instinct was that Ku had been shot through the lungs—how, he didn't know—maybe a random round from the ground. From the amount of blood, it was the only thing that made sense. Riley ripped off Ku's gear, tearing his shirt open.

Leaning against the back wall of the chopper, Seeger was filming the entire thing.

Lieutenant Vickers watched Chandler kick in afterburners and evade the missile. She was lying in two-foot-high grass on the side of a gentle swell in a large open area. There were scattered groups of trees in all directions. She'd disconnected her parachute and the breeze had blown the green cloth away to the south. She was seated, one leg extended straight out, the other tucked underneath to support herself. In her right hand she held her 9mm pistol, ready for action. She knew that in this type of terrain, someone with a rifle could pick her off well before they came within pistol range. She held the survival radio in her left hand.

The radio hissed. "Is it a compound fracture? Over."

Vickers looked down at her straight leg. "I don't see any bone." She put the pistol down and felt the ankle. "I don't feel anything sticking out. I just can't move it. Over."

"Roger. Any other injuries? Over."

She thought she heard a truck engine off to the north. "Nothing serious. But if you don't get here soon, I anticipate some more serious ones. Over."

On the Black Hawk, Comsky was still talking to the pilot as he joined Riley. They were manhandling the sergeant, searching for a wound, but there was nothing.

"Three minutes out!" Lorne screamed at them. "What's wrong with him?" he added, pointing at Ku.

"I don't know," Riley said.

"Fuck," Lorne said. "I need all the bodies I can get on the ground."
Riley picked up Ku's M-16. "I'll take his place."

Lorne looked at Riley for a second, then nodded. "All right. Tell
your camera friend and the lady to stay on the bird. We want to go
in and get out fast."

The radio broke in on their conversation. "Uh, Rescue One, this
is Cruiser One. How far out are you guys? Over." The woman's voice
was flat, but they could read the undercurrents.

"Two minutes," Comsky said, slamming Ku back against the wall
and tightening down the man's seat buckle. "Hang tough. We'll be
there. Over." Comsky cut off the radio and pointed at Ku. "He isn't
hit. Must be sick. Nothing we can do for him now. Just leave him."

"Roger," Vickers replied. She released the transmit button and
spoke to herself. "Two minutes. I guess I'll wait. I've got nothing better to do." She could see men running through the grass to her right,
about two hundred yards away. She twisted her head, but the rising
ground blocked her view to the rear. She checked her pistol one
more time. Her heart lifted when she heard the distinctive thump
of helicopter blades.

"It's a hot LZ," the pilot of the Black Hawk announced.

"All right," Lorne replied, sliding back the bolt on his weapon.

"No," the pilot said. "I mean it's *hot*. Missiles and heavy-caliber machine gun hot. If those guys took down an F-18, they got some heavy
shit. I don't want to hang around. In and out. *Fast.*"

"Just get us there," Lorne said.

Riley pulled back the charging handle on Ku's M-16, making sure
there was a round in the chamber. He looked at Conner, who was
covered in red. She was trying to clean some of it off with a rag. "Stay
on the helicopter! Keep Seeger on board."

She nodded.

"Thirty seconds!" Lorne yelled.

A string of bright green spots flashed by the helicopter. The door
gunners replied with their M-60s, sending red tracers back at the
source of the green in a grove of trees.

Riley felt his stomach muscles tighten. The ground came rushing
up. He grabbed hold of a strap and leaned out. He could see the

pilot lying on the ground, firing away with a pistol. Riley followed her aim and spotted the figures of three men in camouflage moving through the grass.

At that moment a ball of fire came out of the midst of the three men. "RPG!" Riley yelled.

The helicopter pilot tried turning at the last second. It was too late. The RPG rocket tore into the helicopter, to the rear of the cargo compartment, and exploded, severing all the controls leading to the rear rotor disk and stabilizer. Fortunately, they had just been about to land and their altitude was only twenty feet. The Black Hawk slammed into the ground, the wheels buckling as they'd been designed, taking up much of the impact along with the left front of the bird, the copilot dying instantly as the instrument panel crumpled into his chest.

Riley's grip was torn from the strap and he was thrown onto the ground. He lay stunned for a second, then rolled and came up on one knee, the stock of his weapon tight against his shoulder. He was disoriented momentarily. He heard people yelling behind him and the sound of gunfire.

A stream of tracers oriented him. He fired three rounds into the men who had fired the RPG. A heavy roar just over his left shoulder joined his firing and the three men wilted under the fire, their bodies jolting from the impact of the bullets.

Riley ceased firing and slowly lowered his weapon. He looked left. Lorne had one of the door M-60s cradled in his large hands. The team sergeant put the gun down and turned back to the helicopter. Riley joined him.

"Rescue One is down," Colonel Harris said in a flat voice. He was listening to four different frequencies in his headset. "Pilot reports they're on the ground and have a secure perimeter. One dead." Harris's eyes flashed at the Plexiglas status board to his right, where an enlisted man stood on the other side, writing different notations in grease pencil backward, so that they appeared correctly to Harris.

"All right, Rescue One. Hang tight. I've got people moving." He switched frequencies and his tone changed, snapping out orders in a voice that brooked no questions.

* * *

Lorne had Tiller and Oswald along with the two uninjured crew-men in a tight perimeter around the crash site. Riley could see that Comsky was busy, so he stood at the medic's shoulder and assisted. Besides the jet pilot's leg, the surviving helicopter pilot was bleeding from a gash across his forehead where his helmet visor had shattered. He had pulled out his headset and was staying in contact with the AWACS on the aircraft's SATCOM radio. The other pilot's body was still inside the aircraft. And then there was Sergeant Ku, lying where they'd carried him, unconscious.

"How is she?" Riley asked Comsky, who had cut open the leg of Vickers's flight suit.

"I feel fine," Lieutenant Vickers said. "Just won't be dancing for a while."

Riley smiled. "Sorry. We'll get you out of here," he added. Comsky was wrapping a metal splint that looked like chicken fence around her lower leg, holding it in place with an Ace bandage.

Vickers looked over at the helicopter. Smoke was still coming out of the large hole in the tail boom. "Looks like the cavalry threw a shoe." She peered at him, searching his plain jungle fatigues for any insignia. "And you are?"

"Dave Riley." He jerked a thumb at Conner who was kneeling with Seeger as he filmed the scene. "I'm with them."

Vickers nodded.

"You'll be all right," Comsky said. "I've immobilized your ankle." He reached into his aid kit and took out some pills. "These will help."

"Transmit," Conner ordered Seeger. They were in the shadow of the helicopter, protected by the drooping tail boom.

"Now?" he asked, surprised.

"Now." She gestured. "This is hot." She looked over at Lorne, who still had the M-60 in his hands and was searching the horizon, look-ing for targets. "And there's always the chance we might not be get-ting out of here."

Seeger shrugged and took out the small satellite dish, hooking it into the back of his camera.

* * *

Ku gave a strange, choking sound. Riley and Comsky moved over to him just in time to see him vomit a vast quantity of dark red blood.

"Jesus," Riley muttered as they stared at the sergeant.

Comsky quickly donned a pair of surgical gloves. He thrust a pair at Riley. "He's choking. Hold him down," he ordered as he pulled a tube out of his bag.

Riley slipped the gloves on and grabbed Ku's shoulders. Comsky leaned over and put his hand into the man's mouth, sweeping around with his fingers, trying to clear it out. He wiped off a mass of black goo on Ku's shirt, then put the tip of the tube inside the man's mouth. Ku violently threw up again. This time a mass went around the tube and splattered into Comsky's face and over his chest.

"Fuck!" Comsky yelled, wiping across his eyes to clear his vision. Riley kept his grip as Ku thrashed about.

"Turn him on his side," Comsky ordered. He pushed the scope farther in. Ku's chest began rising and falling. "All right. He's got air," Comsky said. The medic reached inside his aid kit and pulled an IV out. "But he's lost so much blood, he's going into shock. He'll be dead if I don't get something in him."

There was a tearing sound from inside Ku.

"What was that?" Riley asked. It was the most nauseating thing he'd ever heard.

"I don't think we want to know," Comsky said as he slid the needle into Ku's arm.

More blood came up out of Ku's mouth around the tube. There was material mixed in the blood.

"What's that stuff?" Riley asked.

"His guts," Comsky said. "That's what we heard tearing. His insides are just disintegrating." He kept working. "Fuck," Comsky muttered. "I can't get this going." The needle hadn't taken and blood was seeping out around the hole. He tried again, with the same result. "Christ, I'm killing him trying to save him. He's going to bleed to death while I try to get blood expander into him."

Ku's eyes flashed open. It looked to Riley like he was trying to speak, but the tube prevented that. The sergeant's hands dug into Riley's arms with amazing strength and he half sat up. More blood and guts poured out. Then Ku's head flopped back and his eyes rolled up.

Comsky reached forward and felt the man's neck. "He's dead."
Comsky peeled off his gloves and threw them down next to the body.
"Fat lot of good those did us."

Riley looked up as Lorne fired a long burst with the M-60. "We
have other trouble right now."

A new voice spoke in Colonel Harris's headset. "I've got the helicopter. Are you sure all friendlies are in the immediate vicinity of the
crash site? Over."

Harris called the helicopter pilot and confirmed it. "Roger, all
friendlies are within twenty feet of the crash site. Over."

"Roger. I've multiple targets on thermals outside of that perimeter. We'll take care of this. Out."

The AC-130 Spectre gunship was developed around the C-130
Hercules transport plane frame. Inside the spacious cargo hold, instead of paratroopers or pallets, there were three large guns, their
snouts pointing out holes in the left side of the aircraft. Between the
three—a 20mm cannon, a 40mm cannon, and a 105mm howitzer—
the aircraft could fire several thousand rounds a minute and put a
round in every square inch of a football field in less than ten seconds.

The pilot who had just finished talking to Colonel Harris had the
plane in a counterclockwise racetrack at over a mile of altitude. His
targeting officer was using an amplified thermal imager to scan the
ground and acquire targets. The guns were computer controlled,
and the officer was feeding in each one outside of the perimeter of
the people around the crashed helicopter.

In the rear crewmen waited. Not to fire the guns, the computer
would do that on the command of the targeting officer, but with shovels to clear away the mounds of expended brass that would pile up
around the guns once they did begin firing.

On the ground Riley cocked his head. There was a familiar sound
in the air. He looked up, but in the hazy sky he couldn't see anything.
Still, he knew what was coming. He'd seen this before.

"You might want to point that thing out there," he called out to
Seeger, indicating in the direction of the UNITA rebels who were

cowering behind a disabled pickup truck, popping up occasionally to fire an errant shot in their direction.

"I think I've got them all," the targeting officer said.

"Let 'er rip," the pilot ordered.

The targeting officer flipped a switch and the plane shuddered as all three guns began firing. The 20- and 40mm cannons had Gatling-type barrels and were fed by belts of ammunition. The 105mm howitzer ate a stack of rounds fed from overhead, one at a time.

On the ground it looked like two solid lines of red came out of the sky and touched down. First on the pickup truck closest to them. Intermingled among the lines was the crump of a larger 105mm round.

In three seconds the truck, and the men around it, disappeared. The firing shifted and, one by one, the troops that had set the ambush had the tables turned on them. There was no escaping under the cover of trees, as the thermal targeting of the Spectre saw through the trees and the weaponry tore apart the foliage, destroying what was underneath.

It was all over in thirty seconds.

"We're clear," the helicopter pilot called out. "There's a Chinook en route to our location to pick us up and sling-load this aircraft out."

Riley put down the M-16 he'd been using. The adrenaline rush was wearing off. He could tell Conner was ecstatic. She had footage that would most certainly make people sit up and notice. Right now, she was talking into the camera, giving her after-action wrap-up.

Riley walked over to Comsky, who was looking down at what remained of Sergeant Ku. Little more than a red lump of flesh in a vaguely human form. "What happened to him?"

"I don't know," Comsky said. "I've never seen anything like that. It's like his body was just eaten up." He was rubbing his hands together nervously. "I think he had some sort of disease. He didn't look too good when he got on board the chopper."

Comsky looked over at Conner and Seeger. "Hey, bring that camera over here."

"What do you want?" Conner asked.

Comsky pointed at the body. "Take a close-up of him."

Conner flinched. "Why?"

"Just do what I say," Comsky said. He was searching through his aid kit. He pulled out a scalpel.

"What are you going to do?" Riley asked.

Sergeant Lorne had walked over and he echoed Riley's question. "What are you up to, Comsky?"

The medic was pulling on a new pair of gloves. "I don't know what killed him, Top, but there's people back in the States who might. We need to give them something to work with." He looked up at Seeger. "Keep the camera on the body." He placed the tip of the scalpel on the center of Ku's chest.

"What the hell do you think you're doing, Sergeant?" Lorne demanded. "You can't go around cutting people up!"

Comsky raised his eyebrows and looked up at his team sergeant. "Top, he's dead and he isn't going to get any deader by me cutting him. Trust me, I know what I'm doing. This is important. Very important."

Lorne glanced around. Other than the pilots, he was the ranking man on the spot.

"We might have whatever killed Sergeant Ku," Comsky said, thumping his chest. "That's why it's important that I do this. To try and get an idea of what it is."

Lorne hesitated, then nodded. "All right. Go ahead."

Comsky slid the blade through flesh. Ku's stomach was full of black blood with traces of internal tissue mixed in it. Comsky reached through the goo with his hand, pulling up dripping internal organs. Conner turned away, retching, the meager breakfast she'd had coming back up.

"His kidneys are gone," Comsky said. He pulled something up. "That's his liver." It was the color of urine and partly dissolved. Comsky put it back down on top of the mass of blood and guts that had been Sergeant Ku. He looked up at the camera. "I don't know exactly what killed this man, but the people who might know are at Fort Detrick. Whoever's looking at this tape back in the States, please get a copy to Fort Detrick."

Comsky stood and pulled a poncho out of his rucksack. "Let's bag him. Bag him tight. Then I suggest we clean up as best we can."

# Chapter 9

**Fort Detrick, Maryland, 15 June**

A madman working in a wax museum could not have set a more fearsome scene. The bodies were twisted into grotesque shapes. Mouths were open; silent lips that would never know the passage of a final scream were pulled wide over fangs. Their chests had been opened, red blood frozen and caught hanging like threads of red.

The eyes were the worst. Black orbs staring aimlessly out, framed in red blood like cheap eyeliner that an epileptic makeup artist had applied.

Dan Tyron didn't like dealing with frozen bodies. Not out of any sense of aesthetics, but because frozen objects have pointy parts and pointy parts make holes in gloves and flesh. And this frozen locker was hot. As hot as any place on earth. And hot plus a hole in the space suit he wore equaled dead.

Inside his suit, Tyron was a large man. He just barely made it inside the army's weight standards every time his annual PT test rolled around, and that was only after careful dieting and some fudging by the unit first sergeant on both the scale and height recorded. The philosophy around this place was that they weren't going to have one of their own separated from the army just because of some stupid rules that had nothing to do with a soldier's capability to do his job.

Tyron had sandy blond hair and a wide, cheerful face that belied a man who was handling dead bodies. Very carefully, he rolled a cart under one of the monkeys. He pushed a button and the chain that had held the body up lowered it until its entire weight was on the cart. He then most carefully unfastened the meat hook that was jammed through the monkey's back from the chain, leaving the implement in place.

He slowed his breathing. His faceplate was fogging up and the air inside his suit was getting stale. He rolled the cart out of the refrigerator room and shut the large steel door behind him. Then down the corridor to the necropsy room, where he plugged in the air hose for his suit to a wall socket. The familiar sound of the fresh air being pumped in filled his ears and the mask cleared. The sound was as comforting to him as the whine of a smoothly running engine was to a helicopter pilot. It meant his lifeline was working. He locked the wheels on the base of the cart so it wouldn't move. Every action was slow and deliberate. He double-checked everything he did. This was not a place for mistakes.

Tyron pulled extra-large surgical gloves over the space-suit gloves, then glanced at the other occupant of the room and pointed at the monkey. "On three."

The other person had the name "Spencer" stenciled on the chest and a woman's voice echoed him over the radio to confirm she understood. "On three."

"One." Tyron and Spencer each grabbed one end of the monkey. "Two. Three." They smoothly lifted the body and placed it on an operating table, handling it as delicately as they would a bomb, which in effect it could be considered. The monkey was dead, but there were things inside it that existed in a netherworld between life and death, waiting for other living flesh to devour just as they had devoured the monkey's.

"It'll take a couple of hours to defrost," Tyron said. "We'll do the cutting on this one at thirteen hundred."

"All right," Spencer acknowledged.

He turned to the other table, where a second monkey lay. They had taken it out of the freezer the previous evening. Tyron picked up a scalpel and handed it to Spencer. "Welcome to level four. Your first patient, Doctor."

He couldn't see Spencer's face as she bent over the corpse. "Thank you, Doctor." She pressed the blade into the monkey's stomach and sliced. The interior cavity was full of congealed blood.

Spencer watched his subordinate as she worked, making sure that she was noting all key abnormalities, although most were not hard to spot. The kidneys were totally gone. The liver was yellow and part of it had dissolved.

He took the samples she was cutting off and placed them onto glass slides. The only glass allowed on level four. When she indicated, he took a pair of large clamps and cracked open the monkey's chest, holding open the rib cage for her to work in there.

There was a crackling noise in the air and Spencer was startled. She froze and looked at Tyron, trying to guess what the cause was. "Voice box," he mouthed to her, looking up at the ceiling. She looked relieved. Any break in the routine was scary down here.

What the hell do they want? Tyron thought. The speaker crackled again and this time he recognized the voice of the USAMRIID—the United States Army Medical Research Institute of Infectious Diseases—commander, Colonel Martin.

"Dan, we have a development in Angola."

A development, Tyron thought, his pulse skipping a beat. Something was hot there. He remembered seeing the news on SNN about the UN/Pan-African mission into Angola. Something about the 82d Airborne deploying.

"I need you to look at something," Martin's voice continued. "ASAP."

Tyron unplugged his air hose and moved to the air lock. He stepped in. His mask was fogging badly. "Got to have control," he whispered to himself, slowing his breathing. The lock cycled and he stepped through. He ripped off his boots, then stepped into the next chamber. He pulled a chain and the suit was hosed down. He waited impatiently as the shower ran through its sequence. There was no way to make it go quicker. Not if it was going to ensure that all viruses that might be on his suit were gone.

A development. The word echoed through Tyron's consciousness. He was coming out of one of only two biohazard level four labs in the country. The other one was at the Centers for Disease Control (CDC) headquarters in Atlanta. The people who worked at both USAMRIID and CDC around level four agents knew that a development usually meant someone had died and that more people were going to die unless they intervened quickly and effectively.

It was obvious to most people why the CDC had such an interest in disease. It was less obvious why the army had one, except to students of military history. Even in the relatively modern times of the last century, in war more soldiers died of disease than in battle. Whenever masses of men gathered together, pestilence was never far away. Also, biological and chemical agents had been used before as weapons of war and they would be used again. USAMRIID's job was to try and stay one step ahead.

The shower finally shut down. Tyron walked into the staging area and took off his suit. He rapidly threw on his Class B uniform and went to the elevator, still tucking the light-green shirt in.

The door opened and he rode it up to ground level. When the elevator opened, Colonel Martin was standing there waiting, dressed in sweatpants and a faded green surgical shirt—his normal work uniform. "This way," Martin said. They went directly to his office. Four other people were gathered there: the other top experts in the office on bioagents.

"We've already seen this once," Martin said, pointing at the TV. He picked up the remote and turned the VCR/TV on.

"What is this?" Tyron asked as the screen showed a crashed helicopter and people shooting.

Colonel Martin had all the information on a classified fax that he read from. "A Navy F-18 Hornet was shot down over northeast Angola at eleven twelve hours today, Greenwich Mean Time. This helicopter was sent to recover the pilot. It, too, was shot down at approximately eleven twenty-three hours."

The camera panned over to two men leaning over a supine figure. It closed in and Tyron leaned forward to see. The man was vomiting blood and in convulsions. There was a breathing tube stuck in his throat and blood coming out of the eyes. He watched one of the men trying to get an IV going only to have blood pour out of the needle punctures. Tyron recognized the symptoms, but he'd never before seen them in a human, only in monkeys. "Oh, shit," he muttered.

"That was our conclusion," Colonel Martin remarked dryly.

He continued to watch as the man died. Then the scene cut to the medic who had been working on the man cutting him open.

"His kidneys are gone," the medic said. "That's his liver." The medic turned to face the camera. "I don't know exactly what killed this man, but the people who might know are at Fort Detrick. Whoever's looking at this tape back in the States, please get a copy to Fort Detrick."

The tape went blank.

Tyron looked around the room and then focused on one man. "Ebola?"

There were two varieties of the deadly Ebola virus: Ebola Sudan and Ebola Zaire. Zaire had a kill ratio of 90 percent of those infected, the Sudan variety not too far behind. It might not be a virus, Tyron hoped. It might be nothing—but he knew nothing didn't kill like that. It had to be something.

"Maybe," the man replied. He was dressed casually in cutoff jean shorts and T-shirt. He appeared to be in his mid-thirties but Tyron knew that Michael Kieling was only twenty-nine. He'd had a tough life. He had black hair hanging down to his collar, and framing his face was the outline of a two-day beard—Tyron wondered how Kieling always managed to look forty-eight hours from his last shave.

Kieling was the resident genius on level four bioagents at USAMRIID. He had a PhD in epidemiology and four years' experience in the field. "Could be Marburg, but I don't think so. He has those welts, but they don't seem to be the same as Marburg lesions. It's hard to tell from this feed," Kieling continued. "Plus he has his hair." Marburg virus usually caused the victim's hair to fall out. Just like radiation poisoning.

"Who's the case?" Tyron asked, realizing he was no longer referring to the victim as a person.

"An Angolan native," Martin said. "We don't have anything on him yet, except that he was assigned to the American Special Forces as an adviser."

"So he was on the helicopter?" Tyron asked.

"Yes."

"Where are those people now?"

"They're returning to a camp at Cacólo. A town in northeast Angola," Martin said.

"How'd we get the video?" Tyron asked.

"An SNN crew was also on the bird. Their feed goes through military satellites, downlinks at the Pentagon, where the censors take a look. They saw this and someone with a few brains gave us a call."

"This is out on the news?" Tyron was stunned.

Martin shook his head. "No. They're holding it at the Pentagon."

Tyron turned back to the screen. "Are they quarantined at Cacólo?"

Kieling laughed. "Come on, man, get real. We just saw this. They don't have a clue over there, although whoever that medic was who did the quick autopsy for our benefit, he's smart. He definitely has a good idea what he's got there. The brass at the Pentagon don't know. The only ones who really know right now is us. And from this, well, we really don't know too much either."

Kieling could speak like that, Tyron knew. He was a civilian on contract with USAMRIID. Inside the tight community of scientists who dealt with deadly infectious diseases, Kieling was known as a virus cowboy. Someone who traveled around the world looking for microscopic bugs that killed. Corralled them. Brought them back to level four. Then tried to take them apart to find a way to beat them.

Tyron backed the tape up to a picture of the man just after he died. "Have you ever seen this before?" Tyron asked, aware that Colonel Martin was watching him carefully. Martin wasn't an epidemiologist. He was a regular army doctor, sent here to overwatch the bunch of scientists and doctors to make sure they could still remember how to put on the uniform and salute and to remind them every once in a while who paid their salary. Except of course, as it turned out, Martin had been absorbed by the Institute rather than the opposite happening, hence his casual outfit. Regardless, Tyron knew, as the ranking army epidemiologist, this was his problem to make decisions about.

Kieling looked at the screen. "I can't see a damn thing on that other than they had a crash-and-burn."

A *crash-and-burn* was the Institute's term for the final stages of a victim carrying a deadly agent. The bug had taken over the body and consumed it and was ready to move on, having killed its host.

"Could it be X?" Tyron asked, referring to the fourth of the deadly filoviruses to come out of Africa.

"Don't know." Kieling scratched his chin. "Only way we're going to find out is to go there."

"I'll contact the Pentagon," Colonel Martin said. "I'll have them hold the footage indefinitely and close down Cacólo." He pointed at Tyron, then Kieling. "I'll get you a plane. Be ready to move in an hour."

## Angola-Zaire Border, 15 June

"That's the spot," Trent said.

Quinn looked at the border crossing. The rest of the mercenaries were farther back, hidden in some low ground. There was only the faint impression of a trail cutting across the ground. No border post. No sign that there even was an international border.

"We'll keep surveillance on it," Quinn said. "I wouldn't put it past Skeleton or some of those ghouls who work for him to have a trap set for us now that they no longer need us here to work the rebels or diamonds."

Trent turned to him. "You think he'd do that?"

Quinn shrugged. "The less said about what's been going on in this country, the better, would be their outlook on things, I suppose. We haven't exactly been legal here."

Trent glanced toward where the other men were. "Some of the men are jumpy. They've seen the jets. They know the Yanks are here. They want to get out before we run into something we can't handle. And six are sick. Killibrew is in real bad shape. He's throwing up blood."

Quinn had been thinking about that. "All right. I've changed my mind. I think it's better for us to go small. The rebels got more to worry about right now than us, and this big a group is sure to catch some American interest. Let those go who want to and get rid of all that are sick. They can go to a clinic in Zaire and get treated." Quinn checked his map. "Here. At Sandoa there's some of those international aid people running a clinic. Tell them to go there. We'll keep about four good men who you trust and who want some extra money." He looked about. "Also, if we do have a tick from Skeleton, let's hope we're getting rid of him."

Trent paused. "What about pay for those who go?"

"They got their half up front. The other half is waiting in Kinshasa. Give them the codes for their accounts." He paused. "Unless Skeleton has reneged on everything, in which case it won't matter much."

"If Skeleton reneged on their money, we've got the diamonds,"

Trent noted. "We can always black-market them. We won't get as much, but we'll get something."

Quinn's hand strayed to the pouch around his neck, but his mind was elsewhere. "We'll have something better than the diamonds."

Trent was puzzled. "Eh? What's that?"

"Whatever this guy is coming after, it's worth a million to Skeleton. And, after we get him where he wants to go," Quinn added, "we'll have both the guy and whatever it is."

### Cacólo, Angola, 15 June

Riley looked across the cargo bay of the Chinook. Comsky was staring down at his hands, and beneath his stubble of beard the medic's face was pale. It had taken a while for the Chinook to show up, then a bit longer for them to get the disabled Black Hawk hooked up for sling-load. The smaller helicopter now hung below the double-bladed Chinook and they were just about back to Cacólo. The pilots of the Chinook had to fly slower than normal to keep the load from getting out of control. Ku's body lay in the center of the cargo bay, tightly wrapped in waterproof ponchos. The Black Hawk's copilot's body was still trapped in the airframe suspended below.

Riley stepped over Ku's body and squeezed in next to Comsky. "What's up, Ape Man?"

Comsky pointed at his hand. There was a gash on the back, running from his middle knuckle to his wrist. "I cut this in the crash." He nodded at the corpse. "I'm fucked. I had his blood all over me."

"AIDS?" Riley asked.

Comsky laughed, but it was not a pleasant sound. "Shit, Dave, that's the least of my worries right now. Yeah, there's always a chance he had HIV. But whatever took Ku down wasn't AIDS. I've never seen anything like that."

"You sure it was a bug?" Riley asked. "Maybe he had cancer or something." Conner had come over and she knelt down next to them, listening in on their conversation. Captain Vickers was lying on the floor, just in front of Comsky, her eyes closed, strapped in tightly to a stretcher.

"I pray it wasn't a virus," Comsky said. "But there was no wound or anything from the outside. And it wasn't cancer. The way he was bleeding and his insides getting torn about. I never heard or seen anything like it. *Something* ate him up from the inside out. When that happens it's usually some sort of virus. That's why I wanted them to get that footage to Fort Detrick. That's where the army has its specialists on viruses."

Riley grabbed hold of Conner as they felt the helicopter jerk. The sling-loaded Black Hawk had been put down. The sling was released. The Chinook moved over, then set down, and the back ramp was opened; but they were halted before they could get off. Major Lindsay was the first man up the ramp into the helicopter, and he did not look happy. Captain Dorrick was behind him. He indicated for everyone to remain in place. They all waited as the pilots shut the helicopter down. Dorrick was holding back, afraid to come too close to anyone, but Major Lindsay walked right up into the middle of them.

Silence descended. Lindsay looked down at the form in the poncho, then back up. "I don't know what is going on, but we've got big trouble." He looked at Conner and Seeger. "Whatever you filmed lit a fire under somebody's ass in the Pentagon. We're shut down here. Nobody comes in or goes out of the AOB. Beyond that, I'm to keep everyone on this helicopter separate from the rest of the population here at Cacólo. Captain Dorrick will take you to your new billets. I'll be by to debrief you in a half hour."

Riley turned and looked at Comsky. The medic's face was now ashen and he was looking at his hand as if it were some strange specimen he'd discovered.

"Excuse me, sir," Comsky said. He pointed down at Lieutenant Vickers. "She needs medical attention."

"My orders are to make no exceptions. You're going to have to take care of her yourself," Lindsay said. "Your medical kit is in the isolation area."

### Andrews Air Force Base, Maryland, 15 June
Since viewing the videotape, Tyron had been on the move, gathering equipment together and packing. Two helicopters had landed on the lawn in front of the Institute. One for Tyron and Kieling and their personal baggage, and the other for the specialized gear they would need to take biosafety level four precautions to Angola with

them and to try and find out what had killed the man in the video. They were now flying to Andrews Air Force Base, where the colonel had arranged their overseas transportation.

Tyron had let Kieling take charge. The other man had much more experience in traveling and going places. In fact, Tyron was now counting his blessings that Kieling had gone on the "jaunt" three years ago. The jaunt was part of the lore at the Institute, and Tyron had heard more than a few stories about it.

There were two things that were of primary importance to be discovered when a new virus appeared. The first, of course, was to determine exactly what the virus was and to isolate it. The second was to find out where it came from. With those two facts, they at least had the basics needed to try and defeat the bug.

In 1994 a virus had erupted out of southern Zaire. Of course, since southern Zaire wasn't a media hotspot, the word got out slowly. The disease burned along the Zaire-Zambia border with a kill rate of over 90 percent of those infected. Thousands upon thousands of people died.

After two weeks ripping through the countryside, the virus made a toehold in the Zambian city of Ndola. The Zambian president had the city cordoned off by troops. Roads were blocked, the airport was shut down, and travel was prohibited. The president was prepared to lose the city to save the country.

And just as swiftly as it had appeared, the virus went away. The last of the victims died and their bodies were burned. Life went back to normal along the border, save for the forty thousand people who had died. But forty thousand dead in Africa barely made a blip on the world media. Except among those at the Institute.

From Zairean doctors, they managed to get samples of the virus in the form of frozen tissue samples sent by plane. They quickly isolated the deadly agent. It was a filovirus, a cousin to Marburg and the two Ebolas. But it wasn't any of them, and for lack of a better name the new virus was christened X. The name *filovirus* was derived from the Latin—"thread virus." Had they not already seen Marburg and Ebola at the Institute, they might not have so quickly caught on to X, but as soon as the strange, thin, elongated forms showed up in the electron microscope they zeroed in on it.

They had X, but they didn't know anything else about it other than that it killed. So Kieling proposed to go and track down where the virus had come from. He took a trip to Zaire and investigated. Like a detective, he backtracked the line of death that the few survivors remembered. As best as Kieling could determine, X had probably originated not in Zaire but somewhere on the southeast side of Lake Bangweulu in Zambia. He managed to hire a small-plane pilot to fly him up there. They flew over mile upon mile of swampland bordering the lake. It was a dismal-looking place, full of wildlife and little visited by man. Kieling tried to get the pilot to land at a small town on the edge of the swamp, but as they descended, the odor of rotting corpses was so great they could smell it in the cockpit of the plane and the pilot refused to land.

Kieling came back to the Institute and proposed an expedition to Lake Bangweulu to try and find out the birthplace of X. His justification was that if it had come out once, it might come out again, and the next time it might not go away. Forty thousand dead and a 90 percent kill rate made for a very effective argument. The funds were appropriated and Kieling went back to Zambia with a team of experts and the proper gear to work with level four bioagents in the field, something that had never been done before.

They went into the swamp and, after two weeks of searching, found an island where Kieling suspected the disease might have originated among the local monkey population. A few local survivors told him that swamp people went to that island occasionally to capture monkeys for export to medical labs for experimentation. That might help explain how the disease got out of the swamp, Kieling reasoned. They suited up and went onto the island as if it were hot. But they found nothing on the island and eventually Kieling had to order them to pack up and head back.

Kieling never found out where X came from, thus the nickname the "jaunt" for the entire exercise. But he had learned a lot about taking the lab to the field, and for that Tyron was now very grateful, because most of the equipment on the second helicopter was prepackaged gear that Kieling had used on the jaunt. Kieling had used his expertise to put together easily movable equipment that they had stored in Conexes in back of the Institute. If ever there was a need to go virus hunting again, Kieling had wanted to be ready.

And now they were off hunting. One dead man in a video didn't necessarily mean they had another X on their hands, Tyron knew. But if they did, at least they wouldn't be starting from scratch preparing this expedition.

In the past several decades X, Ebola, and Marburg had broken out occasionally in Africa and killed with ruthless efficiency—or propagated with amazing strength, depending on one's outlook, Tyron thought. Then they had disappeared. There was still no vaccine for those known scourges—never mind something new. It was a sore point at both USAMRIID and the CDC in Atlanta that they hadn't broken any of the filoviruses' codes. The only thing they had accomplished in the past several years was to come up with a field test to determine if someone had Ebola or Marburg. X was still an unknown.

The choppers came in the flight path for Andrews Air Force Base and landed near a group of hangars. Several air force officers were waiting for them.

"Major Tyron?" the ranking man asked, running up to the chopper.

Tyron nodded. "Yes."

The man pointed at a hangar. "We've got your ride in here." He looked at the other chopper where men were taking off the lab gear. "Might take us a couple of minutes to get your stuff loaded. This whole thing is kind of unorthodox, but we'll get you out of here as fast as we can."

Tyron looked around, wondering why there would be a problem loading the gear. "What type of plane are we going to use? C-141?"

The air force general smiled and gestured for Tyron and Kieling to follow him. "No. We were told to get you there as fast as possible."

They walked in through a small door on the side of the hangar. A sleek B-1 bomber painted coal black sat inside.

"Cool" was Kieling's comment.

"The B-1 normally has a crew of four," the general explained. "We're taking off the offensive and defensive systems operators and replacing them with you two. We're putting your gear in the bomb bay. That's what's going to take a few minutes as it's not exactly configured for cargo."

"How long will it take us to get to Luanda?" Tyron asked.

"At Mach one point two five," the general said, "about eight hours. You've got enough fuel to get there without in-flight refueling." The general looked around, making sure that no one else was in earshot. "If you don't mind, could you tell me what the big rush is?"

"In eight hours," Kieling said, his eyes still on the bomber, "certain viruses can replicate themselves almost six million times. That is the rush."

# Chapter 10

**Cacólo, Angola, 15 June**

"Go slow and explain it so that we can all understand," Riley said.

"Who the fuck put you in charge?" Master Sergeant Lorne demanded.

The group gathered in the GP medium was tense and confused. Major Lindsay had had several tents set up a quarter mile away from the main encampment. The isolation area was surrounded by rolls of barbed wire, but Riley had the feeling the wire's purpose was to keep those inside where they were rather than to protect against attack. Everyone who had been exposed to Ku's blood on the mission where he had died was there: Riley, Conner, Seeger, Lorne, Lieutenant Vickers, Comsky, Brewster, Oswald, Tiller, and the crew of the Black Hawk.

Prior to entering the quarantine area, Riley had assisted Comsky and Lorne in extricating the copilot's body from the wreckage of the Black Hawk. It was not a job anyone from the AOB was going to volunteer for.

Given that no one really seemed to understand what was going on, Riley had suggested that Comsky explain the need for the quarantine, and Lorne's patience had worn through.

"No one put me in charge," Riley replied in a steady voice. "But you're not in charge either. Not of me or Conner or Mike," he added, pointing at the SNN crew. He looked at Comsky. "He's the man who has the most knowledge about what we might be dealing with here, so if anyone should be in charge he gets my vote."

"Who said this was a democracy?" Lorne snapped.

"Oh, give me a break," Conner Young said. "It's a democracy because we're all in the same crap pile. Equal risk. Equal vote. Get it?"

"I don't need to take any shit from you civilians," Lorne said.

"Sergeant Lorne," a woman's quiet voice called out from a cot in the shadows near the tent wall. "As far as I can tell," Lieutenant Vickers said, "I am the ranking person in this tent. So let Sergeant Comsky answer the question."

"Ma'am," Lorne said, refusing to give in, "you might outrank me, but standard operating procedure says that while you are in charge in the air, in an emergency on the ground, it is the senior army person who is in charge."

"That's standard operating procedure only in case of an aircraft crash for escape-and-evasion purposes," Riley countered. He looked around. "You don't have an SOP for this situation and Lieutenant Vickers does outrank you. Do you want to go to Major Lindsay with this?"

"Fine," Lorne snapped. "The lieutenant is in charge. Go ahead."

Vickers turned her head toward the medic, who looked as unhappy as a man could appear and wasn't showing much interest in the feuding. "What makes you think Sergeant Ku died of a viral infection?"

Comsky blinked and made an effort to focus in. "I didn't think it at first, but as I ruled out other causes for what was happening to him, that came to mind. There was no external wound. He'd been appearing sick for a while. The vomiting. The bleeding from everywhere. I'd read about the bleeding around the needle that happened when I tried to run the IV. That's what happened in some cases of severe viral infection."

"So he had a bug," Sergeant Oswald said. "Does that mean we have it? I heard what you told Top at the crash site."

"We're not *sure* he had a bug," Comsky said. He looked around gloomily. "But the fact that someone back in the States ordered Major Lindsay to quarantine us isn't good."

"So he *probably* had a bug," Conner Young said sarcastically. "Are we all agreed on terminology?"

"Going back to the original question," Vickers said. "Does that mean we have it?"

Comsky shrugged. "Depends on the transmission vector. For example, AIDS requires body-fluid—blood or semen—contact. If this has the same type of vector, most of you are okay." He looked down at the bandage on the back of his hand.

"Unless we have an open wound," Vickers said, running a finger along one of the cuts on her face.

"And had contact with Ku's blood," Comsky added. "But if it's like influenza and it's transmitted through the air, then we're all fucked."

A long silence descended.

"Hell," Comsky finally said. "On the positive side, most deadly viruses are not easily transmitted. The odds are great that it isn't transmitted through the air, because most viruses don't last long when exposed to ultraviolet light. That's why they usually go through a body fluid. And anyway, we don't even know if it is a virus."

"I might be a little slow here," Riley said, "but would you explain what a virus is?" Riley knew that he had to get Comsky's and everyone else's mind away from dark thoughts, and the best way to do that was to get their minds working on something professional. Besides, Riley knew, people worked better when they were aware of the facts of a situation.

Comsky collected his thoughts. "There are different types of invasive organisms. The two major forms are bacteria and viruses. Tuberculosis is a bacterium. AIDS is a virus."

Comsky's demeanor had changed. He was back in the classroom at Fort Sam Houston in Texas, where he'd received his basic and advanced medical training. Riley knew that Special Forces medics were highly trained professionals—not functionaries who simply handed out bandages. "Most people think of these things as little bugs that are out to kill humans, but really they're just creatures trying to live. In some cases we just happen to be the host through which they live and reproduce." Comsky paused. "Well, actually, bacteria are alive. Viruses aren't and they are."

Riley looked around. The medic certainly had their attention.

"Bacteria," Comsky continued, "are living cells. They cause problems in humans because our bodies mount a response to their infection, and in many cases the response is so strong it destroys good cells along with the bacteria.

"Sometimes it's the bacteria cells themselves that cause the problem. Cholera is a good example of that. The toxins from the bacteria attack cells in the intestine, causing severe diarrhea, which dehydrates the body to the point where many of those infected die.

"We didn't spend as much time on viruses in our medical training," Comsky said. "If I remember correctly, a virus is genetic material—DNA or RNA—inside a protein shell. They sort of just hang around and exist. Then they come in contact with a host. The problem, for the host that is, is that to reproduce, a virus needs a living cell. In the process of reproducing, a virus kills the host cell."

"Why didn't you spend as much time on viruses?" Riley asked. It seemed to him that if they were so deadly, there would be more attention paid.

"Because you can treat most bacterial infections," Comsky said, "although there are more and more strains appearing that have mutated and are resistant to traditional drug treatments such as penicillin. But there are very few antiviral drugs. The best defense against viruses is vaccination." He looked down at his hand. "And you have to have a vaccination *before* you get infected for it to be effective. So, most of the time, finding out that someone has a viral infection doesn't do you much good, because in many cases there are no cures."

"So if we got some sort of virus from that guy," Sergeant Oswald said, bringing the entire conversation full circle, "then we're screwed."

"Roger that," Comsky said.

So much for improving morale, Riley thought.

"How long do we have if we got this thing?" Oswald demanded, cutting to the chase.

Comsky shook his head. "I don't know. Ku went down fast out there, but it must have been in him for a while." He laughed, but it was not from the humor of the situation. "That's the paradox of viruses that has saved mankind from being wiped out. The quicker a virus kills its host, the less chance it has of being transmitted. If a virus takes someone down in a day, it only has a small window to be passed on. If it takes years, like AIDS, then it has more of a chance to be spread. Thus the more effective a killer it is, the less chance that a virus will propagate.

"To really answer the question," Comsky continued, "we need to find out where Sergeant Ku might have picked this thing up."

Sergeant Lorne liked that. It was a course of action, at least. "I'll tell Major Lindsay to get on it."

Lieutenant Vickers turned to Comsky. "I think you'd better get to work on my ankle and set it as best you can."

### *Abraham Lincoln,* 15 June

"Say again, sir?" the galley steward wasn't used to the ship's executive officer coming into his domain in the forward mess unless it was for an inspection. And he wasn't quite sure he had heard the officer's request correctly.

"I want you to load the largest coolers you have with ice and get them up on the flight deck right now!" the officer repeated.

"Yes, sir." The steward appropriated several large coolers used to transport frozen food on the ship between the forward and aft galleys. He had his shift position them one by one underneath the massive ice-making machines in the kitchen. The galleys were capable of providing over ten thousand meals a day, so they had every piece of equipment imaginable.

They trundled the coolers to an elevator and went up to the flight deck, where a C-2 cargo plane waited. The ship's XO was waiting there, anxiously waving them up the back ramp, where they secured the coolers. As soon as they were done, the ramp closed and the plane was rolled into place and launched.

As it disappeared to the east, the crew was left to ponder what the urgent need for ice was in Angola.

### Oshakati, Namibia, 15 June

General Nystroom pulled his reading glasses out of the case in his breast pocket and slowly read the message that had just been transmitted to him. It was succinct and to the point.

TO: NYSTROOM/EYES ONLY
FROM: HIGH COMMAND/SILVERMINE
CEASE ALL OPERATIONS NORTH OF BORDER—HOLD
IMPLEMENTATION OF JACKET THREE PENDING FUR-

THER ORDERS—REVIEW CONTINGENCY PLAN THAT
FOLLOWS AND PREPARE TO CARRY IT OUT
  END OF MESSAGE

Jacket Three was the operations plan for the invasion of southern
Angola. It was the entire purpose of all their actions for the past four
months. Nystroom shook his head. Why were they stopping him now?
His forces were ready to go. Every hour they delayed gave the rebels
more of a chance to reconsolidate their forces from the destruction
the planes had wrought.

And how was he to cease all operations north of the border? Was
he supposed to just order his scouts up there to hide? Or was he supposed to pull them back?

"Is there more?" Nystroom asked his communications officer.

"No, sir. Just that one page."

Where was the contingency plan, then? Nystroom wondered.
Were the Americans backing out? He'd heard nothing. The 82d was
deploying as planned according to his liaison officers.

If the Americans were still on schedule, was there some change
back in his own command? Or was there another factor? Nystroom
threw the message down. Damn political bullshit.

### National Security Agency, Fort Meade, Maryland, 15 June

Waker read the text of the message that had been transmitted from
Silvermine to General Nystroom one more time. Breaking the South
African code had been easier than he had expected, but he wasn't
too thrilled with what he had just uncovered. He didn't know why
the South Africans were holding up on their part of the operation,
but he knew he needed to pass this information along to his higher
headquarters. Waker put the appropriate address on the decoded
message and e-mailed it along a secure network.

### Cacólo, Angola, 15 June

It was one of the strangest things Conner had ever watched. She'd
had Seeger film Comsky packing Ku's body—or rather the lump
wrapped with ponchos—in ice inside a large cooler the plane had
brought in. They put the body of the copilot in another cooler. She

knew her film was being intercepted by the Pentagon and that everything from here on was going to be held until this thing, whatever it was, played out. She also knew that the recent action would probably never make prime time. It had not been a pretty sight.

"Comsky!"

They all looked out toward the wire. Major Lindsay stood there in the darkness.

"Yes, sir."

"I found out something about Sergeant Ku."

Comsky walked over to the wire, the rest of them following. Conner noted the six feet of air that separated them from the man on the other side. Was that enough to keep Lindsay safe? Was there even something on this side to worry about?

"I talked to Major Gungue and we tracked down the officer who was in charge of Ku before he got picked up to be your team's liaison. A lieutenant Monoko. They were stationed at the Angola-Zaire border at a town called Luau."

"Has anyone checked that place?" Comsky cut in.

"Yeah, we called out there on the radio. No sign of disease. But we did find out something interesting. On their way back from Luau it seems that Lieutenant Monoko got lost. They wandered around the Lunda Norte region for a while before Monoko figured things out and got them here. Hell," Lindsay said, "they weren't even supposed to be here.

"But anyway," he said quickly, "they came across a village where everyone was dead. A bunch of bodies had been stacked and someone had tried to burn them, but the job hadn't been finished. Lieutenant Monoko said Ku got some blood on him from one of the bodies."

"Have you found the village?" Riley asked.

"No. Monoko's not exactly sure where it was. We just have the approximate area."

"How long ago did this happen, sir?" Comsky asked.

"Six days."

"Anything else, sir?"

"The people from Fort Detrick will be here before dawn," Major Lindsay offered. He stood for a few moments, shuffling his feet, then headed back to the AOB.

"Six days," Comsky muttered. "That's fast." Comsky turned away from the wire and walked off into the darkness on the other side of the tent, pondering the new information.

Slowly the rest of them wandered away inside the small area allowed them.

Conner Young returned to the tent and lay down on a cot. She was bone tired but couldn't get to sleep. Riley had been right. The biggest story was probably going to be out here—and she was beginning to believe that she might end up wishing he was wrong, something she could not have imagined twenty-four hours ago.

### Airspace, Atlantic Ocean, 15 June

"We're three hours out," the pilot announced. "We have some secure incoming messages for you guys on the computer link."

For such a large plane, the crew space inside the B-1 was surprisingly small. Tyron and Kieling were seated behind the pilots, faced with rows upon rows of instrument panels. They'd spoken little since taking off because there'd been nothing to talk about.

They both watched as words scrolled up. The information on Sergeant Ku's last week alive, as much as had been found out so far, was displayed.

"Six days," was Kieling's first comment.

"If the ninth was the day he was infected," Tyron hedged.

Kieling turned and looked at him. "This isn't the lab, Tyron."

Tyron ignored him. "They don't have the exact location of the village."

"We'll find it," Kieling said.

"How?"

"We'll find it," Kieling said. "But that's not important. This thing didn't start in a village." He pulled a map out of his briefcase and unfolded it in the cramped cabin. "That border post the case came from—" He pointed. "It's not far from Lake Bangweulu. Maybe seven hundred miles."

Shit, Tyron thought. Was Kieling going to use this trip to recoup the jaunt? Was he going to get focused on X? Tyron tapped the screen. "There's no sign of this in the border town."

"They have the body on ice, at least," Tyron added. "We can get samples back to the Institute on this plane's return flight. We can also look with our equipment and determine if it's a known like Ebola."

Kieling was studying the map. "Uh-huh." He looked up. "Well, we know this Ku fellow wasn't patient zero. They had corpses in the village."

*Patient zero* was the term for the disease's human starting point. If they could backtrack and find patient zero, then backtrack patient zero's steps, they could find what the disease had jumped from to get to humans and they could be that much further on their way to understanding not only the disease itself, but how it started.

A virus had to have a "reservoir"—a living organism that it resided in that it *didn't* kill—or at least kill as quickly as the filoviruses killed humans. Otherwise the parasite would destroy its own source of survival. If they could find the reservoir, then they might find out how that organism held off the effects of the virus, and that might point in the direction of a vaccine or cure.

"Is there any way we can send a message?" Kieling asked the pilot.

"Sure," the pilot replied. "You use the computer. It's just like sending e-mail." He then gave them directions.

Kieling typed into the small keyboard in front of him.

"What are you doing?" Tyron asked.

"Getting a hold of Colonel Martin and seeing if he can get someone to take a look around the countryside where this case came from. Maybe find that village; see what else is out there."

Major Tyron sat still for a while, listening to the sound of the jet engines. "Hey, Kieling," he finally said.

Kieling looked up. "Yeah."

"What if it is a level four? Maybe a filovirus?"

"Yeah?" Kieling waited. "What if it is?"

"What will happen?"

"A lot of people are going to die," Kieling said.

"I know that," Tyron replied. "My question is, how do we handle it?"

Kieling snorted. "We aren't going to *handle* it, as you so elegantly put it. It'll burn, Tyron, until it's burned everything in its path. We just have to hope it doesn't jump the ocean, that's all."

**National Security Agency, Fort Meade, Maryland, 15 June**
Waker read the information request and felt useful for the first time since he'd been assigned to cover Angola. He quickly began typing out a series of numbers and letters that assigned tasks to NSA assets to get the job done.

Within fifteen minutes of the request, his computer began receiving real-time imagery, in various modes, of Eastern Angola. Teal Ruby was a system of telescopes armed with cameras that could take photos from space of both air and ground down to such a resolution that individual cars showed up clearly. This regular photography—not very helpful given it was night there, but part of the standard package—was in the form of a picture mosaic that the computer put together—a job that used to take days by hand.

Of more use, he had two-dimensional arrays of sections of ground taken by supercooled infrared sensors aboard the KH-12. This thermal imaging didn't care if it was night or day. It displayed everything in each section according to levels of heat, the computer separating out ground clutter and then analyzing what was shown to give it a signature. It could differentiate as little as a half of a degree difference in objects on the ground.

That done, Waker wrapped up the information inside an e-mail secure package and sent it back to the return address—USAMRIID. He had to go to his *Directory of Federal Agencies* to find out what that was, and when he did, he had to wonder, not for the first time, what exactly was going on in Angola.

One other thing Waker noted, as he keyed the message off, was that the same request had also gone to the NRO—the National Reconnaissance Office—and that meant that USAMRIID was going to get the entire package of top-of-the-line material that the U.S. intelligence community had to offer, because Waker was one of the few people with a high enough clearance to know that the NRO was in charge of Aurora, and he'd seen what Aurora could do.

**Nellis Air Force Base, Nevada, 15 June**
Hidden deep inside the Nellis Air Force Base range is a highly classified facility known by various names—Area 51, the Ranch, the Skunkworks. UFO enthusiasts believe that the government test-

flies UFOs there. At the present moment, the vehicle being wheeled into place at the end of the longest runway in the world might well be called a UFO, although it was not made by aliens, but rather by human hands, and designed by the best minds in the aerospace business.

The plane began rolling forward. The successor to the famous SR-71 Blackbird, Aurora had made its maiden flight in 1986. At a billion dollars a plane, there were only five in the inventory. To the public that had financed it, the plane didn't exist, one of the most closely guarded secrets in the air force.

Shaped like a rounded manta ray, the two-man reconnaissance plane's most significant features were its huge intakes under the front cockpit and large exhausts behind the engines. Capable of Mach 7, over five thousand miles an hour, or almost a mile and a half a second at maximum speed, it could get to a target in a hurry. Even a target on the other side of the Atlantic Ocean and in the southern hemisphere.

With sufficient thrust built up, Aurora suddenly bounded up into the air and accelerated while climbing at a seventy-degree angle, gradually turning toward the southeast.

An hour and a half—and one in-flight refueling—later, the plane was approaching the coast of Africa just opposite Western Sahara. In the cockpit, the pilot kept his concentration on flying the plane while the reconnaissance systems officer (RSO) in the backseat fed him navigational guidance. "All systems on. We'll be in range of target in seventy-five seconds."

The fact that they had to overfly—and thus violate the airspace of—a third of the countries of western Africa didn't disturb the crew. They were moving so fast that by the time anyone realized that something was overhead, they'd be long gone.

"Fifty seconds." They were now over land. Niger flitted by underneath, then Nigeria.

"Descending through fifteen thousand," the pilot announced. "Slowing through two point five. The look will be right," he told the RSO, giving a direction to orient all the sophisticated reconnaissance systems on board the aircraft.

"Pod deploying," the RSO said as the speed gauge continued to go down. Now that they were under two thousand miles an hour, the surveillance pod could be extended. Doing it at higher speeds would have destroyed the necessary aerodynamics of the plane and caused it to break and burn. Even now the skin temperature of the aircraft was eight hundred degrees Fahrenheit. "Twenty seconds. All green."

"Leveling at three thousand," the pilot said. "Steady at Mach two."

"All systems on."

The RSO activated their low-level light television (LLTV) camera. The LLTV was no ordinary television. The camera enhanced both the light and image, giving it the ability to display an image at night, while at the same time carrying a magnification of over one hundred. The RSO began scanning ahead, using the information fed to it from the satellites above to confirm their location.

"Sixty miles from the border," the pilot announced.

"I'm rolling film," the RSO said.

The plane traversed Angola from north to south, the entire country going by in just a couple of minutes.

"One more pass, this time over a bit to make sure we cover the border with Zambia and Zaire," the pilot said.

He banked the plane and began making a sweeping turn that encompassed most of the southern tip of Africa before he was through. Once more they flew over Angola and the RSO took pictures.

Done, they turned for home while the RSO transmitted in digitized form the videotape they had just taken.

# Chapter 11

**Cacólo, Angola, 16 June**

Conner didn't feel the need to do any voice-over as Mike Seeger filmed the Chinook helicopter coming in to land in the open field to the south of the quarantine area. Beanbag strobe lights flickered from the ground, and the large chopper's searchlights gave the scene an eerie glow. The thump of the massive blades and the swirling dirt and grass kicked up by their downdraft further added to the eerie effect.

But when the back ramp on the chopper came down—that was when Conner truly felt like she had entered the twilight zone. Two men clad in blue full-body suits with large backpacks waddled off. Their heads were totally enclosed by hoods and masks. The second the men were clear, soldiers from the AOB ran on board the Chinook and started unloading gear.

Conner glanced at Riley. His face was impassive, his dark eyes watching the two men walk around to the gap in the wire. "They seem to be taking this pretty seriously," she said.

"I told them to do this so you could film it," Riley said. "Looks pretty impressive, doesn't it?"

"Next time, don't do me any favors," she said. She followed Riley as he walked over to their side of the gap in the wire. Master Sergeant Lorne didn't seem to be too happy about the men's gear either.

"Who are you?" he demanded.

The voice that came out of the small box that hung on the first man's shoulder was coldly mechanical. "I'm Major Tyron." A blue arm briefly lifted and pointed at the second figure. "This is Dr. Kieling. We're from the United States Army Medical Research Institute of Infectious Diseases at Fort Detrick. We saw the video your medic filmed. We're here to check things out."

Lorne stepped back from the opening. "This is Sergeant Comsky," he said.

"I recognize you from the film," Major Tyron said. "You did a good job."

"Lieutenant Vickers is in command here," Lorne added. "She's in the tent, unconscious. Sergeant Comsky just finished setting her ankle."

"We need to see the body," the second suited figure with "Kieling" stenciled on the chest spoke up. "We only have a limited amount of air in our suits and there's a lot that needs to be done."

"I can help you with samples if you need them," Comsky said.

"We'll do the body. No need further exposing you to it. But, we need samples from everyone who might have been exposed." Kieling held up the kit in his right hand. "Blood, stool, and urine from everyone." He put it down on the ground and stepped back.

"What? Are you afraid he's going to attack you or something?" Conner said as Comsky moved forward and picked it up.

"We're just using proper protocol," Major Tyron said. "We're not used to working in these suits outdoors and we're being careful."

"The body is this way," Sergeant Lorne said.

"Everyone with me," Comsky called out.

Tyron listened to the quiet thump of the rebreather tank on his back. He'd never worn a field suit before and didn't feel secure in it. Everything had happened so quickly once they had landed in Angola. There was the rapid transfer from the B-1 bomber to the Chinook under arc lights at the Luanda airport. Soldiers had hustled the gear out of the bomb bay while others stood around, staring, wondering what the hell a B-1 bomber was doing here and who the two men were who were getting such treatment—one of the two looking like a civilian at that! Then had come the rigging of the suits in the back of the helicopter on the way in. Tyron hoped he'd gotten it on correctly. He could all too easily remember the video of Sergeant Ku dying.

Tyron looked around. Jesus Christ, the idiots had barbed wire all around the damn place! All they needed was one nick and the suit's integrity was gone. He could just as easily trip and cut through his three sets of gloves on a rock. Kieling was right; this wasn't the lab.

Tyron followed Kieling around, through the gap in the wire. The quarantined people were watching him. They were armed and didn't look very happy. He didn't imagine he'd be too happy, either, to be stuck on their side of the wire.

They edged their way into a tent, brightly lit on the inside. Two big coolers took up most of the center. The large black soldier pointed at one of them. "That's Sergeant Ku." He then left.

Kieling threw open the lid of the cooler. He carefully opened up the ponchos hiding the body. Despite all his autopsies of monkeys and his medical training, Tyron had to control himself to prevent his revulsion from showing. Immediately he realized the stupidity of that—Kieling couldn't see his face behind the glazed plastic of the suit mask.

"Classic Ebola symptoms," Kieling said, his gloved hands already into what remained of the man. "But that doesn't guarantee it's Ebola." He pointed at Ku's chest. "Look at the rash we saw in the video. It's all over him. We've never seen that with Ebola." With the tip of the scalpel he touched flesh. "Notice these pustules—I've never seen anything like them before."

"The chopper's waiting for samples," Tyron reminded him.

"Yeah, and we can test here with what I brought," Kieling said. "The thing that bothers me is the timing." His fingers were probing Ku's internal organs. "Ebola takes two weeks. Here it sounds like a week, maybe six days, according to the information we received on the way over. I've never heard of anything working that quickly." He carefully cut with a scalpel. "Tube."

Tyron held out a sample tube and Kieling dropped in a bit of flesh and blood.

"Another."

The process was repeated several times, from different parts of the remains.

"We'll know shortly what it isn't," Kieling said as he lowered the lid on the cooler and headed for the tent exit.

Twenty minutes later, Conner was more irritated than scared. GP medium tents didn't allow for much modesty, although Comsky had cleared everyone else out when he'd gotten her samples.

"What now?" she asked as Comsky packed her samples in one of the small coolers the two space-suit men had brought.

"Get some sleep," Comsky suggested, walking toward the exit.

"Get some sleep?" Conner repeated, incredulously.

"It's a good idea," Riley was holding up the tent flap. He'd been waiting outside.

"Great, just fucking great," Conner muttered. She walked past him. The two men were walking back out the wire, carrying their loads of flesh, blood, and other specimens. Their arrival was played out again in reverse, except they only put some samples on the helicopter and it flew away to the west. The two men continued on to the special habitat that they had brought with them and that had rapidly been set up by AOB personnel about two hundred meters away. All it needed was to be inflated. The two scientists disappeared into the entrance of the habitat.

Conner walked to the edge of their compound and watched until they were gone. She noted that Riley had followed her. As the Chinook disappeared, silence descended.

"Scared?" Riley said.

"Are you?"

"Yes."

Conner turned and faced him. "Aren't you supposed to never be scared?"

"You saw me scared in Antarctica," Riley said.

"This is different. You were getting shot at down there."

Riley nodded. "You're right. This is different. I'm *more* scared now."

Conner didn't say anything to that. She waited, wrapping her arms around herself, feeling cold in the dark.

"I think all of us are," Riley said, gesturing around at the tents. "Fear is always the strongest when there's nothing you can do and you aren't sure what the threat is."

"That pretty much pegs this situation," Conner agreed.

They walked around, following the inner curve of the wire.

Riley halted and looked up at the night sky. "I used to think sometimes about warriors in the old days. You know, Vikings and people like that. The Romans. When men hacked at each other with swords and you looked your enemy in the eye.

"I thought it took real balls—no sexism intended—to do that. To have to stand toe to toe and use cold steel on your opponent. But then I turned it around and imagined what one of those warriors would think about the way we fight now. To have your enemy be over the next hill and lob a shell at you. To never see or hear the man who kills you. I think that would have terrified those men. Did you know that in this century more soldiers have been killed by artillery fire than by direct rifle or machine-gun fire?

"But this." Riley took a deep breath. "To face an enemy that isn't even human. That you will never see. That you can't fight with a rifle or with airplanes or bombs. That, according to Comsky, we can't even fight with medicine. To be helpless. It's bad. Real bad.

"I'll tell you one thing," he added. "The generals who planned this operation didn't include this in their contingency plans." He pointed at the habitat. "I hope they know what they're doing."

The habitat had not been designed for this use, Tyron knew. It was an inflatable tent designed for MASH units to be able to operate in a chemically contaminated environment. It had two flexible Kevlar walls—an inner and outer—with the space between filled with compressed air, allowing it to be set up very quickly. On the inside, it was relatively spacious, with just the two of them in there along with their gear.

The air coming in *and* out was ventilated through special air filters. It wasn't the most perfect biolevel four facility, but it was the best thing Kieling had found available in the government inventory when he'd conducted the jaunt.

The entryway was cramped, and with great difficulty Kieling and Tyron disinfected the outside of their suits. Then they unsuited, placing the garments into sealed plastic bags. The samples were inside the coolers and they carefully carried them into the habitat through the air lock. A long metal table had been unfolded there, and the rest of their gear was piled inside.

To handle a level four bioagent required either a full suit or a glove box. On top of the table, Tyron set up the latter. It was a device, two feet wide, by two tall, by three long. It had its own one-way mini–air lock so they could put samples in. Once in, the sample had to stay there until they took the box back to the level four lab and could sterilize the inside.

There were numerous compartments so they could keep samples separate and free from mutual contamination. There was also a microscope built into the box, so they could examine the samples, although getting a good enough look to see the individual viruses would require an electron microscope, and that was one of the reasons they had sent samples back to Fort Detrick on board the B-1. What they did have to look at was a "brick"—a block of virus particles—that they had taken from Ku's body. A brick was a seething collection of billions of virus particles, gathered together, waiting to move on to the next host.

Finished with the mechanical task of getting the box ready, Tyron stepped back and watched as Kieling went to work. Stepping up to the side of the box, Kieling stuck his hands through two openings, flexing his fingers into the heavy-duty gloves inside. Deftly, he selected blood-and-tissue samples of the brick they had taken from Ku.

"I'm going to test it for Ebola and Marburg," Kieling said. He took the samples and placed them into preset tubes containing an agent that would react to the specific virus. The tubes were blue. They would turn red if the virus was recognized.

While they waited for that reaction, Kieling put another sample from the brick onto a slide and put the slide into the other end of the scope and pressed his eye up against it.

Tyron listened to the rhythmic thump of the large air generator on the outside of the shelter. Not quite the same sound as that in the level four lab back at Fort Detrick. He had to wonder whether the shelter was designed to keep them safe inside or to keep the samples they had from getting out. How long could they continue to work in the field suits? That was a question no one knew the answer to. When Kieling had gone on the jaunt, he had only used the field suits when investigating a place where he thought he might find a reservoir for a virus—not to walk around all the time in a place where a virus was already burning. Kieling's earlier comment about not having a lot of air in the suit had not been exactly honest. The suits used a re-breather that, technically speaking, could work for four days, give or take about six hours, without recharging. The problem was basic body functions such as eating, drinking, urinating, and defecating. They were also hot to work in, and in this latitude working under the sun could easily bring on heat stroke.

Kieling's voice startled Tyron. "I don't think it's X." Kieling pointed at the microscope. "Take a look."

Tyron bent over and peered. All he could see was a mass of parti-cles—there was no chance of seeing an individual virus to get a vi-sual ID.

"How can you tell that's not X?"

"I know X and I've seen bricks from X." Kieling said. "That doesn't look like an X brick."

"Ebola?"

Kieling looked down into the box at the four test tubes with the various Ebola reactants. They were still blue. "No."

"Marburg?" Tyron asked, hoping that at least they would know what they were up against. Even though there was no cure or vac-cine for any of the viruses he had just mentioned, knowing the en-emy would help clarify the situation.

Kieling was looking in the box. "No." All test tubes were still blue and the requisite time had passed. "It's not a known. Could be a mu-tation of a known, but we'll have to wait until the boys back at the lab get a look at the individual virus."

Despite the air-conditioning pumping outside, Tyron felt a trickle of sweat run down his back. "Any idea what it is?"

"We can call it Kieling's disease," Kieling said with a laugh. When there was no corresponding laughter, he took Tyron's place and looked down at the microscope again. "We can call it—" He was in-terrupted by the sound of a chime. They had incoming information on their secure satellite radio/fax. They had a military satellite chan-nel dedicated to their use, and it linked them back with Fort Detrick. They could talk by voice or send data/fax. The preference was to al-ways use the fax because it ensured a written record of all that oc-curred.

The two men walked over and watched as a cover letter followed by imagery spooled out. Tyron picked up the cover letter and read it out loud to Kieling, who was examining the pictures.

> To Tyron/Kieling. From Colonel Martin. I'm sending you some of the pictures taken this evening by satellite and over-flight. We're looking at it here and trying to see some sort of pattern, but it doesn't look good.
>
> The imagery analysts say that the places they've circled in blue indicate recent death. The bodies aren't quite cooled to the surrounding terrain. Some of the deaths might be due to the recent air strikes, but we bounced the sites against the target lists and have ruled that out for the ones we circled. Of more concern are the sites where the body temperatures are higher than normal—by a significant amount, several degrees at least. We believe this thing is burning there. Those have been circled in red. Will send more when we know more. I'm trying to get to the chairman of the Joint Chiefs. Be careful.

Tyron put down the message. "What is he referring to?"

Kieling was staring at a photo, his face pale. Slowly he handed it to Tyron. There were a half-dozen sites circled in blue, about twice that number circled in red. The circles covered a wide swath of northeast Angola.

The succeeding pictures showed close-ups of those sites. There were over a hundred cold bodies in one village, visible even through the roofs of the huts by the thermal scanner. In another, the disease hadn't yet completed its deadly work and they could make out the fever burning among dozens of people.

"It's moving way too fast," Kieling said. "We would have had word earlier if this thing was spreading normally. Like we did two years ago in Zaire."

"If it only takes six days—" Tyron began.

"Even with six days from inception to crash," Kieling cut in, "it's still moving too fast. It's got to be passed on quicker than blood contact to hit that many places and that many people that quickly. Notice that in the villages where people are feverish, it's almost *every-*

*one* who has a fever. Even X didn't have anywhere close to that level of infection."

"Could it be airborne?" Tyron whispered, the very thought enough to make him wish he were very far away from here.

"I never thought we'd see an airborne virus that killed this quickly. It doesn't compute in the natural scale of things," Kieling said. "But"—he shook his head—"but it's got to be vectoring some way quicker than body fluid."

"What do you want to call it?" Tyron asked, eager to get a verbal handle on something they couldn't comprehend scientifically.

"Z"

"What?" Tyron asked.

"I said Z."

"Z?"

"Well, it's not X," Kieling said. "And Y would be confusing. I vote for Z." He looked back up. "And because Z is the last letter. The end. And this thing"—he tapped the picture—"it might just be the end if burns as fast as it seems to be burning in these photos."

# Chapter 12

**Angola-Zaire Border, 16 June**

"Flank and far security report in all clear," Trent whispered, one finger pressing the earpiece from the small FM radio into his ear.

Quinn nodded, watching through his binoculars the small clearing on the other side of the border. He wouldn't have put it past Skeleton to arrange an ambush to wipe out both himself and his men. Now that things were changing in Angola, who knew which way the hurricane would blow? The job he had been doing for Skeleton for the last several years wasn't exactly legal and would most certainly be embarrassing if it came under public scrutiny.

They were lying in a shallow trench they'd dug the previous evening. Quinn had dismissed most of the patrol, keeping only four other men besides Trent. All people that he had worked with before and trusted, as well as you could trust anyone who was a mercenary. Which, Quinn had to admit to himself, wasn't very far.

There were other reasons for going light. Several of the men were ill and he didn't want to be burdened by them. More importantly, he hoped he'd gotten rid of a possible spy. Finally, Quinn wanted to travel light to get his job over with as fast as possible. They'd put two of the men on the far side of the clearing and one on each flank to make sure nobody else moved in during the night.

There was a distant noise, getting closer. Quinn recognized it—a car engine. Ten minutes after he first heard the sound, a Land Rover pulled into the clearing. The vehicle was covered in mud.

"Long way from the nearest town," Trent whispered. "They've been on the road awhile."

"Yeah." Quinn had half expected a helicopter. Travel by vehicle was very difficult in this part of Africa. Maybe Skeleton had to be wary of the Americans' no-fly rule this close to the border. Quinn considered that. But the SADF was involved in this Angolan operation, too, and Quinn knew Skeleton had pull there. He could have brought a chopper in if he had wanted to. The only reason not to was because Skeleton didn't want anyone to know what was going on here, not even his people in the SADF.

The Land Rover came to a halt and two white men armed with R4 assault rifles jumped out. A man in a dark blue jumpsuit exited more slowly from the front passenger seat. He began unloading several green cases from the back while looking about the clearing. The two guards moved ten feet from the vehicle and waited, weapons at the ready.

"Professionals," Trent muttered. "Skeleton's boys. Why don't *they* take this fellow in?"

"We know the terrain," Quinn replied, but it was a good question. Any adequate soldier with a map could navigate in terrain he hadn't been in before. There were a lot of pieces that didn't fit together here.

The man in the blue suit was done. The two guards climbed back in the Land Rover and drove away. The man sat down on one of the cases and mopped his brow with a handkerchief. Quinn waited until he could no longer hear the engine. He glanced at Trent.

"All clear," his top kick reported after checking on the FM radio with the security men.

Quinn stood up. "What's in the cases?" he called out.

The man was startled by the sudden apparition. He stood, squinting. "Equipment."

"Step away from it," Quinn ordered. When the man complied, he gave more orders. "Kneel down, forehead in the dirt."

"Is this really necessary?" the man asked. His accent was Afrikaner. A South African, which was to be expected.

Now that he was closer, Quinn could see that the man appeared to be in his mid-forties with graying hair and tortoise-rim spectacles.

The man's skin was pale, indicating he had not spent much time in the outdoors. He was pudgy and Quinn felt an instant distaste for him.

Quinn gestured with the muzzle of his Sterling and the man reluctantly got on his knees and bent over. Quinn walked forward and looked at the three hard plastic cases. They had locks on the opening snaps. He turned back to the man. "What's your name?"

"Bentley."

Keeping out of Quinn's line of fire, Trent quickly frisked Bentley. No weapons.

"You can stand up, Bentley," Quinn said. "Open the cases."

"No," Bentley said.

Quinn closed the distance between the two men in a breath, jamming the muzzle of the Sterling into the soft skin under Bentley's chin. "I didn't fucking hear that. Say it again, asshole."

"I—I meant, I can't," Bentley stuttered. "I'm under orders. You aren't authorized to see what's in the cases."

"Bad answer," Quinn said.

"I can open one," Bentley said. "I have to for us to get where we're going."

Quinn glanced at Trent, who met the look and shrugged. Quinn removed the weapon. "Open what you can."

Bentley rubbed his sore chin as he spun the combination on one of the cases. He flipped open the lid and pulled out a laptop computer with several cables coming out the back. Next he took out a small folded-up satellite dish with tripod legs.

"SATCOM?" Quinn asked. It looked more sophisticated than the rig Trent carried in his rucksack.

"Not quite," Bentley said, unfolding the fans that made up the dish.

Quinn stepped forward, bringing up the barrel of his submachine gun.

"Don't do that!" Bentley cried out. He glared at the soldier. "Do that again, I call this off and you can forget your bonus. Plus I tell Skeleton you blew this. You wouldn't want him after you. Me and my equipment are more important here than you or any of your men. Is that clear?"

Quinn stepped back and gritted his teeth. He waited as Bentley hooked up the computer to the satellite dish.

"What I've got here," Bentley said, "is a terrain map of Angola loaded in the computer. When I hit the enter key here, we get a kick burst up to a satellite, which activates the homing device in the object we're looking for, which bounces back up and gives us a location." With that, Bentley hit the enter key.

Two seconds later there was a glowing dot on the electronic map. "That's where I need you to take me," Bentley said.

Quinn looked at the screen. The dot was located in a narrow strip of land between the Luembe and Luia Rivers. Quinn pulled out his map case and looked at it, comparing it to the screen.

"How long to get there?" Bentley asked, turning off the computer and beginning to repack it.

"About forty kilometers," Quinn said. "My men can make it in two days. Maybe less."

"Good." Bentley snapped shut the case. "I'll need help carrying this."

"Bring in the security," Quinn ordered Trent. He turned back to Bentley. "Mind telling me what we're looking for?"

"Yes, I do mind," Bentley said, shouldering his own small pack.

Quinn smiled, but Bentley didn't see it. Trent did see the smile and it sent a chill through him. He'd seen Quinn smile like that before and it meant trouble.

**National Security Agency, Fort Meade, Maryland, 16 June**
Tim Waker had the graveyard shift, courtesy of the rotating schedule his supervisor had set up. He hadn't even gone home for the intervening time between his last shift and this one. His cat had enough food and water. Things here were starting to get more lively. Two minutes ago something unusual had happened. Someone had bounced a signal off a GPS satellite and then received a back signal through the satellite.

The signal would have been lost amid the dozens of satellite transmitters that were being used by American forces in the country except for two things. It was coming out of the edge of the Lunda Norte area, which Waker had coded the computer to pay more attention to—especially after the request the previous afternoon for imagery— and the satellite uplink went to the GPS satellite instead of one of the NAVFLTSATCOM satellites that handled SATCOM traffic.

GPS stood for "ground positioning system" and it was a series of satellites in fixed orbits that continuously emitted location information that could be downloaded by GPRs—ground positioning receivers. The transmission had been sent up in such a frequency and modulation that it piggybacked on top of the normal GPS transmission on the way back down both times.

Waker looked at the data and made himself a cup of tea as he considered the brief burst. Why would someone do that? The first and most obvious reason was to hide both brief transmissions. But assuming it was the same people who had sent the previous messages: those had gone off a commercial SATCOM satellite and been coded, so that even if they were picked up they couldn't be broken. Waker knew that even a one-second burst using modern encoding devices was enough to transmit a whole message, but maybe this one wasn't a message. The key question was why the change to the GPS satellite?

"Because they want to know where something is," Waker said out loud. But then why didn't the people on the other end simply tell the first transmitters their location? The answer came to him as quickly as he formulated the question: because there was no one at the second site. It was all clicking now, and the more Waker considered it, the more his respect grew for whoever had thought of this. Using the GPS signal allowed the first transmitter to get a fix on the response, which was blindly broadcast up. And there was more. Maybe, just maybe, Waker thought, the second signal was very weak and needed the GPS signal to add to its power.

"Most interesting," he muttered as he summarized the information on his computer and e-mailed it into the Pentagon intelligence summary section. As the report flashed along the electronic highway, it fell in among hundreds of other summaries coming out of the vast octopus of intelligence agencies the United States fielded. And there it spooled, waiting to be correlated and even perhaps read.

### Cacólo, Angola, 16 June

Riley stood at the wire, staring at the medical shelter that had appeared the previous night. The sun had been up for a while, but they had not seen the two men from USAMRIID since their dramatic arrival the previous evening. The soldiers of the AOB were keeping a conspicuous distance and from the time the helicopter had left carrying the samples, Riley had noticed a distinct lack of air traffic into the area.

"Did you sleep?" Conner asked, appearing at his shoulder, with dark circles around her eyes.

"Some," Riley said.

"What's the trick? I didn't get a minute of rest."

"It was more falling into unconsciousness than sleeping," Riley said. "After a while the body can only take so much. Plus I try not to brood on things I can't control."

Conner pointed at the shelter. "Like them?"

"Them and this virus," Riley said.

"I'm worried about Seeger," Conner said, changing the subject.

Riley turned and looked at her. "Why?"

"You'll see."

The door to the shelter was opening and the two men were coming out, dressed in their blue space suits. From the direction of the AOB a party of men were also coming, all wearing their military-issue gas masks.

"Looks like we have a meeting to attend," Riley said. "Better get the others."

The internees gathered at the entrance to the wire while Major Lindsay and other representatives from the AOB—looking very uncomfortable in their protective masks—and the two men from USAMRIID stood just outside.

Riley nudged Comsky. "Will those gas masks work on an airborne virus?"

"I doubt it," Comsky said, "but it's better than nothing. You know the Russians used to issue their soldiers an 'antiradiation' pill to be taken in case of nuclear attack, right?"

"So, you're saying the masks are more for morale than reality," Riley replied.

"Yeah, although they don't do much for *my* morale," Comsky said.

Riley's curse—and his gift—was an ability to project several moves ahead, and he saw trouble in the form of the three groups gathered here in three different states of protection. From those inside the wire who might already be the walking dead, to the AOB personnel in gas masks, to the USAMRIID people in full body suits with respirators. The other bad thing was that the people who understood the threat the best were also the best protected.

Major Lindsay's voice was muffled. "Nothing's changed, other than we have to wear these damn things. Everything's still on hold. No one comes in or goes out."

A mechanical voice echoed out and Riley guessed it came from the man with "Tyron" stenciled on his chest. "We've run tests. It's not Ebola. It's not Marburg. But we believe it is a virus."

"Do you know the vector?" Comsky asked.

"Not for certain," Kieling said. "But it is most likely body fluids. All the filoviruses we've found before are transmitted through body fluids."

That made Riley wonder why the gas masks, then? Comsky had a point with the 'placebo' theory, but it didn't totally connect. Simple surgical masks would have been more practical.

"A filovirus?" Comsky asked.

"A 'thread virus,'" Kieling said. "Most viruses are round. A filo is long. Looks like a jumbled string. Ebola's a filo, as is Marburg."

"So this is a cousin to Ebola?" Comsky asked.

"We don't know," Kieling said. "We're not even certain it's a filovirus. We have to wait for them to look at it through an electron microscope at Fort Detrick."

"Can you test us for it?" the medic persisted.

"We're working on that," Kieling said.

"We sent samples back to Fort Detrick," Tyron piped up, searching for anything to say. "As Dr. Kieling said, they'll have a better look at it and they have the proper equipment to work on it. All we could do here was test to see if it was something we'd seen before. This thing is an emerging virus."

"Emerging from where?" Riley asked.

"We don't know," Kieling said.

"What the fuck *do* you know?" Sergeant Lorne demanded.

"Easy, Sergeant," Lieutenant Vickers called out. She was seated on a crate, her broken ankle sticking out straight with Comsky's field-expedient cast wrapped tightly about it.

"So you don't have any idea what it is or how to treat it. Right?" Comsky said.

"We hope that—" Tyron began but Mike Seeger's voice cut in.

"It is the wrath of God. He is punishing all of us for waging war. You must put down your weapons and accept that which you have brought upon yourself."

Riley rubbed his forehead, now understanding what Conner had meant earlier.

"Shut him up!" Lorne ordered Conner.

"You cannot stop the power of God!" Seeger yelled.

Conner grabbed her cameraman by the arm. "Come on, Mike. Let's go talk about it." She guided him away to one of the tents.

Riley was surprised when Kieling spoke. "He's not too far wrong, you know."

"What are you talking about?" Lorne demanded.

"Well, he may have the source wrong. Maybe it's not the wrath of God we've got here, but it certainly is the wrath of nature," Kieling said. "Whatever this thing is, it's nature's defense against mankind's incursions into places we never were before."

"How did this thing start?" Riley asked, catching on to the idea that this wasn't just a random occurrence. "You say it's nature's defense mechanism. What do you mean by that?"

"We're tearing up the rain forest," Kieling said, "and so far, most of the nastiest bugs we've seen—the two variants of Ebola and Marburg—have come out of the rain forest here in Africa. Humans have upset the ecological balance and these viruses are fighting back against humans to reright the balance."

"Oh, shit," Lorne said. "A damn enviro nut."

"No," Kieling said. "I just look at this clearly and from every perspective. If it can kill you, you'd damn well better try to understand it."

"Are you saying this virus was always there in the forest and we came in and activated it?" Riley asked.

"This virus," Kieling said, "is what we call an 'emerging' one. There are three ways viruses emerge: They jump from one species—which usually they are relatively benign in—to another, which they aren't benign in; or the virus is a new evolution from another type of virus, a mutation, basically. Or it could have always existed and moves from a smaller population to a larger population. In the last case, this thing could have been killing humans out in the jungle for thousands of years, but now it's moved out into the general population."

"Is that possible?" Conner Young asked. "Wouldn't someone have noticed?"

"Not necessarily," Kieling said. "We're now beginning to believe that the AIDS virus might have been around for quite a while. Cases as far back as forty years ago are now being uncovered. They just didn't know what it was back there and called it something else. Plus, when people are killed deep in the jungle, it very rarely makes the news or even garners any attention."

"Which do you think this thing is? How did it evolve?" Riley asked.

"I don't know," Kieling said. "To find that out I need patient zero." He then went on to explain the concept of finding the first person with the disease.

"So you don't think it was Ku?" Major Lindsay said when Kieling was done. "Those people in that village probably had the disease before him and passed it on to him?"

"No, it's not Ku. Ku was the beginning of the disease here in Cacólo," Kieling said. "We're going to have to head out into the bush to find where this thing came from."

"Which brings up another point, Major Lindsay," Tyron said. "Did any of your medics treat Ku? He had to have been very ill for several days before he crashed—died."

"I'll check on it," Lindsay said.

"This is all very nice," Sergeant Lorne said, "but what do we do next, besides sit here and wait to see who gets sick?"

"We sent a plan back to the Pentagon," Tyron said. "We need their approval to begin working on it. We also need to wait for word from USAMRIID on what we're dealing with. There are too many unknowns right now."

"I'll tell you one thing we know for sure. We know it kills." Lorne turned and walked away.

"Let's check on your aid facility," Tyron said to Major Lindsay, and they headed toward the AOB.

Riley watched the others inside the fence slowly melt away and head back to the tents. He noticed that the second blue-suiter, Kieling, was still there, watching everyone disperse.

"You seem to know more about this than the other fellow," Riley said. He could barely make out Kieling's face through the plastic faceplate.

"I've been in the field before," Kieling said. "He hasn't."

"You collected blood and other samples from us earlier this morning," Riley said, "but I noticed neither of you seemed too interested in knowing who we were."

He waited and Kieling waited. Finally, Riley continued. "You don't want to know us, do you? Because if we start coming down with this thing, you want to be able to stay scientifically detached, isn't that right?"

Kieling still remained silent.

"Our medic, Comsky, told us that there is no cure for these types of viruses. If that's so, then you're here to contain this, aren't you?"

"That's correct."

"That's not good enough for us," Riley said. "If you were on this side of the fence, would it be good enough for you?"

"No," Kieling said. He turned to follow Tyron and Lindsay.

"Hey!" Riley called out.

Kieling paused and his mechanical voice echoed out. "Yes?"

"We'll help you. We've got nothing to lose. Remember that."

"I will."

**Oshakati, Namibia, 16 June**

No further instructions had come during the night, and the freeze order was still in effect. General Nystroom had spent a sleepless night, worried about his scouts across the border in southern Angola. By now, his lead motorized elements should have been making linkups with those scouts. Instead they were still sitting here in the desert. Add on top of that an order coming from Silvermine stopping all cross-border flights and it made for a very disturbing situation for Nystroom. He couldn't send in choppers to get his men or to resupply them. The only way out was the same way they had gone in. By foot.

Nystroom threw open the top hatch on his command vehicle and stood on the seat bottom, his head poking out. Small cooking fires burned here and there as his soldiers did what soldiers spent most of their time doing—waiting. But the scouts weren't in a good place to be waiting.

Nystroom radioed his operations officer. "Pull the scouts back."

"Sir, we—"

"On my authority," Nystroom cut in. "Something's going wrong and I don't want to leave those men out there. Notify me the second we get anything further from Silvermine. Send another request to them for the follow-on contingency plan referred to in last night's message."

### Pentagon, 16 June

General Cummings blew into the room, a covey of aides at his side. "Sit down, gentlemen, sit down."

They were in the War Room, deep underneath the Pentagon. Outside the glassed-in conference room, electronic maps lined the walls and personnel manned the various stations. Inside the soundproofed enclosure, Colonel Martin pulled at the collar of his dress-green uniform.

One of the many other colonels in the room was ready with a cup of coffee for the chairman, along with an introduction. "Sir, this is Colonel Martin, head of U.S.A.M.R.I.I.D.," he said, spelling out the letters.

Cummings put on a pair of reading glasses. "And what is U.S.—whatever you call it?" Cummings asked, flipping open a cover labeled "Top Secret" and scanning a report.

The colonel looked at Martin, passing the verbal ball.

"United States Army Medical Research Institute of Infectious Diseases," Martin said.

"Ah, yes, the fellows over at Fort Detrick." Cummings looked up over his glasses. "Someone sick?"

Martin nodded. "Yes, sir." He looked at a sergeant who manned a computer terminal. "Run the video, please."

The glass opposite Cummings became opaque and then the video of Ku dying and Comsky performing his field-expedient autopsy ran. Martin remained silent, letting the pictures speak for themselves. Following Ku's autopsy, there were shots taken from the KH-12 and Aurora overflight. General Cummings had seen enough of those types of photos before.

When it was done, General Cummings looked over at Martin. "I assume that video was shot in Angola. Who was the man?"

"A Sergeant Ku, MPLA, sir."

"And?" Cummings raised his eyebrows. "Very graphic, but is there a point to all this? I've seen people die before, Colonel, if you thought this was going to shock me."

"We believe Sergeant Ku died of a virus. A very lethal virus."

"How lethal?"

"Based on similar viruses, we estimate a ninety percent kill of those infected."

"And the imagery?" Cummings asked. "The blue and red circles?"

"Blue indicated dead," Martin said. "Red those people who have a fever. One of the signs of infection is a high fever."

General Cummings put down the report. "How many of our people are infected?"

"We don't know, sir."

"You don't know?" Cummings snapped off his glasses. "When was this video shot?"

"Yesterday at—" Martin began, but Cummings cut him off.

"*Yesterday!* Why wasn't I informed immediately?"

Martin pulled his tie loose and opened the top button on his shirt. "I tried to get through, sir, but this was the earliest your aides could get me in to—"

"We authorized a B-1 flight for his men," one of Cummings's colonels cut in. "And the imagery to check things out, to include an Aurora overflight. The base camp where the people—"

"Enough," Cummings said. "How communicable is this virus?"

"We don't know yet," Martin said. "We've quarantined the people who were exposed to this man, but we don't know where else in Angola it will break out. As you could see from the imagery, it is burning across the countryside, but so far all the infected villages are inside rebel-controlled territory."

"Give me the worst-case scenario," Cummings ordered.

"Worst case is this is an airborne virus, like the flu. If that's the situation, it's already out of control in Angola and all we can do is hope to keep it from coming back over here to the States."

"The troops already in country?"

"The disease will burn, uh, run through them."

"No antidote? Vaccine?"

"We don't even know what it is yet," Martin said. "We've seen three viruses similar to this one before. There's no cure or vaccine for them, so the chance of us developing a cure for this one, especially on short notice, is very remote."

Cummings spun in his seat. "What's the deployment status on the Eighty-second?"

Someone had that information ready. "Forty-one percent personnel, eighty-six on equipment. Ahead of schedule, sir."

"Get on the horn to the Eighteenth Airborne Corps. Stop the deployment immediately. Anything in the air, turn it around. Then get me General Scott on the SATCOM."

"Yes, sir."

Cummings spun back to Colonel Martin. "What else?"

"As I tried to tell your aide last night, sir, I need support to get—"

Cummings held up his right hand and Martin ground to a halt.

"Colonel, my men screwed up." Cummings's voice was flat and level. "This should have been brought to my attention earlier. If this is as bad as you say, men are going to die because of that. I understand that. My staff *will* understand that. Now that you've brought it to our attention, this is our business, Colonel. What's done is done. Clear?"

A night of screaming into phones and pounding on desktops, trying to get to the chairman, fell away from Colonel Martin. "Clear, sir."

"I want you here with me through the rest of this. You think someone isn't doing the right thing, you tell me right away. My priority is our people. Is that clear?"

"Yes, sir."

"Now. What do you need?"

# Chapter 13

**Cacólo, Angola, 16 June**

"Oh, Jesus," Tyron said, staring at the Cacólo Mission Hospital. They'd confirmed in the morning that Ku had not received treatment from any of the American medics. The next logical step was to check out the local native medical infrastructure.

"It's typical," Kieling's voice came out of the box on his suit. "Last time Ebola broke out in Zaire, it was the hospital where the first patient was treated that helped spread it so widely. The medical personnel always get the worst of it."

*Worst of it* was a mild way of describing what the hospital looked like. There were sick all over the place. Nuns in blood-spattered robes ministered to them. And hospital—that was not what Tyron would call this place. There weren't even the rudiments of medical technology in place.

"I am Sister Angelina." A frail-looking old woman walked up to them. Her English had a heavy accent. She looked up and down at their suits. "I see you are a bit better prepared for this than we are. Thank God you got here so quickly."

"We need to find out if you treated a man. A Sergeant Ku of the Angolan army," Tyron said.

The nun stared at his plastic face mask. "Who are you people? We sent out a request for help to the World Health Organization yesterday. You aren't from WHO, are you?"

"No," Kieling replied. "We're from the CDC. America. I'm Dr. Kieling and this is Dr. Tyron. What's the situation?"

"Over half my staff is down," Sister Angelina said. "High fever, headaches, bloody diarrhea, vomiting, rashes. I am afraid we might have an outbreak of Ebola."

"Sergeant Ku was the case that started it," Kieling said. "We need to find out if he was treated here."

Sister Angelina led them into a building. "I'll show you the records. What day do you think he would have come in?" The Angolans gathered around, staring at the two men in the space suits.

"Anytime in the last seven days," Kieling replied.

The nun flipped open a battered box that contained index cards, wrapped together with rubber bands. She began flipping through.

Tyron took the time to look around. Through a curtain made of a sheet, he could see a ward. There were bodies in the beds and several nuns moved among the people, ministering to them. He felt totally immersed in a different world. The nuns didn't have the slightest form of protection, not even surgical masks.

"A Sergeant Ku," Sister Angelina announced, holding up an index card, "was treated on the morning of the fourteenth. He claimed he was suffering from a venereal infection. He was given a shot of antibiotics."

"Claimed he was suffering?" Tyron repeated. "Wasn't he checked?"

Sister Angelina turned her wrinkled face toward Tyron. "Every morning we average between eighty and a hundred and twenty new patients. That's in addition to those that fill our beds. I have nine sisters to minister to those people, and only four of my sisters are trained nurses. The rest learn as they go. We have no doctor. We send the more critical ones to Luanda on the military flight, if there is one.

"And your man Ku was a soldier. He asked for treatment for what he thought he had and we gave it to him."

"How much sterilization do you—" Kieling began.

"One needle dipped in a bleach-and-water mixture," she said. "We have very little equipment and must make everything we have go far beyond its expected usage."

"Oh, God," Tyron muttered.

"Where is Sergeant Ku?" Sister Angelina asked.

"Dead," Kieling said.

Sister Angelina's face betrayed no emotion. "How?"

"We don't know."

"Ebola?" She pointed toward the ward. "I was in Zaire in '95. This looks the same."

"It's not Ebola. At least not one of the known strains," Kieling said.

"But it is a virus," the nun replied. "Or else you would not be wearing those suits."

"Yes," Kieling confirmed. "It is a virus."

"Can you help us?" Angelina asked.

"We have to track down the source," Kieling said. "I'll have them send you some equipment. Gowns, masks. That will help."

"If it isn't already too late," Sister Angelina said.

To that, the men from USAMRIID had no answer.

"We would like to look at some of your patients," Kieling said.

"You will scare them," Angelina said. "You have already started a panic in town by coming here in those suits. It tells everyone that you are so afraid of something you will wear that. None of the people here are wearing a safe suit, so that means they should be scared, correct?"

"Correct," Kieling said.

"Too late to worry about all that," the nun said. "You're here." Sister Angelina pointed to the ward. "Follow me."

They moved through the archway, careful not to scrape their suits on either side. There were fourteen people in the beds.

"My native support left when they first feared this was a virus," Sister Angelina explained as they moved. "All that is left are my Sisters."

Tyron knew that also meant the native support workers might have run away with the disease in their system. This was the horrifying danger of trying to contain an epidemic. Nobody wanted to hang around in the area where the sickness had taken root, but by running they spread it to new areas.

They walked down the aisle. Tyron was glad that he had the backpack. The smell must be horrendous. The overworked nuns were trying their best, but the soiled sheets from vomiting and diarrhea could only be replaced so often.

They'd seen Ku's body, but at the point at which the virus had been at full amplification, having taken over the host completely. Here they could see what it did to flesh prior to death.

"The rashes," Kieling said briefly.

Tyron had noted that too. Streaks of pustulant red cut across the skin of most of the victims. He leaned over one bed. Blood was seeping out from the child's eyes, nose, and ears. The eyes were looking at him, wide open, rimmed in red, fear and pain evident.

Kieling glanced about. There were no IVs or any other signs of modern medical procedures in sight. Just nuns in their habits, using what they had to comfort the people, wiping sweat and blood from ravaged flesh. Giving aspirin for the sickness and pain.

"We have to go," Kieling said, tapping him on the shoulder.

"Will you help?" Sister Angelina asked.

"We'll get you some help," Kieling promised.

The two men walked back out of the infirmary, onto the dusty street. A crowd had gathered, and the people stepped back from the two men in their suits. A woman began wailing and Tyron increased his pace.

"We know Ku had it and we know the day he came here," Kieling said. "We just got a look at the symptoms. We need to come back and get an idea of the timeline of this thing. Interview some of the patients that are coherent. This is a good break."

"A good break?" Tyron repeated incredulously. "They reused the same damn needle they shot Ku up with and infected God knows how many people, and you call it a break?"

"I didn't start this disease," Kieling said. "And I didn't tell these people to use that needle like they did. It's what's done all over this continent where they spend more money in a day on bullets than on medicine in a year. We didn't create this situation, Tyron, so stop taking everything so fucking personally.

"It *is* a break because we know the date and approximate time some of these people were infected. We have the cases here and can look at them more closely. That rash was unique. Ebola causes a rash, but not like the one those cases had.

"We can see the progression of this thing and also find out how those infected caught it. The needle? Blood? Air vector? We get those answers here."

"Shouldn't we get Major Lindsay to quarantine the hospital?"

"You saw the imagery. It's spread far beyond the hospital," Kieling said. "But we'll tell him. Remember, though, that the hospital is an Angolan problem. Not Major Lindsay's."

"Why'd you lie to her?" Tyron asked as they decontaminated outside their shelter. He felt overwhelmed. There was too much going on and too many things to deal with at once.

"About what?" Kieling replied. "I told her the truth. We don't know what this thing is."

"About being from the CDC?"

"To give her some hope," Kieling said. "Besides, the people who do this work like Sister Angelina—they don't like the military—anybody's military. They hate the military because they have to see and try to save the end result of all the civilians who get maimed and shot and killed in all the wars here. She might not have cooperated with us if she'd known we were from the army."

"What about the vector? We think there's a possibility it *is* airborne, but you told her it—"

"I know what I told her. What good would it do if I told her it might be airborne? There's nothing they can do."

"But she'll find out you lied. You shouldn't have—"

"Did you see her eyes?" Kieling cut in. "Her neck? She's got it, Tyron. She'll be dead soon. So don't worry about what's going to happen in two days. Worry about now."

### Andrews Air Force Base, Maryland, 16 June

"What do we have?" the chief coroner of the casualty identification center at Andrews Air Force Base asked as he suited up.

"Helicopter crash victims," his assistant said. "The Pentagon wants to see if we can't find the body of Jonas Savimbi among that mess. Classified top secret and all that good stuff."

"Oh, Christ," the chief coroner said as he entered the mortuary room. Body parts were laid out on tables. He wasn't upset about the gory scene, rather it was the number and condition of the parts that dismayed him.

"We figure we have eleven or twelve cases," the assistant said.

"What do we have on Savimbi? Dental? Fingerprints? DNA?"

"We have dental and finger. No DNA."

The chief coroner sighed. "Well, we've got a long day ahead of us. Let's get going."

### Luanda, Angola, 16 June

"Yes, sir, I'll take care of all of that," General Scott said into the secure satellite phone. "Cacólo is already isolated and I'll freeze everybody else in country."

"I'm going to the president," General Cummings's voice rang in Scott's ear. "It'll be up to him to decide how to handle this publicly. For now, we're going with a complete blackout."

"Yes, sir." General Scott watched a fly buzzing around his command complex. They'd appropriated an entire abandoned office building in downtown Luanda as division headquarters. Remembering the lesson of Beirut, all entrances into the building were blocked off and heavily fortified.

But the fly got in here, Scott thought. And this virus, whatever it was, was much smaller than the fly. The veteran infantryman felt fear. Not personal fear, but fear for his beloved division. "What about SOCOM's people?" Scott asked, referring to the troops working for the Special Operations Command.

"I'm putting every swinging dick on the ground there under your direct command," General Cummings replied. "I'll talk to Richard about it right after I get off with you."

Scott knew that "Richard" referred to Admiral Richard Peters, the JTF commander in chief, aboard a navy ship off the coast. The man in charge of all the forces involved in this operation.

"That will include the other services too," Cummings's voice continued. "You're the ranking man on the ground and I want you to make the decisions."

"Yes, sir." The fly had landed on the map table and was crossing the acetate overlay that showed all force dispositions in Angola.

"Good luck. Out here."

Scott slowly put the phone down and looked at his waiting staff. What he did know was vastly overwhelmed by what he did not know, but at the least, he had his orders. "Gentlemen, the situation has changed and we have a new priority."

**Cacólo, Angola, 16 June**

Kieling threw down the latest fax from Fort Detrick. "They're still working on the sample, trying to isolate the virus."

Tyron was looking over the imagery again. "This isn't right," he said. "This virus is moving so quickly, yet it's also so deadly. It doesn't add up."

Kieling agreed with that. "The vector has got to be something quicker than body fluids. But it still doesn't have to be airborne. Maybe it's a nonhuman carrier. For all we know this could be getting spread by mosquitoes like malaria and we're looking in the wrong place altogether."

"Rodents?" Tyron offered. He knew Kieling was familiar with the Hanta virus that had appeared in the American Southwest in 1993 and killed more than fifty people. The virus's vector had puzzled scientists from the CDC and USAMRIID until they tracked it down to mice. Finding that source had allowed them to focus on stopping the spread, although there still wasn't an effective vaccine against it.

"We'll have to go back to the hospital," Kieling said. "Interview the people there. They are the only known cases we have, other than these villages in the imagery, and I don't think we want to go out there yet.

"We need to check their history. Where they were. Did they touch anyone who looked sick? Were they bitten by anything? What did they eat before they got sick? The whole regimen."

Tyron looked over at the entrance. He dreaded the thought of suiting up again. Of going out among people who stared at him, protected in his suit, with fear in their eyes. Of going out into a world where death might be as close as a mosquito bite. In his mind, the Kevlar walls of the habitat were growing thicker with each passing hour.

"First, temperature," Kieling said, holding up an electronic thermometer. They duly took each other's temperature. The routine was to ensure they caught as early as possible any chance of onset of a fever. A sign they might have been exposed to a virus. Both were normal.

Tyron followed Kieling into the entryway, sealing the door behind himself. They pulled on their suits, sealing gloves to sleeves and boots to pants with rolls of tape.

"Let's stop by the isolation compound first," Kieling said as he opened the outer door. "I want to see if any of the people there have symptoms. They were exposed yesterday morning. Today's day three for the people we saw at the hospital; day two for the people in the ISO compound. We should be seeing the first signs, if any of them are infected."

"All right," Tyron agreed, following Kieling across the field toward the enclosure.

Inside the wire, Riley watched the two men coming. It had been a restless day so far, and he'd spent a good portion of it simply walking the inside perimeter of the wire. By now he'd made a discernible path in the short grass.

"Good news or bad?" Conner asked, coming up behind him.

Riley knew she'd spent most of the late morning/early afternoon working. Keeping busy to keep her own mind occupied. Filming interviews with the other people inside; doing voice-overs on video already taken; and trying to keep Mike Seeger occupied. The cameraman had done his job, saying nothing except in response to a direct question. When not working, he sat on one of his equipment cases, reading from his Bible, his lips silently moving.

Comsky had spent the time making sure those who had been hurt in the crash were progressing all right. The others had occupied themselves as well as they could. Riley was worried not just about Seeger but also about Lorne and some of the other army people. They did not have the type of personality that accepted inaction in the face of danger.

"Probably no news," Riley said. "One thing I learned a long time ago in the army was that the guy on the ground is always the last to know what's going on."

"You're such an optimist," Conner said.

"At least I didn't say it was bad news," Riley said. "So I guess I'm not a pessimist either."

The two men came to a halt just outside the entrance.

"We found that Sergeant Ku was treated at the local hospital," the man with "Kieling" stenciled on his chest said. "Some of the staff there are now down with what looks like the same virus."

"How long ago was Ku there?" Comsky asked.

"The morning of the fourteenth," Kieling replied.

"Only two days ago," Comsky calculated. "And already they have symptoms?"

"Yes. We need you to take everyone's temperature," Kieling said. "Check for fever."

"And if we have a fever?" Sergeant Lorne's voice was angry. "What then? Do you have a treatment? A cure?"

"This virus probably isn't one hundred percent fatal," Tyron said. "We don't have any idea what its fatality rate is. There are some variants of Ebola that aren't fatal at all. Last year I met a woman who had survived Ebola and—"

"If you're trying to cheer us up, don't," Conner said. "We were with Sergeant Ku and we saw what this virus did to him. Let's just get this over with."

"Do you have any idea what this is?" Comsky asked. "They should have had a chance to look at it back in the States by now."

"We know it's a filovirus," Kieling said succinctly. "We don't know how it's spread. We don't know what its reservoir is. Quite honestly, we don't know a goddamn thing about it."

"Do not take the Lord's name in vain!" Seeger cried out.

"Come on, now, take it easy," Conner said, putting a hand on Seeger's arm. To her surprise, he threw her aside, and the burly cameraman dashed forward to the hole in the wire and through it. He grabbed Kieling and lifted him off the ground, the muscles in his arms bulging.

"Blasphemer!" He shook Kieling.

"Don't!" Riley yelled as he saw what was about to happen.

Seeger tossed Kieling into the barbed wire fence. He then jumped on top of him. The two rolled about in the fence, Kieling encumbered by his suit and unable to defend himself.

"Stop it!" Riley called out as he ran forward. He grabbed Seeger from behind, only to be shrugged aside. Riley could feel tears in his clothes and skin as he waded back into the fight among the sharp edges of the razor wire. Lorne and Comsky joined him and they tried grabbing the civilian. "Take it easy, now," Riley said. "We don't want to hurt anyone."

"It is God's will!" Seeger said, slamming Kieling's head into the ground. "We cannot stop it." He gave one last thump on Kieling, then turned and faced Riley and the others.

"God's-will this, asshole," Lorne said, drawing his 9mm pistol from its holster.

"Put that away," Riley said. He leaned forward, feinted at Seeger's face with his right hand, and, when the man moved to block, slammed his left hand, open palm first, into Seeger's chest.

Seeger lay still, gasping for breath, and Riley, Comsky, and Lorne quickly subdued him. Several men had come running over from the AOB during the confrontation, and they supplied a couple of sets of plastic wrist cinches with which they restrained the cameraman, pulling him out of the wire.

Riley reached down and gave Kieling a hand, pulling him to his feet. "You all right?" he asked as he helped him get untangled.

Kieling didn't answer. He was looking down at his suit. He reached up and pulled off his helmet, showing his face to the others for the first time. "Well, I don't need that anymore." He looked at Riley. "I guess it's no longer *we-they*." He peeled off the space suit and they could see the blood from several cuts, seeping through the jumpsuit he wore underneath.

Twenty minutes later, the situation had calmed down a bit. Seeger was under guard in one of the tents. Tyron had gone back to the habitat, shaken by what had happened to Kieling. Riley and Conner watched as Kieling took temperatures along with Comsky. The two medical men conferred quietly when they were done, then turned to the group.

"Everyone's normal so far," Kieling announced.

"I assume that's good," Conner said.

"So far, so good," Kieling confirmed, "although it's only been a day since you were exposed to Ku's blood. Tomorrow will give us a better idea. The people in the hospital are at that point right now."

"What will you do?" Riley asked.

"I'm going to go where I can be of some use," Kieling said. "Since I can't go back into the habitat without destroying its integrity for

Tyron, I'm going to go to the hospital in town and lend a hand and try to learn what I can."

"Do you two have any more information at all on this?" Riley asked. "Anything from the States? From higher headquarters?"

"We have some imagery of eastern Angola," Kieling said. "It shows patterns of the disease spreading around the countryside."

"Can I take a look at that?" Riley asked.

"What for?"

"I don't know," Riley replied. "Maybe to feel useful. Just like your going over to the hospital."

Kieling shrugged. "Sure. Go over to the habitat and ask Tyron to pass it out to you." With that, he headed toward town. Riley had to admire the scientist. He'd taken what had just happened as if it were no big deal. But then again, Riley reminded himself, of all the people here, Kieling was the best prepared for what they were facing and had probably faced the same threat before. At the very least, Kieling had the advantage of having thought this through and let his imagination do its worst before facing the reality.

As Riley got set to head to the habitat, Comsky grabbed his arm. "We need to talk."

"What's up, Ape Man?"

Comsky led him away from the others. "We have four people running fevers."

"What?" Riley exclaimed. "But Kieling said—"

"I know what he said," Comsky quietly cut in. "I agreed with him that we not tell anyone. What good would it do? It would just add to the stress and panic, and you saw how well Seeger handled it."

Riley could see the logic in that. "Who are the four?"

Comsky gave a weary smile. "Well, me of course. I about ate Ku's blood working on him."

"I'm sorry," Riley said, putting a hand on his shoulder. "Maybe it's—"

"Hey," Comsky said, "I expected it."

"Who else?" Riley asked, half-knowing who the others would be.

"The helicopter pilot who got cut up in the crash."

"But he wasn't in contact with Ku," Riley said.

"I know. Kieling and I talked about that. It's one of the reasons he's going over to the hospital. The way this thing spreads is very strange. Almost like it is airborne to a certain extent. He's going to see if he can get a handle on the vector. Find a common link among those infected."

Riley felt a bead of sweat roll down his forehead.

"Conner's hot," Comsky added.

"Oh, shit," Riley muttered. This had been his idea. His responsibility. He looked at Comsky, who was looking away. "And I'm hot, too, right?"

"One hundred point eight degrees."

## Pope Air Force Base, North Carolina, 16 June

Paratroopers were used to delays. "Hurry up and wait" was the unofficial motto of the 82d, and this morning was proving to be no different. There were planes out on the runway, six C-141 Starlifters, but loading had ceased several hours ago and over two thousand soldiers milled about the green ramp, whiling away the hours, waiting for word to embark. The green ramp was a large building with rows and rows of oversized wooden benches. It was the final staging area for all jumps and deployments, and every 82d soldier had spent numerous hours inside there waiting for an airborne operation.

The carefully choreographed deployment time schedule was already shot to hell, and officers fumed as they saw the little checkmarks on their efficiency reports go down a notch or two. It was bad form to be late showing up for a war.

The PA system crackled, then a voice came on, telling all battalion and separate unit commanders to report to the loadmaster's office. The designated officers quickly complied, eager to find out what the new schedule was. When they came back, the look on their faces was of confusion. The deployment was off.

Even as the soldiers heard the news—welcome for some, not so for others with visions of combat infantry badges and medals to be won—a C-141 swooped in and landed, disgorging disgruntled troopers who had been halfway over the Atlantic Ocean before being turned back.

The official word the commanders passed down was that the operation was going so smoothly in Angola that the troops already there could handle the rest of the mission. Those who had half a brain didn't buy that for a second. Over the past twenty years, the U.S. army had never sent ten soldiers to do a job when it could send twenty.

Something was going on, but from the lowest snuffy in the ranks through the ranking man inside the green ramp, they knew one thing: as Riley had told Conner on the other side of the ocean, they would be the last to know.

## Pentagon, 16 June

Colonel Martin glanced at the digital clock overhead, then back down to the summary he'd just been sent from his people at Detrick. Since the last report, there was nothing new. The most disturbing information was the failure thus far to identify the infection vector. The lab was in the middle of several experiments and had discovered so far that this particular filovirus lasted longer in the open than Ebola or Marburg. After almost ten minutes of exposure to light and air, it was still alive. By twenty, 90 percent was dead and by a half hour, the virus was completely wiped out. But ten minutes was a very long time for a virus to live in the open.

That might help explain the massive extent of the outbreak in Angola. At USAMRIID they were exposing monkeys to the airborne virus. The problem was they would have to wait until the monkeys showed symptoms of the disease to determine how far it could travel through the air. And whether it could infect through the respiratory system.

And time was the problem. The deployment had been halted, but there were still over eight thousand American troops on the ground in Angola—not to mention over ten million Angolans. And the random borderlines drawn on the map wouldn't stop this thing. It was just as likely to burn east and north into Zambia and Zaire. South it would be blocked by the desert. All international travel in and out of Angola had been halted, but there was the possibility that someone had already left the country infected. As international air travel made the globe smaller, it made the possibility of a disease jumping an ocean that much stronger.

The only good news was that, as rapidly as this virus sickened and killed, it could not hide long in those it infected. Martin felt reasonably confident that it would be contained. The problem was the cost of that containment in terms of those already infected.

Martin was startled from his reverie by General Cummings's voice. "What exactly is W.H.O.?" he asked, spelling out the letters.

"The World Health Organization, sir," Martin replied.

"I know that," Cummings said. "My real question is, why are they interested in Cacólo, Angola? I have a report here that WHO is alerting a virology investigative team to go to Angola in response to a request for help from an organization known as Médicins Sans Frontières."

"That's a group called Doctors Without Borders," Martin said. "They're a medical aid organization that works in the Third World. They probably have people in Cacólo who are seeing the disease."

"Great," Cummings said. "This is going to be out on the wire soon. Some smart-ass in the media is going to put that together with the news blackout from Luanda and we're going to have big trouble."

We already have big trouble, Martin thought to himself, but he kept quiet. He had already picked up the pulse here in the War Room, and he didn't much care for it. As best as Martin could describe it, there was more concern over the way this situation *looked* than the way it really was. He thought of those camera commercials: "Image is everything." It certainly was here.

He still didn't think that General Cummings and his staff understood the full implications of this outbreak and he couldn't blame them, because he couldn't give them hard figures to work with.

But *did* it matter how they approached this situation? Martin had to ask himself as he watched Cummings working with his staff. There *was* nothing they could do other than control the image.

### Cacólo, Angola, 16 June
Riley spread the imagery out on the ground and knelt down, studying it in the afternoon sun.

"What do you have?" Conner Young appeared at his shoulder.

Riley checked her out. She seemed okay, but he knew he also looked the same. He hadn't really felt the fever, but shortly after Comsky had told him, he had felt hot. He knew that could be his mind playing tricks on him, and he choose not to dwell on it.

"Overhead imagery of the land to the east of here." He pointed and explained the blue and red circles.

"You mean people are dead or dying in all those places?" Conner was stunned. "What are they doing about it?"

"They who?" Riley said, picking up the sixteen-page intelligence summary for the past twenty-four hours that had been sent along with photos.

"They!" Conner's voice was sharp. "The people who thought of this whole thing. The people who make the decisions and give the orders! The people who are *responsible*!"

Riley's voice was calm. "The people who are in charge are acting. That's why we're quarantined." He pointed across to the AOB. He'd been watching it all morning. "That's why the AOB is closing in on itself. You might not have noticed, but they haven't let anyone in or out for the past six hours, other than when Tyron and Kieling came over here and your man Seeger went nuts. Everyone's scared.

"As far as responsibility goes," he continued, "I don't think anyone is responsible. Seeger's not too far off. This is an act of God, if you believe in God, that is."

Riley watched Conner visibly try to calm herself down. "Do you?" she finally asked.

"Believe in God?"

"Believe that there is a greater plan. A greater power behind everything that happens." She pointed at the imagery. "I just can't accept that all these people dying is random. That it's just the fates playing their hand. There has to be some reason."

"Maybe there is a reason," Riley replied. "I just don't know what it is. I do believe there is some higher power, but I also know that inherent in that belief is the acceptance that I won't know what that higher power is or what its designs are. So I can't tell you the purpose behind this disease, Conner." He paused. He wondered if he should follow Kieling's lead and keep what he knew to himself or tell her.

"If it spread out there this quickly," Conner said, tapping the imagery, "then we have it. We're the walking dead." She laughed, but it was not a pleasant sound. "And my cameraman is off the deep end. At the very least this would be Pulitzer prize material, don't you think? Reporter films own slow demise from viral outbreak during peacekeeping operation."

"It's not certain—" Riley began.

"Ah, ever the optimist," Conner said. "That's the second time to-day I've called you that. By the way, Dave, I don't blame you for me being out here. It should be the other way around. You should be blaming me for dragging you all over the world the last year or so. You should have settled down somewhere. You certainly did enough for God and Country when you were in the service. I'm sorry you're here."

"I take responsibility for my own—" Riley began.

"Give me a break, Dave," Conner said. "Just accept my apology, okay?"

"All right."

"Thank you. Well, back to work on my own obituary. That's a joke, Dave." Conner turned and walked away.

Riley started to get up to follow, then stopped. They were all in the same boat and they could exchange sympathy all day long, but it wouldn't do any good. He looked at the imagery. He was bothered by something. Something he'd said to Conner and something he'd read in the intelligence summary, but he wasn't quite sure what it was. He flipped the cover sheet and began reading it one more time, but it was very hard to concentrate.

### Luia River, Angola, 16 June

There was a distinct lack of aircraft flying, which bothered Quinn. Certainly the Americans couldn't have completely broken UNITA so quickly. There was nothing on the SNN broadcast, other than a re-port that the Americans had halted their deployment. That was cu-rious, but not surprising. Perhaps they were having second thoughts.

The patrol was making good time. Quinn had originally planned on moving only at dark, but the lack of overflights had changed that. They were moving along the east bank of the Luia, making large de-tours around the few villages that stood in their path.

The detours didn't seem necessary. The countryside was deserted. The Americans had certainly done a good job of sending everyone to ground, Quinn figured.

Darkness was falling and he wanted to keep pushing on until at least midnight, take a short break, then continue. His reckoning was that they could sleep when they got back to the border.

Quinn pulled up his night vision goggles and switched them on. He had two of his men out front and one on each flank, twenty meters out. Trent and he were with Bentley, ten meters behind the point. The patrol crested a tall, grassy ridge and Quinn halted briefly to look around. He could see a long way in every direction and there was nothing. No lights, no fires, no sign of civilization. There were no running lights of aircraft anywhere in the sky. They could be the only people on the face of the planet, based on the information his senses were giving him.

Quinn glanced at Bentley's back as the man passed by. Something was wrong with this whole deal. The mission, the terrain, the Americans. There was something happening. Fuck Skeleton, Quinn suddenly decided, giving in to his sixth sense. He'd learned long ago to trust his gut and it was screaming at him right now. Turn back!

Quinn took a step forward to halt his point man and was instantly blinded by a flash of light. A sharp crack of explosion reverberated in his ears and he felt a shock wave blow by, tumbling him to the ground. Quinn struggled to his feet, the goggles slowly adjusting back to normal, twisting his head, looking about.

There was screaming ahead. Quinn jogged forward, weapon at the ready. The screaming came from one of the men who had been at point. The man was lying on his side, hands holding the stumps of what had once been his legs, now gone from midthigh down. Blood squirted out through his fingers.

Quinn looked for the other man. There was a part of a torso about twenty feet away.

"Mine," Trent said, pointing at a three-foot crater. "Antitank, from the sound and the pit. We're lucky it wasn't antipersonnel or we'd all be mush."

"Lucky!" Bentley's voice squeaked. "I was almost killed."

Quinn knelt down to the wounded man, whose screams had descended to gasps of pain-filled breath. "Easy, mate, easy." He shifted around to the side of the man, one hand on his shoulder. With the other he brought up the Sterling, out of the man's sight, and, holding the muzzle less than an inch from his head, fired a round into his brain.

The flank security had come running in at the sound of the explosion and they all stood looking at the two dead men.

"Right," Quinn said. At least he now knew why he had gotten spooked. He turned to the remaining members of his patrol. "No flank. You two take point. Let's move."

As they left behind the bodies, Trent moved over next to Quinn. "Well, another hundred grand for each of us now that Peterson and Dunnigan are dead," Trent noted.

"I know," Quinn repeated. He felt warm and his head was throbbing. This was all fucked up.

"You all right, sir?" Trent asked, peering in the dark.

"No."

# Chapter 14

**Cacólo, Angola, 16 June**

Kieling tenderly wiped the blood off a little girl's chin. He had a surgical mask on and wore two sets of gloves, as did the nuns, courtesy of one of the equipment cases he'd had packed on board the B-1. Too little too late.

He knew a lot about the progression of the virus now. At least its first seventy-two hours. And what he'd learned scared him. It was fast. Faster than anything he'd ever seen that was this deadly. It was violating the basic paradox of virus survival, killing so fast it should be inhibiting its own spread. But that didn't appear to be the case, at least not from that imagery he'd seen earlier in the day.

Kieling still wasn't sure about the vector, but he had one possibility: the rashes that were developing on the bodies of some of the victims. They looked like ropes of angry red crisscrossing the skin. Inside the red, pustules were forming and occasionally breaking. That might be when the virus got into the air, Kieling speculated.

"When will the others arrive?" Sister Angelina was behind him.

She had been on the ward ever since he'd arrived, never taking a break. He didn't know what fueled her. He did know that she knew she had the virus. He'd seen her bend over and retch into a pan a few hours earlier. She'd glanced up at him and smiled, carefully wiping the foamy black matter from around her lips with a stained rag.

"They should be here in the morning," he answered.

She put out a hand and touched him on the arm. "There are no others, are there?"

"There is some difficulty in transportation and entry requirements," Kieling said. "What with the Americans and the Pan-African forces trying to get to Savimbi and UNITA. Things are a bit unusual, so it is taking longer than—"

"You're with the American army, aren't you?"

"I . . ." Kieling halted. Sister Angelina was looking at him, her face calm. "Yes."

"There will be no others coming to help, will there? We're on our own, aren't we?"

"Yes."

"Thank you for being honest." She looked down the row of beds, the sound of people vomiting and moaning in pain filling the air. "I need one more answer. Did your people cause this?"

Kieling blinked. "No."

"I would not have believed that answer if you had not told me you were with the army. And if your army were not soon going to be suffering like these people are. And if you were not here among us without your suit. You have it also, don't you?"

"Maybe."

She pointed toward the door. "You'd better go back to your people and help them. Thank you for your help."

Riley looked up as Kieling entered the tent. He had the imagery and intelligence printout spread out on a table in front of him, but he wasn't looking at it. All it did was reinforce his feeling of impending doom. He'd faced death before but never in a such a drawn-out and certain fashion. Always before there'd been a chance, hope that he could beat the odds, and up until this he had. Conner was seated across from him. They hadn't said a word for the past hour, each lost in their own thoughts.

"How bad is it?" Riley asked.

"It's bad." Kieling looked at him. "How are you feeling?"

"I have a headache," Riley said.

Kieling's gaze shifted to Conner. "And you?"

"The same," she said. "And surprise, surprise, I'm running a slight fever. That was very slick of you and Comsky to decide whether we should know we were dying. Who made you God?"

"I'm sorry. I've made a lot of errors in judgment on this trip." Kieling sat down on a folding chair next to Riley. "Seen Tyron?"

"He's hiding out in the habitat," Riley said. "I went by there an hour ago and he said they had nothing new from Fort Detrick. He just yelled through the door. Didn't even bother to suit up."

"It will take time for the vector experiments to work," Kieling said. "Time we don't have, because we're already ahead of them timewise if we're infected." He rubbed the stubble of his beard. "You know, Sister Angelina at the hospital asked me an interesting question, and I was thinking about it the entire way back here."

"What was that?" Riley asked. He'd taken aspirin, but there was no change. His head throbbed and he felt warm.

"She asked if we'd started this virus."

"You mean biological warfare?" Riley asked.

"Yes."

"Did we?" Conner asked.

"You're joking, right?" Kieling said.

"No, she's not," Riley replied. "I've seen our government do things that are on a par with this."

"Kill people like this?" Kieling said. "Why?"

"To test a weapon maybe," Riley said. "Let me tell you a little story."

With that, Riley launched into the story of his encounter with the Synbats—synthetic battle forms—in the woods of Tennessee three years ago. Creatures that were designed under government contract to replace the infantryman. Except the experiment had gone terribly wrong and the Synbats had escaped and gone on a killing rampage. Riley and his Special Forces team, with the aid of a Chicago police officer, had finally cornered them in tunnels under the streets of Chicago and wiped them out by flooding the entire system.

"So don't tell me that our government isn't capable of something like this," Riley concluded.

"You never told me about any of that!" Conner exclaimed when he was done.

"I couldn't," Riley said. "It was classified."

"What a story. After all we went through in Antarctica, you couldn't tell me—" she began, but stopped as a thought struck her. "So why'd you tell me now?"

"The answer is obvious," Riley said. "It doesn't matter now."

"Do you think the U.S. government could really be behind this?" Conner asked, turning to Kieling.

"No," he answered.

"Why?" Conner asked.

"Maybe the government is capable of doing such a thing, but I'd know if they did this specific thing," he said. "There aren't that many people in the field of epidemiology back in the States—I'd *know* if someone in the U.S. did this," he repeated.

Conner turned to Riley. "What do you think?"

"I don't think our government did it. Not because I know anything about the manufacture of something like it, but because it serves no purpose letting it loose here, especially in the middle of this deployment."

"How about the rebels?" Conner asked. "Could Savimbi have gotten ahold of some biological weapon and unleashed it? Maybe from the Russians?"

Kieling considered that. "Maybe, but I doubt it. It's killing more Angolans than anyone else."

"UNITA would have let it loose in Luanda," Riley noted, "if they wanted to have maximum effect. Not out in the middle of nowhere, in the middle of their own terrain."

"It's not the middle of nowhere," Conner corrected him. "It's the middle of one of the largest diamond-mining areas in the world."

"And?" Kieling said.

"And . . ." Conner bit her lip. "Oh, I don't know."

"Wait a second," Riley said. "There's something in here." He grabbed the intelligence summary. He flipped through. "Yeah, here it is. NSA picked up some SATCOM transmissions out of the Lunda Norte region. Top-of-the-line stuff, but it wasn't ours. And it wasn't the rebels'. The communication was going out of the country."

Riley scattered the photos and uncovered the map underneath. "There's someone out there. Transmitting and getting messages back."

"So what?" Kieling said.

"Wait a second." Riley tapped his forehead, trying to conjure up a memory through the throb of pain. "There's something else." He ran his finger down the page, then the next. "Yeah, here it is. Earlier today at zero seven thirty Zulu time someone piggybacked a GPS—ground-positioning-satellite—signal."

"And?" Kieling asked.

"And someone has to have very good gear to do that *and*," Riley continued, looking at the report, "the NSA analyst thinks that the whole thing was designed for whoever broadcast the first signal to find something on the return piggyback."

"Find what?" Conner asked.

"Something out there," Riley said, tapping the map. The three of them sat silent for a little while, considering the information.

"You mentioned top-of-the-line equipment," Conner said.

"Yeah," Riley said.

"That takes money. And this"—she pointed at the area Riley had indicated on the map—"is the center of the diamond area."

"What the hell are you two talking about?" Kieling demanded.

"Just listen to me," Conner said. "I know it doesn't make much sense, but none of this does. I never told you one of the main reasons I went along with your idea about coming out to this area, Dave."

Kieling rubbed his forehead. "Are we going to play true confession all night?"

"Got something better to do?" Conner countered. "Can you come up with a cure for this thing in the next couple of days?"

"Hell, I don't even know what this thing is," Kieling admitted. He threw a hand up in the air and settled back on his seat. "Go ahead."

"Has either of you ever heard of the Van Wyks cartel?"

"Yeah," Riley said. "They're a diamond cartel."

"*The* diamond cartel," Conner corrected. "The one and only."

"What does—" Kieling began, but halted at Conner's glare.

"Let's put one and one together and come up with two," Conner said. "Dave says that these transmissions are from expensive equipment. They're being made in the region of Angola known for its diamond mines. To me that adds up to the Van Wyks cartel."

Despite the situation, Riley had to smile. He'd seen Conner in this mode before. When she investigated a subject, she left no stone unturned and she committed facts, and rumors, to memory, to be plucked out when required. Of course, Riley noted—as Conner flipped open the lid—she also had her laptop with the information the researchers in the SNN data bank dredged up for her.

"Okay, so maybe it is the Van Wyks," Riley said. "Tell me more about them."

"The Van Wyks empire makes OPEC look like a misguided and inept baby, yet it's managed to stay out of public scrutiny for more than a century. The history of the Van Wyks really starts in 1867, when a boy discovered a diamond on the bank of the Orange River in South Africa. That began the African version of the great gold rush.

"And one fact that is very rarely mentioned is that the battles between the British and the Afrikaners over the next several decades, and the Boer War, had as much to do with control of this wealth as political freedom. Keep in mind, as I tell you this history, the number of people who have died over the past hundred and thirty years in this area, and then think about the present situation.

"Pieter Van Wyks the First, the patriarch of the Van Wyks family, was the first person who understood the new development clearly. During the last decades of the nineteenth century, pretty much the only source of diamonds was South Africa. Van Wyks gobbled up all the mines. Some he bought legally, others he just took when the owners wouldn't sell. Apartheid, besides being a racial instrument, also needs to be looked at through the lens of supplying workers to mines—both diamond and gold."

Conner had been working her computer while speaking. She looked down. "The Big Hole at Kimberly, one of the most infamous diamond mines, was the largest man-made excavation in the world— covering over twelve acres and going two hundred and thirty feet deep. It took almost four thousand workers to keep it going. And you don't have a hefty overhead eating into your profit if you don't have to pay all those workers. But the most amazing thing Van Wyks did was invent a market that his family has never relinquished."

"Invent?" Riley asked.

"If the Van Wyks cartel did not control eighty percent of the world's diamond market and fix the price by regulating supply, diamonds would probably cost one fifth what they currently do," Conner said.

"I thought that diamonds were rare," Kieling said, "and that's why they cost so much."

"Certainly diamonds aren't plentiful," Conner said, "but they aren't that rare. If you controlled eighty percent of the supply of *anything*, you could control the price on the international market. Particularly if you'd been doing so for over a century.

"This is an organization that doesn't care about borders or the international situation. It cares only about profit and propagating itself. Estimated sales of Van Wyks's diamonds last year was three point two billion in U.S. dollars. It controls, at least as far has been uncovered so far, at least six hundred various corporations and employs almost a million people around the world."

"Jesus," Kieling muttered. "That's bigger than many countries."

"And the Van Wyks don't like competition," Conner added. "Here in Angola—since it concerns our present situation—it's estimated that they've spent fifty million dollars a year buying black market diamonds to keep them from hitting the outside world. It is also claimed that they hire mercenaries to try and block UNITA from getting the diamonds across the border to Zaire, paying a bounty for every dead rebel."

"Maybe these transmissions are coming from one of those mercenary groups," Riley said. "I talked to some people in the know before we came over here, and the word on the international merk market is that there's good money to be made in Angola, either working for Van Wyks, the MPLA government, or UNITA."

"Right," Conner said. "The Van Wyks will use any means to further their cause. In World War II, the United States placed a large order with Van Wyks for industrial diamonds. Afraid that those diamonds would create a glut after the war and cause prices to go down, Van Wyks refused. The company claimed that its London vaults had been bombed shut. Despite the greatest pressure from the Allies, the Van Wyks cartel only released a low percentage of what had been requested. There were also rumors—never proved—that at the same time the Van Wyks were supplying the Nazis with industrial diamonds at highly inflated prices through intermediaries in Switzerland.

"But it was after the Second World War that the most interesting alliance occurred. For over fifty years, it has been a poorly kept secret that the Van Wyks cartel has been buying out the Siberian diamond mines. This despite the South African government banning the Communist party and the Russians training ANC guerrillas.

During all this, Van Wyks people moved in and out of Moscow, buying up tens of billions of dollars' worth of Soviet diamonds. All to control the supply and thus control the price."

"So what if these signals are being made by mercenaries in the employ of the Van Wyks cartel," Kieling asked, "and they're out there killing diamond smugglers? What does that have to do with this virus?"

Conner's brief burst of energy came to a halt. "I don't know. But it's—it's . . ." She looked at Riley.

"It's a direction to look," Riley said. "Sister Angelina asked you if we had started this virus. Turn the question. Maybe the Van Wyks cartel started it."

"Why?" Kieling asked.

"I don't know," Riley replied. "Who is the Van Wyks cartel now? I assume Pieter died long ago."

"His grandson by the same name," Conner said. "Pieter Van Wyks the Third."

"We're grasping at straws here," Kieling said.

"You got any better ideas?" Conner demanded.

Kieling slumped back in his chair and closed his eyes. "I have nothing better. In fact, I have nothing at all."

Riley looked at the various satellite and Aurora photos. "This thing started out there to the east. Those transmissions came out of the east. The diamond fields are to the east. It's weak, but it's all we have." He stood. "I'm going to talk to Major Tyron at the habitat and have him see if we can get some more intelligence."

### Andrews Air Force Base, Maryland, 16 June

"That's Savimbi. Or what's left of him," the chief coroner said, pointing at a crushed head that wasn't recognizable, a torso with one arm still attached, and a severed leg.

The coroner stripped off his bloodied gloves and threw them in the trash. "Tell them they got their man."

### Pentagon, 16 June

Colonel Martin walked through the secure vault door into the War Room. General Cummings was at the head of the conference table.

Martin took the seat to his left. As he sat down an aide walked to Cummings and whispered in his ear.

"At least that plan worked," Cummings commented as the aide walked away. He turned to Martin. "Listen to this." He hit the control and the volume on the television was turned up, overriding the murmur of activity inside. Although there were TV sets hung all around the walls, Cummings was watching one inset right into the conference table at an angle, three feet from his seat.

"A Pentagon spokesman denies any knowledge of a viral outbreak in Cacólo, Angola. This despite reports from the World Health Organization that they have received requests for help from an aid foundation in that city to help quell an outbreak of an unknown virus. There are unconfirmed reports of dozens of deaths in the town.

"SNN has been unable to contact any of its representatives in Angola due to a news blackout imposed by military authorities that was implemented last night—at approximately the same time the World Health Organization released information concerning the request from Angola.

"SNN has learned that the deployment of forces from the United States to Angola was halted sometime during the night. Fort Bragg and adjacent Pope Air Force Base have been placed off limits to the media, but sources in nearby Fayetteville confirm that not only has the deployment of the 82d Airborne Division been stopped, but that troops en route that had not yet landed in Angola were diverted and returned to the United States.

"Despite the denials from the Pentagon, Zaire and Zambia have closed their borders with Angola. Both countries have experienced deadly viral outbreaks in the past and their governments are reacting with swiftness to even a rumor of disease.

"In other news, the Japanese—"

Cummings hit the mute button and turned to Martin. "This is going to be blown wide open."

Martin remained silent. That wasn't his concern.

"Do you have anything new?" Cummings finally asked him.

"The first symptoms of Z occur—"

"Z?" Cummings interrupted.

"That's what we're calling it, sir. Z."

"All right, go ahead."

"The first symptoms—fever, headache—occur within twenty-four hours of exposure. Within forty-eight hours some of the victims begin experiencing further symptoms of nausea and vomiting. Between seventy-two and ninety-six hours, bleeding, both internal and external, begins. We do not have much data, but it appears that death occurs six to seven days after infection."

"Mortality rate?" Cummings asked.

"Unknown, sir, but imagery shows no survivors in some of the infected villages. That doesn't necessarily correlate to a one hundred percent fatality rate, though, because survivors would most likely have fled long before the disease reached the critical stage in those it killed.

"We still do not know the way the disease is transmitted, but we hope to have something on that in the next three or four days. We have a few theories that—"

"Three or four days!" Cummings exclaimed. "I don't have three or four days."

Martin put a piece of paper down on the tabletop. "Sir, we don't have any choice."

"I want options," Cummings said. "I don't care how outrageous. I don't want to leave my soldiers sitting there with their thumb up their ass doing nothing, waiting for this thing to come kill them."

"My people have sent instructions to all deployed units," Martin said, "as to how best to guard themselves against this disease." He tapped the paper. "Sir, my people in Cacólo have a . . . well, the best way to put it is that they have a pretty farfetched theory. But since you—"

"Give it to me, Martin," Cummings snapped. "I'll take farfetched right now. I've got the president drilling me a new asshole every two hours. He acts like this is *my* fault. Like I should have known this was going to happen."

"One of my men," Martin said, distancing himself from the words to come, "thinks there is a very slight possibility this virus is manmade."

That caught the attention of everyone in the room. Papers stopped shuffling and voices stilled.

"Biological warfare," Cummings whispered.

"It's only a slight possibility, sir, and there is no proof," Martin was quick to say. He quickly outlined the SATCOM and GPS information that Riley had lifted from the intelligence summary. When he was done, Cummings steepled his fingers.

"It is slim. But it is something. There has to be someone making these messages and moving around out there." The chairman turned to one of his flunkies. "Get on the horn to the NSA and have them give us—and forward—everything they can pick up. Also, get the NRO to put the big eyeball on the areas NSA gives you. If a fucking rabbit farts out there, I want to hear it and see the grimace on its face."

### Luia River, Angola, 16 June

Quinn pulled the small earplug out and slowly coiled it before replacing the radio in its place on his combat vest. He glanced across their small campsite at the sleeping form of Bentley. They had made good time and were less than five kilometers from their destination, when Quinn had called the halt and they'd settled in for the night. He wanted to approach the place in daylight.

Quinn reached a hand up and wiped sweat off his forehead. The headache wasn't quite as bad, but Quinn had been in the tropics long enough to tell the difference between being warm and running a fever and he knew he was doing the latter. "Fuck," Quinn muttered.

"What's up?" Trent asked, sensing his partner's mood change.

"There's a fucking plague going on around here. That's why we haven't seen any planes or run into anybody."

"A plague?"

"Some fucking bug. It's killing people all over eastern Angola. That's why the U.S. has stopped its deployment of troops. Everybody's quarantined."

"Oh, Christ," Trent muttered. "We need to get the hell out of here."

"A million dollars," Quinn said.

"What?" Trent was confused by the sudden switch.

"What's worth a million dollars out here that this fellow is looking for with his high-speed direction finder?"

Trent was still uncertain where Quinn was going with his thinking, so he remained silent.

"Get the SATCOM rig up," Quinn said. "I want to send a message to Skeleton."

### National Security Agency, Fort Meade, Maryland, 16 June

Another look at eastern Angola. No problem, Waker thought. He still had the program he'd run for the first request. He had begun setting it up, when he was distracted by a small star flashing in the upper left corner of his computer screen. He quickly switched programs.

"Bingo!" Waker exclaimed. Another transmission by the same SATCOM rig off the same commercial satellite. This time he—and the billions of dollars' worth of equipment at his command—were ready.

"I may not be able to read your mail," he muttered as his fingers issued commands, "but I sure can get your address down to within ten feet."

# Chapter 15

**Oshakati, Namibia, 17 June**

"Sir, we have the follow-on contingency plan."

General Nystroom had come awake the moment the back hatch on his command vehicle had been opened. He swung his feet, boots still on, to the metal floor and flipped on the overhead red light so he wouldn't lose his night vision.

He took the message from his operations officer without a comment. Pulling his reading glasses on, he quickly read. When he was done, he slowly handed the order back.

"What is the latest on the Americans? Is their deployment still halted?"

"Yes, sir. There is word on the international news media that there is some sort of outbreak of a viral infection in northeastern Angola and that is the reason the Americans have stopped sending troops."

"Northeastern Angola?" Nystroom repeated. He pointed at the contingency plan. "But that plan calls for us to seize that particular area in the American sector."

"Yes, sir," the operations officer said. "But we are on hold for execution. I assume this," he added, holding up the plan, "is for implementation in case the Americans withdraw."

Nystroom held out his hand and the officer gave him the plan back. "Good assumption," the general said, "except for one slight detail. When did the Americans halt their deployment?"

"Yesterday—the sixteenth—around noon our time."

Nystroom's finger tapped the heading on the order. "We might have just received this plan, but it was drafted on the fourteenth of this month." He looked up. "What was the date-time-group of our hold message on the invasion where we were to await this contingency plan?"

The operations officer flipped open his message log. "Fifteen June, nineteen fifteen local time."

"Two days ago," Nystroom noted. "And this plan was done even before we got that. So your assumption is false."

"Which means, sir?"

General Nystroom sighed. "Which means there is much more going on here than you and I probably care to know about, but we're stuck with it."

### Cacólo, Angola, 17 June

"This is the latest," Kieling said, holding out a batch of faxes. "We have approval to take whatever action we deem necessary."

Riley took them and began reading, while Kieling briefed the others gathered in the tent. The glow of the Coleman lamps reflected against haggard faces, drawn with fatigue—several showing signs of their sickness, with red eyes and sweat dripping off of foreheads.

They were almost all here—Comsky, Lorne, and the other members of the team that had been on the helicopter; Vickers and the helicopter crew; Conner—Mike Seeger was in another tent, handcuffed to the center pole; and Major Lindsay, looking very uncomfortable in his gas mask, representing the AOB.

Right now, Lindsay didn't look so foolish to Riley, and he would gladly trade the major's discomfort for his own physical situation. Riley had a pounding headache which the Tylenol 3's that Comsky had given him had done little to alleviate. He was also beginning to feel nauseated. He'd tried very hard the last several hours not to think about the virus that was spreading throughout his body, multiplying and feeding off his own cells, but he had not been very successful. It was hard to ignore the body's signals that something very wrong was happening. And Riley knew that the mind was amplifying and multiplying whatever symptoms he was experiencing.

"Still nothing from Fort Detrick on this disease's vector," Kieling continued. "My theory on the blisters won't get tested until they get blisters on the monkeys.

"They've isolated it and are trying everything they can think of to kill it, at the cellular level, but no luck. I got Tyron to suit up and head over to the hospital to take a look at how things are going there."

Riley held up a sheet of paper. "NSA picked up another SATCOM transmission and they pinpointed the location." He went to the map tacked to the plywood table and looked. "It's here, right between these rivers."

"What now?" Conner asked.

"We go visiting," Riley said. He looked at Major Lindsay. "What about it, sir?"

Lindsay's voice was muffled by the mask. "You all have authorization from the chairman of the Joint Chiefs. The only problem is getting you there."

"Why's that a problem?" Sergeant Lorne demanded.

"We have a no-fly rule that supersedes the chairman's authorization. To keep the disease from spreading."

"Can you get us a helicopter?" Lieutenant Vickers asked.

"We've got three Black Hawks parked at the AOB," Lindsay said, "but I just told you—"

"But nothing." Vickers turned to the Black Hawk pilot. "You are already in this," she said. "Can you take us out there?"

"I can fly," CW2 O'Malley said, "but there's one little problem. The Black Hawk requires two pilots to fly it."

"I'm rotary wing–qualified," Lieutenant Vickers said.

"You've also got a broken ankle, ma'am," Comsky said.

"I'm rotary wing–qualified," Vickers said again. "With the splint, I can handle the pedals if I have to."

"But—" Comsky began.

"End of discussion, Sergeant," Vickers said.

Comsky smiled for the first time in hours. "Yes, ma'am."

A rumbling noise came from outside and everyone's head snapped up. "Artillery?" Vickers asked.

Major Lindsay shook his head. "Thunderstorms are coming in from the east."

"So what's the plan?" Conner asked.

* * *

In the city, Tyron tried to conquer his fear. The streets were deserted, but he could sense eyes watching him from the darker shadows of the shacks along the road. The rebreather sounded abnormally loud in his ears and, despite the temperature drop at night, he was hot. The sky was overcast and he could see lightning flashing to the east.

Ever since the shock of seeing Kieling thrown into the wire and his suit breached, Tyron had hidden in the shelter. That is, until Kieling had come by an hour ago and picked up the latest faxes from Fort Detrick. The conversation had been brief and to the point:

"You're a fucking doctor, Tyron," Kieling had said from the entryway, the inner door separating them. "You took an oath. This is what it's all about. We need you working this like you're supposed to, not sitting on your ass in there, hiding."

"I can't," Tyron had answered honestly.

"You will," Kieling had responded. "Or else I'll have Sergeant Lorne open fire on this shelter and fill it full of little holes. Then you'll have no choice. And the way Sergeant Lorne seems to be feeling, he might not make much of an attempt to miss you."

Fear versus fear. If it had simply come down to that, Tyron knew he would have stayed in the habitat and taken his chances. But Kieling's first words had touched a chord. Tyron was a doctor and he knew he had a duty. Besides the fact that there was no way out of this place until Z had finished burning. Going to the hospital would give him an idea of how long that might be.

Not long, was Tyron's first impression as he stepped into the entryway to the main ward. It was dark inside. No power, Tyron remembered. But the lamps weren't lit either. There was someone sitting behind the old desk: a nun. Tyron reached out his gloved hand and touched her on the shoulder. "Sister?"

She fell over onto the floor, and Tyron stepped back in disgust at the mass of black bile that was all over the front of her habit.

Tyron jumped as a low voice spoke behind him. "I didn't think anyone would come back."

He turned around. "Sister Angelina!"

"I have been trying to move the living to A wing," Angelina said.

Her white robe was caked with blood and other material that Tyron didn't want to identify. She was moving very slowly.

"How many are dead?"

"Thirty-three." Sister Angelina stepped around him and pulled the dead nun's habit over her face. "Thirty-four." She knelt and crossed herself, her lips moving in prayer.

Tyron moved past her and looked into the main ward. There were bodies on the beds. Some on the floor where death spasms had thrown them. Tyron knew better, but he could swear he could smell the odor of death. He forced himself to look. They were all bled out. Blood had exploded out of every orifice of the body, including their eyes and ears. That was the virus looking for a new host, having finished with this one. He forced himself to look more closely. The blisters in the red streaks had broken open on all of them. Maybe Kieling had something.

Tyron turned and moved as quickly as his suit allowed. Sister Angelina was still kneeling, praying. She didn't even look up as Tyron shuffled past, out the door into the street. He had a crazy desire to tear off his helmet and breathe fresh air, but he knew the air was tinged with death. Or maybe it wasn't. "Keep moving," he said to himself. "Keep moving."

**Vicinity Luia River, Angola, 17 June**

"We have a reply," Trent said, holding out the message flimsy.

Quinn put a poncho over his head and used his red-lens flashlight to see the letters. Quickly he decoded it.

TO QUINN

FROM SKELETON

PAY UPPED TO A MILLION A MAN U.S. DOLLARS ALREADY IN YOUR ACCOUNT—TIME IS OF ESSENCE—DO NOT HALT FOR ANYTHING—CALL FOR AIR EVACUATION WHEN BENTLEY CONFIRMS ARTICLE RECOVERED—AIRCRAFT REQUIRES RUNWAY—MINIMUM LENGTH THREE HUNDRED METERS—SIDE TO SIDE CLEARANCE FIFTY METERS—MONITOR FM FREQUENCY 32.30—YOUR CALL SIGN HORSEMAN—AIRCRAFT CALL SIGN GULL

END

"Wake up, Sleeping Beauty," Quinn ordered Trent. "We're moving *now.*"

### National Security Agency, Fort Meade, Maryland, 17 June

"I got you!" Waker yelled out, startling the men and women in the other cubicles in the NSA surveillance room. "I got you!" he repeated, his fingers tapping keys quickly.

On his computer screen the silhouette of the African continent appeared, then grew larger, the edges disappearing, the computer focusing in on the southwest part. It went down south of Angola into Namibia. South of Oshakati where Waker had intercepted messages from the SADF/Pan-African invasion forces that were marshaled there. Still farther south.

The screen halted. The downlink from the surveillance satellite had fixed the location of the origin of the uplink on the return message to the location he had fixed earlier in Angola.

Namibia, along the Atlantic coast. Waker read the name of the region. "The Skeleton Coast." There was a town there. That was where the signal was coming from. "Lüderitz."

Waker quickly summarized the information and sent out a priority intelligence report. Then he reached over to the bookshelf behind his desk and pulled out an atlas. He looked up Lüderitz. There was a red line drawn around the town, extending up the coast one hundred kilometers and south over two hundred and fifty kilometers to the Orange River, the border with South Africa. The red line extended inland about a hundred kilometers. In small red type next to the zone it said PROHIBITED AREA.

Waker put the atlas down on his desk and stared at the map. Who the hell controlled that strip of land and why was such a large area prohibited? Waker had a feeling the answers to those questions were going to become very important, very soon.

### Cacólo, Angola, 17 June

Riley had tried to talk Conner out of coming, but she could tell his heart wasn't in it. Priorities had changed in the last forty-eight hours, and things that had been of great concern that short a time ago were no longer important.

She held an M-16 in her lap. Riley had stuck to that. If she was coming she would be armed. He'd given her a quick lesson in its use. She also wore a flak vest and, over it, a combat vest bristling with extra ammunition clips, a canteen, and a knife.

Riley was leaning between the two pilot seats up front, talking to Lieutenant Vickers on the intercom. The engines had just been started and the whine grew louder, the blades overhead slowly beginning to turn.

Riley sat back down next to Conner. He handed her a headset and she put it on.

"Hear me?" Riley said.

"Loud and clear," she replied.

The helicopter's wheels separated from the ground and the aircraft banked forward and to the right.

"The objective is three hundred kilometers away," Vickers called out over the intercom. "ETA in one hour, twenty minutes."

"Dave, what do you think is out there?" Conner asked.

"Somebody who might have some answers," Riley said. She could see that he was looking out.

"And?" Conner pressed.

"Shit, Conner, I don't know," Riley replied. His head turned and he looked at her. "Somebody's out there in the middle of all this death. Using SATCOM radio through a commercial satellite. Encrypting their messages with one-time pads. I don't have a clue whether that somebody has anything to do with this disease."

"Well, that's pretty damn encouraging," Sergeant Lorne's voice cut in on the intercom.

"I'm not here to encourage you," Riley snapped.

"Why are you here, then?" Lorne asked.

"All I know is that I'd rather be on this helicopter going to do something—anything—than back there inside that wire waiting to die," Riley said.

"Amen to that," Comsky said.

"Amen," Sergeant Oswald's voice piped, followed by Tiller's: "Roger that."

"I didn't know you Special Forces guys were so religious," Vickers called out from the front.

"The way Z is burning," Kieling said, "I might even catch a little of that religion soon."

**Vicinity Luia River, Angola, 17 June**
"Wait a second," Bentley said.

Quinn went down on one knee, Sterling at the ready. Bentley flipped open the lid on one of the cases. He pulled out the GPR into which he had programmed the location of whatever it was he was looking for. "That way," Bentley said. "Four hundred meters."

Quinn didn't have to say a word. He stood, the other three men deploying around in a wedge. They were in relatively open terrain, with small clusters of trees every hundred meters or so. By Quinn's pace count they had moved three hundred meters when he saw something silhouetted on the top of a ridge ahead.

Quinn twisted the focus on his goggles. A tree, twisted and shattered by some powerful force, was leaning to the right. Perhaps artillery or an air strike, Quinn guessed. He wondered about that. According to the map, the nearest village was about seven or eight kilometers away.

Bentley checked the GPR one more time. "Wait here for me," Bentley said, his hand straying up to the night vision goggles perched on his head. The straps weren't adjusted correctly and they kept slipping down. Quinn wasn't in the mood to help him with it.

"We should go with you to the top of the ridge," Quinn said. "If there's someone—"

"I said, wait here," Bentley said. He picked up the third case and took it with him.

Quinn gestured and the other three men went to earth, facing out in the other three cardinal directions, weapons at the ready. Quinn watched as Bentley walked up the ridge and past the broken tree. As soon as the man was out of sight, Quinn followed.

As he came up to the tree, Quinn crouched low. He slowly peeked over a broken bough. The terrain dropped off on the other side, but Quinn's attention was focused on the gouge in the grassy slope. Starting from the tree and going downslope, the dirt was torn as if a tank had ripped through. Bentley was at a large piece of crumpled metal at the end of the gouge, opening the third case.

Quinn heard the screech of metal as Bentley leaned into the wreckage. A downed aircraft? Quinn wondered. Perhaps Bentley was here for its black box, or maybe classified equipment or something else that had been on board.

Quinn turned and worked his way back down the slope, considering the possibilities.

"What's happening?" Trent asked.

"There's a plane or chopper crashed on the other side of the ridge," Quinn said, his mind working. "It must have been carrying diamonds. Maybe the U.S. got it enforcing the no-fly rule, or maybe it had a bomb on board in some scheme Skeleton thought up. Regardless, Skeleton had had a homing device placed on board and Bentley is getting the diamonds."

"Must be quite a few to be worth this much," Trent said.

"You and I know Bentley could carry enough diamonds in his backpack to be worth tens of millions," Quinn said.

"What are we going to do?" Trent asked.

"I don't know." Quinn looked upslope. Bentley had appeared, moving quickly toward them.

"Let's get moving," Bentley said.

"Change in plans," Quinn said. "Last message I got from Skeleton said to call in for air evacuation as soon as you recovered what you were supposed to."

"Well, I got it," Bentley said. "So call."

Quinn's head snapped up like a bird dog on the scent. "Hear that?"

Trent's head swiveled on his thick neck. "Yeah. Helicopter."

Quinn stuck the muzzle of his Sterling in Bentley's stomach. "Maybe *you* already called and we're getting double-crossed here?"

"I couldn't—I don't have a radio!" Bentley protested.

"You have that SATCOM thing you used to get this position," Quinn said.

"I left it here," Bentley pointed out. "I swear I didn't call anyone."

"Then who's on the helicopter?" Quinn asked.

"I don't know!"

"It's setting down to the south of here," Trent noted. "Where we were camped."

Quinn removed the gun from Bentley's stomach. "Someone picked up our satellite transmission."

"How can they do that?" Trent asked.

"I don't know how," Quinn said, "but it's the only thing that makes sense." He took a deep breath and cleared his head. "All right. Here's the plan. We call on the SATCOM. If someone's intercepting, that means they get a fix on us here, but we start moving right away. In the message we designate a linkup point." Quinn studied his map. "Here. Eight clicks north." He knew the spot well. It was an abandoned dirt strip that was used occasionally by diamond smugglers. Quinn had run an assault on the airstrip a year and a half ago.

"What if they decode the message?" Trent asked.

"I don't think anyone can break a one-time pad," Quinn said, not even really aware of where he was for the moment as his brain worked. "No, I think our signal's been intercepted. Get the rig set up."

Quinn blinked as Trent threw his ruck down and scrambled to pull out the radio. He focused on Bentley. "What did you get out of that aircraft?"

Bentley was adjusting his pack straps. "What are you talking about?"

"What did you just get? What did we come here for?"

"That's not—"

Quinn drew his knife and slashed, the blade cutting across Bentley's right cheek, a thin line of blood following the slit.

"What did you do?" Bentley screamed, scrambling backward and falling down.

Quinn stepped forward and slammed a knee into Bentley's chest, pinning him to the ground. He pressed the point into the skin under Bentley's right eye. "What crashed over there?"

"I can't—"

The point of the knife edged forward until it was a scant millimeter from Bentley's eye. "I'll take one eye, then the other. Nothing in Skeleton's orders about you keeping your eyes," Quinn said. "Just get you and your cargo back. What crashed?"

"It was a satellite. Well, sort of a satellite," Bentley said.

"A satellite?" Quinn frowned. "What did you get out of it?"

"Film," Bentley said.

"Film of what?"

"The mine areas," Bentley said. "The satellite wasn't supposed to come down so soon."

"That's worth four million?" Quinn didn't wait for an answer. "Bullshit. Skeleton could get photos of the mines anytime he wants."

"Not this type of photo." Bentley spoke quickly, eye still focused on the knife so close by. "The camera used special imaging. The Angolan mines were never fully exploited. With thermal and spectral imaging, the specialists can determine areas that haven't been dug up yet that have a high likelihood of holding diamonds, particularly alluvial flood areas."

"Why the fuck does Skeleton care? He's going to take over anything he wants once UNITA is destroyed."

Bentley started to shake his head, then thought better of it. "No. Not with the Americans there. And the UN charter calls for the mines to be privatized and turned over to Angolans. Well, Skeleton's got enough Angolan natives on his payroll prepared to take over, but he has to have them come in quick and stake claims. This way he can prevent what happened in Canada."

Quinn slowly pulled the knife away. He knew about the fiasco in Canada three years ago. A prospector had discovered a rich field of diamonds. The rush had been on, and as usual the Van Wyks cartel had rumbled in with the best equipment and a big bankroll determined to keep their monopoly. Unfortunately the prospector had joined forces with a local company, and they'd staked claims using the same type of imaging Bentley had just talked about, while Van Wyks had relied on its tried-and-true but slower methods. The result: forty percent of the diamonds mined in Canada now came out of non–Van Wyks mines.

"It's set," Trent reported.

Quinn sheathed his knife and pulled out his one-time pad. He quickly began transcribing. He finished the message and punched it into the SATCOM and burst it out.

"Where did you say for the transportation to meet us?" Bentley asked.

Quinn laughed. "I don't think that's information you need. You just stick with us. We'll get you there."

* * *

Five thousand meters to the south, Riley looked around, weapon at the ready. The Black Hawk was sitting a short distance away, blades slowly turning.

"What do you think?" Lorne asked, looking about in the dark at the rolling terrain around them.

"They were here," Riley said, pointing at where the grass was pressed down. "Someone slept here. Maybe three, four men."

"So where'd they go?" Lorne asked.

"I'm not a fucking Indian," Riley snapped. "They could have gone in any direction. We need help. Let's get back on the bird."

### National Security Agency, Fort Meade, Maryland, 17 June

"Okay, Okay," Waker said as he read the intelligence request. He was pumped. He was hooked in to his electronic network, everything coming in and dancing in front of his eyes in letters and symbols his brain automatically translated.

"Perfect timing," Waker muttered. The KH-12 had picked up the SATCOM transmission as it was being made. Within thirty seconds it had come up on Waker's screen. And now, three minutes later, someone on the ground in Angola wanted the location of the transmitter.

This time, though, he was talking direct back to the man in the field, and that gave Waker a rush. It was as close as he was ever going to get.

He typed, each finger slamming down on the key with authority.

> TO: EAGLE
> FROM: NSA ANGOLA ALPHA ONE ONE
> TRANSMISSION SENT DTG 17JUNE0307ZULU BY SAME
> SATCOM LOCATION UTM GRID 29583578

Waker looked at the message, his finger poised above the send key, then made a decision. He typed a couple of extra lines.

> TERMINUS OF TRANSMISSION LOCATED ALONG
> SKELETON COAST, VICINITY LÜDERITZ
> END OF MESSAGE

Waker hit the send.

**Northeast Angola, 17 June**
In the front of the helicopter Lieutenant Vickers's voice was in Riley's ears as soon as he put the headset on. "We've got something coming from the AWACS."

Riley put his hands over the headset and listened in.

"Army helicopter, this is Eagle. Over."

Vickers replied. "Eagle, this is army helicopter. Go ahead. Over."

Circling two hundred miles to the southwest, Colonel Harris frowned. The woman's voice sounded familiar. Since the quarantine rule his and his crew's job had been simply one of making sure that no one tried to get out of Angola by air.

So far there had been only one incident. In the first hour of the quarantine a Marine helicopter had tried to fly back out to its assault vessel offshore. Harris still wasn't sure whether the pilot had not received the order or had tried to bolt. Regardless, the aircraft had turned around when he'd ordered it.

Harris checked the message he'd just received from the NSA. "I've got new coordinates for you."

The point man stumbled and fell. Trent was quickly at his side. The man reached up, grabbing Trent's arm.

Quinn came up and looked at the man. He was a mercenary who had served with Quinn for the last two years. "Can you go on?"

The man groaned and rolled on the ground. Trent stood, flicking his arm to shake off the black vomit.

Quinn rubbed his forehead. He brought up the Sterling. The man raised an arm weakly. Quinn fired twice, then let his arms slump to his sides, the Sterling hanging by its sling.

"Let's go," Bentley said.

Quinn thought of the two dead rebels in their poncho stretchers. A million dollars. Would he make it out of here in time to buy help? "Let's move." As they went forward in the darkness, he noted that for the first time Trent had not added up their suddenly higher shares.

* * *

"Lock and load," Lorne yelled. The Black Hawk came in fast, the pilot flaring them at the last minute to prevent a crash. They jumped off, weapons at the ready, fanning across the open ground. The aircraft lifted and hovered overhead.

"They're gone again!" Lorne said as he looked around in all directions. He kicked dirt in frustration.

"What's up there?" Conner asked, looking up the ridge at a twisted tree. They ran up the slope and crested it. A pile of twisted metal lay at the end of a trail of torn-up earth.

"What's that?" Comsky asked as the party gathered around the wreckage.

"Helicopter?" Conner guessed.

"I don't see any rotor blades," Riley noted.

"It's burned, whatever it is," Conner said, touching the metal.

"There's Cyrillic writing here," Riley said, peering at a flat piece.

"Cyrillic?" Comsky asked.

"Russian," Riley said.

"They're gone," Lorne repeated. "That's the important thing. I don't even know what we're doing here, chasing after ghosts in the dark. What does it have to do with this thing we've got? We're fucking dying here!"

"You got a better idea?" Conner demanded. The scene was lit by a bolt of lightning. Thunder rumbled a few seconds later.

"We get somewhere where we can find medical help," Lorne said. "Go back to the AOB."

"Go back and wait to die, you mean," Comsky said. "Top," he added, touching Lorne on the arm, "there isn't any medical help for this other than killing the pain in the later stages."

"Ah, fuck," Lorne muttered, and walked off toward the top of the ridge, back toward the helicopter.

"This thing," Riley said, plunking the burnt metal with his finger. "It came from out of the sky. We know that. If it's an aircraft, we can get the AWACS to check records. Whoever sent that SATCOM message was here. This was what they were after. Let's find out what we can about it." He looked about. "And we know they were here less than an hour ago. We need help looking."

* * *

Colonel Harris considered the dual requests. The first he gave to one of his analysts with the order to check the AWACS records and also relay it back to the NSA. The second he had to ponder for a few moments, before he came up with a solution.

Quinn had heard the helicopter set down to their rear. That confirmed to him that the SATCOM transmissions were being picked up. He checked out the sky. He'd seen this before. Heat lightning, soon to be followed by a torrential rain. Perfect. There was no way they would be found, no matter how close their pursuers were.

"Here!" Comsky called out.

Riley ran over, the others following. A body lay in the grass. Comsky shone a light down and they immediately saw the blood splattered all about and the bullet holes. But there was also the sign of the disease. A red welt across the man's neck.

Riley looked out into the dark. The wind was picking up and he could feel dampness being carried with it. "Weather's changing," he called out. "Back to the chopper."

# Chapter 16

**Tshibomba, Zaire, 17 June**

The pilot checked his map one last time, then carefully folded it so that the portion he needed was face up. He used a band of elastic to attach it to his kneeboard. He had no electronic devices on board other than the engine, windshield wipers, and the rudimentary instrument panel, so this truly was going to be a seat-of-the-pants navigation job. He did have a small FM radio to be used to contact the people on the ground when he got close. The pilot was used to such missions and felt confident he could find the target runway.

He'd been waiting here for five days, the aircraft—a specially designed, top secret prototype named the Gull—under camouflage nets, the entire area guarded by a platoon of Skeleton's men. A generous payoff to certain officials in the Zairean army ensured they would not be bothered by any officials.

He flicked the on switch and the engine coughed once, then smoothly started. It was a specially designed rotary engine; quieter than a conventional piston engine and mounted directly behind the cockpit in a large bubble. The propeller shaft extended forward from the engine, over the pilot's head to the high-mounted propeller, supported by a four-foot pylon mounted on the nose. The long shaft allowed a high reduction ratio for the prop, and the very large blades—over eight feet long—turned very slowly. The resulting sound was no louder than a moderate wind blowing through the trees.

The Gull was made by a South African company, from designs

stolen from Lockheed's Q-Star (Quiet Star) program. The entire aircraft was designed with two factors in mind: reduced noise and radar signature. It wasn't built for speed or endurance, but with the target only eighty miles away across the border, the pilot knew he would be there in less than forty minutes.

The runway was dirt and the rain had further complicated what was going to be a difficult takeoff with no lights. The pilot released the brakes and the plane began rolling. Peering through the Plexiglas with his night vision goggles, the pilot ignored the sweep of the wipers and concentrated on staying straight. In two hundred feet he had sufficient speed and pulled back on the yoke, lifting off. As soon as he cleared the trees, he turned due west and headed for Angola.

### Northeast Angola, 17 June

Colonel Harris had moved the AWACS until it was now centered over Cacólo. The Black Hawk was waiting on the ground at the last site they had gone to. The only other aircraft on his screens was moving in this direction because he had ordered it to.

He keyed his mike. "Spectre One One, this is Eagle. Over."

"This is One One. Over."

Harris quickly relayed to the pilot of the Spectre gunship what he wanted. The AC-130 didn't look like a bloodhound, but it was the best Harris could come up with in the inventory. Using its LLTV, Harris wanted the Spectre to head to the Black Hawk's location, then begin a circular search pattern, literally looking for the people they were after.

"Roger that," the pilot of the Spectre acknowledged when Harris was done with his instructions. "ETA at target site, fifteen minutes. Out."

On the ground waiting, Riley was thinking about the last message they had received giving them this location. The second part—about the other end of the SATCOM communications—was what interested him.

"What's the Skeleton Coast?" he asked Conner.

The helicopter's engine was still on, producing a low whine, but the blades were disengaged so they could talk without the intercom.

"The Van Wyks," Conner answered. "Actually, the Skeleton Coast stretches almost fifteen hundred miles. Pretty much the entire coast-line of Namibia with the south Atlantic. It was named during the sail-ing days because there was no place along that stretch that ships could stop and get water. If a ship didn't make good time down to the Cape of Good Hope, it could get stranded—and all that was there was desert and rock right up to the water."

"So why are the Van Wyks there?" Riley asked.

"Diamonds. That's where the diamond fields are," Conner said. "They own a large section of southwest Namibia that is totally re-stricted. It's the Van Wyks' own private country. They have a security force to control the workers. One of the articles I read said that they even rigged the barracks of workers with video cameras and remote-controlled tear-gas-canister dispensers." Conner paused and wiped her forehead with a rag.

"So we know for sure now that these people are connected to the Van Wyks," Riley said.

"Yes. And I think I'm beginning to see a bigger picture here," Conner said.

"Which is?"

"Right-wingers in South Africa have been proposing a new home-land for whites, and Namibia is high on their list of choices."

"What's that got to do with this?" Riley asked.

"I'm not sure," Conner said, "but if there's a connection between Van Wyks and this disease, then there might be a connection be-tween Van Wyks and the right-wingers."

"You're reaching," Riley said.

"I know, but it's my job." Conner said, leaning back against the seat back.

"You all right?" Riley asked,

"Stupid question, Dave." Conner tried to smile, but she suddenly had to lean forward and throw up.

"Another kilometer," Quinn said. He pulled his canteen out and drank deeply while still walking, trying to replace some of the fluid he was losing and keep his temperature down.

He looked over. Trent and the other man weren't doing too well, either, but Bentley seemed all right. Of course, Bentley hadn't been with them at the ambush.

He had not heard the rev of power indicating the chopper behind them had lifted. What was it waiting for?

## National Security Agency, Fort Meade, Maryland, 17 June

Running through the computer records forwarded to him from the AWACS and the records already in the computer, Waker had come up with a big fat zero as to the identity of the wreckage that had been found in northeast Angola. There was no sign of any aircraft flying over—or crashing in—that exact spot. The Cyrillic writing didn't mean much, because much of the equipment both sides used in Angola had been supplied by the Russians.

Waker sipped his tea and thought about it. Wreckage from the sky? He put the tea down and began typing. Two thousand miles to the west another large computer began scanning, and within thirty seconds he had an answer. On the twenty-first of May, at 0959 Greenwich Mean Time, a piece of space debris had come down with a plotted impact within five kilometers of the indicated place.

"Give me more," Waker whispered as the screen cleared and new letters and numbers appeared, outlining the object that had come down.

> RG14: Proton final stage booster.
> Orbit: Free, plotted, and logged.
> Launch: 18 May 1997
> Launch Site: Kazakhstan
> Comments: Final stage booster for Proton launch of communications satellite contracted out to SINCOM, European Communications. Payload is listed as EG36.

A booster? Waker frowned. He could understand if they had the payload, but just the booster? Shaking his head, he forwarded the information to the Pentagon with a copy for the AWACS in Angola.

## Pentagon, 17 June

It was good news. Or at least a lighter lining to a very dark cloud, General Cummings thought. Z seemed confined to the eastern part of the country. Two companies at remote bases reported men sick. Otherwise the division seemed safe, for the time being. Perhaps they had enforced the quarantine in time, Cummings hoped.

But this other stuff that his G-2—intelligence officer—had put together. Add it all up and it didn't make any sense. The message to the Pan-African forces ordering General Nystroom to halt *prior* to Cummings's own halt. The follow-on plan to seize the diamond areas.

And now this information on a Russian booster rocket coming down in Angola back in May, connected with SATCOM traffic in the same place now.

"All right." Cummings raised his voice and everyone in the War Room ceased his or her activity. "I need a total reevaluation on the situation in Angola. Drop your preconceptions about the strategic scenario. Look at all this new information and give me some possibilities. If this disease is man-made I want to know *who* made it. Who stands to gain by it. And I want options to bring some hurt down on the heads of the sons of bitches if we can pinpoint them!"

### Northeast Angola, 17 June

Raindrops pelted Quinn. He had quit using his night vision goggles because nothing could help a person see in this. He was back to the basics he'd learned as a young lieutenant in the Canadian army: compass direction and pace count. He looked down, then knelt and felt with his hand. Dirt, no grass. He squinted into the dark. It appeared that the runway ran perpendicular to their path.

"We're here!" he yelled, reaching out and grabbing the back of Trent's backpack. The signal was passed and the four men gathered in close.

"How will we know when the aircraft lands?" Bentley asked.

Quinn was shivering now—a down spike in his fever—as water rolled down his body. "If I knew what type of aircraft, that would help. We might have to wait until this thunderstorm passes and the pilot gets an opening. When it lands," he pointed, "we'll see it. Don't worry. Let's just hope it gets here."

He hadn't told Bentley about the FM frequency. Quinn had his survival radio in an ammo pocket on his vest. He was using the same earplug that he did for listening to SNN. So far nothing. His stomach twitched and he leaned over as he vomited into the mud.

The pilot of the Gull was circling on the edge of the thunderstorm, just above stall speed, creeping east with this part of the storm. There was another thunderstorm behind him and he estimated he'd have about a five-minute window to hit the landing strip, make the pickup, and get back in the air.

Eight kilometers to the east, Riley and the others in the helicopter listened to Colonel Harris relay the information from the NSA about the rocket booster.

"Could this thing be some sort of space bug?" Conner immediately asked. They all turned and looked at Dr. Kieling.

"Any bug would have burned up coming down," Kieling said. "Besides, the space program has never . . ." He paused as a thought struck him. "Zero g."

"What?"

"Zero g," Kieling repeated. "Things work differently under zero gravity. Biology—physics—at the molecular level the rules change." He was tapping his forehead. "I read a paper—I'm trying to remember who wrote it. It was about manipulation of the RNA.

"There's a thing called 'transduction.' A virus infects a bacterial cell that has a toxin . . ." Kieling shook his head. "Forget about all that, it's not important right now. But this is starting to make some sense. The blisters on the red rashes. I think that's the way the virus moves—the blister explodes, the virus goes into the air. And Z is different than, say, Ebola because it lasts in the air. It holds together under ultraviolet light longer. And zero g would be the only way to manipulate the virus to get that effect. You could . . ." Kieling came to another halt. "Yeah. It all fits. I see it now. I see it."

"Does that mean you can cure it?" Sergeant Lorne asked, caught up in Kieling's excitement.

"Uh, well, no. But—"

"But shit!" Lorne yelled. "What the fuck are we doing, then?"

"Shut up," Riley said.

"Fuck you!" Lorne stood, as well as he could in the cramped space of the helicopter. He leaned over Riley. "Fuck you. Fuck all you ass-holes. We're dying! Don't you understand that?"

"We don't have time for this," Riley said.

"I don't care—" Lorne began. The anger on his face changed to surprise as Riley uncoiled from his seat, left palm leading in a strike right into Lorne's solar plexus, knocking the wind out of him.

Riley didn't pause, following that with another similar blow with his right palm, causing Lorne to double over. Riley then smashed his left elbow into Lorne's right temple and the team sergeant was out cold.

"Strap him in," he ordered. He put his headset back on. "Anything from the Spectre?" he asked Lieutenant Vickers.

"Negative."

"Keep the engine running."

In the Spectre gunship the storm didn't matter in the slightest. The four powerful turboprop engines cut through the wind and rain and the men in the inside were on task, particularly the target-ing officer, watching his TV set. The thermal imaging also wasn't affected by the weather. He could see as clearly as if it were broad daylight.

They were flying low, doing shallow S-turns. They'd started at the Black Hawk and were ranging out in a cloverleaf pattern, always com-ing back and then back out at a slightly different angle.

In the back of the AWACS, a young technician stared at her screen. She played with her computer for a little while, then she reached up to the rack above it and pulled down a three-ring binder. She flipped through, searching. Finding what she was looking for, she tapped the man next to her. "Hey, Parker, align with me."

Parker switched to the same radar frequency. "What do you have, Cordelli?"

"Just watch."

They waited. "What am I looking for?" Parker asked after a minute.

"There! See it?"

"A shadow," Parker said. "There's a thunderstorm outside, in case you didn't notice."

Cordelli ignored him. "Look what happens when I let the computer project a cross-section based on the shadow."

"What the hell is that?" Parker asked.

Cordelli handed him the binder. "You haven't been doing your homework. Colonel Harris wouldn't be pleased."

Parker read. "The Lockheed Q-Star. It says here that it's an experimental aircraft, and not in production. Hell, it says this thing was tested back in the early seventies."

"That doesn't mean someone couldn't copy it and make their own," Cordelli said. "And they didn't have the radar technology and computer systems we have on this plane back in the seventies. It would be invisible back then. But it isn't now."

Parker handed back the binder. "Your find, you do the honors with the colonel."

The Gull pilot knew he was very close now. He pressed the send button on his stick. "Horseman, this is Gull. Over."

Quinn sat up, ignoring the pain in his stomach and head. He fumbled, then pulled out the radio. "Gull, this is Horseman. Over." He squinted up into the rain. It was getting lighter. The worst was passing.

"Horseman, this is Gull. I'll be down in three minutes. Be ready to load fast. Over."

"Roger that. Out." Quinn stood with difficulty. "Aircraft's inbound. Let's get ready."

"Got him!" Colonel Harris called out. "Got them both!" He had the small airplane on screen for sure now and they had pinpointed the FM ground source.

"Direct in the Spectre and the Black Hawk," he ordered.

Vickers had them in the air even before the message from the AWACS was complete. "We'll be there in two minutes," she said.

Inside the Gull, the pilot held the stick between his knees as he pulled the bolt back on the MP-5 submachine gun. He only had room for one man, and that man was Bentley.

* * *

The pilot of the Spectre gunship leveled off. "What do you see?" he asked his targeting officer.

"I've got them on the ground. Four people." The man played with his camera controls. "I have the plane too. Off to our left. About a half a mile away."

"Eagle, this is One One. What are your orders? Over."

Colonel Harris didn't really understand what was going on, but the latest he was hearing from Washington was not pleasant. And there was the no-fly rule.

"Put it down. Over."

The pilot of the Spectre blinked. "Say again. Over."

"Shoot down the aircraft. Over."

As far as the pilot knew, no Spectre had ever even engaged another aircraft, never mind shot one down. "Keegan," he asked his targeting officer over the intercom, "did you hear that?"

"Yeah," Keegan said. "Far out. We're a fighter now. The jet-jocks will shit when we tell them this. Give me level flight, azimuth, two one seven degrees."

The pilot of the Gull saw the edge of the runway through his NVGs, just ahead. He nudged the stick forward, descending. He had about a second and a half to try and figure out what was happening as a solid line of tracers appeared just in front of him before the plane—and him with it—was torn to shreds by a combination of 20- and 40mm rounds.

"What the hell is that?" Trent called out as they watched the tracers streaking overhead, parallel to the ground.

"Gull, this is Horseman," Quinn called into the radio. "Gull, this is Horseman!" There was only static.

They all turned to look as a Black Hawk exploded out of the rainy dark and flew by.

"There they are!" Riley cried out. "Put us down!"

They landed hard, a hundred meters from the four men Riley had spotted on the flyby.

"What's going on?" Bentley asked.

"Jesus, these fucking people want us bad," Trent said.

The radio dropped from Quinn's fingers into the mud. His head drooped on his shoulders for a long second, then came back up and he looked around. There was just the slightest hint of dawn in the east and the clouds appeared to be clearing.

The third man from Quinn's patrol was lying in the mud, black vomit coming out of his mouth, blood seeping out of his eyes, nose, and ears.

"This is it," Quinn said.

"It, what?" Bentley demanded.

"Ever wonder where you were going to die?" Quinn asked. "Well, this is it."

# Chapter 17

**Northeast Angola, 17 June**

"Do you have us fixed? Over," Riley asked into the boom mike.

"Roger that," the Spectre replied. "We've got the Black Hawk clear. We'll track each individual as you come off. You have four people, about one hundred meters due south of your position. We can finish them for you. Over."

"Negative," Riley replied. "We need them alive. There is something you can do, though." Riley quickly finished giving instructions, then signaled for the other men on the helicopter to move out.

Riley hopped off and slid through the ground fog and the half-light of a sun just clearing the horizon, weapon at the ready. Out of the corner of his eyes he could see Comsky, Oswald, and Tiller on line with him. The sound of the Black Hawk's engine was fading behind them as it shut down.

Riley sidled to the right, getting off the mud of the runway and into the waist-high grass. He got down on his belly and began slithering forward, his clothing immediately soaked by the wet grass, the others following.

When he had made about fifty meters, he halted. "Stand up," he yelled. "Throw down your weapons and put your hands on top of your heads."

"Fuck you!" A burst of semiautomatic fire ripped a few feet over Riley's head.

\* \* \*

Quinn looked at Trent. Trent returned the look with a glare. "I'm not going to be taken in like some animal." The NCO fired another burst from his AK-47. "I can't be locked up."

"We've got a chance," Quinn said. "They want to talk!" He looked at the third man. He was unconscious now, blood seeping out of every pore, covered in black vomit.

A noise caught Quinn's attention. Bentley was turning a knob on one of the cases. "What are you doing?"

"Orders," Bentley said.

"Everyone just fucking freeze," Quinn hissed. "I'm in charge here and I'll make the decisions."

Bentley didn't stop. Quinn rolled twice to get close, then slapped Bentley's hands away from the case. "I said stop."

"Skeleton—" Bentley began.

"Skeleton isn't here," Quinn said.

"I ain't going in, mate," Trent said. He began to stand. Quinn grabbed him and pulled him down.

"What do you think you're doing?"

"I won't be captured! You know that. We agreed."

Quinn nodded. "Yeah, I know we agreed. But we aren't captured yet, so cool your jets." He looked down. His own hands were shaking.

Quinn didn't have time to dwell on his hands, though, because Bentley began fiddling with the case. Quinn finally understood that he was working on a small keypad—activating a destruct device. Quinn drew his knife, grabbed Bentley's right hand, and slammed the knifepoint through the center of the palm, pinning it to the ground.

"Hands up!" the same voice called out, as Bentley screamed, which caused Quinn to smile at the absurdity.

"Who are you?" Quinn called out.

"U.S. Army."

"Why do you want us? We have nothing against you."

"We want to talk!"

"Talk?" Quinn returned. "You shot our plane down."

"We'll shoot *you* if you don't put your hands up."

A line of tracers came down from the sky and tore into the earth less than ten meters away from Quinn's position.

"Next burst is on top of your position," the voice called out.

"We're fucked," Trent said.

"We were already fucked," Quinn amended. He reached over. The third man was dead.

"You can't surrender that case," Bentley said through a grimace of pain.

"Oh, yeah," Quinn said. "So we blow it up and then we don't have shit to deal with these people."

"You can't deal this!" Bentley said, his one good hand reaching for the case.

"Skeleton's got you brainwashed," Quinn said. "Diamonds aren't worth that much." He raised his voice. "You want the imagery, we'll give it to you, if you'll give us free escort to the border."

Riley looked at Kieling, who had come up during the exchange. "Imagery? What's he talking about?"

"I don't know what they might have," Kieling said. "But we need to see it, whatever it is."

"All right," Riley called out.

"That was too easy," Trent noted. "They could just kill us and take the cases."

"Maybe they don't want to damage it," Quinn said. "Or maybe they're afraid we'll blow it up like smart-ass here was trying to do." He could hear the drone of an airplane overhead and knew there was no way out. "We have no choice."

"You can't!" Bentley cried out. "It's not what you think."

Quinn reached over and with one move withdrew the knife from Bentley's hand. "Next time, I won't be so nice," he said. Bentley tucked his bleeding hand into his stomach. "Move and I'll kill you," Quinn continued.

"Stand up!" Riley called out again. He was relieved when a man stood, a Sterling submachine gun in his hands.

"Put the weapon down," Riley called out.

"You've got the big gun in the sky," the man said. "All we've got is our personal arms. You want to talk, we talk like we are now."

Riley glanced at Kieling, who shrugged. "Your call," Kieling said.

"I'll meet you halfway." Riley stood up. He let the M-16 hang by its sling and noticed that the other man did the same with his Sterling. Riley walked forward—the other man doing the same—until they were five feet apart.

"I'm Quinn."

"Riley."

Quinn looked Riley up and down. "I don't see a uniform."

"I don't see one either," Riley replied. The other man looked ill, with the beginning of a red rash running down one side of his neck—which didn't surprise Riley. Everyone out here seemed to be sick. Was sick, Riley amended in his mind.

"You want the imagery?" Quinn asked.

Riley didn't have a clue what he wanted other than answers. "Yes."

"What assurance can you give me that you'll let us go?" Quinn asked.

"What assurance *could* I give?" Riley asked in turn.

Quinn smiled despite his pain. "Good answer, Yank."

Riley had had enough with sparring. He also was surprised at Quinn's attitude. Where did the man think he was going to go now? The border with Zaire was closed. The world was now aware of the quarantine on Z. If Riley was in Quinn's place then—it suddenly clicked in Riley's brain. He *had* been in Quinn's position before. And when he was there he had not been told the truth about what was going on.

"You know you're sick?" Riley asked.

Quinn frowned. "Yeah."

"Do you know how sick?"

Quinn hesitated. "Why don't you tell me?"

"You'll be dead inside seventy-two hours," Riley said. He was surprised when Quinn nodded.

"Aye. I expected as much." He reached into his pocket and pulled out a picture. He handed it to Riley. "We hit some rebels on the eleventh. She was being carried. I knew something was wrong then."

Riley looked at the young woman, ravaged by disease and bullets. Six days ago—just about right.

"The booster you were just at," Riley said. "We think it had something to do with the disease."

This time Quinn did show surprise. "Booster? I was told it was a satellite."

"Who told you?"

Quinn looked over his shoulder. "You say this has something to do with the disease?"

Riley nodded.

Quinn turned. "Come with me."

Riley hesitated. "Can I bring someone?"

"Who?"

"A scientist who specializes in viruses."

"All right."

Riley gestured and Kieling rose and joined them. Together, they walked back to Quinn's group. Riley looked at the dead man lying there, then at the others.

"This is my top. Trent," Quinn said. "This is Bentley," he added, pointing at the man holding a bloody hand. "He's the one who knows what's going on." Quinn kicked Bentley. "Open the cases."

"I can't," Bentley said without much conviction.

Quinn's hand strayed to the knife on his web gear.

Bentley knelt and turned the combination knobs. He flipped the lid open. Inside sat a large metal box, battered and heat streaked.

Kieling looked at the box. He reached to his belt and pulled off a multipurpose tool and used the Phillips head to work on the screws holding the top on. Bentley sat back down, nursing his wounded hand.

Keiling flipped the top off. Inside lay sophisticated machinery.

"What is it?" Riley asked.

"Could it be a camera?" Quinn asked.

"No." Kieling lifted the machine out and turned it over. "No lens." He was looking it over very carefully; then he pointed. "This canister." It was as large as a gallon milk jug. "I'd say it's a dispenser."

"Of?" Riley asked.

"Z."

"Z?" Quinn repeated.

"The virus."

Quinn's eyes opened wide and he turned to Bentley. "You mean this thing we got. He made it?"

"He either made it or he knows who made it," Kieling said.

"You—" Quinn was speechless. His knife was out and he was just about at Bentley's throat when Riley intercepted him. "Easy. We need answers from him. We need him alive."

"I'm not talking," Bentley said. He glared back at Quinn. "You can use your knife all you want, but I'm not going to say anything more."

"Let's take it back," Riley ordered. "And all of you."

"What about safe passage?" Quinn asked.

"You're free to walk to the border if you want to," Riley said.

Quinn looked at Trent, then at Bentley. "We'll go with you."

### Sandoa, Zaire, 17 June

The young French doctor looked up at the sound of trucks rumbling down the road. Three lorries turned into the dirt courtyard of the hospital and soldiers piled out, weapons at the ready, their faces covered with surgical masks.

"What do you want?" the doctor asked.

"We understand you have men here. Sick men who came across the border from Angola," the officer in charge said in perfect French.

The doctor involuntarily glanced over his shoulder at the hospital. "This is an international—" he began.

"You are in Zaire," the officer intoned. "You are under our laws. There is a quarantine in effect along the border. These men entered illegally."

"They are ill," the doctor said. "They require—"

"Where are they?"

"In the isolation wing," the doctor said. "But they—"

The officer ignored him, gesturing. A squad of men ran forward, kicking open the door to the wing. Inside, the surviving members of Quinn's patrol that had been released at the border two days ago lay on cots, tended to by two local nurses. The nurses were the first to understand what was going on and sprinted for the back door. They were cut down by bursts of fire from AK-47s before they made it halfway.

The soldiers walked down the aisle, spraying the beds with automatic fire, ignoring the pleas of those still well enough to beg. The massacre was over in a few seconds.

"You will be held accountable!" the doctor screamed from the doorway.

"Did you tend to these men?" the officer asked.

"You will be held accountable by the international community!" the doctor repeated.

The officer pulled his pistol and shot the doctor through the forehead. "Burn the hospital," he ordered. "I want nothing left standing!"

### Cacólo, Angola, 17 June

"This," Kieling said, using a ruler to point, "is some sort of chamber in which the virus was manipulated in zero g. I can't tell you much more without taking it apart." He moved the ruler. "The virus was then shunted down this tube, to this dispenser. It must have been held there until the booster came down. Then it was sprayed out. Someone probably saw it come down and came to investigate and they were patient zero."

Riley had the imagery. "There's a village here about twelve klicks from the crash site. It's blue. Everyone's dead."

"That's where it started."

Riley looked up at Bentley. Comsky had wrapped a bandage around the man's hand, but he had held true to his word and said nothing since they'd boarded the Black Hawk and flown back to Cacólo. Riley had gotten on the radio and transmitted everything they'd learned so far to Major Lindsay at the AOB, who was forwarding it back to the Pentagon.

"He doesn't seem too worried about catching Z," Conner noted.

"Do you have a vaccine for this?" Kieling asked. Everyone in the tent turned and stared at Bentley.

Bentley simply looked away.

"We know he works for Skeleton," Quinn offered.

"Who is Skeleton?" Riley asked.

"Security chief for the Van Wyks," Quinn said. "Does all their dirty work. I've met him. He's former Rhodesian SAS. A big fucker. You won't mistake him when you see him. About six foot eight, completely bald, and he'd as soon cut your heart out as talk to you."

"Headquartered in Lüderitz?" Riley asked.

Quinn nodded. "Right. How'd you know that?"

"We intercepted your SATCOM and found out where it came down," Riley said.

"Bentley's got to be vaccinated," Kieling said. "He wouldn't have handled this"—he tapped the device from the booster—"like he did, if he wasn't vaccinated."

"A vaccine don't do us much good," Comsky noted.

"But it will save a lot of lives," Kieling said. "Z hasn't finished burning yet."

Riley walked over to Bentley. "You need to talk to us."

"Let me at him," Quinn said, drawing his knife. "Son of a bitch killed us. I'll make him talk."

"I have a better idea," Kieling said. He stood. "I'll be right back. I have to get something from Tyron at the habitat."

### Oshakati, Namibia, 17 June

General Nystroom looked at the new orders that had just arrived, then slowly put them down on the small folding table inside his command vehicle.

"Where did this come from?" Nystroom asked.

"Silvermine."

"I need to talk to Pretoria," Nystroom said.

"Sir, none of our communications links outside of Silvermine are functioning. Silvermine has closed down all other SATCOM channels."

"It figures," Nystroom said. He looked at the orders again. "All SADF are ordered to deploy southward."

"Southward?" the officer was confused.

"Lüderitz," Nystroom said.

"With what mission, sir?"

"It does not say, but I believe it will have something to do with defending that city."

"From whom?"

"I don't know, but we are now in a place I never wanted to be," General Nystroom said. "Order all our South African forces to be prepared to move within the hour. Tell the allied commanders they are on their own." Nystroom sighed. "Please leave me. I have some thinking to do."

**Pentagon, 17 June**

General Cummings looked at the map. "Lüderitz. What do we know about it?"

A staff officer was ready. "The Van Wyks corporation has a compound there. Paramilitary forces to control the miners and protect the mines. G-2 is coming up with the order of battle."

"What's the status on our forces with regard to strike capability?" Cummings asked.

"Jets from the *Abraham Lincoln* could conduct a limited air strike if they had in-flight refueling."

"What about air force units in Namibia near Oshakati?"

An air force officer shuffled his feet. "Uh, we're having some problems there, sir. It appears that we no longer have ground support from the SADF. The whole logistics train is falling apart. We could probably put some planes in the air, but support for continued operations would not be in place for at least two days."

"You didn't consider the possibility that your forces might have to be self-supporting, did you?" Cummings asked the air force officer.

"Sir, we considered it, but the expense would have—"

Cummings ignored him. "I want the *Abraham Lincoln* to turn south at flank speed. I want the Ranger Task Force on board to be given the latest intelligence. I want the ro-ro with the Twenty-fourth Infantry Bradley task force to go south also."

"Yes, sir."

Colonel Martin had been listening to all this planning and finally he had had enough. "Excuse me, sir, but we seem to be forgetting one thing."

"And that is?" Cummings snapped.

"Z."

"What about it?"

"It's still burning, and if Pieter Van Wyks made it, then he has it there in Lüderitz. If he does have a vaccine—which we haven't determined yet—I would assume that his men are vaccinated. Ours aren't. We can't do a damn thing until we get ahold of that vaccine, because even if we win the battle there, we could lose the war in the long run."

## Cacólo, Angola, 17 June

"What's that?" Riley asked.

Kieling held a small black plastic kit. He didn't answer Riley. He opened the case and withdrew a hypodermic syringe. Then he drew out a small bottle of murky liquid. He inserted the needle into the bottle and drew back on the plunger, filling about an inch of the clear plastic tube with the liquid. He took out another bottle and did the same.

Kieling walked over to Bentley. "We've all got this thing—we call it Z—I don't know what you named it. I think you're vaccinated for Z." Kieling shook the needle. "But this—this is Marburg. It might not kill you. Fifty-fifty on that. But it'll make you very sick even if it doesn't." Kieling looked at the others in the tent. "Marburg seems to especially like the eyes and the testicles. Gets in there and really does a number.

"I also put Ebola in here," Kieling continued. "So if the Marburg doesn't kill you, the Ebola will. I've never seen what the two combined do to a monkey, never mind a human. But it will be nasty."

Bentley was staring at the needle. He finally spoke. "You can't do that to me. You're a scientist."

Kieling laughed harshly. "I'm a human being first. A human being who has Z. And you, you're an animal that deserves to die, if you were in on the making of Z." He pressed the tip of the needle against Bentley's neck.

"Please," Bentley begged. "Take it away."

"Is there a vaccine?" Kieling asked.

"Yes."

"Where is it?"

"Van Wyks has it."

"You've been vaccinated?"

"Yes."

Kieling nodded. "We might be able to get it out of him. Out of his blood. But it will take time."

"Is there a cure?"

They all turned and looked at Conner, who had asked the question.

"Is there a cure?" she repeated.

Bentley looked away.

"Answer the lady, you son of a bitch," Quinn yelled.

Bentley looked around the tent. Half the people there already had the beginnings of red welts on parts of their bodies that could be seen.

"Is there a cure?" Conner demanded one more time.

Bentley looked her in the eyes. "Yes. There's a cure."

# Chapter 18

**Pentagon, 17 June**

The War Room listened to the excited voices from Cacólo, relayed through the 82d Airborne Headquarters in Luanda. There had been a bit of confusion at first, trying to identify Riley and his role in things, but General Cummings had quickly cut through the military hierarchy and accepted the situation on the ground in the quarantine site as it was, with Riley in nominal charge.

"We need to get to Lüderitz and get in there," Riley concluded, his voice abnormally loud over the room's speakers.

"I have forces moving," General Cummings said. "Unfortunately, we still have a problem, Mr. Riley. There may be a cure in Lüderitz, but that doesn't mean there will be one still there after we attack. And if the cure is destroyed and they use this disease in defense, we're back where we were an hour ago; actually in a worse situation."

"Let's not go off half-cocked. The *Abraham Lincoln* has just begun heading down there. The naval task force won't be in position for a while. We have time to come up with a plan."

"Sir, *we* don't have time here. We're dying!"

"A lot of people will die if we go in there unprepared," General Cummings reasoned. "There's more going on here. We have South African Defense Forces moving south in Namibia toward Lüderitz, and I don't think they're going there to be on our side. There seems to be confusion in Pretoria in the SADF headquarters. There's fear some sort of coup may be in progress.

"What I want to do is get you and your people in position to help us. From what you've told me, you think you know the vector this takes, is that correct?"

A new voice came. "This is Dr. Kieling. I'm with USAMRIID. This thing is spread by air—not through the respiratory tract, but by bursting blisters on those who have it in the advanced stage."

Cummings glanced at Colonel Martin, who nodded his agreement. "All right, then, we could isolate you on board the *Abraham Lincoln,* could we not?"

"Yes, sir, we could remain as isolated there as we are here."

"Then you need to take your Black Hawk and have the AWACS guide you in to the carrier. I'll inform the ship's captain to prepare for your arrival. In the meanwhile, I want to get a better look at what's around Lüderitz. I'll contact you once you're on board the *Abraham Lincoln.* Out."

### Cacólo, Angola, 17 June

The mood was very different as the Black Hawk took off and headed southwest. Riley knew that hope was a dangerous thing. It was fuel, but if hope was smashed, then everything could go in a heartbeat. Of course, he reminded himself, in this situation any hope was better than the reality they had lived with the last several days.

He sat with Bentley to his right, handcuffed to the seat frame. Kieling was on the other side of the captive, and Riley wanted to continue the interrogation. Quinn and Trent were with them. The mercenaries had insisted on coming, and Riley saw no reason not to allow them. They were all in the same situation, which meant they had the same goals.

Cummings had had a good point, something that Riley had not considered in his excitement over the possibility of a cure. Invading the Van Wyks compound might lead to the destruction of the cure, and many other noninfected people becoming infected.

"The cure," Riley began. "How effective is it?"

"One hundred percent, if you catch the patient before he has developed other symptoms to the point of irreversible damage," Bentley said.

"What form is it taken in?" Kieling asked.

"A shot. We call it Anslum four. What you call Z we call Salum four."

"Where is the Anslum four kept?" Riley asked.

"In a vault in a level four containment facility in the basement of the main building at the Van Wyks corporate headquarters," Bentley said. "It is well guarded."

"Is it booby-trapped in any manner?"

"Excuse me?"

"If we go in to get it, will the Anslum four be destroyed?"

"There is a manual destruct under Mister Van Wyks's control," Bentley said.

"And they are all vaccinated, aren't they?" Riley asked.

"Yes."

"So they don't need the Anslum four?"

"No."

"The manual destruct. Where is it?"

"On the top floor. In Mister Van Wyks's office. And in the lab itself."

"What else is on the top floor?"

"Mr. Van Wyks lives there. His chief of security, whom we call Skeleton, is also there. A very dangerous man."

"Why?" Kieling said. "Why was this done?"

"What? The destruct?"

"No. The virus. Why did you make it? Why was it put down in Angola? Why?" Kieling demanded. He still had the Ebola/Marburg needle in his hand and he shook it in front of Bentley's eyes. "Why?"

"I do not know," Bentley said.

"Bullshit," Riley yelled. "You went through great effort to develop a deadly virus. Why?"

"It was on orders from Mr. Van Wyks."

"Orders?" Kieling repeated. "You make something that could devastate the population of this planet and say orders were sufficient justification?"

"I did not know why Mr. Van Wyks wanted the virus developed. I was told the booster coming down in Angola was an accident. It was our fourth batch."

"Fourth?" Kieling asked.

"Yes. We had to use zero gravity to mechanically manipulate the genetic code of the virus. Our first capsule went up two years ago. The second and third ones last year. We kept perfecting the process and the product. This one was supposed to be brought down like the others: over the Kalahari, recovered, and examined in the biolevel four lab. It was all an accident."

"I don't believe that," Riley said.

"It is the truth."

"It might be what you think is the truth," Riley said. "It might even be the truth, but I don't think it is. Too many coincidences. It just happened to come down in the middle of the Angolan diamond-mine area. It just happened to occur during this peacemaking operation." He stared at Bentley. "Do you believe those were just coincidences?"

Bentley avoided his gaze. "I don't know."

"Didn't you wonder why he was trying to invent a killer virus in the first place?"

"I assumed it was for control," Bentley said.

"Control of what?"

"Control of the workers."

"You need a killer virus to control them?"

"I do not know Mr. Van Wyks's mind. But, to control life and death, is that not the ultimate control?"

### Ovamboland, Namibia, 17 June

A long dust cloud marked the line of vehicles heading south. General Nystroom stood in the track commander's hatch on his personnel carrier and looked up and down the long convoy of armor and trucks.

He knew he was at a crossroads, but he didn't understand the situation. Always before he had been able to negotiate a careful path in an uncertain world by projecting the agendas and goals of the parties involved and balancing them against reality. In his opinion, most people failed because they tended to get so caught up in their own perspective or agenda that they failed to see when their personal view was not in congruence with the reality of the situation.

The Angolan mission was on hold, that was for certain. This disease—Z—that was breaking in the news media and causing the Americans to isolate their troops on the ground was an unexpected factor.

Nystroom knew that army headquarters at Silvermine was heavily infiltrated by officers who owed more allegiance to Pieter Van Wyks than to the government in Pretoria. That was true even when whites ruled there, and was doubly so now. Further, a significant number of officers on his staff held the same allegiance.

With every mile his SADF convoy traveled south, Nystroom saw decades of adroit maneuvering on his part unraveling. Reluctantly he climbed down from the hatch, closing the heavy metal on top and sitting down in one of the jump seats inside. He leaned back and closed his eyes. There was nothing he could do now but follow orders.

**South Atlantic Ocean, 17 June**
Aurora crossed time zones so quickly that there was only one clock on board that they used for reference—Greenwich Mean or, as it was called in the military, Zulu time.

The RSO had a display of southern Africa up on his computer and was calculating the best avenue of approach. "It's a bit over four hundred kilometers south of Walvis Bay," he told the pilot. "Almost a thousand north of Cape Town, so it's not exactly in a crowded space. Let's do two runs. Come in from the northwest, doing a left look along the coast, then racetrack counterclockwise over the ocean and come back twenty kilometers inland, doing another left look toward the ocean. We should get everything like that."

"Just program it," the pilot said. "What about air defense?"

"Unknown. According to the computer the whole area is under private control."

"Private?" the pilot repeated. "Then we won't have to worry much about interdiction. We should get a good look. I'll descend to ten thousand when we make the run."

Eleven minutes later the pilot reduced airspeed as the coast of Africa rapidly approached. The surveillance pod was extended and they raced down the coastline at fifteen hundred miles an hour, the pod gathering in data. From what they could see in their rapid transit at ten thousand feet, Lüderitz was a small port city in the middle of a desert that extended right up to the water.

As the pilot made a four-hundred-kilometer-diameter circle over the ocean for their second run, the RSO ran the video back at slow speed. "I think this compound just south of the city is what the intel dinks want." He froze the frame and the pilot spared a glance down.

Four sets of fences surrounded a ten-kilometer-square enclosure. Centered in the enclosure was a tall building. There were numerous other buildings, all one or two stories. Rail lines led in and out, and there was even a small airport on the inside.

They made the second run without incident and the RSO immediately forwarded the information by SATCOM back to the Pentagon.

### South Atlantic Ocean, 17 June

Lieutenant Vickers had had to compute their flight direction based on where the *Abraham Lincoln* would be when they got over the ocean, as opposed to where it was when they took off from Cacólo. Since receiving the order from General Cummings over three hours ago, the *Lincoln* and its supporting task force had been steaming south at flank speed and had already covered over two hundred and twenty kilometers.

Vickers had to double-check every calculation because it was difficult to concentrate. Her head throbbed and she could see the beginning of a red welt creeping out from under the sleeve of her flight suit, along her wrist.

"I sure hope this ship is where it's supposed to be," O'Malley muttered, watching the fuel gauges. "We don't have enough gas left to get back to dry land if it isn't."

"It'll be there," Vickers said. "I'll get them on the radio for final vectoring." She dialed up the proper frequency and pressed the send button. "Striker Air Control, this is army helicopter Six Four Zero. Over."

"Army helicopter Six Four Zero, this is Striker Air Control. Over."

"Striker, request final approach information. Over."

"Roger, Six Four Zero. We have you on our screens. You're forty kilometers east of our location. Change heading to two zero six degrees. Over."

"Two zero six degrees," Vickers repeated. "Roger. Over." O'Malley made the slight adjustment in their direction.

Striker Air Control had more for them. "Six Four Zero, we're moving at flank speed, thirty-five knots. That's just about forty miles an hour for you land people. Keep that in mind when coming in for your landing. Over."

Vickers smiled. "Striker, this is Cruiser One on board Army Six Four Zero. I know a little bit about knots and landing on a carrier. Over."

A new male voice came on the radio. "Cruiser One, this is Striker Six. Glad to have you coming back to join us. Over."

"Glad to be coming back." Striker Six was the air wing commander on board the carrier—Vickers's boss.

O'Malley had them moving at two hundred and fifty kilometers per hour, so Vickers knew it wouldn't be long before they saw their destination.

"There," she said. "Straight ahead. Home."

"Damn," O'Malley said. "I didn't realize it was so big."

The carrier grew as they got closer, soon filling the entire horizon. Over four football fields in length, the *Lincoln* was the most modern carrier in the navy's arsenal. Its deck was crowded with not only navy jets but also a contingent of army helicopters—part of the joint packaging system the Department of Defense had come up with for carrier task forces to face the new threats of the late 1990s.

Since the *Lincoln* was where Vickers had been launched from, she knew that on board was the army's 1st Battalion, 75th Rangers, and pilots from the elite Task Force 160, who flew the specialized helicopters they had taken on board.

She had been impressed—as the other navy people had been—on the cruise over from Norfolk, with the Rangers. They looked hard and they had trained continuously, live-firing their weapons off the deck of the ship at targets thrown overboard. They'd conducted air assaults back onto the deck of the carrier, rappeling in from the 160's helicopters, both day and night.

Vickers's memories were cut short as they received their final approach information. "Army Six Four Zero, this is Striker Control. We have cleared the forward flight deck for you. Over."

Vickers pointed at the orange panels laid out. "There," and O'Malley nodded. The warrant officer maneuvered them into position and slowly descended, while matching forward speed with the ship's. When their wheels touched down on the flight deck, two crewmen dressed in NBC protective suits ran forward and secured the helicopter to the deck with chocks and chains, then just as quickly ran back to the edge of the flight deck.

Vickers felt like they were on display, crewmen lining the flight deck and on the ship's island looking down, staring at them.

"Six Four Zero, keep all personnel on board. The ship's XO will be out to speak to you in a minute. Over."

"Roger," Vickers said as O'Malley shut the engines down.

Vickers climbed out of the copilot's seat and joined the others on the flight deck on the side of the chopper.

Riley was pleased that they had finally arrived. Sergeant Oswald was unconscious and Comsky had spent the flight hovering over him to make sure that he didn't choke on his vomit. Trent was also unconscious and he had begun the black vomit. Comsky didn't give the mercenary long before he crashed.

Riley stepped onto the flight deck and looked about. After a couple of minutes two men—both in NBC suits, one army-green and one navy-blue—came forward, walking across the deck.

"I'm Commander Owens," the man in the blue navy suit announced, "and this is Lieutenant Colonel Rogers, commander of the First Ranger Battalion." He looked at Lieutenant Vickers. "Welcome back."

"I wish it was under better circumstances," Vickers replied.

Riley introduced himself, then the others, including an explanation of who Bentley was.

"I'm afraid you are going to have to stay out here," Owens said.

"This section of deck has been isolated, and no crew member is to come within forty feet of your location unless suited."

"What's wrong with them?" Colonel Rogers asked, pointing at Oswald and Trent, who were lying on the floor of the helicopter.

"They've got Z," Riley said. "We all have it. He's just the most advanced among us." Riley pulled open his shirt, exposing a spiderwork of faint red welts across his chest. "These will get worse within the next twenty-four hours, then blisters will form. That's the primary way the disease is spread."

"Jesus," Rogers said. "Is there anything my medics can do to help you?"

"Our medical sergeant, Sergeant Comsky, is taking care of us as well as he can," Riley said. "He'll radio over a request for whatever medical supplies he needs."

"Anything we can do or supply, just ask," Rogers said.

"Thank you, sir."

"We're sixteen hundred kilometers north of Lüderitz," Owens said, laying a chart down on the flight deck. They all gathered around. "Right now we don't have any word on possible operations from the Pentagon."

"I have the information you forwarded on where the cure is stored," Colonel Rogers said. "A surveillance overflight was conducted not too long ago, and we should get some idea of security at the site."

"How long until we're in range?" Riley asked.

Colonel Owens pointed at lines drawn on the map. "We will be four hundred kilometers offshore to the north of Lüderitz— within helicopter striking range—by zero four thirty Zulu tomorrow morning."

"We're going in then," Riley said.

Owens looked up from the chart in surprise. "Excuse me?"

"Regardless of what the Pentagon says, we're going in," Riley repeated. He pointed at Oswald. "We'll all be like that by tomorrow evening. We have nothing to lose. Bentley says the cure is in the main building in the Van Wyks compound. It's our only hope."

"We'll be getting imagery soon of the Van Wyks compound," Colonel Rogers said. "I'll make sure you get a copy."

"I can't have anyone going off half-cocked," Commander Owens said. "We have to wait for orders."

"What are you going to do?" Riley asked. "Arrest us? Lock us up?"

"I won't allow your helicopter to be refueled," Owens said.

"Then you'll have to shoot us to stop us from refueling it ourselves," Riley said.

Owens held up his hands. "We have until tomorrow morning. Let's see what the Pentagon comes up with by then."

# Chapter 19

**Pentagon, 17 June**

"What makes you so sure the Van Wyks cartel is behind this disease, other than the word of this man you picked up in Angola?"

Colonel Martin no longer rated a seat at the main table. Besides the various chairmen of each service, several representatives from the White House and Congress were present, including the vice president and the national security adviser, who had just asked the question.

Z was no longer a hidden topic. SNN had the outbreak as its lead story every half hour. The fact that Z was man-made, and that the Van Wyks cartel was the culprit, was still a secret—one of the few advantages the planners still had.

"We've backtracked that booster," General Cummings said. "It's Russian and was launched in Russia, but the payload was commercial. More than half of the payloads the Russians put up nowadays are for pay.

"The satellite that was the payload was owned by a European communications company. It wasn't easy, but the Defense Intelligence Agency has dug through the layers of ownership. It might not be provable in a court of law, but the company that bought the rocket space is a very distant subsidiary of the Van Wyks cartel.

"We've also checked the three previous missions that Bentley talked about. We have those on record, and Van Wyks had an involvement in each one.

"There is no doubt that the mercenaries Bentley was working with were communicating back to the Van Wyks compound in Namibia. We tracked those satellite transmissions with no room for error."

Cummings checked another piece of paper. "Major Tyron, one of Colonel Martin's men on the ground in Cacólo, confirms that Z was in that device that was recovered off the booster by Bentley. He also confirmed that it is a sophisticated mini–remote-controlled laboratory used to manipulate virus DNA and RNA under zero gravity. We cannot pinpoint the manufacture of the device, but the CIA has given us information that the Van Wyks cartel has recruited epidemiologists from the National Institute of Virology in Sandringham, South Africa.

"We have people checking on equipment needed to construct a biosafety level four facility to see if any was bought by a Van Wyks subsidiary. That will take some more time."

Cummings put the paper down. "I believe we have enough evidence—maybe not enough for a court, but enough with people dying over there in Angola—to believe without a reasonable doubt that Pieter Van Wyks was behind this."

"Why?" the vice president asked.

"Sir, we don't know that," Cummings said. "We may never know that."

"What about the place where you think this cure—Anslum four— is?" the national security adviser asked. "Can you get in there?"

Cummings pointed at one of his officers. "My intelligence officer has prepared a briefing on that. Go ahead, Dan."

"It doesn't look good, gentlemen." The G-2 used a laser pointer on the large blow-up of the Van Wyks compound. "The security inside the target building is unknown. The outer security is the equivalent of an armored cavalry regiment."

"Lay it out for us from outside in," General Cummings ordered.

"The port of Lüderitz is capable of handling landing ships, such as those carried by the *Guam*—the amphibious assault vessel accompanying the *Abraham Lincoln* task force. The problem with that is that it will be daylight by the time the *Guam* arrives at the port. A daylight assault by sea is not advisable."

"Waiting another twenty-four hours isn't advisable," the army chief of staff rumbled. "I've got three hundred and sixty-two confirmed cases of Z in the Eighty-second. Twenty-eight among the Special Forces. Sixteen among other assorted support personnel. Of those four hundred and six confirmed, at least a hundred are getting close to being in the acute phase. Which means death within forty-eight hours."

"We understand the time pressure," General Cummings said. "Go on."

"There are at least twenty tanks, sixty armored personnel carriers, and several hundred wheeled vehicles available to the Van Wyks paramilitary forces. This reduces the probability of an air assault force being successful."

"With proper air support we might be able to do it," the army chief of staff said.

"There are also extensive SAM sites, ranging up through SAM-15s, throughout the compound and covering the harbor and rail lines. We estimate a helicopter force would take extensive losses, even coming in under cover of darkness."

"An air preparation could reduce that SAM threat significantly," the air force chief said.

"And lose us the advantage of surprise," General Cummings noted.

"There's something you are forgetting." Colonel Martin felt impelled to speak.

Cummings held up his hand. "I know what you are going to say. They have Z, correct?"

"Yes, sir. If we lose surprise, Van Wyks will destroy the Anslum four, the vaccine, and probably any evidence that he was behind the virus in the first place."

"And any forces we send in face the threat of biological contamination," General Cummings added, turning to the vice president and national security adviser. "It's like a hostage situation except that if we don't succeed in getting the hostage—the Anslum four—out intact, our assaulting forces will all die from infection."

"You have yet to give me any options," the national security adviser noted.

"We have three options," General Cummings said. "One is to wait until our amphibious units are in position—the day after tomorrow—and conduct a joint seaborne and air assault on Lüderitz and the Van Wyks compound, preceded by a thorough air strike to destroy both SAM and armor. The advantage of this option is that it will result in the least casualties during the actual assault. The disadvantage is that we lose surprise and it allows Z to run its course for another forty-eight hours.

"The second option is to attempt an air assault early tomorrow morning as soon as the *Abraham Lincoln* is in helicopter range. The danger in that course of action is that the assault force will face heavy SAM attack on the way in and then will be outgunned on the ground and face armor forces without adequate defenses. The advantage is that it will maintain surprise and it is the quickest option in attempting to seize the Anslum four.

"On both of these two options, we have the additional problem of a high chance that the assaulting forces will become infected with Z, and if the assault fails to gain entry to the underground vault before it is destroyed, they will not have the Anslum four.

"The third option is to pursue a diplomatic solution to this problem. To approach President Mandela and see if he can get the Van Wyks to give up the Anslum four."

The vice president shook his head. "That won't work. Van Wyks is a separate entity over there. There's no way they'll give up the cure. That would be an admission to the entire world that they invented the disease. There's no way anyone would ever admit to that.

"Mandela's got his hands full with his own military right now. This whole thing seems to be tied in with an attempt by right-wingers to set up a separate state. Conveniently they picked Namibia and its diamond mines for that state. We're not even sure who's in charge of the SADF."

"Contacting Mandela would also lose us any surprise," General Cummings added.

The vice president was looking down at his legal pad on which he had made notes. "You say you have a little over four hundred troops infected. Is that number likely to get higher?"

General Cummings looked at Colonel Martin, who stood up. "Our best estimate is that perhaps another hundred soldiers are infected. We believe that Z has been contained at this point. At least among our forces. In Angola the disease is still spreading, although at a slower rate as people become more aware of the problem."

"So we're talking five hundred Americans?" the vice president asked.

"Yes, sir," Martin said.

The vice president sighed. "Gentlemen, we must consider the possibility that we cannot change this situation. That it will run its course."

"What?" the army chief demanded. "Excuse me, sir, but these are—"

The national security adviser raised his hand, silencing the general. "The vice president and I understand the situation, gentlemen. But the options you have laid out do not have a very good chance of succeeding, do they?" He didn't wait for an answer. "As a matter of fact, from what I have heard, many more American soldiers will die. So tell me, what do you expect me to recommend to the president?"

The vice president stood, the national security adviser joining him. "We will be back this evening with the president. Please have some better options, or else we will be forced to let this thing run its course and pursue international sanctions on the Van Wyks." The two walked over to the elevator and the door shut.

General Cummings turned to the others in the room. "I don't like it, either, but we do need a better option. Work on it."

The men and women scattered back to their jobs. Colonel Martin walked over and sat down next to General Cummings. "Sir, there's something else that has to be considered here."

"And that is?" Cummings asked.

"Z. The virus itself. If the Van Wyks have a cure and a vaccine, once they find out that they are suspected, it is likely they will destroy any evidence that would prove that they are behind it."

Cummings was reading a report handed him by his G-2 "Yes? And?"

"And we won't have the cure."

"I know that, Colonel," Cummings's patience was in short supply since the national security adviser's words.

"But, sir, this virus will not just go away," Martin said. "We can contain it among our forces and after sufficient quarantine redeploy those who have survived and are not infected. It will burn out in

Angola eventually. But that doesn't mean it disappears. It will go to ground in some reservoir and will rear its head again and again."

Cummings put the report down. "A reservoir?"

"There's no doubt that Z has gone into other life-forms besides humans," Martin said. "We have not been able to do a thorough study—given the gravity of the situation and the speed with which it has developed—but Z will not kill everything it infects. And it is highly likely that in at least one of the life-forms it will survive and go into a kind of hibernation. And when that life-form comes into contact with a human again, then we will see Z again. And again."

"So you're telling me we're damned if we do, damned if we don't. Correct?"

"Yes, sir."

### *Abraham Lincoln,* 17 June

"If the destruct control is in Van Wyks's office on the top floor—" Colonel Rogers turned his gas mask toward Bentley—"as he says, then we have to go in from the top. Clear down."

Riley tried to concentrate on the imagery. The Van Wyks building was twelve stories high. It did have a helipad on the roof, but there were guards clearly visible in the satellite picture. There were three sandbagged machine-gun positions and they could also make out several men with shoulder-fired missiles on the roof.

Riley had not yet thrown up, but it was not easy keeping his stomach from spasming beyond his control. He had bloody diarrhea, and the two Porta Potti's that the navy had wheeled out onto the flight deck for them were utilized often. He felt terrible, and his interest in Colonel Rogers and the Van Wyks compound was waning. Pain was one thing—Riley could handle pain. Being sick was something entirely different. He wanted nothing more than to just curl up in a ball and detach from his body and reality.

He knew things were getting critical when Conner no longer showed any interest in what was going on. She was lying underneath the helicopter, wrapped in a poncho liner, a bucket near her head.

Riley blinked sweat out of his eyes. Comsky slowly walked up. "Trent is dead."

"Wrap the body," Riley ordered. He looked at Rogers. No words were necessary.

Quinn walked over. "I want in on this assault."

Rogers folded up the imagery. "I hate to tell you this, but we haven't heard anything from the Pentagon other than intelligence. No strike options, nothing. At the rate things are going, I don't think anyone is going anywhere tomorrow."

"We're going," Riley said.

"Your pilots won't be in any condition to fly in the morning," Rogers said.

Riley looked. Chief O'Malley and Lieutenant Vickers were in the same shape he was.

"We're going," Riley said.

Colonel Rogers stood up. "I was told you're ex–Special Forces." He tapped the tab sewn on the left shoulder of his fatigues. "You Ranger qualified?"

"Yes."

"Then I guess you are going."

## Pentagon, 17 June

"Good evening, gentlemen." The president took the seat that the chairman normally occupied and sat down. The rest of the room took their places. "I apologize for not being able to get here any sooner, but as you know I was in Denver this morning and headed back as soon as the gravity of the situation was relayed to me."

The president turned to General Cummings, who was seated to his right. "I've been briefed by the vice president. Have you come up with any better options since this morning?"

General Cummings stood up. "Yes, sir, we have. It's not perfect, but it's the best we can do."

"Go ahead," the president said.

Colonel Martin watched as Cummings briefed the plan they had pulled together that afternoon. The chairman used maps and a mock-up of the Van Wyks compound to emphasize the plan.

While the briefing was still going on, a sergeant entered the room and looked about. He spotted Colonel Martin and as unobtrusively as possible made his way over. He handed him a folder marked "Top

Secret," then exited the room. Martin flipped open the cover and read. By the time he was finished reading, an icy hand had gripped his heart.

Martin looked up. General Cummings was done with his briefing. He remained standing, waiting for the president's reaction.

"It sounds very risky."

"Yes, sir, it is."

"The mission by General Scott," the president said. "Is that necessary?"

"Yes, sir, we believe it is."

"Do you have a probability of success for the actual assault?"

Colonel Martin was impressed that the chairman's face remained expressionless. "We estimate a forty percent chance of success."

"How do you define success?" the president asked.

"Successful recovery of the vaccine and the Anslum four."

"So even if—by your terms—the mission is a success, the assault force is going to take losses."

"It is inevitable, sir."

"How many losses?"

Cummings didn't blink. "We estimate fifty to seventy-five percent casualties in the initial assault force."

The president shook his head. "I'm not sure I can order men to go on such a mission, General."

"Suppose you ask them, sir," General Cummings said.

The president was surprised at that response. "What?"

"I have the men of the First Ranger Battalion and the Second Battalion, Hundred and sixtieth Aviation Regiment on board the *Abraham Lincoln* standing by in one of the hangars. We have a live satellite feed to that hangar. The men have all been briefed on this plan. They know the risks." Cummings pointed at a video camera and a TV next to it. "Not exactly your standard video conference, sir, but it will work."

The president steepled his fingers and considered General Cummings for a long minute, then he nodded slightly. "All right. Put me on."

Cummings pointed at the technician in charge of the rig. The television screen came alive and it showed a cluster of men gathered in a large metal hangar, painted gray. Navy jets could be seen parked in the background. The majority of the men wore camouflage fatigues and had high and tight haircuts—the traditional cut of the Rangers. A smaller group was dressed in one-piece green flight suits and their hair was at the limits allowed by army regulations.

Apparently a screen on their end went live also, showing the president, because the men all jumped to their feet and stood at rigid attention.

"They can hear you, sir," General Cummings said.

"At ease, gentlemen," the president said.

The Rangers merely spread their feet shoulder width apart and snapped their hands to the small of their back—eyes and heads were locked forward. The task force men became more relaxed, but everyone's attention was riveted.

"I understand you have been briefed on the risk of the mission to recover the cure for this virus and to punish those who unleashed it. I just told General Cummings that I have reservations about ordering you on such a high-risk mission. He suggested that I"—Martin could swear he saw the slightest trace of a smile on the president's face—"ask you. It is rather unprecedented, but this situation is rather unprecedented.

"Gentlemen, I would understand if you do not desire to go on such a hazardous operation. There are other diplomatic options that I am prepared to undertake to resolve this issue. The problem is that time is of the essence. Over four hundred members of the Eighty-second Airborne Division are afflicted with this disease and will most likely die unless we recover the cure very quickly."

The president seemed to catch himself. "You know the situation. No one will think less of you for not wanting to go. All those who volunteer, please hold your hand up."

As one, the entire group of men raised their hands. The president glanced at Cummings, then returned his attention to the screen. "Very well. You will hear my decision shortly." The president indicated cut and the screen went dead. He focused on Cummings. "Was that a setup?"

"No, sir."

"Every single man?"

"They're Rangers, sir."

"What about the pilots?"

Despite the severity of the situation, Cummings smiled. "Oh, the task force? They're just crazy, sir."

The president stood. "When do you need to have a decision?"

"To allow the people on the carrier sufficient time to prepare and launch on time, by midnight." Cummings hesitated. "But I have to tell General Scott what to do right away. He has a long way to travel."

The president sighed. "Tell General Scott to do what he has to do. As far as the rest of the plan—I'll have to get back to you after I do some more thinking."

Colonel Martin saw the opening and took it, standing up and catching everyone by surprise. "Sir, there's something you need to know."

The president glanced quizzically at Martin, and General Cummings quickly stepped forward. "This is Colonel Martin. He's head of the medical team investigating Z."

"And what do I need to know?" the President asked.

Martin held up the report. "Z is here."

"Here?"

"In the United States. We have an outbreak at Andrews Air Force Base."

The president slowly sat back down. He rubbed his forehead. "What's happened?"

# Chapter 20

**Luanda, Angola, 17 June**
"The helicopter is ready, sir."

General Scott stuffed his red airborne beret in his pants pocket and ran out to the waiting chopper. He carried no weapon, not even a sidearm. And aside from the pilots and crew members of the Black Hawk, he was going alone.

The aircraft was fitted with extra fuel tanks on pylons. They had a long flight ahead. "Let's go," Scott ordered. The helicopter lifted and they headed due south.

**Andrews Air Force Base, Maryland, 17 June**
The chief coroner looked out his office window and saw the Air Police cars parked outside and the armed guards surrounding the casualty facility.

A man in a full-body biocontaminant suit drew his attention back inside. "Is this the entire list of everyone you had contact with since you worked on the bodies from Angola?"

"Yes."

The man turned to leave.

"What are you going to do with that list?" the coroner asked.

"We're isolating everyone."

**Fort Bragg, North Carolina, 17 June**
When Delta Force had been formed, it had been stationed on the

main post of Fort Bragg, out near the area where ROTC cadets had their billets during their summer training.

A new compound had been built in the early nineties on a more remote part of the post. It included everything they would need, with training areas, ranges, and mock-ups all inside the chain link fence surrounding it.

The guard at the main gate looked up in surprise as a convoy of trucks pulled up and soldiers in gas masks jumped off, weapons at the ready. An officer walked up to the guard. "I'm Colonel Peterson. I need to talk to your commander. Get him on the phone and out here. But in the meanwhile, no one exits this compound." He shoved a piece of paper under the guard's nose. "Orders of the president."

### *Abraham Lincoln,* 17 June

"We're presently located here." Colonel Rogers pointed at the large-scale map. He was no longer wearing his gas mask, only a blue surgical mask. The whole situation had changed since the president had given the go for the mission. There wasn't as much concern that someone might catch Z from the people on the deck. After all, they were going into the center of the hurricane that had formed Z.

Rogers continued. "We were originally going to launch at zero six thirty Zulu, at two hundred kilometers out. That's been changed. The ship's captain is pushing his engines to the max, so we're making better speed than anticipated. Also"—Rogers looked around the room—"that called for enough fuel to remain for all aircraft to make a round trip. We're going now for a one-way mission fuelwise. We're going to launch the first choppers at zero two thirty Zulu, right here. That will be four hundred and fifty kilometers out. That will put our slowest aircraft on target at zero four thirty Zulu. One hour before dawn local time."

Riley nodded. He was feeling slightly better. Whether it was a slight remission in his fever as Comsky said, or the energy born of hope as Conner had told him a few minutes ago, it didn't matter to him. He looked across the flight deck. Some of the Rangers were rigging equipment. Others were doing a last cleaning of their weapons; honing knives; smearing camouflage paint onto their faces. Pilots were walking around their aircraft, using red-lens flashlights to do a final visual inspection.

"There's no sign that anyone in the Van Wyks compound expects anything," Rogers continued. "We have repositioned the KH-12 that was overlooking Angola to give us real-time imagery on the target. The SADF column is now only two hundred kilometers away. It is expected that it will arrive at the compound just at dawn, which gives us a window of about one hour.

"An AWACS is in position off the coast. It will control all flight operations. I will be the commander of all ground forces. I will be on board an MH-60 until the first air assault wave lands. At that time I will reposition to the roof of the primary target. If I am incapacitated or lose communications, my executive officer will command from the C-2 that will drop the initial assault force."

Rogers folded up the map. "Questions?"

"Who do we go with?" Riley asked.

"Those of you who are up to it can go with one of the air assault Black Hawks."

Riley pointed at a group of Rangers who were rigging parachutes. "Can I go with them?"

"You HAHO qualified?" Rogers asked.

"Yes."

Riley could tell that Rogers didn't want him to go with his recon platoon, which had the most difficult and essential mission. The platoon trained to work together and his addition might disrupt their precision. "I'll jump last and hang above until they're all down," Riley added.

"All right. I'll take you over to the platoon leader." Rogers looked out at the ocean, then turned back. "That is all. Good luck and load up."

# Chapter 21

The C-2 that Riley was on was the largest aircraft the *Lincoln* had in its inventory. It was normally used to move personnel and equipment from the vessel to shore and back. Right now the small cargo bay held sixteen heavily armed Rangers in tight proximity to each other, and it was the lead aircraft in the attack procession. Riley adjusted the leg straps on the parachute rig he wore, making sure that they were as tight as he could make them.

Just before he had split from the others who had accompanied him from Cacólo, Comsky had given him a handful of pills. "You don't want to know," the medic had answered when Riley had inquired as to what the pills were. "They'll keep you functioning for a few hours." So far whatever Comsky had given him was keeping him alert and the sickness at bay.

"Ten minutes!" the jumpmaster called out. They were up high, over thirty thousand feet, and the cabin was pressurized.

What Riley found fascinating was the fact that the Ranger Recon element only had eight parachutes for the sixteen men. He had seen dual rigs—two people hooked together in harness with one chute—used by civilian jump instructors to train novice jumpers but had never imagined they would be used by experienced military parachutists. One man was attached in front of the man with the parachute on his back, the harness keeping the pair tight together for the ride down.

"Six minutes. Switch to your personal oxygen and crack your chem lights."

Riley stood up at the front of the cargo bay, behind the coupled parachutes. He unhooked from the console in the center of the cargo bay that had been supplying his oxygen up to now and hooked in to the small tank on his chest. He took a deep breath and then reached up and cracked the chem light on the back of his helmet.

"Depressurizing."

Riley swallowed, his ears popping. A crack appeared at the back of the plane as the back ramp began opening. The bottom half leveled out, forming a platform, while the top half disappeared into the tail section.

"Stand by," the jumpmaster called out over the FM radio as he inched forward until he was at the very edge, looking out into the dark night sky. Riley knew from Colonel Rogers's briefing that they were still over the Atlantic, outside the twelve-mile international limit to avoid attracting any attention from ground-based radar.

"Go!" The jumpmaster and his buddy were gone. The others walked off, the pairs moving in unison. Riley went last, throwing himself out into the slipstream and immediately spreading his legs and arms akimbo and arching his back, getting stable.

He counted to three, then pulled his ripcord. The chute blossomed above his head. He slid the night vision goggles down on his helmet, checked his chute, then looked down. He counted eight sets of chem lights below him. He turned and followed their path as the Rangers began flying their chutes in toward shore. With over five miles of vertical drop, they could cover quite a bit of distance laterally by using their chutes as wings. Riley didn't know what the current record was, but he had heard of HAHO teams covering over twenty-five lateral miles on a jump. He felt confident that with the sophisticated guidance rigs the front man of each pair of jumpers had on top of his reserve chute, they would find the target. All Riley had to do was follow.

Riley was cold for the first time in weeks. Even at this latitude, thirty thousand feet meant thin air and low temperatures. As he descended, it got warmer. Eventually he could see the coastline through his goggles. The white of the surf breaking on the rocks was a bright line, running north and south. Riley's hands were on the toggles that controlled the chute, both turning and descent rate. He adjusted as the line of chem lights below him changed direction slightly. He checked his altimeter: fifteen thousand feet. Not long now.

Twenty kilometers out to sea, the first wave of the air assault element was flying in toward the coast. Four AH-6s—known as Little Birds—led the way. They were modified OH-6 Cayuse observation helicopters. The AH-6 is one of the quietest helicopters in the world, capable of hovering a couple of hundred meters from a person and not being heard. The two pilots both wore night vision goggles and used forward-looking infrared radar to help fly in the night.

Two Little Birds carried a 7.62mm minigun pod and the other two 2.75-inch rocket pods. In the backseat of each aircraft, two Ranger snipers armed with thermal scopes provided additional firepower. The Rangers wore body harnesses and could lean completely out of the helicopter to fire their rifles.

Ten kilometers behind the Little Birds, four Apache gunships followed. Besides the 30mm chain gun mounted under the nose, the weapons pylons of each bristled with Hellfire missiles. A Black Hawk helicopter was directly behind the Apaches: Colonel Rogers's command aircraft. And ten kilometers behind the Apaches came the main ground force: eight Black Hawks carrying ninety-six Rangers ready for battle.

At a higher altitude and circling, the air strike force from the *Abraham Lincoln* was poised. It was an eclectic group of aircraft, chosen for the job each could do: F-4G Wild Weasels to suppress air defense; F-18 Hornets with laser-guided munition to follow, along with A-6 Corsairs with their heavier loads.

And circling high above it all was Colonel Harris in his AWACS, coordinating carefully with Colonel Rogers to make sure that everything arrived on target at just the right moment.

Riley understood the tandem rigs now. The man in the rear was flying the chute. The man in front, not having to bother with controlling the toggles for the difficult maneuvering to land on the roof, held a silenced MP-5 submachine gun in his hands with a laser scope.

The jump formation broke apart two hundred feet above the roof of the Van Wyks headquarters building. Riley knew the guards on the roof had to be awake, but would they be looking up? Not likely, he knew, and that was what they were counting on.

There was a brief sparkle to one side and below. The only sign that one of the Rangers was firing. Through his earplug, Riley could hear the men call in.

"Machine gun one clear."

"Machine gun two clear."

"Sam Two clear."

"Machine gun three clear."

"Sam One clear."

"Team one down."

The first Rangers were down on the roof, and it was clear of opposition without any alarm being sounded. So far so good. Riley let up on his toggles and aimed just off center of the roof. There was a large radar dish there blocking him from landing dead center. He could see the Rangers clearing themselves of their parachute rigs and moving on the next phase.

Riley pulled in on his toggles and braked less than three feet above the roof. His feet touched and he immediately unsnapped his harness, stepping out of it even before the chute finished collapsing. He turned, looking about, MP-5 at the ready. He could see bodies in the sandbagged pits. A clean sweep.

Then Riley did what the guards had failed to do. He looked up and it was as he'd feared: a video camera was set up on the struts holding up the radar dish. The small red light on top of the lens was on and it was panning the roof. They hadn't spotted the camera in the imagery because it was inset under the radar dish. Riley tucked the butt of the MP-5 into his shoulder and fired a burst into the camera, destroying it.

"We've been spotted by a camera," he called out into the boom mike just in front of his lips.

"Go in now!" Colonel Rogers's voice yelled over the radio. "Everyone move up the pace!"

The Rangers had been carefully placing shaped charges on the roof; four different charges, evenly spaced. Bentley had been unable to tell them which corner Van Wyks's office was in. He'd never been allowed up on the top floor. They abandoned their careful placement at Rogers's order, and hurriedly ran out their detonating cord.

"Fire in the hole!"

The charges blew, searing the night with their explosive crack and brief flash. Four holes appeared in the roof, and Rangers jumped down into each one.

Riley paused, head cocked to the side. A roar of automatic fire reverberated out of the southwest hole. Riley sprinted over. A jagged opening, four feet in diameter, beckoned in the concrete.

Riley pulled a flash-bang grenade off his vest and tossed it in, counted to three, then jumped in, just as the grenade went off. He was firing even before he hit the ground. Except he didn't hit the ground. He landed on the body of one of the Rangers and fell to his right side. It saved his life. A string of tracers ripped by, just above his prone body.

Riley stuck the MP-5 up and blindly returned the fire, spraying in the direction the tracers had come from. He heard the sound of a magazine being changed and was just about to move when he froze. That was too obvious. He rolled onto his stomach and peered about. Both Rangers were dead. There was a desk to his left. A wet bar in the direction the bullets had come from. That was where the man was. Whoever he was, he was using the mirror. Riley fired, shattering the glass.

"Very good," a heavily accented voice called out.

Riley put a couple of rounds into the bar, confirming what he'd suspected. He wouldn't be able to shoot through it.

"You're outnumbered," Riley yelled. "Give it up."

"I doubt that my men are outnumbered so quickly. You came by parachute. I saw you on the video, which gave me time to be ready. Still no helicopters—haven't heard them. I do believe that my people will get here more swiftly than yours. And I'm not outnumbered in this room, am I? I saw only one of you come down. That is after I shot the first two who came through."

Riley checked the angles. "You talk too much, Skeleton," he said.

There was a booming laugh. "You know me. What's your name?"

"Riley."

"Riley," Skeleton repeated. "What are you?"

"Special Forces," Riley said, not wanting to get into a detailed discussion of his status. The clock was running. "Where's Van Wyks?"

"What do you want him for?" Skeleton asked.

Riley heard just the slightest sound of someone moving over broken glass. "We want the Anslum four." Skeleton could come from around either side of the bar, and if Riley picked the wrong one, the other man might get the first shot.

"I told Pieter that he had raised the stakes too high," Skeleton's voice sounded like it came right from the center of the bar. "There was no need for a gamble—but Pieter—he's been living alone with too much money and power for too long. No longer in reality."

A small object came flying over the top of the bar. Rrenade, Riley thought, and reacted, rolling right. Skeleton was right behind the object, vaulting the bartop—which didn't make any sense if it was a grenade. Riley knew he'd made a mistake as he fired offhand with the MP-5, still rolling.

Skeleton was also firing in midair, his bullets trailing Riley's rolls by a few inches, Riley's winging by him.

Riley slammed into the wall just as the bolt in his MP-5 slammed home on an empty chamber. He scrambled to his knees and froze. Skeleton—all six feet eight inches of him as Quinn had described— was standing in the center of the room, a folding-stock R-4 assault rifle looking like a toy in his massive hands. Except the muzzle trained right between Riley's eyes didn't look like a toy.

"I'd like to chat, but I must get my men ready for your follow-on forces," Skeleton said. "Good-bye, Yank." He squeezed the trigger and nothing happened.

Both men reacted instantly, throwing down their empty weapons and whipping out pistols and training them on each other's foreheads.

"Well, well, well," Skeleton said. "Standoff."

"I've got nothing to lose," Riley said. "I already have your virus. Where's the destruct for the biolevel four lab?"

"Well, I do have something to lose," Skeleton said. His left hand slid down to his belt and came up with a wicked-looking Bowie knife. "Man to man—blade to blade," he said.

Riley knew he could kill Skeleton with a shot to the head, but that would still leave the secret to the destruct unknown. He didn't know how the other Rangers were doing, but he had to assume that if Skeleton was in this room, then the destruct was in here. Or at least one of the destructs.

"All right," Riley said. "Man to man."

Skeleton slid his pistol back into his holster. Riley drew his thin, double-edged Commando knife.

"Mine's bigger." Skeleton laughed.

Riley fired twice, both rounds tearing into Skeleton's right thigh and half spinning the big man around. Riley leapt forward, throwing aside his pistol.

Their blades met with a spark, then both stepped back.

"You fuck," Skeleton said, glancing down at the blood pumping out of his leg.

Riley circled left, blade up. "Fuck your man to man shit. One thing I learned on the streets of the Bronx was there is no such thing as a fair fight." He staggered, feeling a wave of nausea.

Skeleton's blade flashed forward. Riley ducked and swung his blade up at the other man's gut, but Skeleton was surprisingly agile for his size, and the knife only caught air.

They both backed off again. There was a burst of automatic fire from somewhere else on the floor. Skeleton smiled. "My men."

Comsky's pills were wearing off. Five feet separated Riley from the other man. Riley stumbled back, and as he expected, Skeleton reacted, coming forward, blade leading. Riley threw his knife in one smooth motion. Skeleton twisted, the knife slicing along the side of his face and blood spurting forth.

Riley's arm continued the motion and he slammed down on Skeleton's knife arm with his left hand. His right elbow came up, catching the big man on the chin and staggering him back.

"I still have mine," Skeleton said, tossing his knife from one hand to the other, then back. Riley backed up until he felt the wall come up behind him.

Skeleton stepped forward. He was circling the knife, looking for the kill.

The knife flashed forward and Riley reacted, swinging his right forearm up and deliberately catching the point in the flesh. Riley twisted his right arm, ignoring the agony of sliced muscle. His left hand clamped down on Skeleton's knife hand. The knife popped out of Skeleton's hand, more from surprise than the strength of Riley's move.

Riley didn't give him a chance to recover. With all his might he slammed a punch—the middle knuckle of his left hand leading the way—into Skeleton's right eye. The orb crunched under the impact and Skeleton screamed in agony.

Riley pulled the knife out of his forearm and dropped it to the ground. He reached down with his one good hand and drew Skeleton's pistol out of the holster, then snap-kicked the man in the chest, driving him away.

Riley pointed the gun at him. "The destruct controls?"

Skeleton's remaining eye saw the gun, but he shook his head.

Riley fired, the round ripping into the other leg and dropping Skeleton to the floor. "The destruct control."

"Fuck you," Skeleton said. "Pieter's got it. It's a remote."

"Where's Pieter?"

"Down in the vault."

Riley aimed and fired two rounds into Skeleton's forehead. A searchlight came in the window from a helicopter hovering just outside. Riley could see the Ranger sharpshooters hanging out the window and the small laser dots creeping around the room, searching for targets. He saw something on a table and grabbed it, putting it into one of the pockets on his combat vest.

He pulled down the boom mike, which had been knocked askew when he'd first jumped down into the room. "This is Riley. Van Wyks has the destruct control and he's down in the basement. Over."

The first rule of military operations was What can go wrong will. Colonel Rogers was improvising, keeping things flowing. Since Riley's first call that the video had caught the recon platoon landing on the roof, he'd been running this by the seat of his pants.

The Little Birds were in without incident, flitting about the main building, unnoticed so far. But reaction was coming. The AWACS was picking up antiaircraft radars being activated—seeking targets. The main air assault force couldn't go in until that problem was taken care of.

And now Riley was saying that the recon platoon had failed in its mission. They didn't have the destruct control. For all they knew, the mission was already a failure. Rogers briefly considered halting and cutting his losses—for all of half a second.

"Eagle, shut down these radars and take out the ground reaction forces. Phase three."

"This is Eagle. Roger. Phase three. Out."

Riley kicked open the door to the room he'd been in, his re-loaded MP-5 in his left hand. He spotted two men in khaki with their backs to him firing around the corner. Riley killed them with one burst.

"This is Riley!" he called out, moving down the hall. Turning the corner he met three Rangers—all that were left of the sixteen who had come down. They gathered by the stairwell, one of them hold-ing his muzzle inside the door, firing an occasional shot to keep more of Van Wyks's men from coming up.

"The floor's clear," a young staff sergeant, the ranking survivor of the recon platoon, reported. Now that the firing had stopped—how-ever briefly—the reality of the situation was setting in and there was a quiver in his voice.

"All right," Riley said. "We have to get to the basement."

"There's eleven floors of people between us and the basement," the sergeant reported. "We blew the elevators." He pointed at the stairs. "That's the only way down."

"No, it isn't," Riley said.

The F-4G Wild Weasel was the only remaining version of the ven-erable F-4 Phantom still in the U.S. inventory. It had one very spe-cific job—kill enemy radar and antiair systems.

Two Weasels came in on Eagle's orders fast and high out of the west. The radar systems of the Van Wyks compound picked them up and locked on, just as Colonel Harris, orbiting far overhead in the AWACS, had hoped.

Missiles leapt off the wings of the Weasels—Shrike, AGM-78, and

Tacit Rainbows—fancy names for smart bombs that caught the enemy radar beams and rode them down to the emitters.

The pilots of the Weasels banked hard and were already one hundred and eighty degrees turned when the missiles struck. Almost all of Van Wyks's air defense went down in that one strike.

The Little Birds were going down the building floor by floor, now that they knew the top was all friendlies and all the other floors were the bad guys. The two armed with 7.62 miniguns were firing through windows, shooting blindly. The Ranger snipers hit anything they saw moving. Windows shattered out and tracers crisscrossed the floor, tearing through walls. The men inside lay low, hiding from the carnage as best they could.

The two Little Birds with rockets had a more difficult job. They were firing up the barracks buildings nearby as troops poured out of them. As the first armored vehicles began appearing, they switched to those.

The four Apaches arrived just in time and fired a salvo of eight Hellfire missiles at the armor. Each one was a kill.

"Balls to the wall," was Colonel Rogers's less-than-elegant order to the pilot of his Black Hawk. The other eight Black Hawks holding his main assault force were right behind him.

"There's the coastline," the pilot said. "We'll be there in four minutes."

Next to Rogers, Conner Young held the camera steady, filming Rogers as he barked out commands. She felt very calm, as if she weren't really there, simply watching a scene play out in a movie. After all that had happened the last several days, she wondered that she could even move.

The Rangers had blown the two elevators the Ranger way—simply and violently by throwing satchel charges into the shafts, which had landed on the cars eleven floors below. Nothing remained of either—just a gaping shaft. With a steel cable running down the center attached to nothing.

"Ever fast-rope a steel cable?" Riley asked. Fast-roping was a way of infiltration from a helicopter—using an eight-strand Pli-moor synthetic rope that soldiers grabbed and slid down.

"We . . ." The sergeant paused and looked at Riley to see if he was serious. The other man was wrapping a dressing tight around Riley's forearm, slowing the bleeding. "Sir, I don't think that will work," he finally said, looking at the thick steel cable.

"Won't know until we try," Riley said. He grabbed a cushion off the couch in the small foyer that the elevators opened onto, then leaned into the shaft. He wrapped the cushion around the cable, then jumped out.

He almost lost his grip—he had almost no control of his right arm. He hooked his left all the way around the cushion and cable and grabbed his harness with his left hand as he plummeted down.

The cushion began shredding and Riley wondered which he would run out of first—cushion or altitude. He hoped the latter.

A pair of SAM-7—shoulder-fired heat-seeker missiles and thus not affected by the Weasel attack—streaked up at one of the Apaches. The craft exploded in a ball of flame.

"Shit," Colonel Harris muttered as he saw the signal for the Apache disappear and heard the pilot screaming before the radio went dead.

His mood didn't get any better as one of his analysts called out. "Sir, the SADF convoy is five kilometers from the west gate of the Van Wyks compound!"

Riley hit hard as the last shreds of the cushion disappeared. He shook his head to clear it and looked about. A letter was painted on the wall next to the doors—B.

Riley unhooked the sling of the MP-5 and held it. He hooked the stock into the doors and pushed. At the pressure they opened like they were designed to in an emergency.

Riley rolled into the room, ready to fire. Nothing. Just a short corridor ending at another set of steel doors. He heard a noise behind him and the staff sergeant came sliding down.

"Fuck, sir," the sergeant said with a grin. "That was wild."

\* \* \*

One of the Little Birds was hit by ground fire and autorotated down. Once it was on the ground, the four men got off and immediately became embroiled in a gun battle with ground forces. The Apache pilots were firing wildly now, trying to suppress any SAM shoulder-fired missiles. They would be out of ammunition in another minute at their current rate of expenditure.

"One minute!" the pilot said.

Rogers grabbed his M-16 and put a round in the chamber. It was going as they had expected—heavy losses—and they still didn't have the Anslum 4. And the SADF armored column was knocking at the gate.

"Two on the roof," Rogers ordered. "The rest on the ground."

Two Black Hawks broke off and gained altitude, heading up to put their men down on the roof. The other six stayed low.

"Up or down?" Rogers's pilot asked.

"Down," Rogers said. He watched, shocked, as one of the two climbing Black Hawks was hit by a SAM-7 and banked over hard, the pilots trying to keep control, then exploded in a ball of flame as it hit the side of the building.

Conner held the camera steady, but she could see the bodies inside the helicopter as it slid down the side of the building. She thought of all the young men with the high and tight haircuts smiling and joking as they'd boarded the helicopters on the *Abraham Lincoln*. The Black Hawk touched down and she jumped off, following Colonel Harris. The chopper was back up and gone just as quickly, the pilots eager to get out of this inferno.

Riley felt the building shake.

"What the fuck was that?" The three Rangers looked up as if they expected to see the roof cave in. One had not done so well on the ride down and his hands and forearms had been ripped open. The staff sergeant was bandaging him as best he could, but it was obvious to Riley the man was out of the fight.

"I don't know," Riley said. He pointed at the door. "I need that open."

"I got just the right tool," one of the Rangers said, shrugging off his backpack. "Shaped charges. Burn through three feet of concrete like crap through a goose," he said lovingly as he held up a conical black object.

At the main gate to the Van Wyks compound the security guards were inside two Ratel-90 armored vehicles, their main guns pointing down the road. They could hear and see all hell breaking loose inside the compound, but their job was the road, and one thing Skeleton had stressed was to do the job assigned.

In the faint light of morning they could see a long dust cloud coming from the northeast. The highest ranking guard stood up in his commander's hatch and peered through his binoculars. He relaxed when he saw the old South African flag flying from the lead vehicle. Help had arrived as Skeleton had promised.

Colonel Rogers's men were pinned down. Two of the Black Hawks were stuck with them in their makeshift perimeter around the headquarters building—too shot up to take off again. One of the Little Birds had joined them on the ground, its hydraulics shot out. The others were gone. Colonel Harris had pulled all helicopters that could still fly out of the fight to avoid more losses.

A Ratel-90 came nosing up a hundred meters from the building. A Ranger fired an AT-4 antitank weapon and missed. Another AT-4. This one hit and the Ratel exploded.

Rogers could see a cluster of armored vehicles massing to the south. AT-4s would only do so much. His men were heavily outgunned. As they had been afraid they would be.

"Steady men, steady!" he called out. "Don't waste any of your antitank shots!"

Riley's head rang from the explosion. He peeked around the edge of the elevator shaft. The steel doors were twisted on their hinges. He ran forward and leapt through into the room beyond, no longer caring if he was met by bullets.

He skidded to a halt. He was in a large laboratory. A pressure hatch on the far side must lead to the biolevel four lab, Riley guessed. But his attention was riveted on the lone person in the room.

Pieter Van Wyks was seated at a desk. Between Riley and the desk was a thick clear wall. The old man held up a hand, displaying a device looking very much like a TV remote control.

"Looking for this?" Van Wyks's voice came out of a speaker in the ceiling.

Riley fired a shot at the glass just to check. The round didn't even make a shatter impact as it just ricocheted off.

"You won't get in here that easily," Van Wyks said. "If you try to destroy this glass with an explosive, I will simply push this button—" the liver-spotted hand twitched—"and the Anslum four is gone. That is what you're here for, isn't it?"

"Why?" Riley said, letting the MP-5 hang on its sling. He signaled for the two Rangers to lower their weapons as they came charging through.

"Why?" Van Wyks laughed. "Why? Because I could. Because there simply are too many people. The scientists whine about it in the newspapers every day. Too many people. Too many mouths to feed. Too much pollution. Too many wars. Too much of everything bad. All caused by too many people who aren't worth a damn.

"You do know, of course, that viruses are nature's defense, don't you? It was bound to happen soon. Within twenty years, according to the information I was given by the best minds money could buy. Either a virus, or our own man-made scourge, nuclear weapons. I just helped it along a bit."

Van Wyks shrugged. "Didn't quite work like I had planned, but there's not much I can do about that now. I suppose I will have to negotiate my way out of this."

"You're crazy," Riley said. "You aren't going to negotiate your way out of this."

Van Wyks turned slightly and pointed. A television monitor was mounted on a bracket. The screen showed the main gate to the compound. "Your force above will not last much longer. Help is just a few minutes away, then I will be back in control. Namibia will be the new homeland. I still have the virus, which means I still have power. Oh, they'll negotiate, all right."

Riley was looking around. The only way into the room Van Wyks was in was through a door made of the same clear material. The latch was solid and looked like it could take a pounding.

Van Wyks smiled. "You've lost."

The lead vehicle in the convoy was a quarter mile away. The guards were waving small flags—the old South African flag, from before the change in power.

The flag flying from the antenna of the lead tank suddenly flew off, the line holding it there cut. Something snapped in the breeze, being held by the man in the top hatch—two pieces of cloth, one in each hand.

The guard post commander snapped the binoculars to his eyes. The new South African flag and the red, white, and blue of the Americans.

"Load the gun!" he screamed. The words were barely out of his mouth when there was a puff of smoke from the end of the muzzle of the lead tank. A second later the round hit the guards' Ratel, blowing the turret off and killing all inside.

In the second vehicle in the convoy, General Scott slapped General Nystroom on the back. "Your boys sure can shoot."

"Let us hope we are not too late," Nystroom replied, then he began issuing orders over the radio, deploying his forces.

Riley looked down from the video monitor to Pieter Van Wyks. "No, you've lost." He reached down on his vest and pulled out a small device, the size of a cellular phone, that was in one of the pockets. He pressed a button on the back side of it.

"Got another of those shaped charges?" Riley asked.

"Yes, sir." The staff sergeant put down his backpack and pulled out another black conical charge.

"I'll destroy the Anslum four!" Van Wyks screeched.

"Go ahead," Riley said.

The Ranger put the convex side of the charge right up to the bulletproof glass opposite Van Wyks's desk. He began reeling out the det-cord used to ignite it.

"Stop that! You can't do that!"

"He's doing it," Riley said. He felt energy draining from his body, and with that loss the return of the fever and sickness. He staggered over to a chair and sat down.

"I'll destroy the cure!" Van Wyks screamed. "We can make a deal!"

"I've heard that before," Riley muttered. He held up the electronic device. "I'm jamming your destruct device," he said in a louder voice. "You don't think we wouldn't be prepared for that?"

Van Wyks's eyes got wide. He looked at the shaped charge, at Riley, at the glass door, and beyond it the level four lab. "Please!"

"Fire the charge," Riley said quietly.

"No!" Van Wyks threw down the remote and stood. "No! You can't! We can make a deal. I have—"

The shaped charge exploded, sending a cone of heat and force right through the glass and obliterating Van Wyks.

The concussion knocked Riley out of the chair and into unconsciousness.

# Chapter 22

**Lüderitz, Namibia, 17 June**

"What?" Riley blinked, trying to focus. All he could see was a face—Comsky's hairy face. "Jesus, hell of a way to wake a guy up."

"You weren't asleep," Comsky said. "You passed out. Lucky to be alive, as much blood as you've lost and all else that's wrong with you," Comsky said as he slid a needle into Riley's left arm.

"What?" Riley muttered. "What's that?" he asked, nodding at the needle.

"Anslum four," Comsky said, expertly sliding the needle out. "We got it. There was quite a bit in the lab. We also found the records that give the process to make it, and we're sending it out. Back to Angola and to the States."

"Conner?" Riley twisted his head. He was still down in the basement of the building. He could see the shattered bulletproof glass and the smear that had been Pieter Van Wyks on the far wall. The door to the biolab was open, and people were moving in and out.

"I'm here," a woman's voice to his right said. "I've already had my shot." Conner reached out a hand and touched his forehead as Comsky went to work on his forearm.

"Shit, Dave, you really fucked this up," Comsky said, peering through the blood at torn muscle.

"Great bedside manner," Riley returned, but his heart wasn't in it.

"Where did you get the electronic jammer from?" Conner asked. "The two Rangers who were down here told me what happened."

Riley pointed with his good hand. "That's it."

Conner picked it up. "Looks like a cellular phone to me," she said.

"I guess that's what it is," Riley said. "I grabbed it upstairs when Skeleton told me the destruct was a remote."

Conner's eyes widened. "You mean you—"

"Van Wyks wouldn't have made a good poker player," Riley said. "What's going on?"

"You'd be better off asking what isn't going on," Conner said. "Let's see. As Comsky told you, we have the Anslum four. Since the antidote is so perfectly tailored to the virus, it works very quickly. I'm already feeling better and you should in an hour or so.

"The South African Defense Force has sealed this entire area and disarmed the remainder of Van Wyks's forces. Apparently General Scott of the Eighty-second linked up with the SADF commander in Namibia and got him to switch sides. If he ever was on Van Wyks's side to start with.

"As soon as the threat from Z has passed, the Angolan operation can be completed. You'll be glad to know your guess about Savimbi was correct. We just heard that he has been confirmed dead in a helicopter that was shot down on the first day. He must have been out checking a village infected with Z and he was shot down on the way back."

"What's the death count from Z so far?" Riley asked.

Conner shook her head. "We don't know that. Based on the imagery, at least two thousand Angolans out in the countryside. For the American forces, we've had sixteen people die. There are a couple dozen more who are on the borderline where the Anslum four might be too late."

"What about here?" Riley asked. "The Rangers?"

"Not so good," Conner said. "Forty-two dead. Twenty-one wounded."

The numbers were people to Riley. "We have to make sure this never happens again."

# Epilogue

**Lüderitz, Namibia, 17 June**

Riley had no feeling in his right forearm. It was tightly wrapped in white gauze and immobilized. He knew from bitter experience that the pain would come—throbbing and aching. But for now it was all right.

Bradley fighting vehicles from the 24th Infantry were mixed in among SADF vehicles around the devastated headquarters building for the Van Wyks cartel. Helicopters shuttled in, bringing additional troops and removing the survivors of the Ranger assault.

Smoke still drifted up from crashed helicopters and the bodies were still there, covered with ponchos and guarded by grim-faced paratroopers. And there was Conner, catching all of it with her camera. Riley watched as she placed it down on top of a destroyed Ratel-90 and stepped in front of it.

"This is Conner Young, reporting to you from Lüderitz, Namibia, where, early this morning, U.S. Army Rangers conducted a daring and courageous assault to secure the cure for the virus that has been ravaging Angola. A virus made by man—a man—Pieter Van Wyks.

"The why and how of the disease—which we called Z and his scientists called Salum four—will come out over the next several days. But that's not the story right now. The story is that a threat to all people was made here. And it was unleashed in Angola. A crime was committed against mankind and this was the response. As it must be in the future.

"Even those who do not believe in war or politics conducted by force of arms must understand and accept that the threat that became real here will continue to exist. And the only way we can keep it from becoming a reality again is to ensure that future responses will be just as swift and fierce.

"Men died here. Brave men. Many of them young and in the prime of their life. But what they died for . . ."

As Conner continued, a shadow came up on Riley's side. He turned his head. Quinn had the stub of a cigar in his mouth, watching her. "Nice words," the Canadian said. He spit out the mangled remains of the cigar. "But words don't count for much."

"No, they don't," Riley agreed. "But they're better than staying silent."

Quinn jabbed a thumb at the headquarters building. "Van Wyks opened Pandora's box," he said. "I don't think we can put the top back on."

"Pandora's box," Riley repeated, "was opened a long time ago. The first time a man picked up a stick and whacked another man over the head. We've lived with nukes for half a century. We always knew something like Z was possible. Some might say what happened here was inevitable." He looked at the smoldering remains of the Black Hawk full of Rangers that had been shot down trying to make it to the roof. "But what is also inevitable, and something no one ever really talks about, is that as long as there are men like Van Wyks, who will invent and let loose something like Z, there are men and women just as determined to stop him. Whatever the cost."